TAYLOR KENDALL:

EVIL INC.

K.T. ERWIN

For information on obtaining permission for use of material from this
work, please submit a written request to:
Par Press
PO Box 2073
St. Petersburg, FL 33731
email: writedoc@verizon.net

ISBN-10: 0-9831173-0-6
ISBN-13: 9780983117308

Second Edition

10 9 8 7 6 5 4 3 2 1

This story is dedicated to anyone who faced a crisis and made the moral choice instead of the convenient choice.

EVIL IS THE PRIVATION (LACK) OF GOOD.
  - Augustine (Confessions, Book 3, Ch 7)

DO NOT BE OVERCOME BY EVIL,
BUT OVERCOME EVIL WITH GOOD.
                                        - Romans 12:21 NIV

PROLOGUE

"Who are you? Are you one of them?"

"What kind of wacked-out chick are you? You nearly knocked me off my bike!"

The woman reached for his bag, jerked it from his shoulder and flung it into the bushes. "No monitoring devices allowed. They'll hear and they'll find me."

He dropped the bike and attempted to push the woman aside but she latched onto his stiff arm as if clinging for her life. Beads of perspiration streamed down her high cheek bones creating ripples in what appeared to be carefully applied makeup. Although standing still, she was panting like a runner.

"Look lady, I didn't mean to upset you. Chill out while I get my bag and we'll forget the whole thing happened."

"My name isn't lady; it's Harriet. Please take me away from here, away from them."

"Okay, okay. . . I don't know what your problem is, but I can't help you. I don't even have a place to live so don't tell me about your problems. I got trouble of my own."

"You aren't listening to me! I want a new doctor, a doctor to help me. But they won't let me leave. They won't listen. I don't want to be sick anymore!"

Like a mouse trap snapping, two men lunged, pulling Harriet from his side. She screamed and twisted. "These are the people who make me sick. They want me to stay sick. Help me!" Harriet wailed struggling in vain against the muscular attendants.

He grabbed the messenger bag, jumped on his bike and refused to look back even when a green shirted woman called out to him.

Harriet's protests echoed from down the hallway past the security guard. Normally he ignored these outbursts, preferring instead to watch movies on his contraband portable DVD player. Today he lowered the volume on his earpiece and watched with mild interest as the attendant in green held firmly to Harriet's arm and dragged her down the hall.

"No. I won't go. You can't make me. I demand to be taken to another psychiatrist," said Harriet.

"The MACS treatment is what you need. That's why you came here. Stop whining and do what you're told."

"I am doing what you say. I take my medicine every day, even at home."

"Oh, sure, you think you do. That's what they all say."

Harriet's tone became assertive and her pace deliberate, "No, you're wrong. I take my medicine. I was getting better and suddenly I'm worse. I want to leave MACS. I'm not being helped here!"

The shadow of another figure joined Harriet and the attendant. Harriet's reaction was immediate, "You're the last person I ever want to see again in my life. You can't make me go back either. I've been hospitalized enough to know about patient rights."

A low, guttural voice indistinguishable as male or female said, "Okay, we'll play it your way. You have the right to remain silent and I've got something to help you to do precisely that." The face of the tall figure was obscured by shadows but the action of the hands was clear; administering an injection then placing the protective cap onto a hypodermic needle.

The security guard turned back to his movie and raised the headpiece volume. Finally he could focus on the movie without the background noise. As the story droned on toward the predicted laser battle conclusion, he was oblivious when Harriet ran past him out the front door. For a guy who thrived on blood and guts endings, he missed the real show outside.

CHAPTER 1

I can't be late, not today!

Cutting sharply in front of a sputtering station wagon, Taylor Kendall guided her car into the only open space for three blocks.

So what if half a fender leans over the Fire Lane line. With any luck the meter maids are on coffee break. Besides, a parking ticket is nothing compared with being late for the interview that might rescue my future as a psychologist.

Her walk pace quickened as she approached the corporate headquarters of Medical Alliance for Community Services, a rising star on the community mental health scene. MACS purports the image as a proud independent, appropriately housed in a five story yellow stucco building planted defiantly amid the shiny glass high rises in downtown St. Petersburg, Florida.

As she stood to admire the building, Taylor's attention was diverted by the squealing of tires, screaming and the horrific crunch of human bones shattering against a hunk of Detroit metal on the street corner at the north side of the building. A policeman on bicycle patrol pedaled across from the opposite corner. He used his body as a shield to deflect traffic away from the woman's crumpled form. A green shirted man ran toward the sidewalk, standing amid the gawkers with a blank expression on his face. As Taylor approached, she noticed the MACS logo on his shirt and a hospital type name band on the victim's limp arm.

Was he calling for assistance or making dinner reservations? His indifference toward this scene was nauseating.

"Stupid girl. Never looked up at the traffic light," a man in a navy pin stripe suit said aloud.

"Excuse me, sir. Can you tell me what happened?", Taylor asked as she squeezed her thin frame through the growing crowd.

"Are you a newspaper reporter?" he asked straightening the knot on his designer tie.

"Not locally," Taylor replied, hoping to stretch the truth to gain more information.

"That girl must be doing some serious drugs. She ran out of that building and into oncoming traffic, bounced off the fender of that taxi, staggered a little then got hit again by that old geezer driving the ancient rocket fin Caddy."

"What makes you think she was on drugs?"

"She wasn't making any sense. I told her to wait for the light, but she was as jerking weirdly like she was on a bad trip. Then she shouted at me, 'They made me sick all over again. I have to get away. I don't want to be sick anymore.' Well that did it for me. I don't want anything to do with druggies so I stepped aside."

He paused, checking out Taylor; "Want to go for a drink later and find a way to help each other forget this sad situation?"

"Umm…no thanks, I have to go to work." *What could possibly be sleazier than a pick-up line at an accident scene?*

Taylor glanced at her watch. She was twenty minutes late and did not have any more time to spend on the opportunist in the navy suit or the MACS employee that appeared to be a quart low on empathy. *I think I can do a better job than that with the other MACS patients.*

A blast of cool air hit Taylor as she entered the MACS building and made her way to the front desk.

"Don't sign unless you have a delivery," The security guard said. He was about fifty pounds too heavy for the small seat he was straddled on and clearly too engrossed in his alien movie to even look at Taylor.

"I'm here to see Dr. Girard."

"Take the elevator to the fifth floor," he said with a dismissive wave toward the hallway.

She could have been a terrorist in combat fatigues with a grenade between her teeth for all the security guard knew. He barely broke eye contact with the screen.

Taylor knew when she stepped into the elevator that she had to stop analyzing that horrible accident scene and focus on the reason she came here. *After nine years of undergraduate and graduate school, my future detours through this building. Not the bustling corridors of South Bay Medical Center's pioneer Psychology in Critical Care residency. No, those prizes went to Bratton, Sewell, and Evans.*

It was a pep talk she had given herself many times since the day she realized how the residency system really worked. Bratton's grades were far below her own, but the preppie suck-up happened to be the son of the chief of pediatrics. Sewell was the quintessential platinum blonde bimbo with an overdose of silicone who scored high with the male interview committee because she had so much hands-on experience on a couch. *At least Evans got a spot – between his residency and his genius I.Q. he should finally have a ticket out of that New Jersey housing project.*

Losing the South Bay residency set the stage for that "day of disaster" two weeks ago as she watched all her bid choices evaporate. Taylor counted so much on getting into South Bay that she had merely gone through the motions at three other interviews. Now those places were filled by more enthusiastic candidates.

During the last round her advisor, Dr. Sebastian Dale, called her into his office with a late entry. A new residency was being offered by Medical Alliance for Community Services, a private mental health consortium doing research and partial hospitalization treatment programs. A newcomer to the bid process, the company known as MACS, missed the deadline and was late in contacting several nearby universities. With no viable opportunities in sight, Taylor recalled one of Dale's laws of life, "Something is better than nothing."

The alternative was to teach undergraduates and try for a residency next year. A left over candidate has the unmistakable stench of overripe fruit amid the fresh crop of the newly graduated doctoral students. Taylor vowed to stop analyzing why she was passed over for the South Bay residency the day she grabbed the MACS letter of intent, sighed and signed.

As the elevator door opened at the fifth floor, she repeated Dale's words. "Any credible residency counts. It's only a year and then you are ready for the license exam." Mama often said in adversity, "Shoulders back, chin up and walk like the Southern lady I raised you to be." Dr. Taylor Kendall consciously repressed her doubts, anger and desperation behind an accomplished Scarlett O'Hara smile.

She straightened her posture and walked purposefully to the receptionist's desk. "I'm Dr. Kendall. I have an appointment with Dr. Marco Girard."

The receptionist nodded while pushing buttons on a blinking console and pointed to the sofa. Taylor scanned the fine antique furnishings in the parquet floored reception foyer. The massive chandelier was extreme for a corporate office, yet the soft tone of its crystal drops swaying in the air conditioner breeze was hypnotically soothing.

Taylor's attention was drawn toward the recessed lights illuminating life size portraits on the wall opposite the seating group. She walked over to see if her prospective boss was among the subjects. Captured on canvas as he perched at the edge of a mahogany conference table between two women was the head of MACS, Dr. Marco Girard. The gold plate on the frame identified the chubby petite blonde leaning alluringly against his left shoulder as Serena Girard. The dark gypsy looking woman with folded arms, stern expression and ragged nails at his opposite shoulder was Victoria Girard.

Sisters? No, they don't look anything alike; besides the body language of both women shows a connection in a possessive, even intimate way with him.

The next frame featured one bleached blonde and three dark haired, trendy young adults whose names were also Girard sitting around the same conference table.

This must be the next generation.

Taylor was drawn to the final portrait of a fair haired young man in tan riding pants, shiny black boots and a white shirt with enough buttons open to reveal his chest. He stood alone beside a wooden gate as if returning from an afternoon ride. His mesmerizing blue eyes clashed with a steel set chin and the expression of aloofness that made his presence incongruent among the others. The frame plate identified him as Blake Andres Girard. In smaller print beneath his name was the quote, "Building on what is his own and not on what rests with others. - Machiavelli"

Are we required to bow to the junior lord of the manor? Just my luck I'll have to work for wonder boy.

"Dr. Kendall, welcome to MACS."

Taylor spun around to face Dr. Marco Girard. He was certainly a commanding presence. Taylor extended her hand only to find that Dr. Girard declined to shake it. Instead he bent to kiss her hand with slick lips and a hold that lasted too long for comfort. Normally such a gesture would have elicited more than a few sharp words of disapproval, but Taylor needed this residency so badly that she held her tongue and forced a slight smile. His warm olive-toned fingers moved upward to caress her arm, guiding her toward the archway to the area marked "Executive Suite".

The smell of success was intoxicating. Custom designed mahogany secretarial stations were positioned as sentinels at the base of three paths leading to tabernacle-style bronze doors. Entering the middle door, Dr. Girard's private office, Taylor breathed a silent prayer that this was not going to degenerate into a grab and grope session where she angrily exits and annihilates her last chance at a residency.

Motioning for Taylor to sit, not on his lap, but in a perfectly respectable arm chair at the nearby small conference table, Dr. Marco turned back to his desk and pressed several telephone buttons. Instantly, the bronze door parted to reveal a young woman pushing a tea cart.

She identified herself as Sally, Dr. Marco's administrative assistant. She arranged the fine china cups and saucers, placing a silver demitasse spoon on the Battenberg lace napkin beside each cup. Then she transferred the double tiered, sterling silver server laden with petit fours and scones onto the center of the table. "Shall I pour, Dr. Marco?"

"No my dear, Serena likes to direct our tea time. Please hold all calls during this meeting," his words nearly lost to the sound of the bronze door opening again.

What a study in contrasts, Taylor thought as she saw the two women from the foyer portrait step into the room and sit in chairs on opposite sides of Dr. Girard. If they were personifications of his demon and his guardian angel, it would prove difficult to determine which was which.

"May I present my wife and associate, Serena Girard and our business partner, Victoria Girard. This is our newest member of the MACS team, Dr. Taylor Kendall."

Serena's hand raised in a half wave the way the Queen Mother acknowledges the crowd on state occasions. Taylor smiled, stopping short of rising for a proper curtsey, though she felt Serena would have preferred it. Victoria reached across the table to grasp Taylor's hand for two hardy pumps. While Serena deftly poured tea, Dr. Marco launched into a well rehearsed monologue about MACS.

Looking at them from across the table, Taylor saw even more peculiar contrasts. The scene was reminiscent of debutante parties where rapt attention to self-serving storytelling around the banquet table was as much of the process as dancing with an endless line of left-footed escorts. Mama taught her to maintain an interested smile while inwardly laughing at the insipid chatter going on around her. *Thanks Mama, it's a skill I may have to use often this year.*

"As my husband was saying, Dr. Kendall," Serena raised her voice tone sharply, "The education and research divisions of MACS are increasingly important in our organization. We have trained several social work interns. You represent a new educational partnership as our first psychology resident."

"How fortunate," Taylor replied pleasantly, gritting her teeth to stifle the scream echoing inside her head, *The FIRST! I'm a freaking guinea pig.*

Dr. Marco, as he asked to be called, seemed to anticipate Taylor's unspoken concerns. "While this position is new, our training programs are established. I assured your university committee that we have consulting psychologists and psychiatrists in our programs that were trained at superior universities in the states and Europe. Speaking as a physician with advanced psychiatric training, I know we can provide a residency to satisfy your university and the state license requirements."

Taylor sipped the jasmine tea slowly to give her lips a needed rest from smiling. She hoped Dr. Marco's bravado was good enough to convince the psychology board of MACS' suitability as a residency site and parlay this disappointing year into a coveted ticket to sit for the license exam.

She found herself captivated not by what the Girards said, as by what they did not say. *Do they know about the accident and the woman who died in front of their building? Was she a patient? If she was, then why wasn't anyone concerned about her? Do they leave this carefully crafted nirvana long enough to know what really goes on in their treatment programs? I'm not sure what, if anything is going on in MACS, but it certainly feels odd.*

Taylor knew that they were studying her while she was playing the same game. *Marco and Victoria have such similar*

penetrating dark brown eyes and strong Hispanic features as to pass
for brother and sister, yet he called her a business partner. Serena's blue
eyes and blonde hair are more difficult to access. She could be from the
Netherlands or Nebraska, having no discernable accent to give a hint.

Taylor's effort to make sense of them was interrupted by
Marco's gaze, which seemed to mentally undress her while his
wife's indulgent monologue continued.

Serena picked at her tea cakes, making exaggerated gestures
with her long sunset pink nails. The color would be prissy on
a woman as tall as Taylor but it suited the short, Rubenesque
Serena. Victoria finished her tea in a few gulps and reached for
a second scone. Taylor didn't miss Serena's disapproving stare
or Victoria's salute with the butter knife. They chatted casually
about the great issues of mental health with ample references
to MACS' "groundbreaking programs for the challenging
schizophrenic population." Tea and shameless promotion aside,
Taylor was fighting her natural instincts to prod this protracted
meeting back to the subject of her residency.

Finally, Dr. Marco pushed his cup away and handed Taylor
the set of corporate folders which Sally had placed on the lower
level of the tea cart. Each of the four dark green folders was
embossed with the MACS logo in gold foil.

Her first assignment was to review the contents of the folders
to learn the basics of this sprawling mental health consortium.
For better or worse, Taylor took this to be her formal acceptance
into the MACS program. With an unspoken understanding that
this interview was over, Serena and Victoria offered final words
of welcome and rose from the table.

As they walked out, a disheveled woman in a wrinkled lab
coat brushed past them. Scurrying to Dr. Marco's side she handed
him a closed envelope marked "Confidential" in large red letters.

"Thank you for your usual efficiency," he replied giving
more interest to the envelope than to the bearer. Nevertheless
she beamed as if receiving an exalted compliment. "Dr. Taylor

Kendall, may I present my oldest daughter, Gina Girard. Gina is a chemist with pharmaceutical experience and director of our research labs."

Taylor recognized her as one of the young Girards in the center portrait and smiled. Gina scowled and turned on heel toward the door.

"No, no, Gina, don't leave," Dr. Marco called after her, "I have a special request."

"Certainly Father," she snapped to attention.

"Dr. Kendall will be working directly with our chief psychologist and program director, Dr. Samuel Locke. Unfortunately, he is at the Lakeland program and could not greet her personally. I want her to gain an understanding of our multi-faceted programs, thus I'd like for you to spend the rest of the afternoon and tomorrow morning giving Dr. Kendall a proper introduction to MACS." Having issued his decree, he took a seat in his leather desk chair and began rummaging through messages on the massive desk.

For several awkward minutes, Gina didn't move. The adoring expression she gave to her father quickly slid into a disdainful scowl as she faced Taylor.

Hope you are a good chemist, Gina, because you have no future in public relations.

Gina seemed surprised that Taylor did not blink first and suspended the locked eyes combat. "Well, Dr. Kendall, I'll show you around so I can get back to real work."

They walked rapidly through the Executive Suite as Gina made passing reference to the secretarial staff which, in her view, were not worthy of introduction. Although Taylor was seven inches taller than what she guessed was Gina's 5'3" height, keeping up with her rapid pace was an effort. They paused at the reception desk where Gina scanned the message bin. Taylor tried not to seem curious when Gina took messages out of the bin for Dr. Locke. With a black marker retrieved from the bulging pocket of her lab coat, she scratched Locke's name off one message and wrote in "Lorraine", then placed it in the L. Lewis bin.

Waiting for the elevator, Taylor attempted to make polite conversation, "What a nice touch to have the founding family portraits here."

"That's one way to put it," Gina responded, "In fact, let me use these as an object lesson. Maybe you'll spend less time analyzing our twisted family tree if you know the principal players." She pointed at the people in each portrait to illustrate her explanation, "You've been given a more than generous greeting by my father, my mother, and Serena. I'm in the next portrait, along with my younger sister, Carla, my half brother, Felipe, and his useless shopaholic wife, Tiffany. We all work here. Well, some of us work, others merely occupy desks. You're the psychologist, you figure it out."

"What is Blake Girard's job?" Taylor asked, motioning to the portrait of the fair-haired man in the riding pants as they boarded the elevator.

Gina's eyes darkened as menacing as the night sky during a hurricane, "Blake does not have a job here. Blake is 'The Prince,' the worshiped first born son who refuses to work for his inheritance. As far as I am concerned he is a fool, unworthy of our Father's devotion."

"Like the prodigal son?"

"Perhaps, but I hope he remains in the pig pen and leaves MACS to those of us who earn our place." The elevator door opened and the ride down to the fourth floor was blessedly brief.

CHAPTER 2

Gina bolted out of the elevator motioning for Taylor to follow. "This level houses the MACS educational components and second tier management. I believe you actually have an office somewhere along the wall across from the maze of desk jockeys," Gina gestured toward a hallway to the right of the receptionist. They walked silently past several offices before stopping in an alcove that led to a door marked "Quality Management" which she pushed open without knocking. As the occupant looked up from her computer screen, Taylor saw a softer, more delicate version of Gina.

"Dr. Taylor Kendall, this is my sister, Carla Girard, coordinator of the Quality Management division for our clinical services."

Carla clicked the "save" icon on her computer screen, then rose to shake hands. "Welcome to MACS, Dr. Kendall. The clinical group is looking forward to meeting you." Carla's tiny hand was as warm as her greeting.

"How delightful for you all," Gina responded sarcastically. "Father wants me to play tour guide since Locke and the PR team are out of the office, but I have no time for this. Carla, you can baby-sit Dr. Kendall for the rest of the day. Be sure she gets the new hire package from human resources. Tomorrow morning, around eleven, bring her back to the lab and I'll tell her the party line about our projects."

"Of course, we don't want Father to know that you defied his order, now do we?"

"Keeping the Nutracuratives flowing for the programs is more important than playing hostess. My 'joy juice', as you call it, pays the bills around here and bought your new car," Gina snapped back. Without so much as a nod in Taylor's direction, she spun on her heels and exited the office.

And it's certainly been a pleasure getting to know you too, Gina.

Carla moved from behind her desk to Taylor's side. "Dr. Kendall, please forgive my sister. Her forte is lab experiments, not employee relations. She works hard at letting everyone know she works hard, if you know what I mean."

As if trying to make Taylor feel less like an outcast, Carla flashed a disarming smile, "Don't tell Gina what good timing she has, but I need an excuse to escape from these Medicare forms. I skipped breakfast and lunch and now I am starved. Let's get a coffee and snack then walk around and see who is still in the office. Anyone I miss introducing to you today, we can corner at the coffee pot first thing in the morning, okay?"

Walking along with Carla through the fourth floor was like a freshman discovering that her sorority "big sister" was the most popular student on campus. Both men and woman greeted Carla's arrival with pleasure. From managers to file clerks, Carla knew everyone's name and inquired about something meaningful to each person.

What a shame to hide Carla in a paperwork office, she's a natural in a public contact job.

In the north corner of the Clinical Services section, Carla gestured toward an office marked "Dr. Samuel Locke, Program Director for Clinical Services." "He's your boss," Carla stated, "And since you'll be doing some work in Community Education Services, you'll also work with the Public Relations Office." She paused at the secretarial station in the alcove, making another introduction then writing a note to be delivered by Brook, secretary to Clinical Services.

"Dr. Kendall, I'm so happy to meet you," Brook let out a small squeal punctuated by rhythmic gum chewing. "I started night classes last semester at St. Petersburg College so that I can get my BA then go to graduate school for psychology."

To tame the "Babbling Brook", Carla interrupted, "Hold the life history until we show Dr. Kendall to her new office."

Brook tossed back her long brunette hair to resume a business-like manner. She pressed a four number sequence on the keypad panel of the credenza perpendicular to her desk. Although Brook continued to talk while entering the code by touch typing, Taylor saw her fingers hit the sequence 2-2-9-7. Then Brook reached into the drawer and pulled out one green plastic card with the gold MACS symbol. She motioned for Taylor to follow her to the door of a nearby unmarked office. She swiped the card thru a slot beside the door but the door did not open. Then Carla tried it several times without success.

"Carla, when is the paranoia level going to chill out around here? If we change lock codes after every employee leaves or a patient freaks out and threatens to kill us, we'll re-key the cards more often than an airport hotel."

"That's okay, Brook. Please have security correct this problem before tomorrow morning. Dr. Kendall can arrange her office then." Turning to Taylor, Carla regained her cheerful countenance, "I might as well give you another of the corporate initiation experiences. It's time to get buried under the paper avalanche from human resources."

Carla and Taylor rode down to the third floor where the archway entrance to the Human Resources department was directly across from the elevator doors. A flickering florescent fixture cast odd shadows on the dull beige walls and folding chairs in the waiting area. They stopped abruptly at the sound of shouting. "I want my check and I want it now," a gruff male voice bellowed. "I'm not going to be jerked around by those broads and their fast-talking stud. I know there's something fishy going on the way we manipulate those patients. I'm ready to talk to the state medical board and..."

The woman locked eyes with Carla then interrupted the man's harangue.

"Wait, Hank, here's your check. It must have been caught between these pages." The sincerity of that sudden discovery within the file folder was seriously lacking. He snatched it from the woman's hand and glanced at it; "There's no payment on my expense money."

"Right you are," the woman replied in a monotone honed from frequent repetition, "I think we can take care of that next Friday. You know we get the big reimbursements from Medicare on Thursday. Call next week and I'll see what I can do."

"Will the check cash this time?"

"Just call next week, okay?"

He jammed the check into his back jeans pocket and marched away muttering a curse. Taylor noticed that while his voice was demanding, his hands were shaking, uncertain whether he could act tough enough to demand his money. He had the look of a man weary from trying.

Choosing to ignore the entire scene, Carla restored her smile and said, "Dr. Taylor Kendall this is Joanie Brock, our Human Resources Director."

"Welcome to MACS, Dr. Kendall," Joanie responded, motioning toward her private office. Joanie took a seat behind a dented metal desk surrounded by beige metal filing cabinets. Four overstuffed, three-tiered in/out baskets lined the sides of the desk. A small copy machine sitting on top of a folding table made a low humming sound as it cranked out more papers. Only a skinny slice of natural light, barely a foot wide, came from the single window partially covered by a bookcase filled with more forms.

The paperwork in this office alone killed ten acres of trees. The hot air balloon and ski posters must help her avoid claustrophobia. Anyone would crave the great outdoors after long hours in a workspace with less elbow room than a camper potty.

While Joanie droned on with more of the MACS corporate line, Taylor kept both feet firmly on the floor. Not a position of rapt attention. No, this was an effort to use her legs to brace the wobbly chrome stack chair in which she sat. The contrasts were inevitable. The fifth floor Executive Suites were opulent. The fourth floor was tasteful. The third floor was trailer park common.

It's like Dante's inferno; every level of hell gets worse.

Joanie continued her new employee introduction speech accentuated periodically by handing various forms to Taylor. The buzz of Carla's pager startled everyone. Looking at the message, Carla jumped up saying, "Sorry, ladies, but this is a sensitive call that has to be returned in my office. I'll take Dr. Kendall with me and she can finish the forms in my office. If there are any questions I can't answer, I'll have her highlight the sections and ask you about it tomorrow."

Riding back to the fourth floor, Carla pointed to a slot beside the elevator buttons. "After working hours, the only way to access the upper floors is to put an office key card in, then press the button for the floor. Your key card will be set for access to the floor where your office is located. There's no reason to have access to any other floors. The second floor also has special access codes that are punched in on numbered key pads at the door to each secured area. Tomorrow you'll get a peek at Gina's chemical kingdom."

"Is the entire floor for the lab?"

"Gina would like that much clout. Actually only a half of the floor is the lab. The rest is patient records. When MACS bought this building last year it made sense to put all the highly confidential work on the same secured floor."

This seemed like overkill to Taylor, but this was corporate mental health, not the university where the psychology lab was part work area and part social club for graduate students. Brook did say something about the paranoia level running high.

Before entering her private office, Carla suggested that Taylor go around the corner to the break room and get a coffee refill for both of them. Taylor recognized the hint as Carla's way of gaining privacy to return the text message so Taylor walked slowly down the hallway, trying to imprint on her memory the names and locations of each office she passed.

The break room was a fully equipped kitchen slightly larger than the one in the guest house where Taylor was living. The appearance of a homey kitchen was compromised only by a snack machine in the corner near the entry. She took her time surveying the too sweet, too fat laden, and sometimes too hard to resist items. Fortunately, she had no coins in her suit pocket that would allow her to indulge her weakness for chunky chocolate chip cookies.

* * * * *

Carla pulled her door nearly closed, but avoided shutting it completely.

Like Brook said, paranoia runs high at MACS and a closed door invites suspicion. Better to make the call in a quiet voice while appearing that its business. At the risk of sounding as paranoid as Brook thinks we all are, Gina or one of her office spies always senses when he calls. And when they tell Father about one of those infrequent, cherished calls, all hell breaks out at home.

Carla defiantly dialed the number that appeared on her phone.

A male voice answered, "Don't say my name, is someone listening?"

Sensing someone outside of her door Carla replied in a businesslike tone, "Yes, sir, that is one of the approaches we take to quality management here at MACS."

"Okay, it must be Gina or Lorraine so keep your cool. Don't write anything down, just listen. Drive to Tampa Airport and stay in the left lane as if you are going to Short Term Parking. At the last possible moment, avoid the turn to parking and veer into the lane leading to the level for Arriving Passengers. Leave the office no later than quarter to five and you'll make it to the airport in about an hour. The evening rush is good cover. When you get to the Arriving Passengers area, slow down at the last section but do not get out of the car. I'll find you."

"All right, sir, I understand and I will personally see that the package is delivered to you." As the office door opened, her heart skipped a beat.

"Sorry, Carla, I didn't mean to interrupt," Taylor said placing a coffee mug on the desk. Then she sat down at the adjacent conference table and opened the human resources packet trying to ignore the telephone conversation.

Carla paused and then whispered into the phone, "I can hardly wait to see you."

Taylor paused a few moments then asked Carla for help in looking over the employee insurance form. Carla picked up her mug and went over to the table.

In a whisper, Taylor said, "When I came around the corner I saw a woman leaning her ear toward your door obviously trying to listen. I said hello as if I didn't see what she was doing. She rolled her eyes and walked away but I saw her name tag - Lorraine Lewis.

"Thanks, Taylor. So that raspy breathing I heard outside my door was Lorraine. She needs to give up smoking if she wants to play spy games."

"Perhaps she was stopping short to give you privacy."

"Not a chance. And you can bet that she went straight to the second floor to tell Gina, who will take great delight in running upstairs to tell Father."

The two women sipped their coffee and reviewed the paperwork. Carla talked about Quality Assurance procedures in the MACS programs. After awhile, she stopped abruptly.

"Taylor, I've only known you a few hours, but you seem like someone I can trust. I don't want to impose, but I could use your help."

"I'll try, how can I help?"

"You heard me on the phone and you know it wasn't business. It was my brother. There's a foolish family feud that makes me sneak around to see him. I'll explain it to you someday. The family still holds a grudge about a blowup years ago when he left."

"Gina made a point to tell me about the brother who doesn't work here. It almost sounded as if she's jealous of him."

"Remarkably accurate observation. In our Father's world, you are either with us or against us. I hate being in the middle of this, but I am closer to Blake than anyone in the world. We were born a few weeks apart and grew up like twins. I guess this sounds peculiar… it's hard to explain."

"Carla, every family has its issues. I have two younger sisters whom I alternately adore and despise. At times it's great to be living nine hundred miles away on my own. But wave a plane ticket in my face and I can't wait to see them."

"Thanks for attempting to understand our complicated life. Why don't you finish the top part of these forms while I wrap up a few emails then I have an idea."

Taylor added the usual information to the seemingly endless pages of the new hire packet while Carla typed frantically.

"Okay done! There's one more thing you can do. Let's walk out together and act like we're going somewhere for a latte and chat after work. I would never ask you to lie, merely pretend. Believe me, I owe you for this."

What a great way to start this second rate residency, now you've got yourself embroiled in a conflict with the reigning royal family. The high sounding retort forming behind her lips was thwarted by Carla's pleading brown eyes.

"Okay, I can do that. My car is parked a few blocks south of the MACS building. That is unless I've got a ticket or been towed."

"Terrific!" Carla's relief brought a warm glow to her suntan face that was more vivid than a fresh touch of blush. "Gather up your paperwork and let's leave. It's already four-fifteen. I'll show you the parking area and we'll dash to our cars. None of your bosses are in today, so I guess I'm in charge of you and I say, let's leave!"

Taylor stuffed the new employee packet into her brief case with the other MACS materials then fished around in her purse for keys. Carla opened the lower drawer in her credenza. She slipped out of serviceable leather flats to black sparkling heels. From a monogrammed satin lingerie bag she pulled out a semi-sheer black scarf with iridescent swirls, the perfect embellishment for her dusty rose dress. A squirt of custom blended perfume from a mini-crystal atomizer and a fast application of mauve lip gloss completed the transformation.

Carla's instant party kit in a drawer is an inspired idea. I need to bring some glitzy scarves and makeup to the office to be ready for an unexpected evening out. Like the fashion magazines show — work to date. No more Dutch treat pizza buffets or sharing soggy sandwiches with other students. Heaven forbid, I might actually go on a real date. What was that like again? After five brain numbing years in graduate school chained to books, Taylor realized that she might once again be on the verge of renewing her social life.

"I'm ready. Let's go."

Carla would have been better off to leave immediately. Unfortunately she wasted time telling two secretaries and the receptionist that she was, "Going to show Dr. Kendall where to enter the MACS parking lot." As they emerged from the elevator into the lobby, Carla literally ran into her nemesis. Making an exaggerated show of checking her watch, Lorraine Lewis stood squarely in their path.

"What kind of example does it set for new employees when the boss' daughter skips out early? Got big plans, sweetie?"

Carla raised her head to stare into the face of a slightly taller Lorraine, "No and if I did, he wouldn't be your type. Not that any guy is."

Taylor felt a sudden impulse to protect Carla by distracting the hawk-like attacker. "My indoctrination wouldn't be complete without checking the after work coffee haunts. Carla, you go ahead and get a good table. I'll follow."

Carla took the hint and walked as fast as her slim skirt and short legs allowed. Lorraine turned on heel to follow, but Taylor stepped in front. The women locked eyes. Lorraine's scowl was as intimidating as her appearance; jagged-cut, coal black short hair with a streak of red, like a flame tip that nearly matched the two inch tear drop garnet in a dagger-like setting hanging from a heavy silver chain, the only color in her head-to-toe black attire. Shock value notwithstanding, Taylor had to do something to distract, so she slipped into an uncharacteristically clueless chatter hoping that Lorraine would buy it.

"Will I also be meeting with you tomorrow when I meet with Dr. Locke? I hear that you have a very important position in Clinical Services. Can you tell me what my first assignment might be? How do you like working with the MACS programs?"

They both knew she was playing for time. Lorraine ended it without a shred of politeness, "You're finished running interference. Why don't you leave now? Better yet, don't come back tomorrow."

Taylor expelled a sigh when she was once again inside the familiar confines of her car. She hoped that she gave Carla enough time to escape. As Taylor pulled away from the curb onto Second Street her car was nearly side-swiped by Lorraine's black MG convertible roaring off in pursuit of Carla's white Lexus convertible.

CHAPTER 3

"If you don't need anything else, Dr. Marco, may I leave?" Sally asked, pressing a bottle into the silver wine cooler.

"Of course, my dear. You have been marvelous keeping the police out of our way. We Girards need time to collect our thoughts and put this tragic event behind us lest it spoil our dinner," Marco responded sliding his desk chair within reach of his assistant. She giggled as his hand slithered up the back of her leg to tug on the hem of her lace teddy, an action halted by the sound of the bronze door opening. He jumped out of his chair, standing to acknowledge the arrival of his wife. Sally adjusted her dress along with her composure. She gathered the ice cube trays and left quietly.

Marco motioned for Serena to sit in the chair next to his. Victoria entered and flopped down on the adjacent settee. "Let's get this over with, Marco."

"Your wish is my command."

Marco waited until he had the total attention of both women before continuing, "Thus far Lorraine has acted decisively to contain the damage. She tells me that only three members of the Clinical Staff were involved. They were dismissed early with two days paid leave and a cash bonus. Upon returning to work, they will be transferred indefinitely to other MACS programs - one to Orlando, one to Brooksville, and the other given a generous scholarship to a graduate school in California. Sally distracted the police investigator while I reached Dr. Locke on his cell phone."

"How fortunate that Locke wasn't here to interfere," Victoria replied.

"Will we be expected to comment?" Serena asked, idly twisting her diamond and sapphire tennis bracelets around her plump wrist.

"Not likely, my dear. I have phoned the St. Petersburg Police Department and offered to meet with the investigator, thus leaving both of you out of this matter. Our attorney feels there is no way this patient's suicide can fall back on us."

"Suicide?" Serena scoffed. "You mean the police actually believe that?"

"Calm yourself, Serena. I have it under control."

"I'm more concerned that the staff sees it your way," Victoria said. "What if they start looking over her chart and comparing stories?"

"As always, my beloved business-minded Victoria, you are right. I have not forgotten Machiavelli's warning that '...the temper of the multitude is fickle, and that while it is easy to persuade them of a thing, it is hard to fix them in that persuasion.' For that reason, I have already started my persuasion with the clinic staff. Lorraine has instructions in how to reinforce my words."

"What trick did you use this time?" Serena asked.

"I merely gave those social worker do-gooders the fix that they crave, a chance to process their feelings. I called an impromptu staff meeting after the patients left."

Serena touched Marco's face, her diamond laden fingers brushing against his five o'clock shadow, "Why darling, how clever of you? Did you instruct the staff in what to say to the police?"

"Certainly not! While the local police are hardly in a league with Interpol even they can recognize when a group of witnesses are coached. It makes them start to look for conspiracies. No, I chose to play the great physician reminding our dedicated staff members of the disappointments we all feel when even our excellent MACS programs fail to reach a patient." Standing up to gesture, he continued, "I emphasized how effective our partial hospitalization programs are when one considers the American Psychiatric Association's own studies showing that suicide is the leading cause of premature death among the poor souls with schizophrenia. Alas, this troubled young woman was merely beyond our help," he paused for effect, "Later I'll apply the same story, liberally dipped in psycho-babble and appropriately contrived to dazzle the police investigator."

"So another schizophrenic refuses to comply with treatment and dies. It happens. Let's drop the subject," said Victoria.

"Indeed we shall, Victoria, now on to more interesting matters. What do you think of our newest acquisition?" Dr. Marco beamed at Serena as he lifted the Dom Perignon from its ice nest in the silver cooler and poured generous portions into three Waterford crystal flutes.

"Which one, the Pensacola - Mobile clinics or these new flutes?" Serena murmured with a coquettish smile.

Victoria groaned at having to watch this game again. Not waiting to be served, she reached for her flute, eager to become one with the bubbly.

"You love to tease me, Serena, Cara Mia. You know that I refer to the acquisition of the idealistic Dr. Kendall. She is the ticket to our acceptability with an accredited university psychology program," Marco replied, shifting to a half-reclining position in the wing chair and placing his feet one of Serena's precious antique side tables. How she hated those gestures of masculine domination. At heart, Marco was a carbon copy of his Spanish conquistador ancestors.

Victoria knew that Serena was seething behind that polite demeanor. Actually Victoria enjoyed Marco's "me-Tarzan, you-Jane" moods. After a few days, Serena would remember that Marco was only good for his professional title and as a front for money making schemes. They long ago discovered that they didn't need him for anything else.

* * * * *

Unfamiliar with the downtown commuters' trick of timing the lights, Taylor caught every red light on First Avenue North. She reached for her cell phone and pressed Dale's number on the speed dial. Hearing his recorded greeting, she realized that he had already left campus. Aggravated that she missed the pep talk she desperately needed, she left a message, "I finished my first day at MACS. Still have no idea what I'm doing. I think the inmates are running the asylum. But thanks anyway, Dale. I hope I can last the year here. MACS is a peculiar place."

* * * * *

Carla breathed easier pulling off the Howard Franklin Bridge onto the Tampa Airport exit. All the way across that four lane east-bound span her eyes darted back and forth. She constantly checked the rear view mirror, scrutinizing every small black sports car. In the same way that sea gulls instinctively recognize an impending storm, she sensed that Lorraine was nearby. As she drove onto the airport road toward the "Arriving Passengers" area, there were no black sports cars in sight among the sedans, vans, taxis and hotel shuttles.

The crush of vehicles and travelers was disorienting. Suddenly the passenger door was opened by a man with tousled blond wavy hair, ocean blue eyes and a smile as warm as a fireplace after a long day snow skiing.

"Blake, I am so happy to see you."

Leaning over to kiss her cheek, Blake settled his 6'4" frame in the seat and fastened his seatbelt. "Were you followed?"

"I am not sure. I thought Lorraine was behind me but she's nowhere in sight now."

"Good. Let's not give the hounds time to corner the fox. Tally ho, sister! Lead them on a merry chase."

"No fox hunting metaphors, please, I've never lived it down."

"Which part - sabotaging Serena's saddle or hiding the fox from the hunters?"

"I think the Earl chalked it up to dumb foreigners, but your mother still blasts me with her killer look at the mere mention of fox hunting."

"Victoria got a kick out of seeing Serena slide unceremoniously from her sidesaddle into the duck pond. Too bad Father missed all the fun. He was practically drunk with satisfaction after trading those fake bearer bonds for that Chippendale desk."

"Please, Blake, the desk story is coming back like bad TV reruns. Every time Father wants to impress someone, he tells the story of going to England to buy the eighteenth century desk. If I have to hear him say one more time that it was custom made for the fifth Earl of Meath as a gift from his appreciative royal lover…"

The two of them burst into laughter.

"This is like old times, Carla. You and I are the only Girards with a sense of humor. The rest take themselves too seriously; and they just take everyone else."

Blake gave directions to a chic bistro in Old Hyde Park. Leaving the road warriors on the interstate, they drove through a section of vintage Tampa homes where old money and young Turks mix easily. Parking on a side street, the tall blonde brother and his short brunette sister joined the fashionably dressed crowd strolling toward the shops and restaurants.

Blake called ahead to reserve a table on the street side window, near enough to see out but with a few indoor ficus trees blocking an outsider's view of their table. Discrete. Upscale. Blake learned from Marco how to choose the right place for the right occasion and to demand only the best. Seated with steamy thick Cuban coffees, Carla felt remarkably at ease.

"Freedom becomes you, Carla."

"What?"

"I know you well enough to recognize the look of tranquility that comes from being out of the family's reach."

"You are right. It's like a mini-vacation."

He studied her expression. Away from the family, Carla was a different person.

Carla interrupted his thoughts, "Okay my near-twin, its confession time; how long have you been in Tampa without calling me?"

"Let's say I'm here between planes with enough time to take my favorite sibling to dinner."

"Favorite sibling? Is there competition?"

"Consider the possibilities: Gina fantasizes about dancing on my grave. Felipe feels the same, but lacks the guts to even admit it. Who knows what Tiffany, love child of the Scarecrow from Wizard of Oz, thinks…if she does think."

"So did you come back to see the family?"

"If you mean am I back to apologize and grovel, not a chance."

"But are you okay? I mean we hear…"

"From a family that manufacturers rumors to order, you know better than to believe everything you hear. Seriously, I'm fine, Carla. I've got enough of Marco's genes to always land on my feet. How about you? How long is it going to be this time before the game is up?"

"MACS makes tons of money so we're more financially secure, and Father says that this time our work is legitimate as well as medically sound…"

"Carla, if you believe that, I've got a bikini franchise in Alaska to sell you."

The appearance of the waiter with an appetizer tray and menus gave them a needed break in a conversation that had taken an unexpected turn.

Blake pushed Carla's coffee cup aside and placed his hand over her smaller hand to get her attention. His expression turned serious and he spoke with emphasis on every word, "Carla, do you trust me? I mean, really trust me?"

"You know I do. I trust you with my life."

"Okay, then you must listen to me. I want to take you away from MACS, away from the family. I can fly you out of here tonight."

"Blake, you know I can't do that. What's the urgency?"

"I can't reveal my sources, but I can tell you that the Girard's empire is headed for a fall. They've crossed the line of decency, not to mention greed."

Carla shook her head in disbelief, "You are overreacting. Our parents are charming deceivers and have been called con artists a time or two, but that's all in the past. This time Father has found a significant breakthrough with the Nutracuratives. People are being helped; people who could not afford treatment otherwise. We have clinicians with real credentials. MACS even received a community service award. What can possibly be wrong?"

The conversation paused long enough for the waiter to serve heaping bowls of black bean soup. A few tastes savored in silence failed to erase the tension.

"MACS is not as benign as the liquid facelift treatments in California."

"Be honest, Blake, no one was harmed! Those women were really paying for a chance to restore their glamour and we gave them that. I realize that the hot oils didn't do anything but the positive attention did. I saw many of those older ladies leave feeling, if not looking, the way they imagined they would. Just because one woman got a rash and went screaming to the state medical board doesn't mean that it was all bad."

"What about the cellular restoration clinics in Montevideo? Wasn't it a general's wife who claimed the treatments gave her skin cancer?"

"Right and the General himself stormed into the clinic in full dress uniform waving a pearl handle pistol," Carla recalled imitating the action with her hand. "He threatened to hunt down every Girard relative and make us use the cellular products until our skin rotted. Gina got right in his face saying, 'Forget that, torture is against the Geneva Convention!'"

"I'm surprised her smart mouth didn't get all of you killed."

"You worry too much. We laid low for a few days then escaped on the back roads. It was easy once Father lost the General's security men over the mountains."

"That's what I mean, Carla, this family is like a bunch of roller coaster junkies who constantly need more danger to get the same high. It's too hard on you."

"Honestly, Blake, it wasn't that bad. The worst part of that whole situation was riding in a rickety van that Father drove the way he drives his Ferrari. All was forgotten as soon as we reached the city limits of Santiago. In no time at all, we were settled in at Tio Pietro's 'mansione' in Vitacuta. We barely had time between parties to reflect on what your mother termed 'The Unfortunate Episode'."

"She does have a way of dismissing anything unflattering."

"Everything worked out for the best. We had a great year indulging our whims with Tio's high society neighbors thanks to the profits from Montevideo. Father spent most of the time in Europe raising money. Mother and Serena huddled together planning the California clinics. Guess that's the Girard idea of a family holiday."

"You overlook one important fact, Carla. Peddling liquid dreams to those who can pay for it is totally different than hustling schizophrenics off the streets with promises you can't keep."

"Don't you see, my overly-concerned brother, that this time the people who are benefiting are not even paying for it? The American government is. And if Medicare and Medicaid don't pay us, they'll pay some other mental health agency who gives less effective treatment. The poor are helped and the government pays. What can possibly be wrong with that?"

Blake leaned toward her. In the soft lights of the bistro she could see his blue eyes turn deeper teal, the way they do when he is intense or angry. His words were calmly delivered with the force of a hammer striking iron.

"The super rich will forgo vengeance to avoid embarrassment. But the people MACS targets are desperate and indigent. They have nothing to lose. People with nothing to lose are unpredictable and dangerous. This time I think you all may be in deeper trouble than you realize."

CHAPTER 4

When Taylor inserted her key card into the elevator slot the next morning and pushed the fourth button, the motor hummed and moved slowly upward. She turned toward the mirrored back wall and finger-combed her golden brown hair back into place. Then she noticed something else in the reflection; a small camera in the upper left corner. *Security camera, what else? Is it to keep more patients from danger, or to keep tabs on the staff?*

The elevator doors opened and Taylor stepped out. Only her second day, she experienced a momentary panic trying to remember which hallway led to her office. Fortunately Brook pranced by, tentatively balancing her slender frame on four-inch stiletto heels as she managed to keep three coffee mugs from sliding off a metal tray.

"Hey, Dr. Kendall, we've got your office ready to move in. Follow me." Brook chatted on in excruciating detail about the door key repair.

Taylor decided that the way to deal with her is to say "uh huh" or "really" at sufficient intervals to make Brook think that she was hanging on every rambling word.

They reached her office after a few twists and turns down the hallway. A name plate on the door proclaimed "Dr. Taylor Kendall". She quelled the urge to run her fingers across the name. *Act sophisticated and professional. Do you want to just let everyone in the world know that this is your first office?*

Taylor surveyed the room. There was a fruitwood veneer desk with matching credenza that was certainly nothing fancy, but it had generous drawers and file space. Facing her desk were two sled chairs - the kind that defy comfort in waiting rooms. She tested the high back desk chair and swiveled toward the computer stationed on the credenza. The color monitor came alive with a distracting techno-chorus paying homage to Bill Gates. Her hands assumed the proper touch typing position over the keyboard ready to find out what programs were installed.

BUZZ!

"I haven't even touched anything yet, computer, why are you screeching at me?"

BUZZ! BUZZ!

"Stop it or I'll pull your plug."

The door opened.

"Dr. Kendall, that's your intercom buzzing," Brook said pointing to the phone on the right corner of the desk, "Press the flashing button and say hello."

Fumbling under scrutiny, she followed Brook's direction, "Hello."

"Good morning, Dr. Kendall, I'm Dr. Locke. Look forward to meeting you. Come over to my office as soon as you are settled." The conversation ended with a click and Taylor holding the receiver, half wondering what had just happened.

He sounds nice enough. Didn't mince words. Must be busy after a few days away from the office. With that thought, Taylor checked her hair, applied lipstick and straightened her pearl necklace. Reaching into her monogrammed burgundy leather briefcase, she pulled out a matching notepad holder and approached the secretarial station.

Brook glanced up briefly, then pointed a blue glittered fingernail toward the office two doors to the left.

The door was half open, so Taylor spent a moment scanning Locke's office. His furnishings were similar to hers except for two floor-to-ceiling, jammed-packed bookcases. Not the decorator kind of matching books, but the worn-binding, well-read type of books that she favored. Diplomas on the wall and a few pieces of eclectic art were all that covered the back wall. Unlike the other offices she had seen at MACS, Locke's office demonstrated his professionalism and personal style in a way that made the glitz of Dr. Marco's space seem like an expensive pretender. Rather than stand around like a voyeur, Taylor knocked on the half open door. A masculine voice invited her to enter.

Locke's handshake was firm and his greeting sincere, but Taylor couldn't help but wonder what it was about this field that compelled them to grow a goatee and wear tweed jackets with jeans.

He motioned for Taylor to sit across from him at the small conference table to the right of his desk and began immediately, "We are pleased to have you on board as our first psychology resident. Although Dr. Girard cut the deal with your university and will probably want to sign off on your work, I'm your actual clinical supervisor."

Taylor nodded politely to disguise her overwhelming relief. *Locke appears to be the safer choice. Too much time in close quarters with Dr. Marco's visual assaults would go beyond the call of duty. If only Mindy Sewell had drawn this residency instead of SouthBay, her warp drive libido could send Dr. Marco running to Human Resources crying sexual harassment. Or as Mama says, "Turnabout is fair play."*

"First I need to acquaint you with some of the basics. Dr. Kendall, are you following me so far?" Locke brought her attention back from her daydream. He gave her a wire bound booklet with thirty pages of organizational charts, program summaries and report forms. Pointing to a series of three-inch notebooks on the adjacent credenza he said, "These volumes are the complete text of patient care manuals, program protocols and so forth ad nauseum. You are welcome - make that encouraged - to review these manuals. What you have in your hands is the short version with enough information to bring you up to speed on clinic procedures fairly quickly."

For the next two hours, Dr. Locke painstakingly went over

each page of the smaller protocol booklet with Taylor. So much for planning to impress him with her command of theories and techniques, she was drowning in the acronyms and jargon of professional psychology in the real world.

Brook's voice interrupted Dr. Locke's review, "Hey, Sam, did you know that Taylor is supposed to be at the caldron by eleven?"

"Pardon her misguided humor, she means the lab," Locke quickly corrected. "This is a good time for a break. I'll go to the washroom and be right back. We'll stop in at the lab and then we'll go to the clinic so you can see what we do."

When he was out of sight, Brook elaborated on her warning, "Be careful down in that pit they call a lab. And don't touch the Nutracuratives. I think it doubles as paint thinner. It's all super hush-hush stuff."

"Secrecy is not unusual with proprietary formulas," Taylor said.

"Sounds like you've been practicing the PR department's official spin. But let me tell you, I've been here working late at night and seen some strange looking characters stop at the second floor. Not to mention that they have the lights out, spooky music playing, and lots of flickering candles. How high tech is that?"

"There must be a logical explanation."

"Wait 'til you're on the receiving end of Lorraine's temper. And catch the wardrobe: light black, medium black, and dark black. Always black. She's a walking shadow. Wish I had the nerve follow her into the rest room. Then I could find out if she has a reflection in the mirror. Analyze that one, Doc."

"I have to admit she's a bit old for the teen gothic crowd." Taylor didn't want to tell Brook about her encounter in the parking lot last night.

"The whole Lorraine thing reminds me of this movie I saw about these women who were competing for a chance to run the major entertainment division of some media company and one of them sold her soul to the devil to put a curse on the other one..."

"Brook, get a grip. You make it sound like Lorraine is a character from a horror movie. Why would an educated woman get involved with some cult?"

"You're half right. There's no way Lorraine worships anything. Besides, rumor has it that Satan worships her." Brook delivered her parting shot just as Locke returned.

Left with the peculiar image of Lorraine in the underworld, Taylor followed Dr. Locke to the elevator. Silently they descended to the second floor, Gina's lab kingdom. Taylor was acutely aware of the sound of the elevator doors closing behind them. The second floor lobby was deserted aside from a few pieces of sculpture, one Dali-like painting and an unoccupied reception desk. The door to the right was marked, "File Room – Authorized Entry Only".

Locke moved toward the lab door on the left. He placed his right hand over a number pad and typed in a four digit code. From her vantage point, the code began with 2-2 like the code to Brook's keycard drawer. A disembodied mechanical voice announced, "Access approved. Enter rapidly."

* * * * *

He shuffled his feet aimlessly near the curbside hot dog vendor at the corner of Second Street and Second Avenue North, a prime spot for watching people stream in and out of the nearby office towers. That's when he saw her leave the building across the street. Her stride was crisp and her expression tense. She seemed to be headed nowhere fast.

He tossed the sports page into a nearby trash can and jogged down a parallel alley on the opposite side of the building to intercept her without being obvious. By the time she followed the curving sidewalk leading to the waterfront yacht basin, he was already stationed at the corner as if he had been there for hours.

Taylor was so consumed with her own circuitous thinking that she bumped into him mumbling, then by reflex said, "Sorry."

"That's okay, I've never been the hit and run victim of a guinea pig before."

"What are you talking about?"

"That's what you said. To be specific, you said, 'Freaking guinea pig.'"

A coral flush came over Taylor's ivory complexion.

"Hey, lady, it's okay. I've heard worse. Looks like you need to get away from something or somebody."

Taylor struggled to regain her dignity. Instinctively she backed away.

"I bet your mother told you never to talk to strangers. But I'm not that strange."

Taylor took a moment to look him over. He was tall and lean with slicked back brown hair and nondescript gray eyes. He wore chino pants with a well-worn navy knit shirt. He could be a young millionaire escaping the ladies lunch groups that pack the St. Pete Yacht Club at noon, or maybe he's a bum who found used Italian leather loafers at a Central Avenue thrift shop.

He pulled the lining out of his side pants pockets, "See, no weapons."

She laughed and relaxed her defensive stance. The walk signal flashed as the traffic light changed.

He seized the moment, "If you have fifteen minutes, I'll show you the best view in downtown and promise not to snatch your purse."

"I'm not carrying a purse."

"See, that settles it. Now you know I have no desire to snatch your purse. Besides if that was my intent, I'd dump you for bigger game," he pointed to a garishly dressed woman on the opposite street corner with a duffle straw tote.

They walked toward the marina, stopping at a green bench under two stately royal palms. "This is my official thinking spot.

Welcome to my home away from home."

Taylor was still glancing around a bit nervously, but sat down beside him and took a deep breath, clearly trying to relax.

"Now listen, lady, I have my standards about strangers too. Not just anyone is invited to my bench. It's time we were properly introduced. I'm Gabe."

"Hello, Gabe. My name is Taylor."

"You must work in one of those glass jungles."

"No, I work in that 1930's restoration building two blocks away."

"Don't tell me what you do, let me guess."

She watched him give her the once over again.

"Expensive suit, probably Ralph Lauren, so you're not from the secretarial pool. The bold scarf is too much for a banker. Those heels are too fancy for a government worker who has to stand all day behind a service counter. Too serious looking for a real estate agent. Too proper for a topless dancer. Am I getting close?"

"No, you aren't. It's apparent you're not a psychic," she responded not letting him have all the snappy retorts, "I'm a psychologist. Well, almost."

"An almost psychologist? Have you failed to shrink enough heads to be taken seriously?"

"You're surprisingly close to the truth. I graduated last month with a doctorate in counseling psychology. This is the first week of a one year residency."

"Dr. Taylor, I like the sound of that."

"No, its Dr. Kendall, Taylor is my first name." It was clear from her expression that she was scolding herself for letting down her guard. Shifting the conversation she asked, "What's your name?"

"Gabe. Just Gabe. You know, like Madonna or Prince."

"Why? Are you hiding your identity?"

"Only when I'm working," he replied with honesty that she failed to appreciate.

"What is your line of work?"

"Officially, I'm an actor. But for the time being I'm helping out at an art gallery up on Fifth Avenue. You know, trying to earn a few bucks between acting jobs."

"Do you have any training for the stage?"

"Doctor, your academic snobbery is showing. Yes, I even have a college degree. But I prefer my flexible lifestyle to wrapping a silk noose around my neck everyday and joining the corporate worker bees in their cubicles."

The mention of corporate workers jolted Taylor back to reality. A glance at her watch told him that she must get back to the office.

"*Tempus does fugit.* Or simply, we both need to get back to work," Gabe said as he rose slowly from the bench and extended his hand for a business-like handshake.

"Thanks for letting me share your thinking spot, Gabe," she said.

"Anytime. By the way, this bench does double duty as my lunch spot most days. Feel free to bring your brown bag and join me. Shall we meet here tomorrow?" He wanted to kick himself. That was rushing her. As many times as he has done the casual encounter with a target he knew better than to move too fast.

"My schedule isn't established, but thanks anyway. Maybe we'll see each other around."

"Some days I'm not even here, Taylor. Take over the bench for yourself. And if I am here and you want privacy, tell me to get lost. With your kind of work you need a stress break more than I do."

His words rang true. She reflected briefly on the irritation that drove her to leave the building for fresh air. "Don't give away my seat anytime soon," Taylor said with a glowing smile.

Gabe paused, watching her walk back to the MACS building until she was out of sight. The first contact is always the hardest. He knew the rules. Be friendly, but not too intimate. Create a charming lure, like the waterfront bench. Be available without being pushy.

No need to worry there. Her co-workers will be pushy enough. The stress level in her environment will produce many reasons to flee. Maybe tomorrow. Maybe a few days. No matter. When Taylor needed someone to talk to, he'd be there. Yes, indeed, he made a valuable connection today. Time was running out and he had to establish his connection to Taylor Kendall quickly if she was to be used as his eyes and ears inside MACS.

* * * * *

The last place Taylor wanted to go was back inside that building. Leaving was only a fleeting thought. Her car keys were in her purse and her purse was in her office. Besides, like it or not, MACS owned her for the next year.

As she entered the lobby, a green-shirted therapist was leading a group of eight patients from the ground floor MACS clinic to the waiting van outside. She read in the corporate manual that patients must always be supervised by a staff member when entering or leaving the building. Was that one of the schizophrenia treatment groups? Dale said treating schizophrenia was a lot like predicting the weather in Florida. If you don't like what you see, wait an hour and you'll get something different.

Taylor was glad to find Brook's desk empty. She was not in the mood for perky. Entering her office, she found Sam Locke sitting in the guest chair. She startled.

"Sorry, Taylor, I didn't mean to frighten you." Locke pushed the door closed with his foot. "I want you to know that I had no idea about this switch-pitch in your schedule. For what it's worth, I was as surprised as you."

"It's okay, Dr. Locke, I don't blame you."

"No, that's not good enough. If we are going to work together, I want you to know that I look out for my people. I'll get this thing straightened out as soon as possible. And I give you my word that it won't compromise your training."

Compromise. This very residency is a compromise. Dale warned me not to obsess over taking a last chance residency. Work out the time and get licensed. Better professional opportunities would come along. Now it's another compromise within a compromise. No point in taking it out on Locke. Maybe he can help. Taylor responded, "I want to be a team player but I'm disappointed to have my clinical time limited by a research assignment that any master's level student can do."

"I understand completely. As I told you this morning, we need to replace our program entry assessment tools with more sophisticated methods. That's an area where I see you doing some solid work. Let me talk with Dr. Marco when he returns next week and see what can be done," Locke tried to sound upbeat, but his tone sounded more like a congressman making a wishful campaign promise. He excused himself and left her office.

Alone again, Taylor jotted a note on tomorrow's page in her agenda to bring the tired old statistical calculator that saw her through Descriptive and Advanced Research classes and the program evaluation text. *This project might redeem the wretched term when I learned more about the chaos theory of the universe than program evaluation. There's at least one whacked out instructor in every program except here at MACS where losing touch with reality seems to be a job prerequisite. One thing is certain; this so called research assignment is vague and meanders between experimental and quasi-experimental formats to review old cases and keep up with treatment results in current cases. The goal seems to be to prove that the PR spin actually matches the research for MACS programs. Let me take a wild guess - scientific rigor falls to results*

She shrugged at her screen saver and said aloud, "Who gives a royal rat's butt about research details as long as I get it done fast and they don't know the difference?"

* * * * *

Balancing two of her favorite Starbuck's™ Grande lattes in the crook of one arm and a briefcase hanging from the opposite shoulder, Carla knocked on Taylor's office door, "Coffee time!"

Brook turned from the grinding copy machine to shout, "She's not in the office."

"What do you mean not in?" Carla glanced at her Cartier watch. Ten-fifteen. After wasting over an hour of her Thursday morning at the attorney's office, she was more than ready for a break.

"You were about to tell me where Taylor is?"

Brook emerged from her self-imposed fog to respond, "She went off somewhere with Tiffany."

Nodding acknowledgement, Carla moved on to her own office to set down the briefcase and purse. She pressed the intercom for Nursing Services.

"Yeah, it's nursing, whadaya want?"

"Good morning, Tiffany. Sounds like you are really using what you learned at the seminar on business communications."

"Yo Carla, what's up?"

Carla stifled the urge to reprimand her sister-in-law. Experience has shown how impossible it was to insult the gold-digging bimbo. The only thing that she and Gina agreed on was that Tiffany needed a one way ticket to Outer-Mongolia. "I'm looking for Dr. Kendall."

"She's still in the fifth floor conference room."

"Still? Since when?"

"Since Tuesday afternoon when she got roped into some project for your mother and Gina."

Carla jammed the receiver back on the phone. She picked up the coffees. Without breaking her stride, she announced to Brook, "I'm the rescue party bringing provisions to Dr. Kendall. I'll be on the fifth floor if you need me."

"Naughty girl! You're interfering with the latest grand plan."

"So what? I've been an interference to my mother and sister

all my life."

Once on the executive level, Carla peeked out of the elevator noticing that Sally was occupied with a phone call. She waited until Sally began speaking again and then made a dash into the Executive Conference room to avoid being challenged. "Coffee break, anyone?"

"Carla!" Taylor exclaimed, feeling relieved at the sight of a friendly face, "How did you find me?"

"Better question is how did you get kidnapped from the clinic and stuck up here in la-la land?"

Taylor's reply was cut short as Victoria Girard pushed open the conference room door. "Carla, are you interrupting Dr. Kendall's work?"

"Good morning, Mother."

"Go back downstairs and tend the work at your desk, Carla." Victoria gave her daughter a disdainful glance before turning her attention to disengaging a heavy gold chain bracelet from its snare at the edge of her lilac lace cuff.

"Mother, this is America. Employees get coffee breaks. Besides, I have some important Medicare forms in my office for Taylor to sign. Remember the way it all works - forms lead to billing and billing leads to money," Carla came as close to a taunt as she dared.

"Very well. Go and attend to business immediately. Keep in mind that Dr. Kendall needs to return to her research. I expect her back here before the coffee gets cold," Victoria rotated her short frame on black alligator heels stomping an imprint of each shoe into the plush emerald carpet along the path to her private office.

As soon as Victoria was out of sight Taylor said, "Please don't get in trouble on my account."

"No big deal. In time you'll become immune to Mother's dictatorial ways. My mother can make Evita Perón seem like a Sunday school teacher. The fact is, she's at her worst when

Father is out of town. Here, take your coffee and let's escape to my office."

Inside Carla's office, Taylor kicked off her shoes and felt relaxed, "So what do I need to sign?"

Carla fished through the middle stack of papers on her desk. She handed a memo to Taylor and said, "Sign here."

"There must be a mistake. This is a memo to Brook about ordering my business cards."

"Sign," Carla insisted, pointing to a line below Dr. Locke's signature authorizing the cards.

Taylor felt a thrill at writing her professional name: Dr. Taylor Kendall. She pushed the memo across the table.

"Okay. That's done. Enjoy your coffee and tell me what's going on."

"Hold it. What happened here? Where are the important Medicare documents that can't wait?"

Carla laughed vigorously enough to make her curly black hair appear to dance, "Taylor, you are so straight laced. There are no documents. I just wanted to get you out of Mother's clutches. I don't want you to feel guilty, so I gave you something to sign. Besides, lying in the line of duty is a Girard family tradition."

CHAPTER 5

On the drive to work, the disc jockey interrupted various songs to scream out, "TGIF!" Never before, even during comprehensive exams week did Taylor feel so thankful to have survived until Friday. The days were endless. Walking down the hall to the rest room prompted Sally to follow. She even brought Taylor's coffee because she insisted that, "the special Jamaican Blue, fresh ground coffee beans we use for the executive suite coffee maker are the best in the company." *Good try, Sally*. Kindness notwithstanding, Taylor still felt that Sally was her jailer. Clearly Victoria did not want Taylor to wander around the clinic or the office.

After a few hours of mind-numbing work it was Tiffany, oddly enough, that provided Taylor cover for the escape to lunch. Taylor crouched behind the palm fronds to peek out the conference room mini-window near Sally's desk. Tiffany was whining about wanting more money or a credit card for lunch since her husband, Felipe, was busy in the billing system meeting. Then her opportunity came. The elevator door parted for the mail clerk and his rolling cart. That gave Taylor enough time to bolt from the conference room and into the elevator. As the doors were closing, she shouted, "Going to lunch. See you later."

* * * * *

Outside the MACS building, the bright sun glared onto the pavement forcing Taylor to squint. The sidewalks were filling with the first wave of the lunch crowd. She turned her head as if responding to her name being called and then practically ran toward the waterfront. She was out of breath when she reached the green bench.

After a few moments of sitting in the calm breeze, a mellow masculine voice spoke, "Welcome back to the thinking spot."

Taylor opened her eyes and her face instantly lit up with a welcome smile, "Hello Gabe."

He sat down on the bench and placed a medium size bag between them.

"You must be working hard. I haven't seen you for days."

"More like chained to the conference table."

Gabe reached into the sack and opened a box of fried chicken. The sizzling odor made Taylor's stomach growl audibly.

"How about sharing my lunch?"

"Oh no, I can't do that. I'll get something back at the office."

"Junk food from the snack machine? Absolutely not! You spread out the lunch things and I'll run over to the marina for another cola."

Taylor paused a moment as if to consider the etiquette of accepting his offer, but hunger won the day. She began rummaging through the bag and barely noticed that it was already packed with two sets of utensils.

She savored the wonderful coleslaw and lukewarm barbeque beans, "That fried chicken is close to what my Mama makes."

Gabe watched her eat. *She hasn't been eating well. Probably downing anything available inside that loony bin and hurrying back to work.* He scooped the last bite of beans from the paper container and fed it to her. Then he pulled a bag of M&Ms™ from his pocket. He slowly tore open the top. *Look at that expression. She's a chocoholic all right.* He poured some candies into his hand and held it out to her. As she reached for some, he closed his hand.

"Wait a minute. You don't show up and eat my lunch without a price, lady."

"Okay, kind Sir, what's my share of the tab?"

"Truth."

"About what?"

"About what is bothering you. Did you think I didn't notice?" Gabe paused and let his availability and willingness to listen sink in. Surely she needed someone to talk to, someone outside of MACS.

"Remember when we met on Tuesday? You said I looked stressed. Well, it's been a disappointing week and I've got fifty-one more of them to go," Taylor sighed.

"Maybe you need more time to adjust to working with MACS patients. I've seen the vans unload in the morning. They are pretty odd looking characters."

Taylor shrugged her shoulders, "I don't know if I like their patients or not. I spent less than two hours in the clinic before getting shanghaied up to the Executive Suite for some stupid statistical study. As if I didn't do enough of that in grad school. I didn't sign on to be a number-cruncher. Not to mention working with Gina. She's creepier than any of the patients. And Victoria Girard, one of the owners, what an in-your-face control freak she is."

"So you haven't worked with any patients?"

"No, I've only seen patients at a distance."

"Anything unusual about the patients?"

"The worst I've seen is a poor woman who must have had a psychotic episode the day I arrived. She ran into traffic and was killed. You probably heard about it."

"Was that the woman who was killed at the intersection across from your office building?"

"Yes. She must have been hallucinating to run into the street as the light turned green. She was batted around between cars like a rag doll. It was horrible. And yet nobody at MACS talks about it. I guess they don't get reimbursed for critical incident debriefing and grief therapy." Taylor felt relieved to say aloud what had been churning restlessly in her thoughts.

Like a bartender rushing to refill an empty glass, Gabe kept supplying M&Ms™ as Taylor's story spilled out. She told him about her expectation to work in the MACS clinic. She was so happy when Dr. Locke suggested that she begin by conducting entry and exit evaluations for the patients as well as facilitating group sessions. He reviewed the basic treatment objectives for each group in the rotating daily schedules for MACS Partial Hospitalization Program (PHP) located on the ground floor of the corporate headquarters. Locke wanted her to conduct two groups each day to get started. She chose to do a bibliotherapy group and a problem solving process group for the young adult schizophrenia treatment groups.

The plan was for her to observe the social workers who currently lead those groups for a week, sit in as co-therapist for the second week, and take over the groups by the third week. That would give her time to get familiar with the MACS approach. Along the way, she would be involved in the treatment, team meetings, diagnostic conferences, assessments and some individual therapy sessions. It was the chance to do the work for which she had trained so many years. Locke expressed confidence in her. What was even more amazing was that instead of being treated as an interloper, the other social workers she met welcomed her. And then there was the summons from on high.

Locke took her to the lab where Gina gave a cursory explanation of the Nutracuratives that gained so much positive press for MACS. Psychopharmacology is an increasingly important part of training, so she knew a fair amount about current medications for psychiatric and mood disorders. She asked a lot of questions, partly out of curiosity and partly to give Gina a forum in which to be superior. Maybe she asked too many questions. Although Locke seemed detached about it, the vein in Gina's neck throbbed noticeably when Taylor asked if the woman who was killed in the traffic accident was receiving treatment with the MACS Nutracuratives. A few hours later, she was called out from the clinic and sent to the fifth floor.

Tiffany Girard accompanied her. What a cretin! Brook may

babble out of enthusiasm, but she has the brains to get back on track. Taylor doubted if Tiffany could concentrate long enough to pass a simple mental status exam. Whatever that girl did to entice the Girard's youngest son, Felipe, it had nothing to do with cognitive abilities.

Taylor recalled how Victoria Girard strode overbearingly into the conference room. She took her place in the leather swivel armchair at the head of the conference table. Speaking louder than necessary in a room with only two occupants, she rambled on expansively about MACS. Her arms moved in static gestures, failing to keep pace with her rapid speech. Taylor's mind went on split screen with Victoria on one side and on the other, old news reels of Hitler haranguing for hours as his subjects struggled to stay awake.

After an hour that felt more like three, Gina arrived with an armload of file folders which she dumped onto the table. Victoria continued with a flight of ideas whose topics changed so unexpectedly that Taylor put down her pen. When Victoria's speech slowed down and her wide-eyed expression turned droopy, Gina took over. She presented a list of items to be reviewed from each patient file for the study of treatment effectiveness. Distraction notwithstanding, Gina could not keep Taylor from noticing that Victoria was giving a textbook representation of a manic mood swing, sliding off a high into the next valley of despair. Taylor listened, curbing her irritation. There were maybe a forty files to be reviewed. It's a boring task but tolerable if that's what it took to appease the hierarchy and get on with clinical work.

Such was not the case. The next day, more files appeared. The suggestion of bringing the files downstairs to her office was met with discouragement. Sally even brought fresh bagels with cream cheese set on a gold rim china plate to accompany the special brewed coffee. The next day, Sally ordered pizza delivery for lunch. A little treat, she claimed, courtesy of Victoria. At least this was a high class jail. Water was plentiful in the Waterford crystal pitcher on the table. And bread, well, it came disguised with four choice toppings and extra crispy crust.

The file review was dull enough, but the confinement was ridiculous. Taylor swore on the hot blueberry muffins Sally brought for coffee break not to spend another full day inside the conference room. Thanks to the mail clerk's cart wheel getting stuck in the elevator track, Taylor had time to escape.

As Taylor told her story, Gabe had no difficulty imagining the people she described. When she paused, he asked, "Are you going to continue working at MACS?"

"I have no choice," she responded, completely missing his sigh of relief.

"The last thing you want to do around that bunch of piranhas is to let them know they have your cornered. Power only respects strength. If you let them think they can push you around, they will."

"But I have no power there, Gabe."

"Oh yes, you have. They handed it to you."

"How do you figure that?"

"Knowledge is power, Taylor."

"And exactly what do I know that is so powerful?"

"Maybe nothing. Maybe everything."

She cast a puzzled look at him, "Are you testing out dialogue for some free form play? You aren't making any sense."

He broke forth with his broad smile, but this time with a slight bit more dimple showing.

"Gabe, you look like the cat that fell into the cream barrel. Come on, no fair plying me with chocolate to hear my story then sitting there like a sphinx."

He had successfully peaked her curiosity. "The true story of whether MACS treatments are as good as they claim to be is waiting to be discovered in those patient files. If it is good, write a journal article about it. If it's a crock, then write about that.

Either way you get published which is bound to look good on your vitae right?"

Taylor mulled over the possibilities. "Do you know anything about the MACS programs? Have you heard Dr. Girard singing his programs' praises around town? He's in Fort Lauderdale this week getting an award for their work with indigent schizophrenic groups. I'll look a day late and a dollar short with my half-baked version of how to glorify the sacred cow."

"Then look for the cloven hoof."

"Please, no more weird metaphors. You sound like Brook."

"What I mean is, look for the flaw. Let me give you an example. Do you realize that the most sophisticated airplane can crash because of a flaw in a single part; a part small enough to hold in your hand?"

"Hey, I don't like some of the people running MACS, but it's not my job to ruin an effective program that helps the people who rarely got any kind of treatment before coming to their clinics."

She is not a rabble rouser or a scandal chaser. She honestly views the world from the positive angle. No doubt, she could be passionate in defense of a good cause. Like any good psychologist might do, it's time to reframe the message.

"Let me put it this way, have you ever watched on television as the ground crew at Cape Canaveral prepares for a space shuttle launch?"

She nodded, finishing the last swallow from her drink can.

"Who hasn't been disappointed when the countdown clock was stopped minutes before the launch? Sometimes it's because of a small flaw like a crack in a bolt or a tile that didn't stay in place. As frustrating as that is, the ground crew is focused on keeping the astronauts safe and the shuttle flying at peak performance. The result of all those safety concerns and corrections is many successful missions," he paused to give her time to visualize the scene he had described.

He continued, "Imagine what a service you could do if you

identify and assist in correcting any flaw that might alter the future of the MACS? They certainly can't thrive as a program with the bodies of patients littering the street in front of the corporate headquarters. What if that disturbed woman's death happened because someone wasn't vigilant enough? Or some fail-safe procedure failed? You are new to their system. That gives you the advantage of a fresh perspective." *Look at those eye movements. She's replaying the accident scene in her mind, exactly as I need for her to do.*

"Gabe, I would do anything to keep that from happening to another patient. What you're suggesting sounds like what Dale, my advisor, would say. He's drilled into us the importance of bringing in another consulting professional to see a puzzling case from a different viewpoint. He says it's one way to get beyond your own therapeutic blinders. I think you have a great idea. I'm going to look intently at those files."

"If you want to know whether the dead patient's accident was in any way related to the program, don't you need her file too?"

"Absolutely! And I'm going to find that file for comparison. This make-work project to test my patience may surprise them all with what I can do."

"That's the spirit, Taylor!" *Appealing to the helper instincts that drew Taylor to psychology is the best way to keep her from grasping the big picture of the role I have for her at MACS.*

* * * * *

"She did what? Where did she go? You better hope she comes back after lunch!" Gina shrieked into the telephone.

Lorraine looked up from her sandwich, "What are you having a panic attack about this time?"

"Dr. Kendall skipped out and Sally doesn't know where she went!"

Lorraine stretched like a cat, "You don't suppose she went to get lunch? I warned you and Victoria that excessive restrictions don't work on higher level personnel."

"You said that we needed to keep her away from possible contact with the police while they nosed around doing interviews."

"Yes, but I had in mind something less obvious than a time-out chair in the conference room. If she wasn't suspicious after Harriet's death, then she must be after a few days with Victoria's mania and Sally's guard dog routine."

Mulling it over, Gina became frantic, "If we screw this up, I won't get another chance to break that bastard's hold on Father's approval."

"Is everything in your life tied to this mythical struggle with Blake for Marco's crown and scepter? Besides, Blake's not a bastard. You told me that Marco held Victoria's hand during Carla's delivery in Miami two weeks before he jetted off to Mexico City to arrange a quickie divorce and arrive in New Orleans to marry Serena the day before Blake's legitimate birth. Did you ever consider that it's Marco who's the bastard in this family?"

The facts irritated Gina yet she never failed to defend her father, "My father was duped by that New Orleans whore whose only talents are between the sheets."

"How did she dupe your mother?"

Gina picked up a mortar and pestle paperweight and hurled it toward the door.

"Temper, temper."

"I don't know why you refuse to see what a stumbling block Blake is for my future, for our future," Gina replied trying to bring her anger under control.

"Our biggest problems right now are a dead patient, a police inquiry that could trigger a Medicare inspection and a psychologist-wannabe who stumbled onto the accident scene and may have heard something damaging. How you can make all that Blake's fault is beyond rational thought."

She walked behind Gina's desk chair and began to massage the muscles in Gina's neck and shoulders. She had to bring Gina back to reality so they could work together on short circuiting the problem.

"We don't actually know if Harriet said anything to Dr. Kendall or anyone else. Do you think we ought to ask her?"

"Don't be stupid, Gina. I agree with Victoria that the entire situation must be downplayed. As far as we know Dr. Kendall hasn't contacted the police and the investigator doesn't know she exists. If she heard something incriminating, I think she would have spoken up. Let's wait for the private detective's report to find out where her skeletons lie. Then we'll have something on her to secure her silence if it comes to that," Lorraine felt increasingly comfortable with her plan. "Remember, we promised Victoria that we would handle everything during your father's absence. This is your chance to make points with your father and your mother."

Lorraine rearranged Gina's collar and gave her a quick kiss on the forehead as she headed for the door. "One more thing, about that syringe I gave you Monday, you did put it in the lab's bio-waste container, didn't you? Tell me it went out with the hazardous waste collection yesterday."

Gina nodded her head and smiled as Lorraine walked out and closed the office door. Reaching into the pocket of her lab coat, Gina pulled out the syringe that was inside a plastic zip-top sandwich bag. She appreciated the reminder as she often forgot to empty her lab coat pockets until time to drop them into the laundry cart. Carefully she stashed the baggie in the middle of a silk plant next to her file cabinet. *Father always said that love was grand but covering your butt was better. That syringe with Lorraine's fingerprints might be my insurance, or least a 'get out of jail free' card.*

CHAPTER 6

D r. Sam Locke could see the employee parking lot from his office window. As he expected, Victoria was alone when she got into Marco's red Ferrari and gunned the motor for a quick take off onto First Avenue. Mid-morning he overheard secretaries in the kitchen passing the warning that Victoria was in "one of her moods," so he knew it was only a matter of hours before the inevitable stormy departure. Perfect. He bypassed Sally's intercept and dialed direct to Serena's private office.

Putting on his jacket, Sam picked up a legal pad and stopped at Brook's desk to say that he was going to the fifth floor.

"Got your fluff stuff?"

"Thanks for the heads-up. You're getting good at this." Sam dashed back into his office, picked up two new journals, and walked out again.

"You always say that you need to bring something to deflect attention from the real purpose when you get an audience with Serena."

"How true. In this situation, I'm going for an approach much like drowning the barbeque grill in liquid fire starter before lighting."

"Are you on the hot seat again, Sam?"

"No. Not that I know about. I'm trying to liberate Dr. Kendall."

"But she's under house arrest. Why not wait until Victoria gets back from her three daiquiri lunch and ask her?"

"No thanks, with Marco gone, this gives Serena, the rebel princess, a way to look like a peacemaker as she restores equilibrium to the kingdom. That's usually worth a diamond bauble or two from her grateful husband…and maybe a threesome with their partner."

"Don't go there, Sam. I'm much too visual."

* * * * *

Exiting the elevator, Sam noticed a new Aubusson rug in the reception area. He paused reverently to appreciate how many of the finer things in life his PHPs produced for the Girards. Then he saw Taylor in the conference room. She was so focused on those files that she paid no attention to the chime-like tone heralding the elevator's arrival on the Executive floor. Sam remembered the big deal Serena made about altering the sound of the elevator bell. Heaven knows how much extra money that customized jingle cost.

Although three secretaries and a receptionist made the Executive floor function, it was Sally, stationed in the middle like a sentry, who regulated access to the three Girards. Sam approached and announced that he was here to see Serena.

Sally punched up a computerized day book and entered Serena's file code, "But Dr. Locke, that's not possible. You aren't on our schedule for today."

"I think she plans to see me."

"I rather doubt it. I keep all the Girards' schedules and I would know…"

BUZZ! BUZZ!

Sally picked up the telephone. Her self-serving grin turned to a frown.

"It seems that Serena will see you after all," Sally choked out each word.

Sam's sardonic expression was his best response.

Following the established ritual, he took a seat in the wing chair to the right of the grand dame's desk. He preferred the right chair since discovering how to use a picture frame on the opposite wall as a mirror reflecting the door. It helped him see whether Lorraine was lurking around the corner before he said something that he did not want her to hear. Triangulation was MACS' most popular sport.

Serena finished signing several letters before looking up to acknowledge her visitor. "Good afternoon, Dr. Locke, what is the nature of this urgent matter about which you telephoned?"

"First of all, the programs are operating at 92% capacity this week. Take a look at the preliminary monthly patient census," he said removing a worksheet from his folder and placing it on her desk. Like the business gurus say, give the good news then ask for what you want.

"Does this mean more transfers into our Live Anew Wellness Centers?"

"Yes, it certainly does. Quite honestly I think that your Live Anew concept will get at least 60% of the people who are released from MACS PHPs," he replied knowing how much Serena wanted to hear encouragement for the new venture.

"And of course you will instruct your therapists to begin presenting the value of Live Anew as transitional care to the patients well before their release to increase that number, correct?"

"Certainly!" okay, *one butt-kissing exercise down, one to go.* He pulled another show and tell item from his folder and opened to an article he found on the elevator ride upstairs. "Serena, I knew you would be interested in this article in the latest issue of *Psychology in Community Treatment.*" He pointed at the headline and abstract. "Here is another study supporting your ideas about the importance of follow-up care for community dwelling older adults with schizophrenia, particularly those with no family support system." He handed the journal to her.

She read the abstract intently. Then she did what the typical untrained person would, skip to the recommendation. Fortunately she had no clue about psychological research methodology or she would have realized that the only connection this study had with her Live Anew concept is that both involved chronic mental health patients living independently.

Sam knew that in feeding Serena's ego about her pet projects, relevance was never as valued as perceived agreement. Marco would know the difference. However, he rarely devoted time to serious study. It was not for lack of knowledge. Marco was a well trained psychiatrist, when he had to be. Like he told Sam once over too many brandies, "Keep the women out of the way of serious deal making by occupying them with running trivial details of the businesses we create. After all, that's why God made them…and of course, for our pleasure."

Sam looked at Serena while she rattled on yet again about attaching Live Anew centers to all the MACS' clinic sites in Florida. His mind wandered during these diatribes. *Serena is an acceptably attractive woman whose face comes from the hands of the best cosmetic surgeons money could buy. Too bad the tummy tucks didn't work as well. But it's well disguised in very expensive clothing. She is like a swan carved in dry ice; pretty to view, yet burns when touched. Maybe Marco likes the challenge. Or he enjoys upsetting the balance by alternately cavorting with his wife, Serena and his ex-wife, Victoria during his infrequent stops at home.*

"Sam, was there another matter to discuss?"

He cleared his daydream and began to explain how Taylor had been taken from the clinic and reassigned paperwork tasks. Carefully moderating his words to diminish the actual irritation he felt, he kept bringing the story back to how this will appear to her university.

"I assume that Marco has a good reason for this introductory approach. Did he discuss it with you before he left for the Atlanta conference?" she asked.

At last! She's finally taking the bait.

"To my knowledge, Dr. Marco is not aware of this change in Dr. Kendall's assignment. I understand it was Gina's idea and Victoria issued the order to support it. I guess I thought that

Victoria would have told you about it. I assumed you knew all the significant decisions at MACS," he replied slamming shut the trap. Her Mona Lisa smile fell into a sullen pout.

"What if Dr. Kendall goes back to the clinic after the project is completed?"

"Not a problem for me. I can work around it from a personnel perspective. After all, I didn't imagine the luxury of having a psychology resident when I made the quarterly schedules. But I know that the standards for a resident training site are high. If Dr. Marco is out of town when the university committee pulls an unannounced site visit, will you be the person to explain why we are out of compliance?" *If you want something done at MACS, go for money or ego. Let them think that either is at stake, then sweeten the deal by altering reality with some high sounding principles.*

"Precisely what, Dr. Locke, is the downside?"

"Serena, you and Dr. Marco and our Public Relations department have done so much to develop a positive image of MACS in the community and beyond. Now you are on the threshold of launching your Live Anew programs. I don't want to have all your hard work tainted by losing our first psychology resident. Imagine how impossible it would be to bring on board joint ventures with any credible university if we are disgraced as an advanced training site." That was about as thick as he could spread this load of manure. He sat back in the chair waiting for her to process his words and reach her predictably self-serving conclusion.

"How do you think we best handle this?"

"I'm sure that we can work out a schedule that returns Dr. Kendall to the clinic and gives her some time after program hours to do Gina's patient research. The research may take a little longer to finish, but the overall residency will remain in compliance."

Noticing a favorable expression on her face, he continued, "If Dr. Kendall has a good residency experience that will encourage her university, as well as others, to send more doctoral graduates. That's good for business and very good for public image. I'm sure there is promotional value to our first resident being a female from a respected regional university.

Serena took the bait. "Thus in your professional opinion, you think it would be suitable to include some time to learn about Live Anew in her training experience?"

"Definitely. Besides she'll have the advantage of already knowing the PHP program when the patients are stepped-down to the least restrictive treatement."

The Mona Lisa smile reappeared. She nodded indicating the audience was over.

He stood up, took two steps then turned back toward her. "There's one problem left. Who's going to clear this with Gina?"

"Gina does not make decisions in MACS, no matter how much she tries to play the heir apparent. I'll settle this with Victoria. Dr. Kendall will be back in the clinic on Monday."

He walked out knowing that the battle had been transferred to higher ground. As a bonus he set it up so that Gina would likely be chastised by Serena. Even a hint of Gina's attempt to usurp the power that Serena coveted for her precious, yet notably absent son, Blake, would put her in the attack mode. Past experienced showed that was not a pretty sight.

Leaving Serena's office, he walked into the conference room and whispered, "Taylor, stay cool. Your deliverance is in progress."

Before she could assimilate his words, he walked away and entered the elevator. When the doors closed and the motor engaged, he let out the belly laugh that he had repressed for the past hour.

Sam felt smugly satisfied as the elevator door opened at the fourth floor. Taking a step to exit, he was broad-sided by Lorraine rushing to enter. He caught his breath and said in a mellow voice, "If you want me that badly, just ask."

"Get out of my way, Sam."

He moved aside and watched the doors closed.

"Hey, boss, you are cruisin' for a brusin'," Brook said walking up beside him. "And since you are here, be a gentleman and carry some of these supplies."

Following Brook down the hallway, he asked, "Where is the princess of darkness off to in such a hurry? Is there a problem at one of the PHPs?"

"Don't think so, she was looking to see if you were in your office when she got a call on her cell phone. Acted mysterious, even for Lorraine. And then she revved up her broomstick and headed toward the elevator."

CHAPTER 7

Not the athletic type, Lorraine disdained the downtown walking crowd. Although her destination was less than a half mile from the office if traveled directly on foot, she drove the MG. The one-way streets managed to keep downtown drivers alert, but took a few extra blocks of driving to get where you were going.

She parked in the side alley and glanced around the entrance before walking up the stairs to the front door. This trendy spot was formerly a greasy spoon buffet where old folks and hungry college students sat side by side listening to the sound of their cholesterol rise with each bite. The new owners kept the white gingerbread front porch and pale green clapboard siding. At a distance it looked the same. Fortunately the dumpling special was long ago replaced by Nouvelle Cuisine appetizers. She shook her head in disbelief wondering why the new owners lost all sense of discretion with that swirling script sign on the front door in day glow purple paint: "Chez Sway".

Even during the afternoon cocktail hour, the ornate Victorian bar room was dimly lit with the warm glow of imitation gaslights and shielded from the hot Florida sun by heavy pull down shades. The deep claret upholstery made Lorraine feel quite at home. She motioned for the bartender.

"Hey Mojo Woman, too early for your action," he said as he sauntered up to her.

She reached over the bar, grabbed his left wrist and gave it a sudden twist.

Grimacing in pain, he whispered, "What do you want?"

Enjoying his discomfort, she slowly released her grip, "That's

MISS Mojo Woman to you, dude. Now where's Cutter?"

The bartender pointed toward a back booth then jammed his throbbing wrist into an ice bucket.

Cutter wasn't difficult to find; six foot six with washboard abs and shoulders the width of a 1958 Buick. He made eye contact with Lorraine, motioning for her to sit down. With a quick peck on the cheek, he dismissed the young man nestled beside him.

"Good grief, Cutter, are you still picking up chickens at the high school gym?"

"Hey babe, if you need your action older and slower, that's your deal. I've been telling you to work out with weights. Makes the nights last longer."

"Enough mutual sexual harassment. Have you finished the report?"

He reached inside a leather biker saddlebag and pulled out the thick manila envelope. Holding it beyond her reach, he saw her dark eyes burn with impatience.

"Is this worth the ridiculous price I'm paying you?"

"You know how to hurt a guy. My work is impeccable. No one does your dirty little jobs faster or more accurately."

He continued to clutch the envelope observing her irritation rise, "Do you realize how many private detectives hand over streaky copy machine duplicates and handwritten notes? Or worse yet use that disgusting erasable paper run through an ancient electric typewriter? Not for my clients. Look at that table of contents and matching dividers with each section in narrative form. Did I ever tell you that I was an English literature major in college?"

"Hand over the report!"

He grinned as he tossed it over to her. There was nothing to make a client more willing to pay a high price quite like a high demand for the product. It was like the infomercial guys turning viewers positively evangelistic over a new kitchen gadget.

Lorraine scoured the introductory section, ignoring Cutter's smooth rhetoric in favor of the facts. Taylor Dodd Kendall, age twenty-seven, born in Jackson, Mississippi and raised in Memphis, Tennessee. Oldest daughter of Dr. Thomas Edward Kendall and Julia Sterling Dodd. Attended the same private girls' school as her younger sisters, Savannah Sterling Kendall, age twenty-two and Paige Creighton Kendall, age seventeen. Received BA in Sociology from Vanderbilt University, graduating with honors in three years. Active in Alpha Omicron Pi Sorority, Pan Hellenic Council representative, tennis team and held several offices in student government. Member of the Cotton Carnival court. Presented along with her sister, Savannah, at the annual debutante ball during her second year at the university. Accepted at Vanderbilt for graduate Psychology program. Made a request to delay admission while traveling for a year as a chapter consultant for her sorority. When the year's break was over, Taylor passed on her option to return to Vanderbilt for graduate studies and enrolled in the Counseling Psychology program at Knight University in Sarasota.

Impatient to find more, Lorraine skipped to the tab marked "Relationships". Taylor was obviously one of those fashionably dressed privileged teenagers whose perfect teeth came from genes instead of years of orthodontia. Copies of articles in the *Memphis Commercial Appeal* chronicled her successes. Winning horse show ribbons. Winning debate tournaments. Winning trophies at piano competitions. Winning several academic scholarships. Winning - winning - winning. Lorraine fought back the inevitable comparison of Taylor's youth to memories of her own gawky, loner teenage existence.

Throughout the articles of Taylor's triumphs were enthusiastic accolades from her friends and teammates. There were still more articles of the "Buy One - Give One" school supply drive that Taylor organized as a service project her freshman year in high school. She received the Citizenship Medal and scholarship money along with the key to the city presented by the Mayor. The

newspaper even printed crayon scrawled letters of appreciation
from first graders who were thrilled to have pencil bags and
new tablets like the other children. The project that provided
these school supplies for underprivileged children grew each
year until, before leaving for Vanderbilt, Taylor persuaded a local
radio station to take on the sponsorship.

Another series of newspaper photos showed Taylor and
her high society friends at cotillions, bridesmaids' luncheons
and several victories in the Colonial Country Club's mother-
daughter tennis tournaments. Always smiling, Taylor appeared
amid equally attractive girlfriends in cashmere sweater sets and
on the arm of some tuxedo-clad young man. Clippings from a
society column featuring "Young Memphians" told of Taylor's
sorority initiation, election to various sorority offices and the
ceremony announcing that she wore the fraternity pin of Trey
Hamilton, a pre-med student at Vanderbilt.

There were more photos of the magazine perfect couple and
then suddenly Trey disappeared. The year she moved to Florida,
he transferred from Vanderbilt to Tulane in New Orleans. *No
serious relationships during graduate school, no messy divorce, no
live-in lovers, no abortions, no drug use, no traffic tickets, no jail
time, no police reports. . . the most dysfunctional part of this woman
is that she probably color codes her linen closet and alphabetizes the
cans in her pantry.*

"That's the best you could do? Where's the dirt?"

"Unlike the other employees I've been paid to investigate,
this Taylor is different. She's a real lady; dedicated student, loves
her family, an all around nice person. If I were straight, she's the
kind of the girl I'd bring home to meet my mother."

Lorraine shook her head, reached over and guzzled a large
swallow of Cutter's imported beer.

"Don't shoot the messenger if the result isn't what you
wanted. But the price is the same, even if there's no dirt to dish
out," he said pointing to an invoice clipped to the report cover.

"All right," she sighed as she reached for a trim line wallet from her inside jacket pocket. She counted out four hundred dollars in fifties, twenties and tens. He preferred small bills. No checks.

"Aren't you forgetting the extra fee for a rush job?"

She rolled her eyes and counted out another two hundred dollars.

"Nice doing business with you, Lorraine. I thrive on corporate distrust. Keep hiring new employees. I need your kind of steady investigative work to support me while I train for the fall bodybuilding competitions."

On the way out, Lorraine tossed a ten dollar bill into the bartender's tip dish. He flinched. She laughed.

Outside Cutter caught up with her. He opened her car door, which she was too preoccupied to challenge with her usual feminist rhetoric. She tossed the report on the passenger seat and drove back to MACS.

Cursing the elevator's slow speed, she practically pushed her way out of the doors at the second floor. Galloping down the hallway in large strides, she tapped the shoulder of the nearest lab assistant and demanded that he, "Tell Gina to meet me in my office immediately!"

Lorraine stretched out on the half-size sofa and dangled her long legs over one side. Moments later, Gina burst through the door. "Where is it?"

"On your desk."

"Is it what we wanted?"

"Read it for yourself."

Lorraine maintained a blank expression while Gina painstakingly read each page. Twenty minutes later, Gina threw the report at the trash can.

Lorraine sat upright, "So what did you learn about Dr. Kendall?"

"That twit is the prototype for a Virgin Mary lack-of-action figure."

* * * * *

Blake swung his nondescript sedan into a parking spot across from the restaurant where the MG roadster parked. He pulled the weather beaten Panama hat low on his forehead. He had been waiting beside the MACS parking lot to see where Gina would go after work, but when he saw Lorraine's MG dart past him in such a hurry he decided to follow. Using pocket-sized binoculars he read the name and description on the door of Chez Sway. That, along with the sparse crowd likely to be there at three o'clock, was enough to make him decide against trying to blend in with the regulars.

While he waited, he unfolded a city map and rested it against the steering wheel. He looked like another tourist sitting in a dull brown car trying to figure out directions around town. Establishing that image, he punched in a familiar phone number. He never failed to feel relief when the soft, melodious voice answered, "Quality Management, Carla Girard."

"How are things at the little shop of insanity?"

"I'm so happy that you called. I need to hear a sane voice occasionally"

"Are you all right? Is anyone bothering you?"

"Back up the brother-protector mode. I'm only bothered by paperwork today. Otherwise there's Mother's screaming, Gina's manipulating and general corporate paranoia. It's business as usual." Much as she tried to make light of her surroundings, the descriptions were, if anything, an understatement and he knew it.

"What's new with the gruesome twosome?"

"Nothing. Gina obsesses and Lorraine lurks, but it works for them."

"How's your new friend, Taylor?"

"She's terrific. In fact, you'd like her. Tall, attractive and totally unpretentious. She comes from a nice, normal old southern family. I need to introduce you."

Blake stifled a laugh, thankful that his sister could not see his facial expression. "Is this woman Marco's new bait to bring me back into the fold? In case you're wondering, I'm not lacking for female companionship."

Exasperated, Carla retorted, "If Taylor ever figures out how outrageous our family really is, she'll run like a gazelle from this job much less any other connections. I said she was a great woman for you, Blake, not for the family."

"Please, no matchmaking."

Carla remembered a situation certain to make her brother cringe, "So rather than listen to your sister, you might like to see if Cousin Micheline and Tia Isabela's goddaughter are still willing to cat fight over you?"

Blake would never forget the summer after his freshman year at Princeton. Marco sent him plane tickets to Caracas and directions to hire a boat for the short journey to the island. Tia Isabella, Marco's youngest surviving aunt, invited the entire Girard family, including wife and ex-wife, to holiday at her summer place in Porlamar, a chic island resort off the coast of Venezuela. Unknown to Tia, Serena had already invited her cousin's youngest daughter, the highly marriage-minded Micheline to visit.

If Tia Isabella was surprised at the extra guest, Serena was equally stunned by the constant presence of Elena, Tia's goddaughter. So much for a few weeks of rest and lounging on the beach as Blake spent most days trying to avoid being cornered by the petite New Orleans cousin and the smoldering eyed Venezuelan girl. For a week, it was a feast of feminine delights. Each girl found outlandish ways to gain his attention, no doubt coached by their respective sponsors. Then the good times turned serious. Both girls had designs on Blake far beyond his body. They wanted to trap him. Marry him. Own him.

Finally he enlisted Carla's help. She distracted the hopeful brides with shopping trips as she befriended each girl separately to gain information about their sponsors' latest plots. Finally, she sent a telegram to Father, after pleading with his manservant to reveal the location of his high stakes poker game at a mainland club.

Fortunately, Carla guessed right. Marco wanted to sanction every aspect of the future for his son and heir. He actually dropped the winning hand as he read her terse message: "The Prince is under siege. Serena's French cousin or Tia's choice? Who shall be the Princess bride?" Carla knew that selecting a wife for Blake was to be under her father's direction, not the whims of his thrice-married aunt and certainly not by the woman Victoria called "the little Creole tart who schemed her way into Marco's bed and into his life."

Marco arrived in Porlamar with his usual flair, driving a borrowed jeep through the rose garden directly onto the patio. Seeing his father's arrival gave Blake the same relief that battle fatigued soldiers felt when reinforcements marched over the hill. The next day, Marco made excuses about pressing business matters that he and his son must attend. With all the rush to depart, the women who remained behind would have been surprised to discover that Marco and Blake took a slow boat ride back to Caracas, doing a little fishing off the deck along the way. Then they flew to Cancun, Mexico for the final week of Blake's vacation.

Marco went along as far as Miami International Airport where, in the usual emotional farewell, Marco embraced his son and reminded him of his great destiny as the Girard heir. Blake was thankful to be on the way back to his dorm room instead of waking up with a drugged hangover in the heart shaped bed of a tacky mirrored bridal suite.

Still smiling at the thought of that frantic vacation, Blake said, "Do you think Micheline and Elena ever found husbands?"

"Shall I ask your mother and Tia Isabella for an update?"

"No! I'd rather join a monastery than to be chained to either of those gold diggers."

"Great idea!"

"Join a monastery? I've been there; not my style."

"No, silly, but I'll make some off-the-cuff comment to Tiffany about you in a monastery. Then she'll mix-it up in her usual stupid manner. By the time it gets back to your mother, she'll have the fit of the century thinking you have gone celibate."

"Not half as much as Marco will," he laughed at the dilemma this notion would cause for his father. "Imagine having to depend on Felipe and Tiffany to produce the Girard heir."

He glanced up in time to see Lorraine and an unknown man leaving the restaurant.

"Sorry, Carla, but I have to get back to work right now. Call you soon." With that he pressed the end button to disconnect the call and grabbed his camera from the case on the passenger side. *Sloppy work, Blake. Got so involved in a personal conversation that you weren't ready with the zoon lens when your target came out. Rookie mistake. But Girard luck is a wonderful thing.*

Not only did Lorraine stop to talk to the man, but they moved off the shaded porch and onto the open driveway where he could take a series of photos until the man turned away. Then he started his car and drove away.

That film had to be developed immediately. He wasn't completely familiar with downtown stores. Besides, it was too close for comfort. He might be recognized. From Fifth Avenue, he turned onto Fourth Street North and looked for the nearest Walgreens Drugstore with a one hour photo developer.

* * * * *

The photos turned out clear yet didn't tell the whole story. Even under a magnifying glass, the identity of the man who was with Lorraine remained a mystery. Blake summoned a colleague to meet him for happy hour at Tio Pepe Restaurante on Gulf to Bay near Courtney Campbell Causeway. It was always worth the drive to Clearwater. The Latin American style Spanish cuisine choices were similar to what Victoria used to make during times when they were low on servants and waiting for another scheme to pay off. With Marco's snobbery about eating Spanish food at any American owned restaurant north of Miami, he wasn't likely to run into any of his family here.

A medium built, reddish-blonde haired man slid into chair opposite Blake. Although thirty-something, Jack Sims looked like a college kid with his Kansas farm-boy wholesomeness. Situations had to be extremely serious to wipe away his chronically cheerful expression.

"Bring on the chips and salsa, my man, and let's talk," Jack said, slapping his friend on the shoulder.

"Park it, hayseed, and give me your full attention. This is business."

Jack picked up the photos and quickly scanned a few, "What were you doing hanging around outside Chez Sway?"

"Company business. Do you know anything particular about that place?"

"Not me, man. If I'm ready to howl, I'm more likely to be at the new club on Ulmerton Road than over there in fairy land."

"Did you miss the memo on political correctness?" As soon as he asked the question, Blake knew the answer. Jack was the plainspoken type who did his job by the numbers. He was also the proverbial "man's man" with strong moral viewpoints from that Midwestern upbringing.

Jack ignored the question, adjusting the magnifying glass over a photo, "Sure I know the guy. He's called Cutter. Although I think his real name is something old school like Archibald."

Blake stared at the photo. *Big fellow. Not fat, but strong. Might have been a good linebacker in younger days.* "What's his game?"

"Cutter started out as a bounty hunter after mustering out of the Army. I heard that he earned that nickname. Rumor has it he used to do some fancy knife work when the repo job turned ugly."

"Has he done time?"

"No, not hard time. He's spent his share of nights cooling off in the city jail on some minors. Oddly enough, he has a charming side capable of smooth talking his way out of most scrapes."

"Charming would not have been the word I would have chosen."

"Come on, Blake, be open- minded. My neighbor, Pete, works vice for St. Pete Police and he's known Cutter for years. Pete got him interested in bodybuilding."

"Is Pete that kind of friend?"

"No, Pete's married with two kids. Besides he said that the time he was recovering from a gunshot wound, Cutter brought complete gourmet-style dinners over to his house every night for a month and kept a protective watch over his family until the shooter was caught. Since then, he and Pete's wife, Bonnie, are big buddies. They sit at the kitchen table drinking coffee and debating the relative merits of Tupperware™ versus Rubbermaid™ for storing leftovers."

"A three hundred pound bouncer with kitchen fantasies? I doubt his clandestine meeting with Lorraine had anything to do with homemaking. He may have a feminine side, but she doesn't."

Jack burst out laughing. Sometimes Blake took the work too seriously. "Meanwhile back to answering your question. After Cutter got into bodybuilding, he had to protect his hide so he gave up the bounty hunting and took computer courses at the technical school. Now he runs a specialized investigative service getting the down and dirty on folks by letting his mouse do the walking."

"What does this have to do with MACS and Lorraine?"

"Beats me, but I have heard that he gets a lot of work from white collar clients; a suspicious boss, a competitive coworker.

Makes his contacts at Chez Sway, his unofficial office."

"So we have Mike Hammer with a tight butt and visions of young men dancing in his head."

"Blake, my man, you are out of touch with the alternative lifestyles."

"You can honestly say that knowing my family background."

"Sorry, I didn't mean that like it sounded."

As he had done so many times, Blake pushed the whirlwind of thoughts about his family's odd entanglements and their entitled attitudes back into a safe corner of his subconscious. Try as he might, he could never predict when those memories would burst out of their mental vault and intrude on his effort to live a reasonably normal life.

"Okay, Jack, if you really feel like a jerk, then atone by rounding up information on Cutter's recent clients. I want to know who he has been checking up on and what he found," Blake fired back in his usual do-it-yesterday tone.

"You mean hack into his computer and follow the trail."

"Who says you can't lead a Jack-ass to water and make him drink?"

"Very funny. You don't care how I get this done. Just get it done, right?"

"Right."

"And if somebody pulls my chain about this, are you going to cover me?"

"Don't I always?"

"Man, you don't come from aristocrats, you're a pirate."

"No real difference."

CHAPTER 8

Taylor never thought of herself as a clock watcher, until today. At five o'clock she bolted from the Executive Conference room leaving files scattered on the table. She pushed open the fire exit door and ran down four flights of stairs then out the side door. If the exit alarm rang, that's too bad. Heels clicked in steady rhythm as she sprinted across the parking lot to her car.

Unfortunately the thousands of other downtown workers pouring out of parking garages and curbside spaces were equally intent on leaving. The slow moving traffic gave her too much time to replay all the irritations that compounded during the first week at MACS. Finally breaking away from the pack, she turned onto Fourth Street North. Her plan was to attend exercise class followed by grocery shopping, but her stomach wanted food and her wounded ego cried out for chocolate.

She pulled into Publix Market off 38th Avenue while trying to recall the sparse options in her refrigerator. She steered her cart straight for the Bakery. *Food must never govern mood. That's what Dr. Travis taught. Well, let Dr. Travis pig out on bean sprouts and wild berries. Grandma Dodd said that a freshly baked cookie won't cure what ails you, but after a few bites, who cares?*

Taylor selected a handful of soft chocolate chip cookies at the self-serve counter. Then she picked up two samples of cream cheese coffee cake to curb her hunger. Fortunately Friday and Saturday were great days for food samples. As she wheeled around the store, she managed a mini-buffet by noshing bite-size pieces of cheddar cheese, fried chicken, spinach quiche and tofu burger. Normally she hated shopping during the evening

rush hour, but today it was a blessing in disguise. Nibbling her
way through the aisles and using the time in the checkout line
to read the latest trash magazine headlines proved to be quite
relaxing.

The grocery was only minutes from home, or what was to
be home during this year. After pulling out onto 38th Avenue
North, she turned south on Ninth Street and another short
distance to 41st Avenue, onto one of the city's few remaining
brick streets.

The residents in Allendale were staunchly protective of their
brick streets. Ordinary pavement would be déclassé in this stately
neighborhood. Taylor turned into the side driveway and used
her newly acquired remote to open the gate. The same remote
opened the four car garage attached to the main house, but she
didn't want to park there and walk across the garden. Parking in
the turnaround area was the easiest access to the poolside guest
house that she called home.

The single story bungalow wasn't where she planned to
live. After graduation, she had made reservations to stay in a
hotel while she looked for a small apartment and a few thrift
shop furnishings. As usual, Mama had other ideas. Among the
stack of graduation gifts was a small box which Taylor assumed
to be earrings. Instead it was a black enamel key ring with a
V-monogrammed charm and two gold keys.

Mama announced that the keys fit the pool house at Mary
Etta Vanderveer's St. Petersburg home which was on loan to
Taylor for the residency year. Taylor turned to her sisters, who
shrugged their shoulders with that "she's done it again" look.
Feeble attempts to promote her own plans were overrun with
Mama's insistence that Taylor would be doing Mary Etta a
favor. After all, she and M'Etta became best friends in the same
sorority where Taylor pledged as a legacy, and everyone knows
that Alpha Omicron Pi's look after their own.

Yielding to the inevitable, Taylor actually won one by

overcoming Mama's objections to let her youngest sister, Paige stay for a week and help with the move. After driving Mama and middle sister Savannah to Tampa Airport, Taylor and Paige went back across the Sunshine Skyway Bridge to spend a few days lounging on Siesta Key. Taylor had been so busy during her doctoral training at Knight University that she missed Paige's early teen years. The little girl whose hair she braided for elementary school was a stunning young woman starting her senior year in high school.

Tanned and rested, the sisters packed the car and waited for the moving truck to pick up the remaining boxes of books, linens and other assorted stuff from the graduate student's apartment complex. Taylor led the way to St. Petersburg following the detailed map and pre-arranged moving instructions. If Mama had been a little older, Taylor would have suspected her as the mastermind behind the Normandy Invasion. Mama left nothing to chance. Since Taylor's father Tom died three years ago, Julia Kendall's desire to weave a hedge of protection around her three daughters was stronger than ever.

The sprawling two-story dove gray stucco home was as classic a representative of Florida style as the Kendall family's Memphis colonial home was of the old south. Tall windows with French doors ringed the lower floor. Every doorway opened out onto lush greenery and cascades of hot pink oleanders. Following the curving driveway to the rear past a rose garden, the guest house came into view. Paige saw it first, "Oh, Taylor, it's a perfect doll house. Way cool!"

M'Etta's handwritten note that came with the keys described it as a two bedroom, two bath guest suite with spacious living room and efficiency kitchen. Paige's description was better; it was a miniature of the big house. The guest house even had a set of white wicker lounge chairs with plump blue/green floral cushions that matched the outdoor furnishings around the main house.

They approached the center French door and found it unlocked. Paige ran back out to the side driveway and signaled the moving truck to drive in. The two burly men who probably spend their days unloading pianos and refrigerators took less than twenty minutes to drop Taylor's five heavy boxes and two wardrobe crates inside the living room. As the movers drove away, a short red haired lady in a flowing orange and yellow chiffon sundress appeared. She hugged Taylor and Paige like long lost relatives.

"What a delight to have Julia's little girl come to stay in at my home!" she exclaimed demonstrating that thirty years in Florida failed to diminish her Natchez, Mississippi drawl. She phoned the main house instructing her housekeeper, Sigrid, to bring over sandwiches and lemonade. Pushing aside a box of books, she draped herself elegantly in a side chair and motioned for the girls to sit on the sofa beside her.

"I do so regret that I didn't get back in time to visit with Julia during your graduation," Mary Etta sighed. "You see, normally I hate to waste time on airplanes so I take a night flight and sleep my way across the Atlantic. When I couldn't get a first class seat on the flight I wanted, I had to stay an extra day. Fancy that, having to stay one more day in Paris! To keep me from getting bored, the Concierge, that darling man, got me a last minute invitation to the Carolina Herrera runway show. Two things I love most are fashion and my late husband's virtually unlimited credit cards. I was such a trooper that I only bought enough clothes to fill one extra suitcase."

She even laughs like Mama; robust yet dainty, a technique developed by southern ladies before Scarlett was old enough for her first ball. As they talked, Taylor realized that the guest house was not merely furnished and decorated, but exquisite down to the last detail. She tentatively voiced her concern, "Mrs. Vanderveer, everything here is so lovely it can't be improved on. But would you mind if I put up a few personal items if I'm really careful...."

"Honey, this place is yours for the year. Act like it. If you hate the color scheme, I'll call my decorator and we'll do it another way."

"Actually, I only meant to put up a few family pictures or some knick knacks."

"Taylor, when I said this is your place for the year I meant it. Do what you like. Besides, I change decor here every few years so I can stay on the A-list with my decorator. But there is one condition to my generosity."

"What's that?"

"You must kindly remember that Mrs. Vanderveer was my mother-in-law, God rest her miserable, interfering soul. Please call me M'Etta." She rose from the chair, cramming a wide brimmed yellow garden hat on top of her erratic red curls. "And there's one other thing. I don't do bed checks for you and you don't do them for me," she said with a wink.

Paige winked back, "Sounds great."

"I'm leaving Sunday afternoon for a few days in Vancouver then on to Alaska for a cruise. Then I'm flying to Italy to meet friends for another cruise. I live to travel. When my Hubert retired, we vowed to see every corner of the world and we saw a lot. Before he died six years ago, he made me promise to finish that dream and he left me an outrageous pot of money to do it with. Like Hubert said, since our only son died and we have no grandchildren to spoil, there's no reason to save it for the distant relatives. But if you need me, Sigrid knows how to reach me."

"I'm sure everything will be fine."

"Don't hesitate to ask for anything you need. Sigrid manages my house and her husband Lars supervises the gardeners. They have an apartment off the east wing and a little cottage at Indian Rocks Beach where they go for weekends. If you need anything, anything at all, they'll take care of it." M'Etta hugged the sisters leaving the bright orange print of a motherly kiss on each girl's cheek, like Grandma Dodd used to do.

She turned suddenly, "There is just one other thing. Please invite your friends over to swim or throw a party. This pool house saw some wild times when Hubert and I were a young couple."

With that final directive, M'Etta disappeared into the foliage on a path to the main house like an oversize Monarch butterfly heading for the next flower.

"Wow! That's the kind of old lady I want to be," Paige said.

"After meeting her, I'm sorry that she's going to be away so much while I'm living here. I bet she has great stories to tell."

"Don't say anything about all her traveling. Mama will be happier if she thinks you are well chaperoned now that you'll be living alone for the first time."

"Living alone without a chaperone and only twenty-seven years old. What a scandal for the family!"

The sisters laughed. Then they locked hands, turned their wrists sideways left to right, followed by three claps in the manner the Kendall girls used as children to seal a secret.

* * * * *

Taylor recalled that scene as she unpacked the groceries in the kitchen. It seemed hard to believe that she moved in here less than two weeks ago. Paige flew back to Memphis. M'Etta Vandeveer and nine pieces of Louis Vuitton™ luggage left in a stretch limousine. Sigrid and Lars were practically invisible.

Sigrid was an organizer after Mama's own heart. Before Taylor left for the first day at MACS, Sigrid had already taped an envelope to the guest house door containing a typed agenda detailing all activities in and around the property for the coming week: pool cleaning, dishwasher repair in the main kitchen, tree surgeon checking the recovery of the date palm on the south lawn. Nothing happened that was not scheduled by Sigrid. Glancing again at that agenda, Taylor realized that she would have the whole place to herself over the weekend. Sigrid and Lars were at their beach cottage, their cell phone and pager numbers noted in red on the agenda.

After a week of getting up early and staying up late to read program materials, Taylor was ready for a weekend of peace and quiet with absolutely nothing to do. However, that was part of the problem; a weekend in paradise and no one to share it with. Her mind wandered to the narrow windows above the Fifth Street antique gallery where Gabe worked. *I wonder if he's seen me driving by there on the way home from work. It looks like there's a cramped upstairs apartment. I wonder what he does on the weekend.*

* * * * *

Gabe was watching when she bolted from the building. Turning her Mustang into oncoming traffic with hardly a sideward glance was the most reckless maneuver he had seen her do.

There went my chance to get her attention as she left work and invite her to for an innocent happy hour chocolate sundae. I know it's too soon to ask her for a real date. Her conservative upbringing would make her back away if I get too pushy.

He sat on a green bench in the shadows of the Bay Plaza Building where he had a prime view of the MACS building and parking lot across the street. He pulled the baseball cap down to shade his face and watched the exodus. He made a game of trying to match each employee with his or her car as they left to pursue the other side of their lives.

A white stretch limousine with a gold MACS crest on the side pulled up to the rear door of the corporate headquarters, arrogantly blocking two handicapped parking spots. The chauffeur scanned the cars the way that a bodyguard does for a rock star. When he seemed satisfied, he flipped open his cell phone and made a quick call. Minutes later a woman carrying an alligator briefcase emerged from the building. She paused to speak to a well dressed young man and his companion. The chauffeur's body language showed that he didn't consider the couple to be a threat.

As the older woman spoke to the young man, the younger woman twisted her long blonde hair and shuffled restlessly on platform heels. Then she took off her white lab coat to reveal a black leather mini-skirt and a flimsy excuse for a gold sequin tank top. She looked like a hooker gathering props to play doctor. The older woman shot a disapproving glance at the girl and her companion before turning away from them to slide gracefully into the limo. The couple recognized their dismissal and walked over to get into a Mazda Miata with the vanity plate, "Felipe".

Two years ago when MACS opened for business, so did Serena Girard's checkbook. She was buying her way to acceptance and money was no object. Over the past year, her photo appeared frequently with patrons of the Salvador Dali Museum, a fledgling ballet company and a tutoring center for underprivileged children.

There was a time when Gabe thought a woman like Serena Girard epitomized the height of chic. That was before he met Taylor Kendall. Both women dressed well, choosing classic clothing that accentuated their best features. Both displayed finishing-school posture and perfect manners. Yet compared with Taylor's natural elegance, Serena was a hollow porcelain figurine.

Gabe watched the MACS limousine blend into the commuter traffic until it was out of sight. He stood up, took off the baseball cap and ran his fingers through his brown hair to diminish the hat-head line.

Darting across Second Street, he headed west on Central Avenue. It was five-twenty and already the after-work party crowd was rocking. Several renovated restaurants in the ground floor of old Central Avenue buildings put out plastic tables and chairs on the sidewalk to accommodate the overflow of Generation X'ers. The Baby Boomers tended to remain inside, hugging the bar stools, comfortably within range of air conditioning, especially

after the humidity skyrocketed in the early afternoon and
lingered at sauna level after nightfall.

A pair of chattering girls wearing similar navy suits with a
company logo on their blazers fell in step on either side of Gabe
trying to talk him into joining them. He shrugged them off.
The short one with streaked hair shouted, "Artsy fag!" He didn't
bother to respond.

What is it with women these days? I don't want a drink. And I
definitely don't want to become their Friday night prize. I've spent my
life dealing with aggressive women and have nothing to show for it.
No more. Now, assertive women, that's different. Women like Taylor
are smart, sassy and stunning. Even more, she's classy, refined and
demure. Demure. There's a word that doesn't apply to many women
today.

Feeling hungry from the scent of hors d'oeuvres at the
sidewalk happy hour parties, he went into the Sub Shop on
the next block. Nothing fancy, just fast food that actually tasted
good. With dinner in the bag, he walked two more blocks to the
gallery. Entering by the door off the side alley, he climbed the
stairs to his retreat, flopped on the suede sofa and unwrapped
the turkey sub.

The apartment was convenient for work, but definitely not his
style. When the gallery's former owner turned part of the upstairs
storage room into an afternoon trysting place, she apparently
went wild over Chinese red with black lacquer furnishings. The
sofa was the only concession to comfort. Gabe cleared a large
lamp table as a pedestal for his own television and DVD player,
a small twentieth century intrusion.

The u-shaped bar with conventional black chair-
backed bar stools opened onto the living room area. The narrow
cabinets, microwave, hot plate and motel size refrigerator were
the only semblance of a kitchen. What passed for a bedroom
was divided from the living area by a pair of imitation Chinese
screens. Another Chinese silk print served as the headboard

over a double bed. A set of matching highboy cabinets on each side of the only window on the alley side provided drawers and closet space. Gabe stashed the fading red brocade bedspread in a bottom drawer.

Once he set his mind to mentally block out the decor, Gabe found the apartment acceptable. Compared to some of the places he had to live when working in different cities, this was practically the Ritz. A bookkeeper/manager and two part-time fine arts majors from University of South Florida Bayboro Campus kept the gallery going. Gabe wasn't expected to work much. The manager had no problem giving Gabe use of the apartment and a loose job description with no questions asked in return for a generous cash rental payment in advance.

Kicking off his loafers, he stretched out on the sofa for a twenty minute nap. He closed his eyes and tried to focus on a tranquil scene like the beach in St. Thomas or fresh snow at Vail. Wherever his mind wandered, Taylor was there. Taylor in a plush lined parka throwing snowballs. Taylor in a silky brown bikini stretched out on a sugar white sand. Instead of catching up on sleep after a busy week of late night reading and studying for his part, he couldn't get her out of his mind.

Yet he had no viable excuse to see her again until Monday. He couldn't very well show up at her place since he wasn't supposed to know where she lived.

Blake stormed out, slamming the door. Enough reports. He was ready to start a new phase of the operation next week. Anything else he needed to know he would find out as he went. His father taught him that he must know his enemy but not too well. Marco often said, "Too much preparation makes the hunter overconfident and that blunts his edge." In those terms, he was ready for the hunt, but enough for today. It was the weekend and he was alone.

At first he thought about driving along Gulf Boulevard. No, he wasn't looking to pick up girls or drown his agitation at a beach bar. He couldn't even phone Carla. By now she was locked into the family dinner ritual. Calling would put her on the spot. Without much thought he drove to the most likely place to lose himself.

Grabbing a small black case out of the trunk, he went into the building toward the front parking lot near the FBO at St. Petersburg/Clearwater Airport.

"Hey, Travis, I need a favor."

"Blair! I hardly see you anymore," the wind burned man responded enthusiastically to Blake, whom he knew as Blair Andrews.

"Listen, I'm here plenty. Don't you see my fuel bills?"

"You keep my cash register humming, but you usually fly out before the red-eye special. What brings you out in the evening?"

"I need to unwind."

"Sorry but I only have one mechanic still here. The rest will be three sheets to the wind at the bar up the street. I don't know how fast I can get your plane ready."

"I'm not taking the jet tonight. What I really want is a few hours in your biplane."

"Captain Speed wants to play Snoopy with the Blue Baron? It's already six-ten. No radar. No fancy gear. You'd have to come home on time."

"Yes, but it's daylight savings which leaves an hour of flying time and the weather looks clear. Come on Travis. I'll owe you. I'll even pay for the Baron's next full tilt overhaul. Add it to my account."

It was Travis' turn to look smug, "And you'll also give me some flight time in the Citation?"

Blake bristled. Grudgingly he admitted to himself that Travis was as protective of the vintage biplane as he was of his sleek, powerful business jet. He extended his hand to Travis and said, "It's a deal. But I have to go along; you aren't jet rated."

"Okay, okay. Let's not fax the FAA about it. And speaking of the FAA, if you head for the Skyway Bridge, try flying over it, not under it. I hate those cranky bureaucrats screaming at me."

"Now Travis, it's been years since I did the Skyway stunt. Besides, that takes more power than I can get from your old tub."

"Go ahead and make fun of the Baron; we can take it. If you're looking for thrills, stick to barrel rolls. But if you do anything really crazy, you'll have to pay for a fresh paint job and figure out how to sneak in a new N-number."

They walked around the side of the building and together made a preflight check before moving the biplane out from its portico. Blake climbed into the rear seat and started the engine. Travis slapped on the side of the plane to get his attention. Shouting to be heard over the prop noise, he gave a final warning, "Buzz a chicken coup up in Hernando County if you have to release some aggression. Stay out of trouble and bring her back in one piece."

Blake saluted and turned the plane toward the taxiway. He could hardly wait to get clearance to take off. Only a Cessna 150 stood between him and miles of cloudless sky. In minutes he was airborne and feeling the rush of wind in his face as he turned toward the bay.

"Hey, Travis, wasn't that the Blue Baron taking off without you?" the mechanic asked holding his hand up to his eyes to shield the sun. "I thought you never rented that plane to any customer."

"That's so. The Baron isn't in the rental pool. But this guy's a friend who used to fly out of here. Didn't see him for several years and then a few months ago he showed up asking for a place to park his plane. You know him."

"No I don't."

"Well you need to, Mike, because you pant over his airplane every chance you get," Travis let out the clue waiting for his co-worker to make the connection.

"Is that the guy who owns the Citation Jet in the main hangar?"

"Right you are."

"This guy's a friend and you never told me? You jerk."

"I'll be sure you get the workup on the Andrews Corporate jet next time and I'll tell Blair what a great job you did."

Mike pulled a grease-streaked rag from his overall pocket. He wiped his hands and the sweat from his brow with the same corner of the rag. He craned his neck to watch the biplane fly out of sight.

"I'll tell you one thing about your jet-jockey friend. He's out there trying to get his head straight with some old time, bugs-in-your-face flying. It's either a money problem or a woman problem."

"I don't think it's a money problem. Blair Andrews pays his bills on time and he never complains about prices."

Mike nodded knowingly, "Yep, then it's a woman problem."

* * * * *

Serena creased her linen napkin to a fine point dabbing any stubborn crumbs that dared to cling to her collagen-plumped lips. Dropping the napkin on the table beside her place setting, she waved her hand in the direction of the patio and told the maid, "We shall have coffee on the patio."

"Do we have to stay? I want to go dancing," Tiffany whined.

Felipe nudged his wife and whispered to her, "Mother might be more generous with us if you showed better manners."

Gina jumped up from her seat and walked around the table to lean over her half-brother's shoulder, "Your bimbo only knows what's in the junior department at Dillard's. Courtesy is beyond her ability." She patted his head, flashed a snarl at Tiffany and walked away.

Felipe rose defiantly to follow Gina.

Carla stepped in front of him and gently touched his arm, "Felipe, don't fall into her trap. She's trying to bait you into an argument. Then you'll end up looking like the fool."

"I don't care, Carla. I'm going to do something to make your sister change her attitude toward my wife."

Carla rolled her eyes. She heard his big talk before. He'd threaten and crow like a rooster to her or to Tiffany or to the servants, but face down Gina? Not a chance. No wonder Father relegated him to an innocuous accounting position. Felipe was such a disappointment. He could never take Blake's place as heir. Prestigious families rejoice when two sons are born, which they refer to as an heir and a spare. Felipe was closer to being a spare pawn than a substitute heir. He would never be the Girard heir, no matter what happened. Cruel as Gina was to him, she was correct in saying that Felipe wasn't fit to shine Blake's shoes.

"Are you coming outside?" Victoria bellowed from the patio breaking Carla's thoughts.

"Yes, Mother." She suddenly realized that everyone had left the dining room. She crossed the patio to the coffee cart. *Such a lovely family evening: Serena's choice Handel CD is being drowned out by Gina and Tiffany locked in another insult tossing contest. Unfortunately, the best insults are so far beyond Tiffany's comprehension that she just smiles appreciatively when she misses the meaning. Victoria and Serena are totally engrossed in some document, probably another business deal. Predictably, Felipe is sulking and mumbling into his cognac-spiked coffee.*

Carla took her coffee and went over to the edge of the patio wall. She tried to appear attentive to her family's interests while politely ignoring them, a skill refined over time. Her ears perked up when she overhead a familiar name.

"This investigator's report shows that there is no viable reason to perceive Dr. Kendall as a threat. I agree with Dr. Locke that she needs to spend more time working in the clinic."

Carla spun around, "You had Taylor investigated? Wasn't the university's recommendation enough? Does she look like some common criminal? Never mind - if she did she would look like us!"

Victoria stared disapprovingly at her daughter, "How naive you are, Carla. We are sitting on a gold mine. Plenty of people would like to steal our success or use the unpredictable actions of our patients against us."

Serena could not resist chiming in, "Unequivocally! We must protect MACS against industrial espionage. Our Nutracurative formula alone is practically priceless. Professional staff can be as tempted to steal corporate secrets as the lesser paid workers."

Gina saw an opportunity to score points with both mother and stepmother, "Our parents are merely protecting the family's interests. Can you honestly say that you don't enjoy living like this, Carla?"

"Yes. We all do. But I would like for us to try living without constantly looking over our shoulders to see who is out to get us. Even the employees sense our corporate paranoia. Have any of you ever considered that there may be some trustworthy people in the world?"

"It takes time to be sure and we cannot afford to be wrong," Gina said.

Carla raised her usually soft voice as she stared at Gina, "Now I understand why you and Mother kidnapped Taylor on her second day and then buried her under a pile of meaningless paperwork! It was so Sally the watchdog could keep her in sight. You thought she was here to spy on our company?"

"Exactly," Gina responded, exchanging nods of approval with Victoria.

Seeking to diffuse the tension, Serena presented her best diplomatic smile, "Of course, dear Carla, we meant no harm to Dr. Kendall. We merely had to be certain. The death of that young woman was hard on everyone. Someone not familiar with our patients and the complexities of treating schizophrenia might rush to erroneous assumptions."

"Like thinking we have some responsibility for the people we treat? Is that the erroneous conclusion Taylor might draw?"

"Be realistic, Carla. Dr. Kendall has no real psychotherapy experience. Anyone fresh out of graduate school could misunderstand the situation, but she'll be brought up to speed soon."

"What is your point in all this?"

"I'm pleased to say that the private detective's report Gina commissioned shows that Dr. Kendall is a woman of good character with an excellent academic background. She'll be busy in the clinic starting Monday." Shifting effortlessly to the facial expression that meant "subject closed," Serena reached for the silver coffee pot, "Come now children, let's refill our coffee cups and enjoy this delightful sunset."

Carla knew it was time to tune them out. She walked around the patio taking the stairs that led down to the boat ramp. In spite of its absurd inhabitants, Carla loved this house as much as any place she'd ever lived. The pale peach stucco and burnt orange clay tiled roof reminded her of the finer Spanish compounds, like those in Santiago.

Father was equally enamored with this house. The real estate agent gave them a booklet explaining the house's history. Designed in the early 1920's by the famous Palm Beach architect, Addison Mizner, this sweeping structure on Brightwaters Boulevard remains distinctive even among the newer, ostentatious homes on Snell Isle. The house sits at a slight angle relative to the street. In a copy of an old letter from Mr. Mizner to the original owner, he recommended this placement on the lot to take maximum advantage of a sunset view over the canal. He was right.

Carla's thoughts were interrupted by Tiffany's shrill voice, "Look at that funny old airplane."

"That's a biplane," Victoria explained. "My father bought one of those from an aviation surplus dealer shortly after Marco and I married. He and Marco spent a week flying that crate from Texas back to Chile. They had a fine time with it until Marco crashed it doing stunts."

"I never knew Father was in a plane crash!" Gina exclaimed. "Was he hurt?"

Victoria threw back her head for a hearty laugh, "Not by the crash but by the bulls. He loved to fly low over their pasture, get their attention and then soar upward over their heads. He said that red bi-plane was as close to a matador's cape as he ever planned to get. One day he misjudged the distance, caught a tree top and went down. He had some nasty bruises from those bulls."

"That was acceptable out over pasture land," Serena observed watching the blue biplane roll and turn. "What I want to know is why planes today are allowed to fly low over elite waterfront neighborhoods?"

"I don't think they can, Mother. I will summon the police," said Felipe.

"Sure, Felipe, you do that. Better yet, call MacDill Air Force Base. Or why not Batman?" Gina goaded him.

"I was trying to be helpful."

"Then pour an extra shot of cognac in your coffee and pass out early tonight."

As the verbal battle continued in the background, Carla stared at the plane. It swooped low enough so she could see that there was only one pilot. Whoever it was, he was enjoying the freedom of being above it all. Blake wanted her to go flying recently, but she turned him down. On reflection, she wished she had gone. She liked to fly with him.

Many times when they were teenagers in South America, they took to the air to escape the nonsense going on in their family. Blake was flying before he learned to drive. He offered to teach her, but she was afraid of failure. Poor flying angered Marco, even though his piloting skills were as unnerving as his driving. Flying with Blake was different. Even when he climbed several thousand feet high and did stomach-clenching acrobatics, she loved it. He was daring, but competent. She watched the blue biplane make a final pass near their canal, then turn northwest. Oh, how she wished it were Blake.

* * * * *

By mid-Sunday afternoon, Taylor had done all the laundry, sunbathing and relaxing that she could tolerate. Although she solemnly promised herself not to think about MACS over the weekend, she reached for her briefcase and pulled out a notepad. Pouring a fresh glass of ice tea, she looked over the statistical array made from data in the patient files. Something about that information nagged at her. Something didn't fit. She had to find out what it was. Maybe it was the flaw Gabe challenged her to find.

As the sun was beginning to set, she went back inside the pool house and turned on her laptop computer. Rummaging through an unpacked box of books, she found the CD file box. *Never thought I'd have to use this vile statistics program again!*

While the cumbersome program loaded onto her computer, she went to the kitchen to refill her tea glass and grab a piece of cold chicken. She knew from long nights of dissertation preparation how much time it took to enter the basic information to run statistical analysis. She opened a new file and started typing in numbers from her handwritten grid. The initial entry was the grunt work; tedious, boring and demanding. She recalled how her descriptive research professor likened the importance of this part of the work to a defense attorney who fails to check all the facts and thus makes the wrong argument that lands his client on death row.

He'd say that if a researcher, like an attorney, works with partial or incorrectly entered information, the conclusions are dead wrong. But this time someone is dead, a real person, a person I don't know but somehow can't get out of my mind.

Two hours later after checking and re-checking, all the data was loaded into the program. She punched the button to begin the analysis. Amazing. Her three-ring notebook in high school weighed more than this computer, yet it sorts and cross-multiplies with a speed that would make Albert Einstein hyperventilate. Eager to see the results, she printed out a set of graphs.

If these figures are believable, the retention rate for completion of the MACS Partial Hospitalization Programs equals or exceeds 84% with a relapse rate of 15%. Didn't Dale say that relapse rates for schizophrenia among community dwelling individuals without monitoring are over the moon? Why is the relapse figure so low at MACS?

Speaking of the moon, Taylor noticed that the light from the full moon was reflecting off the pool through the French doors. She closed the windows and checked the door locks before going to the bedroom. Then she taped three pages of graphs to the mirror so she could study them while taking off her makeup and brushing her hair. Tired as she was, she was transfixed by these graphs.

Mentally exhausted, she slipped into the bed and drifted right to sleep. Even in her sleep, she pursued the data which began to morph into odd characters like those from *Alice in Wonderland*. Every time she thought she was close to finding its secret lair, the answer escaped. The chase was on.

CHAPTER 10

BEEP! BEEP! BEEP!

Taylor awoke Monday to the sound of her back-up clock. She was raised with the belief that tardiness was the eighth deadly sin, so she followed her Mama's habit of setting two alarm clocks.

With no time to spare, Taylor reached for comfort clothes, one of those outfits that can look professional with minimal effort. Besides, if it was going to be another day immersed in file folders, whom did she have to impress? Making a turn in front of the full length mirror, Taylor inspected her navy knit pants, matching cardigan jacket and lime green shell. Most of the female therapists wore pants outfits, but this needed a little punch. She rummaged in her scarf drawer. *Aren't sisters wonderful? Savannah's lime and navy print scarf is still here. Wonder if she's missed it?* With a quick twist and tie, the scarf lent an air of corporate respectability.

Grabbing her briefcase and a boxed juice, Taylor pushed the front door closed with her hip and dashed for her car. Fumbling for her seatbelt, she was startled by a tap on the driver's side window.

Sigrid reached into her apron pocket and pulled out an envelope, "Good morning, Miss Taylor. Here's your weekly agenda."

"Thank you, Sigrid. Did you have a nice weekend?"

"Ya, we did. I'm baking bread today. When you get home after work, ring the bell by the patio entrance and I'll bring out a fresh loaf for you."

"I'm looking forward to it already!"

Sigrid watched and waved as Taylor backed out of the driveway. Taylor wondered if Sigrid was motherly by nature or if she had instructions from M'Etta on behalf of Julia to keep a watchful eye.

Merging into the traffic on Ninth Street, Taylor recalled how she once thought that going away to Vanderbilt University was living on her own. True, it was away from her family. But there were always roommates. When she traveled for the sorority, she often stayed with sisters or at an on-campus sorority house. Even when she moved into the graduate student apartment complex at Knight University, she lived in a cramped student apartment with two other women. Although the paths of an incoming experimental psychology student, second year social work student and Taylor as a counseling psychology doctoral student rarely crossed, it wasn't exactly living on her own.

This was different; home alone in the privacy of M'Etta's pool side guest house. Of course, it was a superb neighborhood and her quarters looked like a photo layout from *Architectural Digest. I can't even brag about this to my friend, Lauren. She loves working in the New York psychiatric hospital and merely tolerates that single window, one room walk-up apartment on the fourth floor of an ancient brownstone. In her email last night, she says she acquires a new appreciation for Post Traumatic Stress Disorder every time she rides the subway to work. Here I am living in a mini-mansion and working in an office within walking distance from the St. Petersburg waterfront. All that's left is to commiserate about what we have in common; starting a new job, leaving friends, hoping to find the right relationship.*

In spite of its high sounding name, Medical Alliance for Community Services is a strange place, filled with even stranger people, and that doesn't even count the patients. But, maybe it isn't so bad after all. Perhaps it really is what the promotional brochure claims, "On the cutting edge of group psychotherapy for the twenty-first century." The graphs certainly demonstrate that MACS is outrageously successful, at least in statistical terms. What about the people those numbers represent? How many fall through the cracks, and are there more situations like the woman in the accident?

Daddy always said that it's people, not numbers that matter in health care. The newspaper report said her name was Harriet but it's as if she never existed in MACS; ignored or blotted out of an otherwise pristine corporate image.

Taylor kept her eyes on the road, but her mind was transported back to summer days in Daddy's office. From the time she was twelve years old, she had an unofficial summer job keeping his bookcase arranged, filing medical journals and sorting medication samples. She remembered the times that Daddy took a coffee break to listen to the latest pitch from a pharmaceutical salesman.

He always came back with the same question, "I don't care what you think it does or what it does for your lab rats, I want to know if this drug can be effective and do no harm to my patients?"

"To do no harm," was the admonition from the Hippocratic Oath that hung above Daddy's desk. She memorized that oath years ago. Even though she chose to become a psychologist instead of following generations of Kendalls to medical school, she could still recite every word.

Turning into the parking lot, Taylor snapped out of her daydream. She knew what she had to do. She had to find out if the MACS programs could actually deliver the results claimed without harm to any patients.

I have to concede one thing to Dr. Marco. People with schizophrenia are an incredibly complex population to treat. What they perceive in some highly delusional phase as harm can be necessary medication. How can you rely on a hallucinating patient's perception of "harm"? What caused the greatest "harm" to Harriet – the illness or the cure?

A woman with a mission, Taylor inserted her key card in the elevator slot and defiantly pressed the fourth floor button. She decided to start the day in her office then talk with Carla.

Rounding the corner, she saw Brook hunched over the fax machine.

"Good morning, Brook."

"Dr. Kendall, I presume. Glad to see you back in your own office. Want some coffee?"

Dr. Locke leaned out of his office and interrupted, "Bring her coffee to my office and maybe a cup for me too?"

Taylor walked into Sam's office and sat down. She expected a lecture on why she didn't report directly to Sally on the Executive Floor.

"Taylor, you have been liberated."

"What do you mean?"

"According to my watch, you have barely fifteen minutes to drink your coffee, stow your briefcase in your office and get down to the clinic. I like for my program staff to be on time."

She studied his expression trying to confirm his words, but he kept a poker face. After a minute or so of silence, he burst out laughing. "Lighten up, Taylor. This is on the level. You report to the MACS clinic downstairs today, and tomorrow and everyday thereafter as far as I know."

"How did you do it? Did this cause any problems for you with the partners?"

"Occasionally I win one around here. Actually you can thank Serena."

"Serena? I hardly know her. Why would she intervene for me?"

"Serena fancies herself to be a haute-couture version of Mother Teresa. She'll interfere in any part of MACS where she can look like a savior." He paused and handed a daily schedule of the partial hospitalization groups to Taylor. "Of course, there's always a price to pay for Serena's favor."

"But if you believe the society column, you'd think she is a great philanthropist."

Lowering his voice noticeably Locke gave a stern warning,

"Serena never does anything unless it benefits her, directly or indirectly. Remember that when you deal with her. She's a user."

"You mean she does drugs?"

"No, Taylor. Serena is a user of people. Power is her drug of choice; she wields the power to design, sculpt, display and then destroy her creations when they become tiresome."

"What creations?"

"She sees her employees as her creations. She moves them skillfully to form a human shield around her. Loyalty is expected, but rarely rewarded. As long as she needs you then you have her protection, but she will cut you off at the knees in a heartbeat. I only tell you this, Taylor, because I may have set you in her sights by asking her help to get you away from Victoria's project."

"But I work for you and my clinical work is under Dr. Marco's supervision."

Sam looked grave enough to give Taylor a shiver, "I offered you up on the sacrificial altar of public image as the newest MACS phenomenon, our first psychology resident. It's part of the new era for the MACS community education programs, and so on. Then I guided Serena toward the conclusion that your promotional value, not to mention a photo op, was higher working in the clinic than in a conference room buried under file folders."

"Well, that can't be all bad. Besides, my university would be happy for positive press."

"Let's hope it stays that way. It's time for you to get to work, Dr. Kendall. I'll be downstairs later for the treatment team meeting."

Taylor stopped briefly in her office to retrieve her clinic name badge. Brook came in and thrust a white lab coat toward her. "Clip your badge to the upper pocket."

"I don't need a lab coat. That's a bit stuffy for group work."

Brook nodded, "Actually, it's old fashioned, pompous and downright macho; at least that's what most of the therapy staff say. But it's also required. So, Dr. Kendall, if the lab coat fits wear it."

Taylor took off her cardigan and put on the starched white symbol of authority. Formal or not, she decided to wear her bright scarf to tone down the austere medical look. Brook straightened Taylor's badge, patted her on the shoulder approvingly, and watched her break into a sprint to catch the elevator.

* * * * *

The morning routine at the MACS clinic reminded Taylor of changing planes at a metro airport during prime business hours. In short, it was controlled chaos. Green shirted people darted back and forth out the side door to meet the vans and escort patients into the clinic. A nurse and an aide were checking charts. The phone rang incessantly. An unshaven man with flowing salt and pepper hair who arrived on the first van was hanging over the nurses' station counter repeating his litany; "Is it snack time?" "Where is everybody?" "Can we go home now?"

Taylor approached the station realizing that she was as confused about where she was suppose to be as he was.

The nurse looked up, "Can I help you, Doctor?"

"Good morning. I'm Dr. Taylor Kendall and I…"

"Right, we heard you were coming in today. I'm Neva. Here are your intakes for this morning. Ray, can you show her where to go?" Barely looking up, Neva thrust two notebooks at the middle aged green shirted man and resumed charting.

Ray extended his hand to Taylor, "Welcome, Dr. Kendall. I'm Ray Dwyer. Follow me. I have to wheel this patient into the community room; then I'll take you to the intake offices."

The corridors were narrow so Taylor dropped a few steps behind. As they walked along, she noticed that Ray carried on an upbeat conversation with the sullen older woman in a manner that was encouraging without being patronizing, an effective therapeutic approach to encourage communication. Errand completed, he motioned for Taylor to follow him to a side office. Cramped and ordinary, the sea foam green walls were typical of a testing or intake setup with a few moderately comfortable chairs. He opened the top file drawer in the small cabinet next to the desk.

"Here are the intake packets and your report forms. Extra file folders and note pads are in the back. Use one folder for the workup you complete on each patient. If the patient already has a chart, stick the completed folder in the front of the chart and take it to the nurses' station. If there's no chart, turn in the folder. Testing materials are in the bottom drawer. We use routine test instruments, nothing exotic, but you know that stuff better than I do."

Taylor glanced at the file labels. She was familiar with most of the psychological testing materials. What she needed was to know more about the daily schedule.

"Do you do any part of the intake, Ray?"

"No, I'm not a therapist. I'm a techie."

"A what?"

He chuckled, "Officially, a mental health tech which is actually, a glorified gopher. I have enough understanding of aberrant behaviors to herd the patients into groups on time and keep them from wandering out to do lunch with the pigeons in Williams Park."

"Or running out into traffic?"

His cheerful expression turned sad, "Guess you heard about Harriet. Crazy things happen around here, but that was inexcusable."

"I know what you mean. It was my first day here. I didn't even know her, yet I felt sad for her. I suppose no one on staff was able to do anything to prevent it."

"Well I could have," his modulated voice rose to a higher pitch, "If only Neva hadn't assigned me as escort for that patient we sent on a plane back to North Carolina. If I had been here,

I could have stopped her, I know it. Harriet wasn't like most of them."

"In what way?"

"Harriet wasn't even that bad off as far as her schizophrenia goes. She was cooperative about taking Nutracuratives. She really wanted to prove to her family that she could get her life back together. She had a goal, a reason to be compliant with treatment. Doesn't that make a difference, Doc?" His eyes pleaded with Taylor to grant absolution for Harriet's fatal mistake.

"It usually does, but I don't know enough about that case to have an opinion."

"Did you hear anything? Did anyone hear her say anything?" Ray's eyebrows raised, "What did she say? Please, it's important to me. I have to know."

Taylor wasn't sure how much to reveal about the second-hand comments she heard at the scene. His concern seemed sincere, but she wanted to get more information before she gave any, so she carefully crafted an answer, "People on the street corner were saying that she was rambling on with what seemed to be persecutory hallucinations. It's hard to know if her hallucinations had any meaning."

"If you think of anything more, please tell me. The official explanation of her death is too cut and dry for me. The two techs who worked with her earlier in the day were transferred to MACS programs in Orlando and Brooksville the day after it happened. And the social worker who was at the accident scene suddenly found money to go back to grad school in California. A lot of things happened too fast if you ask me."

"Ray, you know that everything an individual says during a psychotic episode doesn't square with reality."

"That's textbook talk, Doc. Get to know your patients and you'll find grains of truth even in psychotic ramblings. You have to pay attention. Too many professionals don't want to take time to pay attention. They diagnose, drug and move on. We techs and the social workers are with these patients day in and day out. We get to know them. I knew Harriet as a person, not as a paranoid schizophrenic." He paused to observe Taylor. She was listening without interrupting him or correcting him the way the nurses did. "You don't know this, Doc, but before he got fired, my buddy Hank, a social worker here, said that Harriet was asking for a second opinion from an outside physician. If that witch did anything to harm Harriet, I'll personally throw her into oncoming traffic."

"Do you really think anyone here would endanger a patient?"

"I've said too much already. You'll have to see for yourself. Just remember that the glory of the program is everything. Anything or anybody who threatens the success of MACS gets put out like Hank or silenced permanently like Harriet." Ray pushed up from the chair, stretching his lanky body. His welcoming smiled returned. "Sorry, Doc, if I got too intense. It's a sore subject."

"Not at all, Ray. I believe in having compassion for our patients. My father was a family physician and I remember seeing him get upset when patients died," Taylor disclosed, attempting to establish empathy. "I didn't know Harriet like you did but I do feel your sense of loss for what her life might have been."

"Thanks, Doc. You're okay. Watch your back around here. The sooner you size up the players, the better off you'll be. And if you need anything, ask me," Ray winked and left the room whistling a melancholy tune.

Taylor leaned back in the desk chair reflecting on what she heard. *In the fifth floor Executive Suite, Harriet's death was ignored. But down here in the clinic, staff actually knew this woman, and so did other patients. Here's where I can subtly glean information.*

A knock on the door shattered Taylor's concentration. A green shirted woman stepped in, coaxing a shaking young man to follow.

"Come on, Bobby. Come on in and meet Dr. Kendall. She'll have some candy for you," the woman said, finally dragging the man to a nearby chair.

"Hi, I'm Devon. I'm a floating nurse-assistant helping out here for a few days," she said handing an envelope to Taylor. Much to Taylor's surprise, the envelope was half filled with peppermint candies. Devon looked at Taylor while talking to Bobby, "Remember Bobby, if you work nicely with Dr. Taylor, she'll give you some candies." With that, Devon breezed out the door leaving a dazed patient behind.

Bobby was as silent as a sphinx, not uncooperative, more like emotionally absent. His presence would hardly be noticeable but for the sporadic twitch of his legs that radiated down to make his feet move with a syncopated tapping sound on the linoleum.

Taylor scanned a page with his social history desperately looking for some topic of interest. Nothing she tried gained his attention. Fifteen minutes into the intake session, Taylor relented and handed over a peppermint. Bobby popped the candy into his mouth savoring the sugar rush. For the length of time each candy lasted, Bobby was verbal. Taylor hated the idea of bribing a patient with candy, but for some odd reason he was more willing to talk with each sugar fix. She made a note in the chart to discuss substitution of alternative healthy treats like yogurt raisins or dried fruit. The last thing this bedeviled man needed to further complicate his life was diabetes.

As Bobby was talking about the voices he hears and what they tell him, Devon opened the door with a cheerful, "Time for group, Bobby."

"We aren't finished yet. He can join the group later."

Devon tapped her fingernails impatiently against the door frame, "Dr. Kendall, I have to deliver Bobby to group. If you want to make another appointment for him, see Neva." Without waiting for Taylor's reply, Devon held out a peppermint in one hand and motioned for Bobby to follow. He shuffled toward the door, a trembling arm reaching for the candy.

Taylor walked out behind him to the nurses' station. She

waited for Neva to finish a phone call then asked, "I need another appointment for Bobby's testing and I prefer to do it today. What time slot is open?"

"No time today. He has a full schedule of groups."

"But I can't do testing piecemeal; it's not the proper procedure."

"Doctor, that's your problem," Neva snapped back. "Right now I've got physician calls to make and you've got another intake. Learn to stay on schedule."

Taylor was summarily dismissed. She glanced over to see someone else in her office. *Maybe Dr. Locke will be down later and this can all get straightened out. No need to make an enemy of the charge nurse after finally getting into the clinic.*

Devon was waiting at the intake room with another patient. "Alva, this is Dr. Kendall, she's going to talk with you. You like to talk, don't you?"

Taylor took a seat across from the woman as Devon left. The frail woman reminded her of the old comedy skit her Mother liked to see on reruns where Lily Tomlin played a little girl sitting in a huge chair.

"Hello Alva. I'm happy to meet you," Taylor said extending her hand.

Alva reached out her tiny hand, and then drew it away quickly before making contact.

No problem. Easy to understand why a diminutive woman who could slide in unnoticed in the lunch line of an elementary school might be wary of being deposited in a closed room with a 5'10" woman who was a total stranger.

Alva's chart recorded her weight at eighty-one pounds, down from eighty-nine pounds two weeks ago. Odd, there's no mention of anorexia or medical complications that would account for escalating weight loss. Schedule or no schedule, Taylor knew that she had to take time to build rapport. Alva responded with a slight smile when Taylor complimented her dress and asked what she liked to do for fun. That got Alva talking about her garden and the colorful flowers. Taylor listened attentively for a few minutes then explained, "I need to ask you about some other things."

"What kind of things?"

"Things that will help me get to know you better. I'd like to know how you feel about yourself. Can you tell me how you feel right now?" Without breaking eye contact, Taylor reached for a silver ink pen near the legal pad.

Alva started screaming, "No, no. Don't touch it. The bugs will get on you."

She drew her matchstick legs up under her dress and buttoned her ragged sweater.

Taylor slowly moved her hands away from the pen and placed them in her lap out of sight. "What bugs do you mean, Alva?"

"Those bugs, can't you see them? There they are on your tissue box. Turn your head quickly, one's flying toward you!"

Taylor turned her head and then felt silly. She tried to display calm and follow what she was taught about dealing with hallucinations. *Don't acknowledge what isn't real, but don't diminish or belittle the patient's fears about what she believes she sees.*

"Alva. Look at me. I know you think that you see bugs. I don't see what you see."

"They are all over your desk. Get them, please, or they will jump on me!"

Therapeutic approach notwithstanding, Taylor decided this was the time to improvise. She looked around and saw a medium size glue stick in the pencil container. She pretended to spray the desk area with it. "See, Alva, the bugs are all gone now." That charade worked for about half hour before the de-bugging process was repeated in order to continue testing. She was nearly finished with the initial series when door opened again. This time it was Ray.

"Sorry, Doc, but I came to get Alva for the next group."

"Ray, I could use about fifteen more minutes and we'd be done."

"If it were up to me I'd agree, but I'm toast if I don't get her into group on time."

"Is it so terrible if she arrives a few minutes late? I'll escort her there."

"And will you explain it to Medicare? Patients have to be present in the group for so many minutes of the allotted time or the program can't bill for it. If they lose money upstairs, we get in trouble downstairs," he replied helping Alva to her feet and trying to keep her moving around the bugs that she insisted were running across the floor.

Taylor sighed and handed the glue stick to Ray. "Take this bug repellant. You may need it."

"Now you're getting the hang of it, Doc. Sometimes it makes more sense to work with the delusion rather than to fight it."

* * * * *

Taylor reviewed the two intake forms. She could make a partial report from Alva's testing along with recommendations for additional monitoring. As for her time with Bobby, there wasn't enough of the assessment completed to make a report. She noted her conclusions on the summary page in each patient's folder, placed the folders inside the chart and dropped them at the nurses' station. She also left a yellow sticky note asking to speak with Dr. Locke. She stopped at the makeshift food service counter to scour leftovers from the patients morning break. Picking up a lukewarm orange juice and a slightly crumbled cheese roll, she went back to the intake room to make notes of the questions she needed to ask Locke.

Deep in concentration reading a test manual, she was startled when the door crashed open then slammed shut. A scowling Lorraine Lewis appeared suddenly, as if she had beamed into the room. She threw down two chart notebooks.

"What is the meaning of this, Dr. Kendall? Can't you finish a simple intake report in a reasonable time?"

Lorraine's standing posture with folded arms confirmed that this wasn't a question; it was a confrontation. Two can play at that game. Taylor stood facing her.

"As you certainly must know, the erratic behaviors consistent with these patients' disorders can make assessment difficult."

"Lose the excuses. This isn't grad school. No treatment, no payment. No payment, no program. No program, no residency. Do you get my drift?"

"I hear you, Nurse Lewis. Are you suggesting that I compromise professional standards and score a half completed test just to finish a report on time?" Taylor intended her remarks to be a sarcastic reality check, but it missed the target.

"What I'm suggesting is that you learn to keep within our schedule and I don't personally care what it takes to do it. Don't make any more incomplete reports like these."

"I think we need to take this up with Dr. Locke."

"And that's another thing; don't think you can go running to Locke all the time. I thought you were a smart girl. Don't you know he's only a figurehead? This is my program. I'm head nurse here and the support staff report to me."

Taylor straightened up her posture, trying to add another inch of stature to face off her equally tall adversary.

"I think Dr. Locke would like to hear what you said about him."

"Go right ahead, but remember that I control the nurses and they control the patients. Let's see...you have a process group to do in two hours. If we got behind because of some interfering junior psychologist, then we'd be late for lunch," Lorraine paused for emphasis, "I want to see you try to handle a dozen schizophrenics when their blood sugar crashes. Of course that would be about the time the aides would be called in for an impromptu meeting so you'd be on your own, hotshot. Think about it."

"You'd manipulate the patients to get back at me?"

Maintaining her chilly exterior, Lorraine replied, "That's your take on it, but then who can prove it? Sometimes things happen in these programs. You said yourself that it's a difficult and unpredictable population."

The silence between them oozed like maple syrup. Their eyes locked in motionless combat. Lorraine turned to open the door, staring over her shoulder at Taylor.

"Listen to me and listen well. Locke is just another guy with a Ph.D. whose name looks good on the corporate letterhead. He may be the one who gets credit for designing the MACS PHPs, but I've found ways to make them more profitable. More and more the Girards are realizing how valuable I am to this operation. I expect to be in charge of the Clinical Division long before your residency is finished. So don't count on Locke to protect you. Either he'll get bumped up to some high sounding administrative position or tossed out the door. Or maybe you'll go first."

"Play your corporate politics all you like, but remember that I'm under Dr. Marco's supervision for this residency. He wants me here to open the door for MACS to become an approved residency site."

"You really are naive, girl. Marco, Victoria and Serena only want to make money, lots of money and they don't ask questions about how it happens. You're only here because psyche residents like social work interns are cheap labor that gets billed out at full tilt rates. Now don't cross me again or I'll see that every day you spend here is more miserable than the one before."

Feeling like she wrestled with a bear, Taylor's heart rate was just beginning to return to normal when she was startled by the door opening again. Ray ducked into her office and moved toward the file cabinet to avoid being seen from the hall. In a whisper, he said, "I heard Lorraine's searing tone. Are you all right?"

"Yes, Ray. Thanks for your concern."

"Come on, Doc. I know what it's like to be on the receiving end of her venom. Go take a break. You have at least a half hour to gobble down lunch before your group."

"Ray, I could use a walk to clear my head. I'll hurry back."

"Don't worry. I'll cover for you by getting the group started batting around the beach ball. They'll never notice if you're a few minutes late."

"Neva will notice and she'll tell Lorraine."

"Come on, now. Even psychologists get a potty break. I'll make it sound convincing."

"Thanks, Ray. And I'll return the favor. In fact, I think we can help each other on something that's important to both of us."

He glanced at his watch, "Later, Doc, the clock's ticking."

Taylor grabbed her wallet and sunglasses from her purse and walked casually toward to staff exit to avoid attracting attention. She heard Alva's pitiful screams coming from the back corner of the nurses' station. Taylor sneaked over on tip toes to lessen the tapping of her heels on the tile floor. Peeking around the half open door, she saw the backs of two green-shirted techs who attempting to restrain a squirming Alva. Apparently she was fighting an injection because she kept crying out, "No needles. The bugs live in the needles."

A guttural voice interrupted, "I said hold her still and I mean it!" The voice came from a person who paused to raise the needle and check for air bubbles, casting a shadowy outline against the side wall. As the figure moved closer to grasp Alva's bony arm, Taylor realized that it was Lorraine. Whatever was in that needle was powerful because Alva's body reacted almost immediately by becoming limp. Lorraine checked Alva's pulse and said to the techs, "Prop her up on the sofa in the lounge and let her sleep it off until the van arrives." Taylor didn't need an engraved invitation to bolt for the exit.

CHAPTER 11

The bright sun beaming on her face energized her, sending a surge of power through Taylor's body to make her shaky legs move faster. She darted through a line of cars that stopped for the red light then ran down the sidewalk toward the waterfront. She saw him. At least she hoped it was him sitting on the bench. She shouted, picking up her pace, "Gabe! Gabe!"

He turned, dropped his lunch sack and ran to meet her. He was both startled and delighted when she threw her arms around him and rested her head on his shoulder. The pounding tempo of her heart beat crashed against his rib cage. It was more than running, it was a fear based adrenaline rush that he'd known plenty of times in his own life. He shifted her to his side and with arm firmly around her back, guided her to the bench. Even sitting still, she was struggling to catch her breath. He handed her his soda and she drank greedily. "Taylor, what's wrong? Did someone hurt you?"

"Gabe, I'm sorry to be so ridiculous, but I need to talk to you."

He reached down to pick up the dropped lunch sack. "Lunch is served, Madame."

"No. I can't stay," she said glancing quickly at her watch. "I have to be back soon to start a therapy group."

She took another swallow of the chilled soda and continued, "Is there any way you can meet me after work? Can we go somewhere private to talk?"

"Do you want to come over and see my etchings?" he asked with a silly grin, then realized from her tense expression that she was in no mood for humor. "I'm sorry, that was flip. Forgive me."

"It's all right. I know I'm not making any sense because I'm not sure it makes sense to me."

He held her soft warm hands between his, "Okay, here's the plan. After work, you drive north on Central Avenue to the gallery past the Fifth Street traffic light. Pull over in the taxi lane and honk your horn. I'll come out and we'll go somewhere for dinner."

"I didn't mean to sound like I'm...I'm..."

"Asking me out on a date? I wanted to ask you out anyway, but for the record we'll call this a meeting. Next time I'll ask you out properly."

The mention of time prompted her check her watch, "Oh no, I have to hurry back for group. See you later." She jumped up and ran toward the intersection.

"Wait," he shouted, breaking into a sprint to catch her where she waited for the traffic light to change. He handed the sack to her, "At least promise me that you'll eat the other half of this sandwich during your break. See you tonight." He crossed the street with her.

She turned up Second Avenue to cut across the MACS parking lot. He sprinted over to First Avenue, anxious to get back to the gallery. Something was about to break loose on this situation. He could feel it. He had to make a few calls.

* * * * *

Taking a deep breath of fresh air before going back inside, Taylor at least appeared to be calm. *As Mama always said, act like you're above it all and people will assume you are.*

She walked casually past the nurses' station. No one was at the desk. As she entered Group Room 3, a multi-colored beach ball sailed toward her. She caught the ball, and then set it spinning on a single finger the way Daddy taught her to spin a basketball. While not the most profound therapeutic intervention she knew, the trick engaged the group's attention, which was a feat in itself.

In what seemed like no time at all, a bell sounded indicating five minutes to wrap up group. The younger members jumped up and headed for the door; some to take a quick smoke break and others to grab more cookies at the snack cart.

Ray was helping an older woman steady herself on the walker when Dr. Marco Girard strode in front of them. Deeply engrossed in the summary paperwork, Taylor didn't see him enter nor Ray's efforts to gain her attention. Clapping his hands, his bass voice rang out, "Bravo! Bravo!"

Taylor sprang to her feet so suddenly that the clipboard fell from her lap sending papers flying across the floor, "Dr. Marco, what a surprise to see you."

He bent down to help her gather the papers. Then he pulled a chair next to hers, deftly adjusting his position so that their knees touched.

"What a delight to see my favorite psychology resident busy at work! And I hear you are doing a splendid job. You and I must arrange a regular meeting time to discuss your progress. After all, my dear," Dr. Marco said reaching over to touch her shoulder, "I am your senior supervisor."

Blessedly Ray appeared, "Excuse me, folks, but I have to rearrange this room for the final session. You can talk in the community room." He smiled at Taylor. She understood what he was doing. Unless the meticulous schedule had a sudden change, this room was free. However, it was also the most isolated, at the end of the hallway with only a thin window beside the door. The community room was in a high visibility area off the main hall and a frequently used short cut to the staff restroom. She hoped Ray noticed her lips mime the words, "Thank you."

Entering the community room, Dr. Marco sat down on a sofa and asked her to join him. He proceeded to nudge closer to her while talking about what he observed in the group. Inches before he reached thigh-rubbing closeness, she had an idea.

"Why don't I get a coffee for us?" she asked, hopping up

without waiting for his answer. When she returned, she handed him a coffee mug then sat in the arm chair next to the sofa. He leaned toward her, gazing with dark eyes that penetrated like a surgical laser through her lab coat down to make her skin blush beneath the peach lace camisole.

"Tell me, my dear, how is your training experience progressing thus far?"

Thoughts swirled. *Dare I tell him about my concerns for Alva, Bobby and the other patients? How much does he know about day to day operations? How much does he care? Is Lorraine right when she says the Girard family is only in this for the money?* She ventured an honest yet edited evaluation, "Frankly, Dr. Marco, my first week got off to a peculiar start."

"In what way, my dear?"

"I was a bit disappointed to get wrapped up in a research project before I even spent time with patients, but Dr. Locke took care of it so I suppose he cleared it with you. Anyway, I'm really happy to be working in the clinic."

"Has the staff treated you appropriately?"

Her first image was that of Lorraine, reading the riot act. "The support staff are wonderful. They welcomed me graciously. Lorraine Lewis does seem to have a style of management by intimidation that I find out of place between professionals," the words leaked out of her thoughts before she was ready.

Dr. Marco didn't appear surprised or dismayed. "What is the issue between you and Nurse Lewis?"

"I'm sorry I said anything. We'll work it out. I don't think that I can do an adequate intake with every patient and keep on the tight time schedule she demands."

Marco paused, making the effort to sound scholarly, "Alas, young Dr. Kendall, you have discovered that great chasm between doctoral programs and actual mental health practice. There is so little time to do all the wonderful things for which you were trained."

"You understand what I mean?"

"Yes, there is so much I would like to do for these poor souls, but we have to keep pace with the schedule. We are paid only for the treatment that is documented. Empathy is not reimbursable. You must realize that the vast majority of these patients would get no treatment at all if not for MACS pioneering programs and our ability to collect from the Medicare system."

Taylor recoiled at the hollowness behind his sincere sounding words. "So we do what we can and we slide a little on protocol? I guess my university committee didn't know about your standards of practice when they approved my residency."

"Now let's not see problems where none exist. No one at MACS is asking you to compromise your standards. You simply must learn to be more flexible to operate within our system."

"Exactly what do you mean?"

"Adapt your testing times. Write the best report you can write. We already know the symptoms and the problems of the schizophrenic population. The intake and evaluation is merely part of the routine," he said casually. "There are never any real surprises. Each patient we keep in the MACS clinic who completes the therapy program and transfers into our Live Anew follow-up program is one person whose life is a thousand percent better than before. Take satisfaction in small victories."

He watched her consider his words as she slowly sipped coffee. He turned toward Taylor, lowering his voice, "Lorraine informs me that you observed the unfortunate incident involving a female suicide from our program?"

Taylor resented the way that he referred to this human being as the "suicide," as if she had no identity. "The crowd of onlookers was blocking the entry to MACS the day I arrived. I guess I'm as guilty as the next person for staring at the accident scene."

"Think carefully, Dr. Kendall, did you hear anyone mention anything she may have said?"

She knew she couldn't brush him off as easily as she did Ray, so she gave a censored version. "Like any accident scene, every bystander has his or her own version. Probably nothing more than paranoid ramblings, at least that's what I got from the *St. Petersburg Times* story the next day. Are you trying to find out if what happened to her could be happening to our other patients?"

"Certainly not!" he recoiled at the question. "If you are going to survive in the medical field you must learn to accept the loss of patients, particularly the chronic mentally ill. Surely you know that suicide is the leading cause of death among schizophrenics."

"Yes, Dr. Marco, I read your extremely detailed memo on the subject."

"Good. Now let's put this distasteful matter to rest. That is, unless you think of anything, anything at all about the accident scene… Naturally, anything you recall might help us work better with other patients in future crisis situations."

He's smooth. He is arrogant enough to think that he can use my interests and what he perceives as my inexperience to set me up.

Neva walked in juggling several chart notebooks. "Sorry if I'm interrupting, but I've been looking for Dr. Kendall. I need your signature on the two morning intakes."

Grateful for the excuse to leave, Taylor said, "As you said, Dr. Marco, I must get moving to stay up to speed with the program."

Neva handed the top two notebooks to Taylor. "The paperwork you need to sign is marked with red clips. You can work on them over at the nurses' station desk. I'll be there in a minute." Neva said, exchanging glances with Dr. Marco until Taylor was out of sight.

* * * * *

"She's going to be a pain, a protocol freak."

"Deal with it, Neva." *She's going to be more difficult to bring into the system than anticipated. Usually the candidates who are passed over on their prime training choices are the ones who are so grateful for a chance to work that they'll do anything. But not this woman. She's not as desperate as I expected. What are you trying to do, Sebastian Dale? You stole Blake from me. Now I'm stuck with one of your do-gooder disciples spouting the same ethical swill you used to brainwash my son, my Prince.* Feeling the tension tighten in his shoulder muscles, Marco grasped control of his rising anger to complete the more important task, "Let me know immediately if she continues her preoccupation with the Logan woman's death."

"Too late, Ray's been bending her ear."

"Ray? Who is he?"

"Ray is a tech. Very experienced. He can handle these patients when no one else can. Please don't transfer him. I don't want to lose him."

"Then manage him. Keep him busy. He'll get over the bleeding heart soon enough."

"Don't be so sure, Marco, I think he was in love with Harriet. That's why I sent him on escort duty the day Lorraine decided to terminate."

Marco's warm hands cupped Neva's face. "Let's be careful with our clinical jargon, my dear. Using the word 'terminate' could give someone the wrong idea of how we move patients between levels of treatment."

He grabbed her shoulders, pulling her toward him for a rough kiss; the way he knew she liked it. As he walked away, Neva was breathless but not from the kiss. The Nutracuratives may have been a harmless crock, but the substance inside that syringe that day was a very real, legal prescription medication. Apparently Dr. Marco either didn't know or wasn't bothered by the idea of something good used for something bad.

CHAPTER 12

Grateful to put this peculiar workday behind her, Taylor was walking out of the clinic door when she heard her name.

"Taylor! Wait up. What do you say we go out to my favorite coffee place that we missed?"

"Thanks, Carla. Maybe tomorrow, I have dinner plans tonight."

"Tall, dark and handsome?"

"You're close. Tall, slick brownish haired and handsome."

"What department does he work in? I must be slipping to miss him."

"He's not connected to MACS. He works downtown."

"Look out for those stockbrokers. Once the market closes and the first scotch is poured their libido rises faster than the Dow."

"Thanks for the tip, but this guy's mellow. That's part of his charm. I could use mellow after a day in Lorraine's shadow," Taylor replied, opening her car door.

"Have fun. Let's do lunch tomorrow so I can hear all the details."

Stepping aside as Taylor backed up her car, Carla mumbled, *No matter how Taylor tries to look casual, her eyes give her away. She's excited about seeing this man again.* Not unlike the excitement that once made Carla's dark Spanish eyes dance at the mention of Jay's name. Candlelight dinners. Sunset walks. Stolen embraces in the stairwell. That's the way it began. He listened to her complaints about being stuck as summer replacement in the Girard's Buenos Aires psychiatric clinic while her father took

Blake on a European jaunt disguised as a business trip.

That was Blake's gift the year he graduated from Princeton. As a consolation prize, Carla got a new car and too much unpaid overtime in the billing department. But working late had its benefits. In a matter of weeks, Dr. Jayant Nandan became her first serious love affair. The slightly built Indian doctor was a man of few words, and Carla hung onto every one of them.

Nosey Gina once caught them kissing in the file room. That night at dinner Victoria unleashed a fury normally reserved for berating servants. Marco telephoned from Rome. He exerted his fatherly influence to reason with Carla, suggesting that she drop this embarrassing infatuation. Carla called her parents bigots and racists. Marco ordered her to stop seeing Jay. The scene was repeated several times on nights when Carla came home late without an excuse. She and Jay talked about eloping, but Jay was in Argentina on a special work permit obtained under Dr. Marco Girard's sponsorship. Completing this psychiatric training could lead to certification in Mexico or the Caribbean, and eventually allow him to be able to work in the States. Jay was a man in love, but he was also a practical man. His widowed mother, eight siblings and a disabled uncle depended on the money he sent back to India every month.

Serena stepped in, appearing to play the devil's advocate. She invited Jay to dinner, acting as if she were trying to help. After twenty-one years of distance and distrust, Carla let down her guard allowing Serena to be her confidante. Serena convinced Carla that a brief cooling off period until Marco's return would allow her father to see this relationship in a better light. She even let Jay drive them to the airport.

Serena, Carla and Gina spent ten days shopping in Miami and Grand Cayman. Supposedly Serena was investigating another business opportunity on the island. At first it was good to get away from her mother's screaming accusations, even if it meant spending time with her stepmother and her betraying sister. Then Carla began to get suspicious of the delay.

As soon as they cleared customs at the airport, Carla insisted on going straight to the clinic. She ran down the hall to the small office on the left. Seeing the door ajar, she burst in shouting, "Jay, I'm home!"

Two men wearing police badges were rummaging through his desk. They told her that Jay was in jail, pending deportation, for gross negligence in the care of several clinic patients. Tears flooding her eyes, she turned away from them and ran down the hall. Her father stepped into her path.

"I'm so sorry you had to find out this way, my darling," Marco said with feigned sincerity, guiding her into his private office.

She pushed away his embrace. "You did this, Father. I know you did. You ruined Jay's career because you didn't want a Hindu in the family. I'll never forgive you for it."

Blake stood up from a nearby chair to see his sister dissolve in tears. He opened his arms and she ran to him for protection. "What have you done, Father?"

"My son, my Prince, I exercised fatherly concern for your sister. She was used by that Indian doctor. With your mother's gracious assistance, Victoria and I were able to prevent Carla from turning a summer romance into a misguided alliance."

Later Blake heard his mother's version of the story. Then he realized that his gut instinct was accurate; Carla had been duped. A year later on a trip to Greece, he detoured thousands of miles out of his way to look for Jay in Calcutta. What he found was a poor family huddled in a cramped apartment. They shunned him. On the way out, a younger brother who spoke credible English told Blake that Jay returned home in disgrace and joined the Indian army. He was a medical officer whose last letter placed him near the India-Pakistan border. In one of countless border skirmishes, Jay was killed, becoming another casualty of hatred and despair.

Carla shook her head to break the hold of those memories.

How different things will be for Taylor and her magic man. She's confident and secure. When she falls in love, nothing will separate her from her man. Opening the car door, Carla started the engine and reached for a cassette at the bottom of the glove box. It was sitar music, Jay's favorite. Driving away Carla wondered what kind of man Taylor's soul mate was.

* * * * *

There he was, waiting outside the gallery. *He needs to lose the slicked down hair style. Overall, handsome, with potential for debonair if he would exchange those old polyester golf shirts for a snappy Puma polo or a button down collar shirt. Still he's handsome in a ragged sort of way.*

"Drive all the way down Central and cross over the Treasure Island Bridge."

"Where are we going?"

"To a little out-of-the-way seafood place on Pass-a-Grille with fresh fish and all the local color you can stand."

On the way Taylor told him about her day in the clinic, including her puzzling encounters with Ray, Lorraine and Marco. As they reached the tacky strip of flashing neon light motel signs that herald Treasure Island, they agreed to postpone further discussion of MACS until after dinner to avoid ruining their appetites.

The Fish Joint was clearly not a candidate for the Golden Spoon award. Tattered red check tablecloths were slapped over ancient wooden tables sitting on cracked vinyl floors, whose dull brown color was partially concealed by sawdust mixed with peanut shells. Tee shirts, cutoffs and flip flops seemed to be the dress code, but the grilled grouper was Cordon Bleu delicious.

They shared a basket of onion rings which they reached for simultaneously. His fingers brushed hers. She slowed down her usual hurried eating style, trying to make the moments last longer. By the time they finished their meal, the used candle on their table burned so low that the flame was barely visible below the lip of the recycled tuna can which served as its holder. He asked for the check along with two deluxe brownies and coffees to go.

She reached for her wallet, "I thought this was a meeting, so here's my share."

"Put away your money."

"I don't want you to feel obligated. You said this wasn't an official date."

"Okay, you can pay for your entree, but I'm buying dessert. It's worth it to watch that contented look on your face when you eat chocolate," he said reaching across the table to hold her hand. He was feeling an overwhelming desire to be open with her and yet he knew it was in direct conflict with the reason he needed to get close to her.

He led her out through the restaurant's back door and down the wooden stairway to the beach. A few feet away, they found an old bench nearly obscured by tall sea grapes moving in a waltz tempo to the soft evening breeze. The wood was partially rotted on the left, forcing them to sit close together on the right side. Feeding her the last bite of brownie, he kicked off his loafers.

"Let's go dip our toes in the water."

"I can't do that, Gabe. My stockings will be ruined."

"That might be true if you were wearing stockings, but you aren't. Let's risk being a touch less proper and act like the natives."

Her mouth almost dropped open in surprise. "How did you know I wasn't wearing stockings?" she demanded, pushing up her slacks and pulling down knee high hose.

He smiled, "Lucky guess?" He decided this was not the time to tell her how many women he had undressed - some in the line of duty, but most purely for pleasure.

They waded ankle deep into the warm gulf water. Taylor was grateful that she wore her knit pants to work today. Even if she had worn the tan linen that cost a mint to dry clean, she would have followed him into the water. The warm gulf waters slithering around her toes felt wonderful.

"You're a water baby, aren't you?" Gabe watched her kick at the waves.

"You bet! That's one of the greatest treats of living on the Florida coast; never too far from water, either the gulf or the bay. My family thinks that's silly. Mama says we have enough waterfront view right at home; the swimming pool and the lily pond. And if I need more, it's a short drive to the fake beach at Sardis. Since I've gotten used to Florida beaches, I can't settle for less."

"Sounds like you are becoming a real Floridian."

"I think so. I suppose that's why I didn't seriously pursue any of the residencies out of state, even two that were offered through University of Tennessee Medical School in Memphis. My father used to teach there so I would have been as much the favored candidate as Bratton was at South Bay," Taylor said, wincing at the thought that she might have benefited from the kind of favoritism she disdained.

"Did you get aced out of South Bay by some good ole boy?"

"Actually it was a second rate good ole boy, a bimbo and one truly great guy."

"Three residencies?"

"Yes and I struck out; no runs, no hits, no errors. And that's how I ended up at MACS."

He paused grateful that the conversation, interesting as it was, finally returned to business.

"Let's go back to the bench," he said tentatively putting his arm around her waist to guide her back across the moonlit sand. "While our feet dry, you can finish telling me what bothered you at work today."

Once again, Taylor found it easy to pour out her concerns to Gabe. He listened to her account of the confrontation with Lorraine, the subtle manipulation from Dr. Marco and the undisguised pressure to work faster at the expense of quality.

"I can deal with usual workplace irritations. I took a year off between college and grad school to work as a traveling representative for my sorority, so I get the corporate world. But I have never worked around such an odd group of people. Brook is right; the place runs on high octane paranoia."

"How's your program review coming?"

"I didn't work on it today, but I did try to get Harriet's file. My request got back to Neva, the charge nurse, who told me in no uncertain terms that the file was not available to me now and never would be."

"Sounds like you struck a nerve."

"Apparently. I've already learned that Neva is another stooge for Lorraine, who in turn reports to Gina. I found a memo from Gina in my box before I left work. She said that Harriet's chart would not be suitable to the study of program effectiveness due to the suicide."

"Do you agree with that?"

"Yes and no. Obviously she couldn't be included in a follow-up with a three-month post treatment recall, but what I don't understand is why no one at MACS is concerned about whether or not any other patients are at risk for self-destruction. Like you said, Gabe, finding and correcting flaws is important to maintaining quality treatment."

"Can you get anyone else to help you?"

"I've already asked Ray, the tech who knew her, to help me find more information. He's very angry about the incident and isn't willing to call her death a suicide."

"Word on the street is that there's something more to the story."

"How could people outside MACS know something when even the staff have been forbidden to talk about it?"

"Taylor, a lot of the street people and folks living in the cheap rooming houses downtown have been patients at MACS. It's a revolving door. Patients come in until the Medicare payments run out, then they get discharged. You know it doesn't take long for untreated, unmonitored schizophrenics to bounce back."

"That sounds as if we keep treating the same people over and over with no lasting result."

"Oh there's a result all right. It's money, Taylor, big money."

His bluntness made her reflect on how evident big money was at MACS. *The antiques in the Executive Suite alone must be worth hundreds of thousands of dollars. Dr. Marco drives a tomato red Ferrari. A chauffeured limousine transports Serena and Victoria.*

And the jewelry! He wears a diamond rimmed Rolex, Serena has sets of jewels to match each of her thirty-five Chanel suits (at least that's how many different suits the secretaries have seen so far this season) and Victoria limits her jewelry to a heavy gold link bracelet and Cartier tank watch, but she flaunts two Salvador Dali originals on the walls of her chrome and glass, hard-edged modernistic office.

Gina, Carla, Felipe and Tiffany drive expensive cars and wear an endless display of designer clothes. Brook says they live in a mansion on Snell Isle with a staff of servants. When they get busy at work, an honest to goodness English butler shows up with food from home. That's a twist on the brown bag lunch.

Taylor tried to synthesize her thoughts to make sense out of it, "The Girards have several MACS programs around the state. Maybe they are reaping the rewards of good business acquisitions."

"Or maybe they're making money the old fashioned way, on the backs of the poor and the distraught. Didn't you tell me that you are already being asked to cut corners on testing and evaluations? And didn't you say your patients and others are hustled into group long enough to be counted on the billing records?"

"Yes, but…"

"Is that the way you want to practice psychology, Taylor?"

"No, but…"

"Don't you have an obligation to your patients? Your name appears as the examiner on these reports. What if a Medicare auditor questions your work? Will you lie for the good of MACS?"

"Of course not!"

"Then I think you need to cover yourself. Any improprieties at the PHPs could tarnish your reputation in the future."

She did not want to hear him say aloud her worst fears. "Gabe, I'm new at the MACS clinic. I'm not responsible for any of this."

"I know, but government inquiries are rough things. Medicare is no different than the IRS. When they smell deceit, they turn over every rock and shake down every employee looking for something not up to code," he paused, watching her assimilate the concept. "Didn't you also tell me that you overheard the nurses wondering if Harriet's death would trigger a Medicare program review?"

"Well the local police don't seem to be too concerned about it. Dr. Marco says he talked with them and they consider it nothing more than a simple suicide of a mentally ill person."

"Is that what you think?"

"I don't know. Even if she intended to kill herself, I have a nagging feeling that something else pushed her over the edge. Maybe it was the walking trauma machine, Lorraine."

"Think about it, Taylor. Why would the head program nurse do something to cause a patient more distress, not to mention send her fleeing into the street?"

"That's what Ray wants to know," Taylor admitted. "The initial explanation made sense. Schizophrenic patients are a high risk for suicidal actions, whether or not they actually perceive the danger, but every other bit of information I get about MACS gives me that creepy sensation that what you see is not what you get."

"Want some help checking it out?"

"What kind of help?"

"You know, the cloak and dagger routine. I've been a second story man, a spy, a safe cracker, a soldier of fortune. . ."

"Gabe, you are too wrapped up in your acting. This isn't a play. This is real. I can't ask someone who has nothing at stake here to get involved."

"I understand what you're saying, Taylor. If it's a risk to you, then I want to be around to protect you. I also have some friends who are skilled at investigations."

"You mean bring in a P.I. to spy on my employer?"

"No. More like some help with background information, that sort of thing."

She looked at her watch. "I can hardly believe it's 10:30. I need to get home."

They drove back to the gallery singing along to an oldies tape. Parked at the curb, Gabe leaned over to give her a series of nuzzled kisses on her neck.

"Until next time, lovely lady. How about meeting for lunch tomorrow?"

"Can't do. I promised to have lunch with Carla. She's such a dear. Probably the closest thing to a friend I'll find at MACS," Taylor replied, then offered an observation that surprised him. "No matter what craziness is going on there, I can't imagine that Carla's part of it."

He offered neither support nor objection, trying to appear open minded. "Okay. I'll yield to a prior commitment. Let's meet after work at the marina. I'll take you sailing."

He jumped out of the car, closing the door before she could say no.

* * * * *

Walking into the apartment, Blake's cell phone was flashing to indicate a message. He dialed the coded number.

"What's up?"

"I got the computer information you wanted."

"Can't it wait until morning? I'm bushed."

"Don't think so, man. Trust me, it's the stuff that inquiring minds want to know. I'm in the back booth in the bar at the sushi place off Tyrone Boulevard."

Blake hung up the phone. Late as it was, he hustled out of his work clothes and into crisply pressed navy chinos with a light blue Polo dress shirt. Slipping into his personal wardrobe felt good. Clothes notwithstanding, it was hard to feel stylish in that clunky brown car. Oh how he missed the unmistakable scent of leather seats in the new Lexus, which was now sitting idle in the garage at his Reston, Virginia townhouse.

When Blake arrived at the restaurant, all but the late diners and die hard drinkers remained. The drinkers were mostly gathered near the bar in view of the television watching baseball. The tables near Jack were empty. *Good choice. The problem about public places is that you never know who might be eavesdropping.*

As he approached the booth, Jack stood up, motioned toward the waitress, and slapped Blake on the back in greeting. "Say, my man, wearing the basic Blake wardrobe tonight. Did I interrupt a hot date with the good doctor?"

"Yes and no."

"Is that yes or no? I'm living my life vicariously through the *bon vivant* adventures of Blake the wonder stud."

The waitress arrived with tea and a sampler plate of sushi. "Can I get anything else for you gentlemen? Appetizers? Extra napkins? My phone number?"

Blake shook his head, and then gave her a lingering smile that was worth her night in tips, "Thanks, you arrived in time to rescue me from my inquisitorial friend. We won't be here that long."

When the waitress walked away, Blake turned back to Jack, "Okay, hotshot, what did you find?"

Jack took a folder out of his briefcase, held it to his forehead saying, "The answer is: someone you want to know better. Now what is the question?"

"Not the ancient Carnac routine again. You've got to stop watching those 'Tonight Show' reruns. Okay, I give up, what is the answer."

"Taylor Kendall."

"What do you mean?"

"The attractive Dr. Kendall; doe eyes, great legs, hyperactive brain cells."

"What did you find?"

"Okay, okay. I found a suitable geek-in-training at the office and set him to work on your assignment."

"Was that wise? Can you trust him?"

"Are you kidding? By the time I gave him the big buildup about secrecy and loyalty, he was Sir Lancelot armed with a mouse. All I had to do was keep the guy plied with root beer and potato chips while he worked all night."

"Did he do the computer search at the office?"

"No, we worked at his place. This kid lives in a one bedroom apartment that looks like an electronics store. He prefers his equipment anyway; says it's better than what he uses at work."

"Why does that not surprise me? What did he find?"

Jack slowly opened the folder and handed it to Blake, "After hacking into Cutter's computer, we found that the last complete investigation he did was on Taylor Kendall. Quite an interesting report. And, get this, it was commissioned by Lorraine Lewis at MACS."

Blake scanned through the report copy. The speed reading he learned in college often came in handy in his work. "What do you think they were looking for?"

"Certainly not what they got. We also found two prior reports on MACS employees, one requested by Lorraine and the other by Gina Girard. He shook a few choice skeletons out of those employees' closets, but don't you know Lorraine and Gina were disgusted after reading the report on Taylor!"

"Why?"

"Because the good Dr. Kendall is exactly what she seems, an intelligent, well mannered young woman from a moderately affluent Southern family who works hard and stays out of trouble."

"And they needed a private detective's report to figure that out?"

"Now, Blake, you know better than anyone how the Girards operate. People they can't buy, they control with velvet handcuffs. What I can't figure out is why they gave the MACS residency to someone with as little blackmail potential as Taylor."

"It's a matter of intersecting convenience. Taylor made the mistake of setting her sights solely on the South Bay Hospital residency. She was sure that she'd get it on ability. That's a problem with being innocent, Jack. She failed to size up the hospital's selection committee well enough to see that she had no chance against nepotism and nymphomania. She nearly got left behind which is a career killer in professional psychology."

"So MACS was the last resort? That's a bad choice, man, not blackmail material."

"You're right. My guess is that Marco assumed Taylor was left behind because of something she did wrong. He must have been too blinded by the idea of billing prime psychologist fees for an unsuspecting novice that he assumed he was getting an ethical derelict who would do anything for a chance to complete the residency."

"Wait a minute, there's a familiar name in this report, Taylor's advisor, Dr. Dale. Isn't he the guy who flew up for our graduation?

"Yes. Dale's been more of a parent to me than the unholy trinity ever was. Without his influence, Jack, we might be adversaries instead of allies."

"You don't think your family knows about what you do?"

"Even my sister, Carla, has no idea that I'm an FBI Agent."

"Man, what a reunion this is going to be."

Blake paused to contemplate the scene he'd so long savored in his imagination.

"Meanwhile, back to MACS," Jack refocused the conversation, "We've got one demigod and two high priestesses who are bitterly disappointed to find that the training demon they hoped for is really the vestal virgin. Do they change the game plan or find a volcano and sacrifice her?"

Jack's barbed humor brought to Blake's mind images of other people throughout the years who were setup to take a fall long enough for Marco, Serena and Victoria to escape responsibility. *I will not allow them to pull the same stunt on Taylor. The noose is tightening around MACS. As soon as Marco feels scrutiny, he will set up the sacrificial lambs. It's also possible that Marco really did know about Taylor's clean record and plans to use her innocence to his advantage. I will never let Marco ruin her professional reputation, no matter what I have to do to stop it.*

"Blake! What are you mumbling?"

"Sorry about that."

"Are you sure that you aren't too close to this case? I know you told the director that your understanding of how the Girards run schemes would help us score more than a surface hit on their operations. If it gets too personal, you know you have to take yourself out of action."

"Do you want to take over my work here?"

"You know me better than that. Cut the offended aristocrat act. You aren't 'The Prince' anymore, just another worker bee like me." The two men glared at each other.

Jack broke eye contact first, "I'm your friend, Blake. I know what this case means to you, personally and professionally. I want you to stay on the job as long as you are clear what the goals are; the bureau's goals, not yours."

Blake knew that Jack was right. It's a lecture he'd delivered to himself several times since this assignment began.

"No point breaking up our waitress' flirtation with those guys at the other table. Jack, would you go up and get our sushi platter while I scan the reports on the other employees?"

When Jack returned, Blake had read the leverage MACS held on social worker, Hank Brand, and medical records clerk, Janelle Sylvester.

"I see there is one other file. What's next?" Blake asked, playing into Jack's penchant for turning mundane aspects of their work into a grand quest.

"Geek Boy pulled off a few isolated pieces of info that he thought might be interesting from Cutter's internet searches. This one caught my attention," Jack said as he held the page so that Blake could see it. "Three emails to other PI's discussing the type of security used by cruise ships sailing out of Port Canaveral."

"You mean weapons checks? That's no secret. They have screening equipment similar to airports."

"No, not weapons. Cutter was trying to find out how carefully the contents of bags were checked. Look at this memo."

Blake studied Cutter's inquiry. "What does this have to do with MACS?"

"Go to the next page," Jack directed, then pointed to the upper right corner. "Copies were sent to Lorraine and to an email at another location. Look at that email address for NICO. Since I don't know where that email goes, I wasn't ready to invade the privacy of some innocent citizen."

"Not innocent at all. NICO is short for Nicollo Machiavelli, author of *The Prince*, Marco's guide for living and my childhood bedtime story."

"Whoa! You think that's Dr. Girard's personal email box?"

"I'll bet you dinner at Commander's Palace and a flight on my jet to New Orleans that it is."

"Don't tempt a man who nearly left the FBI rather than get transferred away from the French Quarter, the world's ultimate food court. This must be a sucker bet."

"I'm afraid it is, my friend. But don't worry, when this gig is over, I'll fly to you and your lady to New Orleans for dinner to celebrate."

"All right!" Jack exclaimed, barely covering the sound of his stomach growl as a tribute to memories of the Big Easy. "Oh and there's one more thing. Geek Boy pulled some passenger records from the ships that sail out of Port Canaveral. In the last eleven months, Marco Girard sailed twice on the Carnival and once on the Royal Caribbean. Gina Girard and Lorraine Lewis sailed twice on Royal Caribbean. Felipe and Tiffany Girard sailed once on Norwegian Cruise Line."

"Where did they go?"

"Every trip was to Nassau, Bahamas. I can't picture your hoity-toity family being fascinated with the merchandise at the Straw Market?"

"They probably do stop at the Straw Market since it's in line with their real destination."

"What do they buy over there?"

"It's not what they buy; it's what they bring."

"I don't get it, Blake."

"Now I see how the pieces fit. Cruise ships dock at Prince George's Wharf in downtown Nassau in tidy rows like a gigantic parking lot. Passengers walk down a short ramp to the dock and right into downtown Nassau. No need to get passports stamped for entry or exit. All that's needed to get back on the ship is a credit card size I.D. inscribed with nothing more personal than your name, cabin number and your dinner table assignment."

"I'm still missing something."

"To get back on ship, passengers go through another metal detector and haphazard visual screening by overworked ship security. Sometimes the non-security staff gets tagged with the duty. Their prime directive is to prevent weapons and stowaways. Whatever else legitimate passengers bring on and off the ship is largely ignored."

"Don't the Bahamian authorities keep a close watch on entry and exit?"

"Not from the cruise ships. It's a user-friendly system. Ships bring tourists with lots of American dollars to spend in Bahamian shops, casinos and restaurants. Like I said, easy come, easy go."

Jack's attention perked up, "Are you saying that's where the missing corporate funds are going? I thought the suave bad guys used numbered accounts in Switzerland or the Cayman Islands? Why wouldn't Marco do the same?"

"Simple. It's too obvious. What many people don't know is that private accounts are also offered in the Bahamas. Set up a certain type of trust and get a connected local attorney to further create distance between the real source of the money and its destination. Why stir up Immigration's attention with a passport trail when you can do a long weekend in Nassau with no fanfare?" Blake explained. "Not to mention the extra tax-evading cash Marco can earn at his favorite gambling sites on Paradise Island."

"Exactly where do you think the money is?"

"I have an idea, but I'd rather check it out first."

"How can you do that?"

"Make them nervous then follow the next messenger to the money."

Jack's face showed his astonishment. "Blake, our job description doesn't extend that far. You're talking about getting authorizations to operate in a foreign country. That's going to drag things out way too long. We're supposed to close in on them fast and get out. The director will never go for it."

"He doesn't have to, because I'm not going the official route."

Jack rubbed the back of his neck to soothe the headache that often flared during these kind of discussions with Blake, "I've already dragged a junior employee into unauthorized computer hacking. Now you want to run a Lone Ranger operation in a foreign country and I'm supposed to cover you, right?"

"Stop worrying. I'm only going to observe. I won't be out of sight more than two days. It's a short flight over and a few hours simple surveillance. All I need from you and Geek Boy is to keep close tabs on the cruise and flight bookings, then let me know which Girard to follow."

"As long as it's unofficial," Jack warned, "You can't bring back any evidence or the Justice Department may not be able to use it for prosecution. We have to play nice-nice with the bad guys. They hire better lawyers to twist our Constitution in their favor if we so much as sneeze on their silk suits."

Blake shared Jack's disgust, "Justice, the IRS and Medicare have been batting the MACS investigation around like Larry, Moe and Curly. If we only concentrate on what's within our reach in Florida, we'll do exactly what Marco expects - miss his nest egg for the next scam."

"Can you do this without getting tagged? If MACS is laundering money in the Bahamas, it's your family acting as couriers. What if they see you?"

"Jack, you may have learned the art of being sneaky during training, but I learned it as a boy. The only member of my family who even poses a challenge to my surveillance skills is Marco. At worst, he would assume I'm scheming my way around the world on cards and women like he taught me. We'd have a few drinks, an expensive dinner and end by arguing over why I won't apologize and return to the family."

"Wait a minute. How will you lure him to Nassau? And even if you put on the pressure, aren't these ships booked way in advance?"

Blake reached for napkin and scribbled down several words. He scrambled the letters and circled three words. He folded the napkin with his notes, placing it in his shirt pocket.

"What was that about?"

"Just a few notes for the trip while the thoughts were fresh in my mind. In answer to your questions, yes, I can lure him to Nassau without revealing my identity. And yes, he can sometimes get on the ship late by traveling as an extra dance escort. Or he can go over from Ft. Lauderdale on the day trip gambling boats like we use to do when I was in college."

"Dance escort?"

"Sure. Cruise ships are safe vacation packages for single women, especially older widows. Cruise directors are always looking for debonair guys like Marco to travel at reduced rates for dancing and entertaining the ladies. Or he can go the private way and get a bargain on a high priced suite that didn't get booked. Either way works."

"Sounds like you've done this before."

"It was a popular father-son outing. Marco and I have made a lot of money on cruises, especially the ships on the Mediterranean; not to mention the gifts from grateful, frog-faced dance partners. Marco always said, 'The uglier and richer the woman, the bigger and more expensive are the gifts she will buy to please you.'"

"Blake! What a cad you've been! Are you sure you're on our side?"

"Thanks to Dale, I know what side I'm on, but I also know how the other side operates. Evil is remarkably predictable and that's how I'll lure Marco to Nassau. Thanks to you and Geek Boy, I'll get whatever else I need from Nico's email."

"More hacking? Do you need help?"

"Not this time. Besides, you don't want to know what I'm going to do next."

Blake rose from the table and walked over to the bartender to pay the check. Jack gathered the papers back in file folders, rushing to catch up with Blake's long strides across the parking lot.

"Wait up! I've got copies of the files for you," Jack called out, pulling a manila envelope from his briefcase.

"Thanks," Blake tossed the envelope through the driver's side window of his brown sedan.

"I can't stand it, Blake. What are you going to do to make

Marco jump?"

"Simple, I'll move money out of one of his accounts."

"What bank? How will you get the password?"

"Trial and error. I'll start with the bank he used to use for gambling winnings. As for the password, my family tends to use familiar names and dates, nothing complex. When Marco finds a chunk of money missing, he'll high tail it over there to trace the move."

"That's what worries me, tracing the move right back here."

"No chance, my rule-oriented friend. I'll fly to Atlanta in the morning and do the transfer from a computer station at the airport. Be home for dinner."

Jack saluted, and then watched his friend and colleague drive away. No one made his job look more glamorous than Blake, and few survived leaning over the edge as often as he did. Maybe all the good guys needed was to be trained first by the bad guys.

CHAPTER 13

ally sat at her work station Wednesday morning monitoring the other secretaries. The clicking of computer keys verified that the women were busy. The florist delivery arrived early, as she planned. The enormous arrangement of orchids and tea roses on the reception hall table was garish and ridiculously expensive, the type Serena prefers.

An aroma of brandy and leather emanated from Marco's office. Sally stayed late last night to supervise the cleaners who reconditioned the leather furnishings. When they finished, she burned a candle with brandy scent. As a finishing touch, she organized the haphazard papers on Victoria's desk, leaving a box of Godiva chocolate truffles in the center. On Executive Staff meeting day, Sally made everything in the inner sanctum perfect. Alerted by the elevator chimes, she rose to receive the accolades she carefully contrived to obtain.

Victoria stomped across the marble entry, "Where is Marco? I want to know what he's up to and I want to know now!"

Sally fell in behind Victoria's Gucci-heeled goose step to her office, "I haven't heard from Dr. Marco this morning. Of course, he'll be here soon. It is Executive Staff meeting day."

Victoria threw her briefcase and leather purse in the direction of the sofa. She flipped on her computer and sat down. Her eyes caught the chocolates. She pounded her fist on the gold box, leaving a dent and a trail of cherry cream oozing from each side.

"So lover boy thinks he can pull a fast one and gloss it over with chocolate covered cherries!"

Sally's mouth moved but no words came out.

"Don't just stand there like a simpering fool! Find him!"

Victoria shrieked, turning toward her computer to curse the slowness of the internet server.

Sally walked out and closed the bronze door. The secretarial area was silent. They were all staring at her. "Get back to work now! This is Executive Staff meeting day. Look like you deserve to be on this floor or I'll ship each one of you to a clinic office."

Being able to return the wrath felt good. The elevator chimed again. Dr. Marco Girard emerged carrying a large bouquet of red roses and that all important gift bag from Saks Fifth Avenue.

"Good morning, Sally," he said with a wink. "And good morning, ladies. These roses are to adorn your desks; as if the office needed more beauty than your smiling faces provide."

After distributing two roses to each secretary, Marco entered his office followed closely by Sally. She shut the bronze door and pushed in the lock. He reached into the Saks bag and pulled out a gold velvet lingerie rollup. Sally smiled and tugged at the satin bow. Her eyes gleamed as she held up a black lace teddy, the plunging front held together by a flower pin with opal petals and a garnet center.

"Naughty girl, you know there's no time for personal modeling on staff meeting day."

"Ooh, I love it!" she purred planting an innocent kiss on his cheek. He clamped his large hands around her waist, pulling her toward him for the kind of kiss he expected his money to buy. From outside the door, Sally could hear her intercom buzzing. She broke away quickly. "I almost forgot. Victoria wants to see you and she's boiling mad. Said she wants to know what you've been up to."

"Time got away from me, so I didn't sleep at home. Why does she care, she's no longer my wife. Let her wonder what I'm up to."

Sally's smile turned to a pout, "Gambling or another woman?"

"Gambling, of course. I've found the woman," he smiled caressing her cheek. "We'll check our calendars later to arrange a personal modeling session for my eyes only. The pin is a gift you can wear for others to see."

She blew him a kiss and opened the door. Victoria stormed past her to face down Marco. "Thanks for showing up."

Sally made a hasty exit, pulling the bronze door closed behind her to muffle the sound of Victoria's tirade. She stuffed the Saks bag into her lower desk drawer. Arranging the opal and garnet pin on her jacket, she was once again the picture of detached efficiency as Serena stepped off the elevator.

Predictably, Serena paused to examine the floral arrangement, making a visual sweep of the reception area. "Satisfactory," she mumbled walking past the secretarial area and motioning for Sally to follow. Sally stood leaning against the wing chair mentally enumerating Serena's moves.

Open the credenza behind the desk, insert alligator purse on the left side, never the right side, of the second shelf and the matching briefcase on the lower shelf. Glance at the silver tray set to see that the Waterford crystal pitcher is filled with ice water and precisely five lemon slices. Sit in the desk chair, turn clockwise, never counterclockwise, to assume the straight back, left hand on top of right hand royal position. Read the appointments noted in the calendar perched on a carved wood stand, often claimed to be a stand for the holy book from some obscure Italian church. Using the thumb and middle fingers only, lightly grasp a monogrammed notepaper from its golden filigree nest and place it at a slight angle ready for writing. Then reach for a gold pen from the crystal holder. At that point - however long the ritual took - Serena raised her eyes as a sign of approval for the conversation to begin.

Sally held out a sheet of paper with phone messages neatly taped in a row, "These messages came in this morning. Nothing major, I can handle them if you like so you can get ready for the meeting."

Serena scanned the messages, making notes on the paper beside each one. "That would be lovely, Sally. Are we prepared for our very full agenda?"

"The Executive Staff will be in the conference room at eleven o'clock. The functionary personnel that you listed will be dismissed at noon. Those you requested will remain for the lunch buffet. Caterers are setting up now in the small conference room and the kitchen. The food will be transferred in after the meeting adjourns. Jordan is picking up the guests at Tampa Airport. If their flight is on time, they will be here at about 12:15 for lunch with the key staff. After the dessert and coffee, the staff will be dismissed and the guests will meet with you, Victoria and Dr. Marco. The caterers are leaving appetizer trays and wine for late afternoon. Dinner reservations are made at the Vinoy," Sally reported beaming proudly at her own efficiency.

"Excellent. Be certain that you scrutinize the staff as they enter. In order for MACS to give the right impression, our key staff must be well dressed and appear affluent. Look closely at Wanda in medical records. She persists in wearing white shoes with dark skirts. If I want to see a cartoon character, I'll go to a theme park. And what about Lucy, has she lost any weight from her latest diet?"

"I'm not sure, but if she has it's not noticeable."

"That won't do. Create some project for her. Send her on an errand, anything, keep her out of sight. Have that petite Jamaican woman represent the billing department."

"But Serena, LaChelle is the second assistant. She's only been here six months. Lucy's primary assistant, Billie, knows more about the computerized billing system."

"No, no. That won't do. Granted, Billie is a hard working older woman, but we're not trying to sell to a geriatric company," Serena replied leaving the internal political implications to fall on Sally. "And be certain that Dr. Kendall is available for the dinner party. That will be all."

Serena pressed the intercom button for Marco's office. The roar of voices caused her to rock back in the chair and put down the phone receiver. "One moment, Sally. Do you have any idea what is going on in there?"

Sally turned around flashing a catnip grin, "Actually, I know part of it. Victoria came in early stomping and ready to do battle. When Dr. Marco arrived, she started screaming at him. Something about where he spent the night last night and whether or not he blew any big money at cards." She held her cheek muscle taut to avoid breaking into a smile at Serena's obvious discomfort.

Marshalling her dignity, Serena kept her voice tone calm, "This must be a mistake. You know how nervous Victoria gets before meetings with potential business contacts. Ask Dr. Marco and Victoria to come to my office."

Sally's eyes blinked. *Do I look like someone with a death wish? Might as well dance among a herd of stampeding elephants as to get involved in an argument between Marco and Victoria.* Then she said aloud, "I was ordered out of the room. This must be a very discrete corporate matter. As the wife and the, uh, friend of the other partner, I suggest you go to Dr. Marco's office. It's only forty five minutes to meeting time, but I'm sure you can handle it."

"Yes, I'll deal with them," Serena grudgingly replied.

* * * * *

As Serena rose from her desk, Felipe burst in. "Mother, I'm glad you're here. What's going on?"

"I am on my way to your Father's office to find out. Who summoned you?"

"Father called and said to drop everything and come up here. Is he angry with me again? Did Tiffany insult another client?"

Serena patted her youngest son on the shoulder. "There, there, my sweet boy. Whatever it is, I'll make it right. What you must do is to avoid contradicting your Father. You know that you can never win by..."

"Of course, I can never win with him. I'm the flawed son, the idiot, the incompetent...always less than Blake the Magnificent."

Serena touched her fingers to his lips, "Now, darling, you know that's the wrong attitude for approaching your father. Take a deep breath and please, stand up straight. Try to appear confident. Follow me."

Mother and son paraded to the center bronze door. Using her master key card, Serena opened the door and entered with Felipe, eyes cast downward, following at her heels.

Marco and Victoria were sufficiently caught off guard by Serena's entrance to cause a lull in their argument. Serena seized the momentary advantage, "I can't even be late from the hairdresser's without finding you arguing again. We have an important day. Save the petty disputes for later."

"Petty! Since when do you call $425,000 petty?" Marco demanded pounding his fist on the desk. "Felipe, what did you screw up this time?"

Felipe's quivering lips froze as his eyes reached out toward his mother for help.

"I'm speaking to you, boy. What have you done?"

Victoria stepped between father and son, "Why are you blaming him? By your own description, he's too inept to be dishonest. I thought you had the numbered accounts scattered and coded?"

"Yes, I do, but Felipe and Tiffany were the last ones to deliver money."

"Did his little night depository of a wife become greedy and push him for more than the allowance we give?" Victoria mumbled.

Serena rose to his defense, "I simply won't stand by while you dissect our son; your son, Marco. He does nothing but work like a slave and you barely notice. Then something goes wrong and you call him in to be the Judas goat. Let us remember that Gina has made the delivery several times. Could it be that Lorraine is as greedy for money as she is for control and pushed Gina to betray the family?"

"That's nonsense, Serena, and you know it. Gina devotes her life to our enterprises."

"Gina devotes her life to trying to become her father's heir."

"So it's about Blake again," Victoria snapped. "Haven't both of you realized that 'The Prince' isn't coming back? He's not around to be your leverage anymore, Serena."

"Stop! I say stop this insane bickering!" Marco shouted. "This is getting us nowhere. Now Felipe, I want a straight answer: did you have anything to do with the movement of the money out of our private trust account in the Royal Bank?"

"No, sir, I wouldn't even know how. As you've said many times, my computer skills are barely adequate."

Marco sized him up. *What a simpleton; too weak to swat a fly much less try to skim off the family's accounts. If Tiffany had enough brains to realize what an ineffective champion Felipe was, she would be out at the clubs trolling for a new meal ticket.*

"Very well, you are dismissed. Say nothing about this, not even to your wife. If you do, boy, you will pay dearly for the indiscretion. Do you understand?" Marco motioned for Felipe to leave.

Ignoring the conversation with Felipe, Victoria used Marco's computer to access the offshore accounts. "Marco, it happened again! Another $222,000 is gone!"

Marco and Serena rushed to look over her shoulder at the computer screen.

"Marco, do you think the government is on to us?"

"No, Serena, my dear, this is the United States. Their police agencies never make bold moves like that. They act slowly and stay within their own rules. That's why it's such a fine country to steal from. The government makes it so easy."

"Then who dares to take us on?" Victoria swiveled the chair to face Marco, "Better check your latest list of enemies, gambling debts and jilted women."

"Why does this have to be about me?"

Serena glanced at her diamond ladies Rolex to discover that a mere thirty minutes remained until the beginning of Executive Staff meeting. "Whatever is going on, we have to proceed with business. No more arguing. No more blaming. We must present a united front for the new investors. This whole matter must be a mistake at the bank."

"Two mistakes in less than twenty-four hours?" Victoria asked.

"If it's not a mistake, then we must discern who has enough inside knowledge of our operations to make such a move. If not the government, then who dares to cross us?" said Serena.

Marco knew that Serena was asking the right questions. *Find the answer and you find the thief. This is not a matter to entrust to Felipe, not even to Gina. Blake could have handled it. Without him, I shall have to handle it myself. After I find the thief and get the money returned, I think I shall treat him to a grand dinner before deciding whether or not to have him killed. A man with such boldness is worth getting to know. He's like Blake and I. It's the type of bold moves we made all around Europe. Ah, in those days we relied on charm instead of computers.*

Serena saw him pause after her inquiry. She pressed on to gain the advantage, "Let's go to the meeting, Marco. You can solve this mystery later. Besides, there is no other mind as clever as yours for making money appear and disappear." She tilted her head, choosing what she considered her best side, toward him.

He dutifully kissed her cheek and lifted her chin, "You are right, Cara Mia. I am the one to solve this mystery. I shall begin immediately before any further losses occur. As we all know, nothing encourages a dishonest person to take more than a quick and easy getaway."

He turned and pushed the intercom, "Sally, I need to go to the island. No time for the usual cruise arrangements. Secure airline tickets with open return."

"But, Dr. Marco, the meeting is about to start."

"Make it happen. I'm leaving for the house to pack. I can be at the airport in ninety minutes. Have the tickets ready for me to pick up. First class, of course."

Serena and Victoria looked at each other with expressions of astonishment.

"But, the investors meeting!"

"Victoria, my dear, it's another fleecing. Get everything you can and give as little as possible. You recall, the way you did when we were married. I'm certain that your usual 'good cop, bad cop' act will work effectively. I'll phone later from Nassau."

* * * * *

Marco preceded the women out of the door. Briefcase in hand, he paused at the elevator to greet several staff members arriving for the meeting. He waited for the second elevator to open. Carla and Taylor stepped out.

"Good morning, Father."

"Good morning, Dr. Marco."

"It is indeed a good morning having seen two shining stars of MACS. I'm pleased to welcome you to the Executive Staff meeting, Dr. Kendall."

"As long as I'm not neglecting my clinic duties, I'm willing to do my part."

"I knew you were a team player. See Sally after the meeting. She will fill you in on some additional assistance we need today."

"What kind of assistance?"

"No time to go into detail, I must hurry to the airport. Talk with Sally."

"Airport, Father? What about the afternoon meeting?" Carla asked.

"Don't worry, my pet. Your mother and Serena can handle the matter. It will probably go late, so why don't you go with the group? That will make Dr. Kendall feel more comfortable," he said stepping in the elevator. As the door closed, he hailed, "Have a grand evening!"

Taylor turned and whispered to Carla, "What evening? How did I get in this?"

"Since you are halfway in, I'll tell you the rest," Carla explained motioning for Taylor to follow her away from the crowd. "We have potential investors coming in this afternoon. You are part of the 'show and tell' package. If all goes well, and Father's research says it will, we will wine and dine them later at the Vinoy. That's basically what Sally will tell you, be available for dinner."

"But, I have plans."

"I can't tell you what to do, Taylor, but you can expect command performances like this. Especially since the PR Department is setting you up as another corporate icon. We better go in, the meeting is about to start. Let's get a good seat out of the line of fire."

Taylor followed Carla to a plush high back chair in the middle of the oval mahogany conference table. *This isn't exactly my favorite room. What a residency! I get house arrest the first week and now I'm expected to play geisha after hours.*

As Victoria gave a rousing welcome speech, Taylor thought of Gabe and their plans for sailing tonight, *I know he'll understand. He's so easy going. At least he's genuine, not like the phonies I'm stuck with tonight. I don't want to socialize with the Girards. I don't even like them, except for Carla. And I don't care a thing about MACS, as long as it lasts one day past my residency year. Maybe the staff rumors about money trouble are true and these investors are the bailout.*

With the fervor of a politician, Victoria stopped only long enough to take off her suede jacket and push up the sleeves of her silk blouse before picking up where she left off, "We've got the best people that money can buy, we've got the best programs in the country, and we are expanding. The Jacksonville medical clinics will be on line in two weeks with a full PHP. Are you hearing me? MACS' PHPs and Live Anew programs are going right under the nose of the Mayo Clinic branch and we are going to teach them a thing or two about modern mental health. Those high and mighty docs will see what our Nutracuratives and our group psychotherapy can do!"

At the first signal for a break, Taylor dashed for the door. She ran down the stairs to her fourth floor office. Feeling bad about making the call, she didn't want Gabe to make elaborate plans for sailing and find out at the last minute that she couldn't come. *Actors are usually on tight budgets and he may be stretching to rent a boat. As much as I want to be with him, I can't let him waste the money if I have to cancel.*

"Hello."

"Gabe. This is Taylor."

"How's my first mate? Did you bring sturdy deck shoes and a change of clothes?"

"That's why I'm calling. I hate to do this but I have to go to a late meeting."

"What's going on at the clinic?"

Taylor didn't want to make it sound like she was choosing to ditch him for a party, but she was not inclined to lie, "Actually, I got railroaded into being part of the corporate showpieces for some investors who are in town today. I'm expected to stick around and go with the group for dinner."

"I understand. Maybe you can duck out at dessert and we'll still get in a few hours of sunset sailing."

"I don't know how long it will last."

"Rumor around downtown is that Dr. Marco is a party animal. You certainly won't have to read the prices on the cafeteria menu when he entertains."

"We aren't going to a cafeteria. Besides, I can't imagine any of the Girards carrying their own trays. Anyway, Dr. Marco won't be there. He didn't even attend the Executive staff meeting. He left suddenly for the airport. Carla thought it was odd, but frankly, most of what goes on around here is odd to me."

"Are you sure Dr. Marco left town?"

"Yes, I was with Carla when he told her that he was going to the airport. She seemed surprised."

"You know, I think that you're right about tonight, Taylor. Your group will probably run late and that would spoil my plan to show you a sunset on the water from the moment it begins until it slides into old Tampa Bay."

"I'm really sorry, Gabe, I was looking forward to sailing with you."

"Me too, but we can make plans to sail on the weekend when your work can't interrupt. How about Saturday?"

"Sounds great. What time?" she asked looking up to see Brook point at the clock.

"I'll call you tomorrow."

"Or we can talk about it at the bench for lunch?"

"I won't have time for lunch today. I'll put in some extra work tonight and tomorrow so I can be free for the weekend. This is probably a good time for me to help the company with shipping. I'll be out of the shop so call my cell phone if you need me."

"Okay, Gabe. I see Brook dancing feverishly in my doorway. Either the meeting is starting without me or she desperately needs a bathroom break."

Brook walked with Taylor to the elevator. "Did you break a date with Mr. Wonderful for the MACS suck-up dinner?"

"Yes, I did."

"Why? Tell them they don't own your life. Think boundaries. If you don't, you'll get used more."

"I get the idea that saying 'no' around here is politically incorrect. Is that what you did? I mean you're young and attractive, an obvious criteria for displaying employees. Why aren't you included in these impromptu dinners?"

"You've been around me and you have to ask? You know I'll say anything to anybody. Tact is not in my dictionary. Serena would have a cow if I said something to embarrass her. Nope. I'm not on the Girard social list."

The elevator opened and Taylor entered, reluctantly pushing the fifth floor button.

CHAPTER 14

"Mr. Sims," the harried secretary called out from her nearby desk, "there's a call on line three that you have to handle right now."

"Take a message, Gloria. I need to show Stan where to find the files he needs…"

"Mr. Sims, I'll help him find the files while you take this call in your office."

Jack gave her a quizzical look walking past her desk to pick up the phone in his office, "Agent Sims."

"Tally ho, the fox is loose."

Jack kicked the door shut and lowered his voice, "Blake, what's going on?"

"Get out of Bug City and call me on your cell phone."

Jack hung up the receiver, reached inside his briefcase for the cell phone and stuffed it in his pants pocket. He stopped at Gloria's desk and whispered, "I'm taking a walk…for my health, you know."

"Is my dreamboat in trouble, causing trouble or breaking up trouble?"

"I'm never really sure about that."

Jack ran down three flights of stairs, out the side door of the Federal Building. Collapsing at a nearby deserted bus stop, he hit the speed dial.

"You must be training again, hayseed. See what running does for your metabolism."

"Yeah, sure. Where are you, Blake?"

"I'm back at St. Pete/Clearwater Airport refueling the Citation."

"Where are you going?"

"Following the trail. Marco left MACS around ten o'clock for Tampa Airport. Take Geek Boy off the cruise line search and have him find Marco's commercial airline reservations. Call my cell phone as soon as you know. If his flight hasn't left Tampa, I want you to pull some strings with the airline security and create a delay. If that doesn't work, phone Nassau and make an anonymous report of suspected drug mules on his flight."

"Excuse me, Mr. G –Man. Are you suggesting that I file a false report with another law enforcement agency."

"I'm suggesting a little creativity to give the good guy a chance to catch up with the bad guy. And while you're at it, have dinner at the Vinoy tonight. Save the receipt and I'll put it on my expense account."

"Why would I want to sip wine coolers and act excited about grilled squid when I can go home to a thick sirloin and baked potato drowning in butter?"

"Because, my Midwestern cow-craving sidekick, the Girards are entertaining another sucker and Taylor will be with them. Keep an eye on her for me."

"Why Taylor?"

"It's a family tradition. Showing off the illustrious staff distracts the mark from looking too closely at the bottom line. Taylor and the other professionals are collectibles suitable for display. They don't know what's really going on. They're part of the show. Be sure she gets home safely."

"Blake, she doesn't know me. I can't exactly tell her who I am without explaining that you aren't who she thinks you are. Get my drift? All I can do is tail her on the way home."

"Fine, do what you have to. Don't let them send her off with some bozo."

"Whoa man, does MACS expect their staff to hook for the glory of the enterprise?"

"Not initially. They'll size her up, see if she likes to party. I don't want her to see that side of them too soon and I don't want her exposed to any danger. We don't know who these so-called investors are or what their game is. I mean it, Jack; protect her no matter what you have to do."

"Shall I strap six-shooters to my hip and fire a warning shot in the lobby?"

"Get serious, Jack. Don't you know how to write a traffic ticket or act like a regular cop? Whatever it takes, pull her away if the crowd is seedy."

"And exactly how many classes did you take in traffic patrol at Quantico? Blake, do you hear yourself? You're getting personally involved with this woman. Where's your professional objectivity?"

Blake drew in his breath and regained control over his scattered thoughts, "What I meant was, if Taylor gets frightened by a rowdy group she might quit on the spot. We need her to stay where she is."

"I'll watch Dr. Kendall like a Mother Superior guarding the convent. You watch yourself. Get back as fast as you can so the old man won't get suspicious."

"Tell him I'm working at my other job. After all, I need to make the cover viable. He's used to my unpredictability."

"Blake, call me at least twice a day. Let me know what's up."

"Jack, I don't want you in too deep on this one. You know I'm going against procedure."

"By the way, how far over the line did you go to get Marco to move so fast?"

"You don't want to know."

"Sure I do. I'll need it to write my memoirs when I retire or get fired for conspiring with you."

"Okay. I made two hits on his Nassau bank accounts. By the time Marco poured his coffee this morning $425,000, then $222,000 mysteriously disappeared from his secret account without a trace."

"Cripes, man! No wonder he's freaking out! Why the odd

amounts?"

"That's the fun of the game, Jack. 4/25 and 2/22 are family birthdays. It's a kind of signature. If he stops to analyze it, he might even think it's me."

"Are you totally nuts? That will blow your cover."

"My parents have no idea where I am or what I do. Once or twice year I make an appearance in Monte Carlo or Cannes where the high rollers play. When I'm too busy to go, I make a generous donation to the lifestyles of a few old friends who can barely afford to remain in those circles. In return, they complain loudly that I recently left town after taking them in Baccarat or hustling their women."

"That's too strange to be real in anyone's world but yours."

"Yes, it's worked like a charm for years and it continues to work because Marco is a creature of habit. He always does his gambling and whore-mongering away from the home base of his current business. Victoria and Serena tolerate his escapades as long as he avoids compromising the upstanding social life that they painstakingly craft. Even if Marco thinks it's me toying with his money, he will head for a favorite gaming spot and try to lure me for the showdown. While he's fixated on setting a trap, he'll be less likely to realize that it's MACS that is under investigation."

"You're both pirates, man."

"That's right, Jack-o, and the only way to catch a pirate is to beat him at his own game. It takes a con to con a con."

"Isn't there some way we can do this officially?"

"That's naive even for you. If I don't step outside the lines on this one, no agency operating by the rule book will ever find all the money that they have swindled from Medicare through MACS. I'm going to push a little from a safe distance. When the time comes, we'll spring the trap with all the proper legal flourishes and hand over a tidy package suitable for prosecution."

"Blake, can you do this and remember what side of the line

you're on? Fact is you could raid his secret accounts for a few of the millions we suspect he's pocketed and we'd never know."

"That's always been possible, but it's not a problem because I don't need their money."

"Face it, man, your hobbies cost more than my mortgage."

"True, my salary doesn't pay to operate a business jet or for my favorite tailor. I guess it's time to let you in on a secret. Long ago I took the ill-gotten gains of my gambling, womanizing adolescence and invested in growth stocks. Thanks to a totally legal and slightly aggressive investment strategy I can afford to do this job because I want to, not because I'm desperate to get vested in the pension plan," he paused changing to a serious tone, "My reward in bringing down MACS is the same as it is for you, to score one for the good guys."

"With a little personal payback on the side?"

Blake didn't want to answer that question aloud anymore than he wanted to admit it to himself, "As my Father often quoted from Machiavelli, 'Where the Prince himself is new, the difficulty of maintaining possession varies with greater or lesser ability of him who acquires possession.' In this situation, I have the advantage."

"How do you figure that?"

"The new and improved Blake brings greater awareness to the game. Marco only knows evil. I've learned the nature of good and evil. I can play it both ways."

Blake pushed the disconnect button to end the cell phone call and headed toward his Citation Jet. Every time he saw that plane, its silver trim sparkling in the sun light, he was seduced again. It was well worth getting shot and pursued by the Sheik's harem that saw him as a new toy. He preferred to characterize those months as an unofficial semester abroad. Working in Kuwait as a security officer for one of the many overnight oil barons earned enough money for the three years of law school in the six months he worked. Call it payment for taking a bullet in the arm while guarding the Sheik's mother. The last two months of his contract was spent recuperating in the guest suite at full pay. The best part was being given a choice from among the Sheik's personal aircraft as a bonus. The plane was overflowing with electronics even though its interior resembled a garish suite in the Poconos.

After the first year of law school, he did some aggressive marketing to sell that plane to a rising starlet who actually appreciated the Sheik's decor. Using the proceeds plus a particularly good run at Monte Carlo, he picked out this smaller Citation Jet direct from the manufacturer. This was his plane and his alone. He set up a personal corporation to justify it as a business expense. There was no line item on a government expense account for jet fuel, but his accountant always found creative and remarkably legal ways to write it off.

Climbing inside the cockpit, he strapped on the seat belt, completed his instrument check and called the control tower at St. Petersburg/Clearwater Airport for taxi instructions. He'd have to deal with a slight delay to slip outside of Tampa radar and give the appearance of following the flight plan he filed for Naples. A few years ago he escorted two drug cartel pilots to federal prison. They offered an intriguing bargain to get a last gourmet meal. He changed their airline tickets and took the pair, still in handcuffs, to the Columbia Restaurant in Ybor City. In return, they told him several impressive tricks for making course changes to avoid detection. He'd use one of those tricks now. At worst, he'd waste fifteen minutes.

Looking at the diagram of Nassau's airport he smiled. *You're in my sights, Father. After all these years you are getting exactly what you want. The Prince is coming for your empire.*

CHAPTER 15

The squeal of a pager interrupted Victoria's erratic ramblings. All eyes turned toward Taylor.

"I'm sorry," she mumbled sheepishly, removing the pager from her pocket. "I thought I set it on vibrate mode."

Carla leaned over and pointed to the pager, "You probably did. Look at the message, 99-01. 99 means an emergency and 01 is our code for the downstairs clinic. I guess no one told you about the override alarm that can send an audible signal to our critical personnel."

Taylor rose from the chair and glanced at Dr. Locke before walking out the door.

"Go ahead. You can handle it," Locke said. "Call if you need me."

She wondered if he was expressing confidence or apathy. No question as to the other strong emotion in the room. Their faces said what they dare not. Most of the people around the conference table watched her departure with looks of pure envy.

Reaching for the door into the clinic, she could hear the problem. Bobby and Earl were at it again. Wasn't déjà vu supposed to take longer than a few hours to recycle? Things sounded the same as at the start of the day when she was standing at the nurses' station looking over her treatment schedule.

An angry van driver dashed in the side entrance shouting, "Get those loonies off my van!" He claimed that Bobby and Earl got into an argument after picking up Earl at the group home on Central Avenue and 56th Street. The shouting and pushing escalated over fifty miserable blocks frightening the other patients as well as the driver.

It took Taylor, Ray, another tech, and two social work interns to separate the combatants and calm the other patients. That incident threw off the start of groups which sent Neva into a tirade. When Taylor announced that she would be away from the MACS clinic most of the morning to attend the Executive Staff meeting, Neva redirected her wrath toward Taylor and away from the beleaguered support staff.

Now, a few hours later, the melee was underway in the community room during a break between groups. "Get away from me! I saw what you did!" Bobby screamed, pointing at Earl.

Earl clinched his fists, "You're a fruitcake. You hear me, fruitcake. Stop breathing on me or I'll punch your lights out!"

Taylor ran toward Bobby, placing a protective arm around his shoulder, "Bobby, it's me, Dr. Kendall. Everything is all right."

Earl struggled against Ray's hold, "See, he's breathing on me again. Make him stop breathing on me! I'm going to die from his germs. If I die, it's your fault! You want him to torture me. I know it."

Ray looked at Taylor, "I'll take Earl for a walk in the lobby. When Bobby settles down, he needs to take his Nutracurative drink."

Taylor nodded wondering for a fleeting moment why she didn't major in experimental psychology where you could walk away from the mice if they became impossibly uncooperative. When Earl was out of sight, Bobby's rigid body began to relax, his breathing becoming more regular.

"Okay, Bobby, let's start all over," Taylor said as she surveyed the remaining cup filled with Nutracuratives. She knew the nurses checked each patient's wrist bracelet to match the name and patient number with the same information on the label of each paper cup containing the highly touted magic elixir. The name matched - Bobby Nabor, Patient Number 2258 - but the alpha prefix on his wrist band was "D" and the prefix on the cup was "R". Taylor asked Angie, a social work intern, to get one of the nurses. Luck of the draw, Neva answered the call.

"What's the problem, Dr. Kendall?"

"No problem, just an observation." To avoid stating her concern within Bobby's hearing, she pulled a soft marker pen from her pocket and circled the "R" on his paper cup. Holding the cup with the label toward Neva, she then wrote on the cup, "D is his wrist code".

"So what? Can you give him the cup or shall I?"

"I merely wanted to be sure that this is the right drink for Bobby?"

"Giving out Nutracuratives isn't even your job, Doctor. If you decide to do it, don't question the process." Neva turned sharply, took a few steps, then cast a disgusted glance over her shoulder, "And to think that you psychologists want prescription privileges? What a laugh. Your patient would croak while you stop to analyze an aspirin."

Much as Taylor wanted to return the verbal fire, she knew this was not the time or the place. Neva's acid tongue was enough to set Bobby on edge.

"Is she going to punish you, Dr. Kendall?"

"No Bobby. No one is getting punished. We were talking."

"That nurse is mad at you. I know it. She gets mad at me too. She hates me."

"Bobby, Neva doesn't hate you. She's very busy today. That's probably why she sounds a little upset. It's not about you," Taylor reassured him while contemplating the situation. *Actually, it's about me. That woman has been on my case since the day I arrived. Maybe she has standing orders from Lorraine to remind me that I'm unwelcome in her domain.*

"Dr. Kendall, is Bobby ready to go to group? I'll take him."

"In a moment, Angie," Taylor responded turning toward Bobby. "We need to finish the juice first and then I'm sure Bobby would like for you to walk with him to group. Wouldn't you like that, Bobby?"

He nodded yes then no, looking deeply into Taylor's eyes for reassurance. She handed the cup to him. He cringed, "I don't want you to be mad at me, but I can't take this. I think Earl put rat poison in my drink."

"Bobby, Earl left the room sometime ago. I've been standing right here beside you. I didn't see him put anything in your drink before he left."

"Then he made that nurse poison my drink. That nurse who hates me. She did it," he insisted, crossing his arms protectively across his chest and clinching his lips shut.

Her mother always said that drastic problems call for drastic measures so Taylor picked up an empty paper cup.

"Watch this, Bobby," she demonstrated. "I'm pouring a little of your drink into my cup. I'll drink first and you'll see that it's perfectly fine."

As she raised the cup to her lips, a hand seemed to come out of nowhere to slap it away from her. Taylor's head jerked, sticky juice sliding down her chin and the remainder of the liquid splashed onto her new linen shoes. She turned to face Gina.

"What was that about?"

Gina's muscular arm grabbed Taylor's free hand and pulled her toward the back of the room as she barked orders, "Neva! Get that patient to drink his juice and move him to the right group. Now!"

Neva and a tech pulled Bobby's arms apart, ignoring his whimpering cries as they forcibly removed him from the room. Young Angie's face turned ashen as she observed the scene. Looking for something to do, she picked up a hand full of paper napkins and brought them to Taylor.

Gina glared at her, "Don't you have something to do? Interns are supposed to stay busy. Get out!" Angie jerked backward as if slapped then ran out of the room.

"What is your problem, Gina? You frighten my patient, terrorize an intern and assault me! I'm calling Dr. Locke."

Gina tightened her hold on Taylor's arm, "Don't you ever, I mean ever, meddle with the Nutracuratives again or I'll have Father toss you and your high and mighty ambitions out the front door!"

"What ambitions? I'm trying to survive around here and so are my patients. Suddenly you come out of your lab hole in a psychotic rage. Whatever that stuff is that you mix in the Nutracuratives, you need a gallon of it. And while you're at it, raid your Father's drug samples for some anti-anxiety pills."

Taylor stared at Gina's flushed face, wondering whether the danger of walking away was greater than the danger of facing her down. The decision was taken out of her hands when Lorraine stormed through the door with Neva at her side.

"That's enough! Dr. Kendall, you have crossed the line of your competence. You are never again to touch the Nutracuratives. And you are never again to question my nurses. If you do, I swear I'll see to it that you are fired and disgraced in the mental health community, do you hear me?"

"I hear you," Taylor replied standing her ground.

"And I hear you too," Dr. Locke said sternly as he entered the room. "In case you've forgotten, Lorraine, I'm in charge of PHP operations and our protocol distinctly dictates that quality control is everyone's job. Dr. Kendall or any other member of the professional staff has the right to do anything and everything to keep our patients safe. If that means asking questions, then they ask questions. If your nurses' egos are so fragile that they can't respond professionally to an honest concern, then they are the ones who need to be replaced."

Locke moved to Taylor's side as Lorraine moved next to Gina. The tension in the room sizzled like bacon frying in hot grease.

Lorraine broke the silence, "Dr. Locke, we have important corporate business this afternoon that needs our attention. We can discuss this incident later. It's not over."

"And it won't be over until only one of us is left standing. However, much as it pains me to say so, I agree that we need to set this aside and take care of business. Be sure Dr. Kendall's group schedule is covered. She's coming with me and she'll be needed at the afternoon meeting also."

His hand pressed against Taylor's back, guiding her toward the door. Not a word was spoken until they were safely inside the elevator.

"Are you all right, Taylor?"

"I am now. I felt like I was being ambushed. Thanks for the backup."

"I knew something was off base from the look on Lorraine's face when she read the screen of her alphanumeric pager. I waited until she was in the elevator then I left the meeting and went down the back stairs as fast as I could. When I opened the clinic door, Ray nearly ran me over. He was heading upstairs to find me and tell me that Gina was hitting you. Are you hurt? I need to know what happened and file an incident report."

"No, I'm not hurt. I don't think she was trying to hit me, but she sure scared me when she slapped the drink out of my hand."

Locke's eyebrows raised in amazement. The elevator door opened to the fourth floor. "Let's take a break in my office. You can catch your breath and tell me the story."

* * * * *

"Get everybody busy! Sort tongue depressors. I don't care what they do, but keep the staff from gathering in little gossip groups. And don't let this happen again."

"But, Lorraine, those two male patients have been fighting since they came in the door this morning. They've been unmanageable all morning."

"Are both patients R-codes?"

"Yes."

"Neva, you know you have to be prepared for some reactions?"

"Maybe with Earl, he's always edgy. But not Bobby, he's so docile. Did Gina get heavy-handed with the chemicals to be sure we get enough patients to recycle?"

With lightening speed, Lorraine's left hand reached out for Neva's neck, digging inch long, pointed maroon fingernails into the skin hard enough to leave impressions. Neva gasped then became still. Sensing fear, Lorraine locked eyes on her prey and spoke in a morose whisper, "I've told you more than you ought to know because you pledged your absolute loyalty. When I take over as Clinical Director of the PHPs, I'll give you my job as Head Nurse. That was our deal, remember? But if you derail this gravy train, you can kiss your Florida Nursing License goodbye. If I go down, you go down and the trip won't be pleasant."

Neva gulped for another breath to speak, "I'm not the one calling the shots here. I simply follow your orders. This isn't my fault."

Lorraine pressed her thumb nail harder into Neva's throat, "Don't play dumb with me. Dr. Marco may be warm between your sheets, but he's as cold as I am when it comes to self protection. And he's a soft touch compared to the women. Victoria will cut your heart out and have it mounted on a gold disc for Serena to hang on her charm bracelet. Do you understand me?"

The sudden release of her grip set Neva off balance. She took a guarded step away. Feeling the indentations in her skin from Lorraine's nails she gasped, "How do I explain this?"

"Say it's a new hickey from your friends at the biker bar. With your slutty reputation, no one will think twice."

Looking at her watch, Lorraine knew she had to finish this matter and get back to the conference room. She hesitated in the elevator, and then pushed the second floor button.

Opening the door to Gina's private office, Lorraine found what she expected, Gina staring at the wall with a glass in her hand. Lorraine walked over and snatched the glass. Taking a sip, she sputtered, "You weak fool. How many times have I told you that you can't find courage in vodka?"

"It's ginger ale."

"Right, and I'm the tooth fairy. Give me the bottle!"

Gina reached into her lower desk drawer and pulled out an over-the-counter cough medicine bottle that was intended as a disguise for the vodka. Lorraine took it, pouring the rest into the planter. She pulled a guest chair next to Gina.

"What got into you down there? Your father wants this whole operation to be low-key. We barely dodged an investigation when Harriet died. We don't need another incident."

"You don't understand; she was going to drink some of that patient's Nutracurative. I had to stop her. What if she had a reaction and went to the hospital and then they found..."

Lorraine grabbed Gina's shoulders shaking her like a rag doll. "Stop this nonsense! You're acting as crazy as your mother. We've got a plan and we have to stick with it. Our plan only works as long as MACS keeps sucking money out of Medicare."

Gina looked up, her lips trembling like a child lost in a department store. Lorraine handed her a tissue, "Fix your makeup and comb your hair."

As Gina reached in her top desk drawer for a compact and brush, Lorraine sighed inwardly. *No wonder she lives in Blake's shadow. If he's half the man they all say he is then none of his genetically defective siblings will ever take his place. Oh, well. I've cast my lot with Gina so I'll have to prop her up. Marco knows that she's devoted to MACS and she's here, the fair-haired boy isn't. Maybe we can still pull it off.*

"Is that better?"

Lorraine surveyed her, then handed her another tissue, "Blot that lipstick."

"But you said I look better with lipstick and that Father would notice if I was more stylish."

"Not in that garish shade of crimson. Your lips arrive thirty seconds before you do."

Gina cowered at the disapproval. Lorraine made a quick recovery, "We'll go to that new cosmetic boutique at the mall this weekend and pick out a better lipstick for you. And if you keep your act together and stop nipping the vodka at work, I'll let you choose some matching teddies for us. Now I've got to get back to the meeting. Stay in your lab and out of trouble, okay?"

* * * * *

Taylor sunk into the chair, sipped hot cinnamon tea and poured out the story of her confrontation with Gina. Locke scribbled a few notes as she spoke. Mostly he nodded and listened in his usual therapeutic manner. In the margin of his yellow legal pad, he wrote Lorraine's name with a line through it like the international no smoking symbol. If only getting her out of the program could be that easy.

"Sam, I'm really sorry if I violated any policies in the way I tried to coax Bobby to drink his juice. I only meant to reassure him. From the program materials I read, I thought that the Nutracuratives were a natural herbal supplement. If that's true, why did Gina attack me to keep me from drinking it?"

Locke tapped his pen against the chair arm. He seemed to be searching for an answer. "Quite honestly, Taylor, I don't know. I want to get to the bottom of this. It's strange behavior even for Gina."

Venturing into dangerous territory, she asked in a whisper, "Do you know what's in the Nutracuratives?"

"No, I don't. It's a trade secret. The official story is that Dr. Marco discovered some herbs in a remote South American village that he claimed gave the natives incredible sense of tranquility. He brought some of the herbs back and began to experiment with them. In his Venezuelan treatment center he found a way to combine the herbs with high quality nutritional supplements to help extremely anxious and delusional patients stabilize without using psychopharmacological agents. He says that in Venezuela, where there are no heavy handed regulations, he was able to expand the use of the herbs. Supposedly he and Gina came up with this Nutracurative formula that's all natural. Since it's not an FDA approved drug, MACS can't even bill for it. We absorb the costs of the Nutracuratives used in the PHPs as research expenses."

"What does the Nutracuratives offer that prescription drugs can't?"

"That's a mystery to most of us. Yet in the year and half I've been here, I've seen amazing progress. We get patients with schizophrenic symptoms so severe that they are unable to function independently - walking the streets in a daze or sleeping on park benches. A few weeks into MACS programs they begin to function better and participate in group therapy. I can't explain it, but I've seen real benefits from the total program."

"I respect your opinion, but the rest sounds a lot like the corporate brochure. That may be enough information to satisfy the PR department and the patients, but my father was a doctor. He always wanted to know as much about the harmful side effects of a drug as its potential to cure. I know that Daddy would want to know more than the hyped version of MACS' miracle cure."

"You have a point. I've trusted Dr. Marco to handle the medical end while I turned all my attention to the psychotherapy aspects of the partial hospitalization programs. Frankly, it's not easy to get a direct answer from him. He dances around a question as well as he tangos."

"Tango?"

"Yes, a memorable moment from last year's corporate anniversary party."

"Somehow I can't picture prissy Serena doing a passionate dance like the tango."

"She didn't. Marco danced with Victoria. For all we could tell, she even let him lead. Quite frankly, I was amazed to see Victoria dance as lightly as a ballerina after hearing how she stomps around the office."

The door opened suddenly, "Don't panic, folks. Keep telling those dirty little secrets."

"Brook! Do you ever think of knocking?"

"Come on, Sam, where's the fun in that?" she replied setting down a tray with a small carafe and a plate of cookies covered with a linen napkin. Then she ripped off the cloth with the flourish of a magician, "Ta da! Let's have more tea and sympathy. Word in the break room is that you and Taylor backed down the High Priestess and her pet demon."

"Brook, let's not get melodramatic."

"You might as well tell me the juicy details since I have to type up the incident report anyway."

Taylor handed her mug to Brook for a refill. "Let's just say that Gina misunderstood my efforts to calm a patient and approached me with a bad attitude."

"Attitude? It's more than attitude. I hear she's waited years on the national organ donor list for a personality transplant."

"Now Brook…"

"Listen up Sam Locke, if anybody knows it's true you certainly do. The last time you called her down when the patients complained that the Nutracuratives tasted sour, she went whimpering back to her protector. Next thing I know Lorraine flies up here on her broomstick and gets so far in your face that she could count your nose hairs."

Taylor burst out laughing at Brook's imagery. The laughter spread.

"Hey Taylor, you really want to know the great secret of MACS?"

"I sure do."

"Well, I'll tell you," Brook eagerly explained her theory, "The secret is that there are more certified lunatics on the first floor but there is more lunacy per square inch on the fifth floor. The Nutracuratives are part of the window dressing. My guess is that it probably doesn't even use fresh Florida orange juice. It's orange flavored swill that Lorraine and Gina mix up in their caldron at night. Whatever it is, it's not what we think it is."

Locke jumped up, grabbing his suit jacket from the chair back. "We've got to get back upstairs, Taylor. We have to be there for the luncheon show and tell."

"The what?"

"I'll explain on the elevator."

Brook patted Taylor on the back. "This is the part where they use your character and your credentials to make MACS look good. It's like the swimsuit parade in a beauty pageant. The more you show, the farther you go in this company."

CHAPTER 16

The reception area on the fifth floor hummed with activity. The select group of MACS professional staff gathered in conversation groups while Baroque music played discretely in the background. Locke was given the high sign to join Victoria and two stocky, Mediterranean-looking men. Taylor paused to survey the scene. Serena was in her element, playing hostess to the guests as well as trying to appear chummy with the employees who typically got near her only when summoned.

"It's show time, Dr. Kendall." Fiona Conner, MACS' genial Public Relations Manager whispered. She told Taylor that there might be opportunities to speak about the treatment programs, but Taylor expected something like a seminar or news interview, not a corporate sales pitch.

"Oh, hello, Fiona, I didn't see you when I came in."

"Guess not; you were gazing at pretty boy's portrait. Probably a good thing he's not here. Who would get any work done?"

"Did you know Blake Girard?"

"No, I've only been here six months and he's never showed up. The rumor is that he broke away from the family years ago. They don't even hear from him. Too bad, he'd probably be a great spokesperson when Dr. Marco is away on business, and not too hard on the eyes, if you get my drift." Fiona opened her small notebook. "I have to brief you on today's action."

"Please do. I can't imagine what I'm doing up here. My job is clinical, not prospecting."

"Taylor, one thing you'll learn is that the Girards consider all of their employees as assets on the balance sheet. They use anything and anybody to further the corporate interests. It's crude but effective." *Count on Fiona to approach a problem objectively. Even if her job is to put a positive spin on everything that involves MACS, she's down to earth enough to separate the dazzle from the reality.*

"Heads up! Her highness is heading in our direction," Fiona mumbled.

Serena glided toward them with the two men following. "Gentlemen, this is our psychology resident, Dr. Taylor Kendall. You know Fiona Conner from Public Relations. Dr. Kendall, meet Mr. Spiros Pappanastas and his nephew, Mr. Theo Pappanastas."

The older gentleman shook her hand. The younger man, bowed slightly asking, "And what is your assignment with MACS, Dr. Kendall?"

Taylor paused, her eyes darting between Serena and Fiona wondering what she was expected to say. Receiving no clues from their plastic smiles, she went with the simple truth, "I conduct preliminary assessments of new patients and facilitate group therapy in the MACS clinic downstairs."

The elder man spoke, "And what about your extensive research into the effectiveness of the programs?"

Taylor was taken by surprise, "What research?"

Serena quickly filled the lull, "It's all right to talk about your work. You see, gentlemen, one of the delightful aspects of having a graduate from such an esteemed university is that she is well-trained, yet modest about her expertise. However, we don't object to giving out a few hints in this instance."

Victoria cut into the circle, "Dr. Kendall is working on a study to demonstrate the effectiveness of MACS programs and our unique Nutracuratives on adults with schizophrenia. She's devoting every spare minute to the research. Dr. Marco says you'll have some results in a month? Isn't that right?"

Taylor saw the set up coming. *Tell the truth and get canned. Play along and be part of the deception. Where's the third option?* "Actually, I may have results sooner than that if I can get your approval to come in on the weekends. That way I can keep up with all my duties in the clinic during the work day."

Victoria flashed a wide, toothy grin, "See what I've been telling you gentlemen? The MACS staff is totally dedicated."

The men nodded at each other, then at Victoria. Spiros spoke quietly, "How fortunate to have such a lovely young woman willing to give up her free time for work."

"Do I have your approval?" Taylor glanced at Victoria trying to determine if this was real and not just for show. To sweeten the deal she added, "I know you'll be excited at the untapped potential being revealed in this study if I can access more of the completed patient files."

"Yes, indeed!" Victoria replied, noticing the reactions of the Greek investors, "Tell Sally to put your name on the unrestricted access list and you'll get a new key card."

The caterer rang a small dinner bell to gain attention, and then invited everyone into the conference room for lunch.

Victoria linked arms with the two men, "Yes, indeed. Did you hear that? Untapped potential..."

Taylor wasted no time getting to Sally to make her request and used the distraction of the lunch seating as an opportunity to head to Sally's desk.

"Are you sure Victoria said unrestricted access? I don't see the point. You are nothing but an over-educated therapist. Why do you need to be here after hours?"

Taylor pulled back her shoulders to accentuate her height and cast eyes downward at the shorter woman, "Because Victoria said so and I don't recall hearing her say that her secretary needed to know the details."

Bristling at the challenge, Sally spun her chair toward the computer. With lightening speed, she typed and printed a memo. Ripping the paper from the laser printer, she rose from her desk and glared at Taylor, "We'll see about that."

Taylor watched Sally enter the conference room and slip the

paper in Victoria's hand. Unfortunately Sally's face wasn't visible as Victoria grabbed a pen from Felipe's coat pocket to sign the memo.

Sally returned, flopped in her desk chair and avoided making eye contact with Taylor. She ran the memo through a small copy machine near the desk and smacked each one with a date stamp. "Here," she thrust two pages toward Taylor, "Give one to the downstairs security desk and the other to Carla. She'll get a new key card made for you."

"Thank you for your kind attention."

"Don't mock me, Doctor. You merely caught Victoria in a generous mood. If you abuse her generosity, I'll be sure she knows. I'm the eyes and ears for the Girards."

"Yes, Sally, I'm aware of your role. I thought people were harsh in calling you the Office Nazi. Seems I have a lot to learn," Taylor replied turning to join the lunch crowd with the papers clutched possessively in her right hand.

* * * * *

Shrimp puffs and quiche notwithstanding, Taylor would rather be sharing a brown bag lunch on the waterfront with Gabe. The dessert tray hadn't even been passed around before her cheeks ached from smiling. *So this is the business side of mental health. How does Fiona stand it? It feels like a carnival midway. Every corner I turn toward in this room sounds like somebody is reeling in players. Victoria is obvious, but Serena is quite the charmer. Felipe is trying way too hard. Bet they miss Dr. Marco's commanding presence.*

"Taylor, you look like you are a million miles away," Carla observed pulling up a chair next to her.

"I was mulling over my schedule, trying to figure out how to make up for lost time today on assessments that I need to do in the clinic. Oh, by the way, I have to get a new key card from you. I've got the authorization memo in my pocket."

"That's fine. Let's stay for the dessert and coffee, and then we'll go by my office. I want to talk to you about what happened with Gina."

"How did you know?"

"A little Brook told me."

"She's a one woman neighborhood watch. How does she do it?" Taylor marveled at the younger woman's ability to keep up with even the slightest detail among the chaos.

"Actually, we ran into each other in the rest room a few minutes ago. Whatever the problem with Gina was, I can't offer any excuses for my sister's behavior. There simply is no excuse for her."

"Hi ya'll, pretty ladies. Got room for one more?"

Taylor looked up as the very epitome of a long tall Texan rolled a chair over and sat right in front of her and Carla.

"My name's James King. Call me Jim. I'm the CFO for those guys over there," he said pointing to the Greek duo.

Taylor met his handshake while wondering if he's called Jim-Bob back home on the range.

Aloud she said, "Nice to meet you Mr. King. I'm Dr. Kendall," placing particular emphasis on the title doctor.

Not deterred by formality, he responded, "Now what's your first name, honey?"

"I'll give you one guess and it's not honey," Taylor said sharply, bumping knees with him as she rose from her chair. "I have work to finish. See you later, Carla."

"See you too, Doctor, at dinner tonight. Let's sit together," Jim called after her.

Taylor pushed past the server who was rolling in the dessert cart. Not waiting for the elevator and a chance for Jim-Bob to catch up, she ran down the back stairs. Thankfully, Brook was away from her desk.

Taylor grabbed her purse and scribbled a yellow sticky note to attach to Brook's computer. The note read, "Gone home to change shoes. Orange spots clash with chic dining. Be back shortly. Taylor."

* * * * *

Gritting her teeth, Taylor drove toward Allendale wishing it were an ocean away from MACS. Brook's words echoed in Taylor's mind like a broken record, "*Whatever it is, it's not what we think it is.*" The more Taylor mulled over those words, the more she was convinced that things were not as they seemed. Finding out exactly what was in the Nutracuratives was essential to understanding Gina's odd reaction. And maybe, just maybe, it would help make sense of Harriet's mysterious death.

The gate opened and she pulled in beside the garden walk, barely missing a startled Sigrid.

"Oh my goodness, you are home early. Are you feeling ill? Let Sigrid fix fresh vegetable soup for you."

"No thanks, Sigrid, I'm feeling fine," Taylor protested, holding out her left foot, "Only my shoes suffered injury."

Ever the efficient housekeeper, Sigrid took the left shoe off Taylor's foot and demanded the other shoe, "I must hurry if we have any chance to keep those spots from ruining the shoes. Many times I've cleaned champagne from Ms. Mary Etta's evening gowns after a party."

"Afraid we're too late. I think the beige linen and orange Nutracurative are together forever."

"I will try to make them good as new, and then I'll make a sandwich for you."

"No need. I already had lunch. I have to make a quick shoe change and get back to the clinic. Don't worry if I come home late. I have to attend a dinner with some MACS people."

Walking barefoot into the pool house, Taylor flopped on the living room sofa. She had an overwhelming desire to turn on mindless game shows and eat cookies for the rest of the day. Instead, she followed her second, stronger impulse and dialed the phone. A familiar soothing masculine voice answered.

"Gabe, it's Taylor, can you talk for a few minutes?"

He ducked into a shop, turning his back to muffle the distinct beat of reggae music from the clerk's radio.

"Taylor? Are you at work? You sound like something is bothering you."

The frustration from this morning's incident finally spilled out as he listened patiently. He steeled his own reaction to avoid responding as strongly as he felt, "Taylor, I wish I could come over tonight, but I can't leave until my work is finished. Why don't you call the office, say you're feeling sick and stay home?"

"I can't do that, Gabe. Besides, I want to know more about these guys who are here as so-called investors. I also want to get my unrestricted access key card from Carla before Sally finds a way to cancel it."

"Unrestricted access? How did you get that?"

"Victoria tried to put me in a corner about the busy work research project she gave me a few weeks ago and I took advantage of the situation. She seems to get even more hyper than usual with these guests in the office. Brook says the stakes are high and MACS needs capital for the north Florida expansion."

"Sounds like you are learning a lot about the MACS business side."

"More than I care about, except that I think I'm onto something. Maybe I can use these visitors, especially Jim-Bob, the Texas tornado, to get more information. Then I'll take the rest from patient files over the weekend."

"Taylor, wait! You can't go rummaging around secure areas alone. Don't you start any of this until I get back. I'll help you."

"I can handle myself."

"Oh yeah, and you probably think you can pop open locked drawers with the swipe of a credit card like the P.I.'s do on television."

"You mean I can't?" she said with feigned shock, "And I

already planned out this great black leotard outfit with ski mask, suitable for early evening espionage."

"Taylor, this is serious. What you find may be more than you expect."

"In less than a month, I've been threatened by Lorraine, seen Gina go psycho over a supposedly harmless drink, and been used to entice strange men to buy into God knows what at MACS. That's enough to make me want to know the truth."

Gabe paused, knowing that she was not the kind of woman to take orders, much as he wanted to insist that she stay away, "Please, Taylor, just go to dinner and listen. No heroics. No sneaking into file cabinets. No second story work. Please let me have more time with you. I want to take you sailing. I want to get to know you better. A few days delay won't make an enormous difference to MACS, but it will mean everything to me."

She was disarmed by his willingness to show vulnerability, the total opposite of most men. "Okay, Gabe. You know how to charm a woman."

"And you promise to play it cool?"

"I promise not to topple the MACS Empire…at least until next week. Meanwhile, I'll attend the party and soak up information like a sponge. I might even bat my eyelashes and sit next to Jim-Bob."

"Now wait, you don't have to go that far. And by the way, do you have any spike heels to wear?"

"At my height? My closet at home in Memphis holds the world's finest collection of silk flats, tinted to match my evening gowns. I grew up in a generation of vertically challenged men. Spike heels were out of the question."

"Okay, some kind of heel will do, preferably with pointed toes."

"Why? Are you into shoe fetish?"

"Not at all, but I want you to make the best possible impact on Jim-Bob's insole if his hands stray under the table cloth."

"Gabe, you ought to be a therapist. I feel so much better after talking to you. I need to get back to work," she paused, "I miss you."

"I miss you too, Taylor. I may have to turn off my phone for a while, but leave a message on my voice mail and I'll call back as soon as I can."

Taylor hung up the phone feeling like a huge weight had been lifted from her shoulders. Gabe was the only person nearby that she could trust. *If Mama had any idea what was happening inside MACS, she would be down here on the next plane. Calling Dale would be even worse. A few years ago he was chairman of the Psychology Board Ethics Committee. He might pull the plug on the residency immediately and investigate later. Even Carla, who is as close to a friend as anyone at MACS, is still part of the Girard family. Brook is too much of a talker to keep a secret. And what's the deal with Dr. Locke? He sounds honest yet he's high up in the Girards' corporation. Is he covering for them? Or is he left out of the loop? Sure sounds like he knows very little about the Nutracuratives that are critical to the success of his therapeutic programs. No, Gabe, is the best confidant. He's totally out of the MACS situation so he can see it from a completely objective viewpoint.*

CHAPTER 17

When Blake landed at Nassau International a few hours ago, the coffee in his thermos was still warm. He congratulated himself on making good time. Landing at Paradise Island's field would have been closer, but not practical. His custom plane attracted attention. Better to be at the larger airport where business jets are commonplace.

Leaving instructions with the ground crew, he checked in at the rental car counter. Minutes later he turned the jeep onto John F. Kennedy Drive to snake along the back roads to downtown. Parking is always at a premium and by midday it's even worse. He settled for a space near the Nassau Public Library on Shirley Street. He waved off the local bus, preferring the long walk up Parliament Street to stretch his legs after the flight.

At the corner of Parliament and Bay Street, his senses became alert. *Time to get down to business.*

He flipped open the cell phone and left a message for Jack. "The Prince arrived. Stand by for visual confirmation of the target." Not expecting Jack to return the call immediately, he almost made a joke when he answered the phone. Fortunately he played it straight. The voice on the other end wasn't Jack, it was Taylor. He received a quizzical look from the clerk as he huddled in a quiet corner of the shop to finish the conversation.

Emerging from the souvenir shop, Blake moved slowly west on Bay Street, his eyes scanning the crowds. "En Garde," he whispered under breath.

From a block away, he recognized his father leaving the Scotia Bank and heading next door into the staid two story gray building that housed the Royal Bank. Blake pulled his well-worn

Panama hat low on his forehead which, with the old faithful
Nikon camera with high powered distance lens hanging around
his neck, made him look like a typical tourist. He learned on his
first undercover assignment tailing an errant politician around
Las Vegas how effectively a good camera dubs as binoculars. The
gaudy windsurfer shirt he bought at Tee Shirt Factory Outlet
completed the ideal look to blend in with a fresh batch of bargain
hunters pouring off the cruise ships.

Within an hour of flying into Nassau, he had the information
he needed to proceed. Not knowing Marco's exact location, he
dared not go into the most likely hotel. A fifty dollar bill and
the promise of its twin persuaded a young Bahamian man to
get information from the bellhops. Yes, the Spanish doctor, big
tipper, got a suite at Atlantis on Paradise Island. Yes, he is invited
to the private card game tonight. No, he's not playing golf this
afternoon. No, he didn't rent a car. Said he had business in town
and the hotel jitney dropped him off at John Bull's on Bay Street.
Blake happily paid his unwitting accomplice. *Surveillance is
easier outside of the United States. Just wave those Yankee greenbacks.
Enough to entice, but not enough to make yourself a target.*

After Marco disappeared inside the Royal Bank, Blake
crossed the street and hurried up the stairs at the International
Bazaar. He found a vacant table on the outdoor patio at the
coffeehouse. From his viewpoint he could see if Marco's next
stop would be Barclay's Bank or back down Charlotte Street
toward the Bahamas Financial Centre. Marco's polite but firm
questioning of the money movement in his account was bound to
take enough time to grab a late lunch. Blake ordered a sandwich
and watched the parade of tourists intermingled with colorfully
clad local vendors and island chic business people.

An hour passed, then thirty minutes more. Marco must
be grilling those bankers without mercy. Blake was bored and
decided to have some fun at Marco's expense. He reached into his
camera bag for the tourist booklet he was handed at the tee shirt

shop. He dialed the number for John Bull, known as "Nassau's jeweler extraordinaire." Marco wouldn't pass up the chance to add to his collection. A prim sounding man answered. Using a proper English accent, Blake asked for the Rolex specialist, then said, "Good day, sir. I am Dr. Marco Girard's man of business. My employer made a purchase in your shop earlier and I need to make a correction immediately."

"What correction? He chose the merchandise himself."

"I know that, good man. Let's not waste time in handling this matter."

"Is the doctor canceling his order? We have already begun the engraving."

"Of course not, we need for you to add to his order; some gifts for the ladies in his life." Blake knew he had the salesman's attention.

"Yes sir! But we only have an order for the two men's Rolex watches. No women's gifts. Will you or Dr. Girard come in later today and make the selections?"

"No time. We are deeply involved in negotiations at this moment. I am counting on you to select suitable gifts to complete the doctor's purchases.

"What do you think the doctor would wish?"

"Let's have diamond and emerald drop earrings set in gold with a matching necklace and a ring in size eight. Then find a large, brash looking set of earrings in black pearl or onyx. And finally, select a small diamond tennis bracelet."

"Yes sir, we can provide those items to your satisfaction."

"Now listen carefully to the way these gifts must be handled. Be certain that the diamond and emerald set for Mrs. Serena Girard is tied with a pink ribbon. The earrings are to appease Victoria, the former Mrs. Girard. Place a green ribbon on her gift. Prepare a gift card on each box with each lady's first name inscribed in calligraphy style. The tennis bracelet is to be tied with white or silver ribbon and no card. The doctor is a very busy man, both day and night," Blake paused for effect, "The Paris jeweler where he shops devised this color coding system to help him remain in good graces with all his women. Do you understand what I'm saying?"

"Indeed, sir. However, these additions may increase the order by as much as $30,000. How will payment be made?"

"Sir, you represent a discrete establishment, that's why Dr. Girard shops here," Blake said with all the expected snobbery he could muster,"I'm not in a place where I can repeat the directions. Secure payment for the additional purchases same as the other items and deliver as instructed." He dropped his voice to a mere whisper to give the impression of secrecy, "And whatever you do, don't call attention to the additional purchases. Dr. Girard would be exceedingly embarrassed to realize that he was so blinded by your remarkable Rolex display as to forget his ladies."

Blake ended the call and burst out laughing. *At least my mother will get another trinket out of the adventure. She will be as pleased by the paltry gift for Victoria as with her own present. And there is something for Father's "fille de joie" as Mother refers to his mistress of the moment. Besides, Marco must have spent twice that much on the Rolex watches and he'd gamble away as much or more tonight. The real fun will be when Felipe tries to cover up these indulgences for reimbursement on a Medicare cost containment report. Talk about being between the devil and the deep blue sea. That's my gift to you, little brother. It's another fraud count if you succeed, and Father's fury if you fail.*

Marco came out of Royal Bank with a large manila envelope under his arm. He crossed the street, stopping briefly outside Fendi next to John Bull's. Blake ran down the stairs and raised his camera to observe Marco's movements while pretending to take photos. Thankfully, Marco did not tarry long in front of the shop window. Blake watched his father fall in step with the crowd moving toward Barclays Bank. Marco was practically at the jeweler's door but walked on by. He would not go in to claim his purchases, considering it plebian to carry his own packages. Using the crowd as cover, Blake followed until he saw Marco enter Barclays.

Taking the chance that Marco would be there for at least half hour, Blake ran across the street to Crown Jewelers. Granted he learned well from his father how to shop for quality jewels and what styles to choose for a particular lady. At the second showcase, he saw the perfect quarter inch wide gold link bracelet with a diamond at the juncture of each link. He could picture how fine it would look against the silky skin of her alabaster wrist. The clerk quickly produced a matching necklace, earrings, and ring.

Blake reached for his credit card eager to buy the lot and then paused. *Unlike mother, she isn't a gaudy woman or a greedy woman. Taylor often wore one, maybe two elegant jewelry items, never more. I want to buy her the world, even if it has to be one piece at a time.* Holding the delicate bracelet in the palm of his strong hand, he was overcome by his feelings for this woman. *She doesn't really know me. Will she ever know the man behind the façade?*

"Excuse me, sir," the saleswoman interrupted his daydream, "I need to see some identification that shows you are connected with the Andrews Corporation."

Blake reached into his wallet for the document that matched the well-disguised credit card.

"Thank you, Mr. Andrews. The bracelet is being wrapped for you."

Every job has its perks. The fake ID for Blair Andrews and the Andrews Corporation business history was the best Uncle Sam could provide to support his favorite alias. He managed to persuade the bureau to let him use that alias in an undercover investigation several years ago and then decided to keep the ID for selective use. No harm. It merely validates the Andrews Corporation credit card that is billed to his financial manager, a former Princeton dorm mate who pays the tab from investment income and never asks questions.

As he reached for the door, he saw Marco on the opposite sidewalk hailing a taxi. No need to follow. The banks were closing and Marco would be on his way back to the Atlantis Hotel to prepare for dinner followed by late night gambling. It was nearing five o'clock, the sidewalks becoming even more cramped and the one way streets a cacophony of horns competing with reggae music pouring out from open shop doors.

Having done the surveillance he came to do, Blake made a final stop at Columbian Emeralds to shop for the other women in his life. He chose a nickel size gold replica of a Spanish coin on a neck chain for Gloria, the feisty agency secretary who called herself Moneypenny to his James Bond. Then he bought a Tanzanite drop necklace for his friend in Washington whom he called on occasionally for work or play. Several emerald rings caught his eye as such an ideal stone to compliment Carla's dark Latin beauty, but emeralds were considered the signature stone of his pale skinned, streaked blonde mother. Much as he found that an absurd barrier, he didn't want Carla to feel Serena's sharp rebuke over a gift. Instead he chose a marquise cut amethyst ring with three diamonds on each side and matching earrings. The regal purple would be a fitting accent to his stepsister's natural Hispanic features. *Imagine how the unholy trinity will become unhinged thinking that Carla might have a secret admirer and a life of her own beyond their control?*

Outside the shop, Blake found a public phone. With his best French accent, he called the Atlantis Hotel. "I, Henri, have a gift of vintage champagne for delivery to Le Doctor Girárd. Which dining room will I find his party this evening, s'il vous plaît?" He heard the sounds of tapping as the concierge checked his computer for dinner reservations, "The Doctor's party is private. Deliver the gift to the front desk and we will take it from there."

Blake hung up the phone, knowing that with Marco spending the evening on Paradise Island he was free to go to his favorite restaurant downtown.

* * * * *

Three college girls in the hotel lobby spotted him first. He tried to ignore their giggles as they picked up free wine coolers from happy hour at the piano bar and edged closer to where he stood alone. "Excuse me, are you someone famous?" the short brunette in a tragically over-ruffled pink dress asked.

He turned toward them, showing his best smile, "No, ladies, I am a business man with a few hours to enjoy Nassau before returning home to the corporate grind."

They continued to hang beside him making conversation.

"Hope you have a grand evening, girls. Now I must get outside before all the taxis are taken."

"Oh, what a coincidence," the bone thin blonde squealed, "my friends and I are going into town too. Maybe we could share a cab and you can show us the best clubs."

All he wanted was an elegant dinner, not to become the Facebook feature story for a trio of twenty year olds. Suddenly he saw an escape. A tall café au lait-skinned woman in a body hugging red sequin gown stepped out the front door heading for the cab stand. Blake made his move, "*Bon Soir, mon ami.* We must hurry to make our dinner appointment."

She smiled, totally unflustered as he hustled her into a cab and sat beside her.

"Graycliff on West Hill Street, driver."

As the taxi pulled away from the hotel, he turned to her, raising her hand and kissing it gallantly, "My deepest thanks. You have rescued me from a dire fate. I hope I did not frighten you."

"Sir, your problem was evident."

"Was my desperation to escape that obvious?"

"Yes," she laughed, "you hardly appear like a man who finds his pleasure with innocents."

Blake smiled, wondering if he was now in more or less

trouble. "If rescuing me has interfered with your plans, may I invite you to dine with me? Afterward I'll take you wherever you want to go."

"Do you have a telephone I can use?"

"Yes," he handed her his cell phone, "It's a U.S. line so dial accordingly."

She spoke rapidly in a French dialect, most of which he understood.

"Merci. I told my friends that I would meet them later. Perhaps you will join us?"

"Perhaps."

"My name is Chantal. I come here every few months from Andros Island as my escape."

"I'm Blair Andrews, here on a short business trip. Actually I return to the states tomorrow."

She placed her left hand on his knee, long fingers wrapped with exquisite jewels. He held up her hand, pointing to a four tiered diamond ring with a round center diamond so large only a trained eye would believe it was real. "Are you married, Madame Chantal?"

"Sometimes."

"Let me guess: your husband is a rich, powerful man who does not understand your needs?"

"No, darling Blair. My husband is a rich, powerful man who understands me completely. That's why he hands me a roll of money and lets me have the occasional week to party and play the tables. When I return to our plantation, I'm the dutiful wife. He never asks and I never tell."

The taxi approached Graycliff, the island's five star restaurant. Offering his hand to help her from the taxi, he whispered, "Let's enjoy dinner together."

Leaning her head toward his shoulder, "I am not here to displace the woman in your life."

"What woman?"

"The one who weaves a spell over you. Do you realize how totally she captivates you?"

"I doubt that she knows it."

"Then we shall celebrate what is yet to be."

"All right, Madame Chantal. What can I do, within reasonable limits, to show my gratitude to you for the rescue?"

"Are you a gaming man?"

"I hold my own at the table."

"Ah ha! I knew it. After dinner I'll take you to meet my friends. I must warn you, they are serious players."

"That's fine, but I have to admit that I am not new to the game. Where are we going? Surely you aren't with the Atlantis crowd?"

"No, no. My friends don't mingle with tourists. Our host has an estate near Lyford Cay where we have private gaming arrangements."

"I generally use my credit card to establish my stake. I didn't come prepared with cash."

"No problem. My friend always has his personal banker on the scene to handle the financials."

"*Très bien, ma* Chantal. I feel lucky with you beside me tonight."

* * * * *

"Lady Luck sure is smiling on me," Jim King said triumphantly as he moved Carla's shawl and claimed the seat next to Taylor. "I usually hate business dinners, but not tonight."

Taylor forced a smile. *How on earth did the two 'rug merchants' as Victoria called them hook up with a cowboy CFO and an Ivy League MBA marketing manager? What's in it for them? Is this a business deal or a set up? Over and over Serena touted "the breadth and vision of Magna Health Limited that's perfectly in tune with the spirit of MACS." Grandpa Dodd would have said, "Pass the hip boots, boys, the slop's getting taller than the hogs."*

After lingering two hours over cocktails and pompous conversation, Taylor went for an extended restroom break. Earlier she had discovered the tranquility of the Vinoy's elaborate poolside patio. Before pressing the speed dial on her cell phone, she looked around to be certain she wasn't followed. Dialing twice got the same result. "The party you are calling is either out of range or not answering at this time. Leave a message at the sound of the tone." She started to speak, and then hung up.

He must be working. He said something about having to attend an auction for the gallery. Maybe cell phones are not allowed, at least for the workers. No point to call and get him in trouble. Besides, he said he would call tomorrow and he's always kept his word. Disappointment registering on her face, she walked from behind the topiary sculpture right into a man balancing a drink and plate of stuffed mushrooms. The drink splashed and the mushrooms slide off the plate onto the stone patio.

"Oh! I'm so sorry."

"No problem," replied the man who looked like a catalog model. He accepted the tissue she pulled from her purse to blot his jacket sleeve.

"Let me at least pay for having your jacket cleaned."

"Not necessary. Actually, the mushrooms weren't that great." Two seagulls swooped down and greedily grabbed the remainder of the spilled food in their beaks. "See, we did the local wildlife a favor. By the way, I'm Jack and being run over by you is more entertaining than the crew of business associates I'm waiting to join."

"I know what you mean. I'm Taylor and I'm with a rather unique group myself."

"Taylor? It can't be. Are you Taylor Kendall?"

"Yes, I am, but I don't know you."

"True, but you do know my good friend, Gabe. He talks about you. He said you worked with some big shot company downtown."

"I don't know about that, but I do work downtown in the MACS clinic."

Looking over Jack's shoulder, Taylor saw Carla walking toward her. "I think my group sent out a scout for me. Again, I'm really sorry about the mess. Are you sure I can't pay for having your jacket cleaned?"

When Jack shook his head, his curly hair moved like waves, "Maybe I'll see you sometime over at Gabe's place and I can spill something on you. No, can't do that. Gabe is too fine a cook. I sop up everything he puts on my plate, but I'll probably see you around the downtown haunts." He left as suddenly as he appeared. Taylor turned slightly as Carla approached.

"Taylor, we were ordering entrees and realized you were gone. Are you okay?"

"Sure. I wandered out here for some fresh air. I'm not used to eating so late."

"We hold to our Spanish ways for entertaining - long preludes with snacks leading up to dinner a few hours later. Father says it's very effective for getting to know business associates."

"At the very least, you find out who has patience to last until dessert."

They walked back through the hotel lobby. Carla paused a few feet outside the dining room entrance. "Taylor, you don't look like you are enjoying yourself."

"To be honest, I'm not. I realize that the business side of mental health supports the clinical side, but I'm not comfortable being on display as a prop in this game of dining for dollars."

Carla listened intently and then smiled, "For someone who claims not to know much about business, you cut to the bottom line fast. I tried to tell Mother and Serena that this wasn't what Locke would call the highest and best use of your talents, but they never listen to me."

"If this is such an important evening for influencing Magna Health's executives, why isn't Locke here?"

"Let's put it this way: he's not as pretty as you are."

"Okay, but he knows a lot more about the operation of MACS partial hospitalization programs than I do. He could answer their questions."

"That's what Mother wanted to avoid," Carla responded, opening the dining room door without indication that what she revealed caused her any misgivings. Taylor was further confused by the Girards' game of subterfuge.

* * * * *

The only game of chance Blake intended to play was to track his father's likely offshore banking accounts without Marco or the Director finding out what was going on. Then a peculiar chain of events catapulted him from a quiet, gourmet dinner to a politely cutthroat card game with Chantal's beguiling friends. He had to admire the way she worked a room. Watching her circulate was like being an extra in the cast for a remake of *Breakfast at Tiffany's. Too bad Marco isn't here. This is the kind of group he savors; tough play, experienced competitors and limitless bankrolls to make the winning sweeter.*

The $50,000 limit that Blake promised himself to keep went out the window when the Brazilian exporter played fast and loose, grasping most of Blake's stake as he was preparing to cash out. Old habits die hard. Marco taught him to play to win, "Gambling, my son, is the method of dueling for the modern man. At times, it may be necessary to vanquish rather than merely defeat, particularly when the opponent is a fool who needs reminding of his perilous condition."

His instincts in overdrive, Blake determined not only to vanquish but to bring the game to an end before dawn. Amazing how youthful thrills were gone from such an evening. Winning became practical, almost mechanical as he let his well-honed skills take over. At three a.m., the host signaled for his staff to bring a round of brandy and set up the breakfast buffet.

Apparently more weary than he realized, Blake barely noticed that in addition to doubling his initial stake, he scored a garish diamond and sapphire necklace, a five carat pear cut diamond ring, a chit for a Rolls Royce custom golf cart parked at the Cable Beach Golf Club and last, but not least, a small house on the west end of Eleuthera Island.

Chantal's long arms wrapped around his waist pressing her body against his back, "To the victor belongs the spoils. Perhaps we can renegotiate the nature of our friendly evening together, n'est pas?"

"No fair tempting a man when he's tired, but I'll make a counter offer." Reaching into his left pocket, he took out the diamond ring and placed it on her right hand. Nibbling her fingers lightly, he turned her hand over and placed the chit for the golf cart in her palm.

"Let me describe for you what I have to trade."

"You have already been generous, ma Chantal. Merci beaucoup for your kind invitation. I have enjoyed a stimulating and, frankly, profitable evening with your friends. We are even."

"It is fortunate that my ego is strong. Few men would pass up what I offer you."

"I can imagine that," Blake said paying homage with his eyes to the way the red gown slithered across her curves.

"Now that you are a Bahamian landowner, our paths will cross again. I want your promise to bring this woman who holds such power over your heart back here to meet me. I must determine if she is worthy of you," Chantal said, taking a personal card from her evening bag and slipping it into the inner pocket of Blake's tux jacket. They walked arm in arm to the driveway where their host's uniformed chauffeur waited beside the white Daimler limousine to return guests to their hotels.

The Brazilian man followed them out of the mansion. "Why leave so soon?"

"I need at least a few hours sleep to fly home today."

"Surely you can afford to book a later flight? Or you may want to sleep in the guest room at my house since you own it."

"Yes, that reminds me, expect to hear from my legal representative who will arrange title transfer immediately. I prefer that you vacate the house by the end of the week. Of course, you will leave the premises in prime condition as a matter of honor, Señor."

The loser gritted his teeth. "Why such a hasty departure? Off to more games?"

"No, I have appointments in the States that won't wait and I need some sleep. You see, I am the pilot of my corporation's business jet."

"A private jet, sir. You never put that in the pot," the Brazilian sputtered.

"Considering the way you play, I never had to."

* * * * *

"I want you kids to stay as long as you like. The MACS account will cover your tab," Victoria said with a slight slurring of her words. "Party hardy!" was her final directive as she was guided between Carla and Fiona toward a waiting taxi.

The two Magna Health owners left an hour earlier, making excuses about time zone adjustments to slip away from the dining room before dessert. Serena disappeared shortly after the cherries jubilee was presented with pyrotechnic flourish. Wondering if the party was finally over, Taylor was swept up in the dwindling group to the bar for coffee. She was willing to stay for a shot of caffeine to wake herself up from that tedious dinner. Jim King walked up behind her, placing a hand on her right shoulder, a hand that kept trying to slide lower, but for her wiggling away.

"My principals are gone and so are yours, so let's dance."

"Exactly how are you spelling that; p-r-i-n-c-i-p-a-l-s or p-r-i-n-c-i-p-l-e-s?"

"I like a woman with a sense of humor. Come on, one little dance, honey?"

Looking over the dance floor, Taylor spotted Felipe and Tiffany in one corner and near the bandstand she saw Neva draped like Christmas tree lights around Mr. Ivy League MBA. Two women and a man she only vaguely recalled seeing in the MACS break room were tossing down drinks and quibbling over computer program details. With Fiona and Carla gone, she felt quite out of place. She was pleased to see Jordan Graham, the Girards' Director of Development, walk back toward the table. He stepped in front of Jim King.

"Dr. Kendall, I need to speak with you for a moment. Excuse us, Jim."

She followed him to a noisier area near the bandstand.

"I don't know what you think is expected of our employees, but there are things happening here on more than one level, if you get my drift."

"I didn't know what to expect or even why I was taken from the clinic to play hostess. Apparently Neva knew the plan."

"You didn't hear this from me, understand? Neva likes to party with guys who are rich and inclined to show gratitude with expensive gifts. Victoria knows how Neva operates so they have an unspoken understanding that is, shall we say, mutually beneficial for the company."

"Is bringing me along for dinner another off-beat loyalty test?"

Jordan searched for words to explain but not indict, "I don't try to understand the Girards, any of them. I merely work around them to keep the companies running. For what it's worth, I recommended excluding you from the dinner guest list and was overruled."

"I have no interest in being part of the corporate seduction team."

"Before I leave, I want you to know that you are free to go

anytime."

"Thank you, Jordan. I'll go back to the table and finish my coffee so it won't look like you had something to do with my departure. I realize that as CFO you have to do business with these guys tomorrow. I don't want to complicate your life by letting Jim-Bob think you thwarted his chance to ravish me."

Jordan made a courtly bow and walked away chuckling over the "Jim Bob" appellation.

Much to her dismay, Jim King was headed toward her, "Okay, little lady, it's dance time!"

She decided that dancing on a public floor was as a lot safer than other options. Surprisingly Jim was an acceptable dancer, or as good as he could be while trying to press his partner close enough to crease his lapels. When the music ended, she dashed back to the table to gather her purse and jacket. Needless to say, Jim-Bob was in hot pursuit.

"Dr. Kendall, you see the MACS programs from the inside. Do you think the treatment regime is worth the $400 per head they bill for it?"

"What $400 are you talking about?"

"You know, the daily reimbursement rate for patients in partial hospitalization. If Magna Health comes in with MACS, we'll be purchasing Nutracuratives, consulting services and a kind of franchising fee for the psychotherapy program protocols. MACS billing division will handle our billing, which is their part of the profits. It becomes a turnkey deal."

"Why don't you do your own programs?"

"Actually, we do. Magna's specialty is sports rehabilitation centers. We cater to serious athletes, marathon runners and those who get injured trying to be athletes. We have twenty-five sites in Texas, ten in Oklahoma and eight in Kansas. Developing PHPs as adjunct programs helps use the rehab facilities for Medicare patients during the day since we treat primetime payers - working folks - during early and late hours. At least that's what Victoria and Serena recommend."

"I don't know about their plans, but I can tell you that most of our patients in the schizophrenia program are very mobile. I can't picture them needing physical therapy. Trying to turn their attention away from running out the door and down the street is a bigger problem. Perhaps the Nutracuratives would have value for your other patients as well. You need to talk with Gina Girard, that's her domain."

Jim took out his pen and wrote the name on the corner of the cocktail napkin, "I was wondering why we haven't met Gina. Dr. Marco mentioned her when he made the first contact with our company. His daughter, right?"

"Yes, his oldest daughter. You met the youngest daughter at dinner. Carla."

"Cute little thing. Not too bright, but not too expensive on the payroll either."

Taylor wanted to challenge his sexist assessment. Perhaps the discussions that he had with Felipe Girard gave him a skewed impression of Carla. According to the rumor mill, Felipe was the dim bulb in the family. The description seemed to fit considering the woman he married.

"Taylor, you are studying treatment effectiveness, do you think the MACS program is a good deal for the money?"

"You really need to talk with Dr. Sam Locke. He got the programs up and running. He probably knows the reimbursement issues as well. Frankly, Jim, I've only been here a few weeks. I don't even know the names of every MACS supervisor we had lunch with today. I'm not trying to hide anything or be evasive. Chances are you know more about MACS operations than I do."

"Thanks for playing straight with me, honey. When we heard that Dr. Locke was already booked to teach a MACS educational program tonight, we were led to believe that you could answer all of our program questions," Jim said looking increasingly irritated. "What do you know about the patient death in one of the programs?"

"Do you mean Harriet?"

"No, it was a man's name. Was there another?"

"Sorry, I must be confused again on names. Do you know which MACS site the patient was in?"

"Sure. It's public record if you know where to look. Our lawyers found a malpractice suit filed by the family of Greg Newman. Said he flipped out after leaving a MACS PHP and took a dive off the Sunshine Skyway Bridge. Suit claimed that MACS, the Medicaid case manager and a few other state agencies were responsible. Do you know anything about that?"

"No. I can honestly say it's the first time I heard that name or the situation," Taylor answered, feeling like the protestations about Harriet as an isolated case were designed to distract attention from other problem cases.

Jim took her hands and held them tight, "You know, little lady, I believe you. In fact, I think you're the only straight shooter in the bunch. Let's drop the business crap and get to know each other better." He squeezed her hand possessively.

Taylor broke his hold, "I have to go. It's way past my bedtime."

"Mine too. My suite is upstairs and I'll even let you have the mint on my pillow."

Taylor realized that Jim-Bob had given up pumping her for corporate information and moved on to the roping event. She had no intention of going anywhere private with him, no matter how much she wanted to get information on the other patient's death. Neva and the MBA were out of sight, probably upstairs checking out each other's numbers. Felipe and Tiffany huddled in a corner table. Taylor also noticed that the three other MACS employees were too drunk to notice anything. She felt cornered without allies. He pressed against her and nuzzled her neck. She blocked out his words concentrating on finding her car keys inside her shoulder bag. Making a fist around the keys with one key protruding from the top, like her Daddy taught her, she was about ready to scrape the side of his redneck.

"Dr. Kendall! Is Dr. Kendall here?"

She turned to see Jack, the man who claimed to be Gabe's friend, approaching. She wasn't sure what was happening, but she decided to play along.

"I'm Dr. Kendall," she said waving her arm.

"Sorry to bother you, Doctor," he said very formally, then he reached for a leather pocket folder with some sort of photo ID that he flipped casually toward Jim-Bob, then re-pocketed saying, "I'm Detective Jacks. I got your name from your license registration. There's been a report of vandalism nearby. I need for you to come with me and survey the damage to your car."

Taylor was certain that this man wasn't a cop. Maybe he was an actor, like Gabe. That's it. He's up to something. "Of course, officer, I'll follow you."

"Wait a minute, buster. Cops travel in pairs. Where's your partner?" Jim demanded. "I think I better come along."

"No, Jim," Taylor was certainly not going to have him follow her to a dark parking lot, "I can take care of my own business. Besides, I have to get home and you need to be fresh for tomorrow's meetings."

"I'll get a cab and follow you."

Jack got right into his face, "This is a police matter. Unless you are the lady's husband or father, this does not concern you. Shall I have hotel security show you the way to your room? Or would you enjoy a night in the St. Petersburg city jail for interfering in an investigation?"

Taylor moved toward the door, "Let's go detective. See you tomorrow, Jim."

Walking silently outside the Vinoy Hotel entrance, he motioned for her to turn right. Taylor was beginning to wonder what was really going on.

Jack sensed her uneasiness. "There's nothing wrong with your car and, as you have certainly guessed, I'm not a police detective.

I hope I've saved you from the proverbial fate worse than death."

Taylor looked at him as his words settled in, then let out a melodious laugh that echoed off the street lamp. "You must be an actor like Gabe. That was a command performance."

"If I misread things, you can go back inside and forget this happened."

"No, you read it exactly right. In fact, you saved Jim-Bob from bodily injury," she said raising her right fist which still tightly clutched the key in striking position.

"Whoa! Don't hurt me, lady. I bruise easily," he replied feigning fright.

"Jack, you are funny, and you have a great sense of timing. Thank you very much. When I got stuck with this crowd from MACS, I had no idea what their agenda was."

"I understand. Even though you're a free woman again, I'll walk with you to your car. Where are you parked?"

"Some kind of law enforcement guy you are! You can't even find my car."

"I can say with complete candor that stolen cars aren't my beat," he smiled, stepping back for her to lead the way along the sidewalk. Accepting her car keys, he opened the driver's side door then handed them back to her. "There you are, safe and sound. Shall I follow you home?"

Her eyes glared at him.

"Wait. That came out all wrong. What I meant to say is would you like for me to follow you home to be sure you get in safely. That's the least I can do for my buddy Gabe's special lady."

"No thanks, Jack. You've been a big help. I don't live far."

He waved, watching as she pulled away from the curb.

Gabe's special lady. Did Gabe tell him that or did he presume? Taylor hoped that he heard it from Gabe. Apparently he heard something about her from Gabe or he wouldn't have recognized her name. *What a coincidence to spill stuffed mushrooms on an innocent bystander only to find out he's a friend of Gabe? How lucky that Jack was still at the Vinoy and was a good enough friend to be concerned about his buddy's 'special lady'?* Taylor was feeling lucky indeed.

Taylor wasn't use to getting to bed after midnight, especially on a work night. What an odd evening. Eyelids drooping by the time she made it back home, she scribbled a few notes that she wanted to check on: *Greg Newman - find his chart, program assignment and notes regarding his death. Newspaper office - check newspaper morgue for articles on the incident.* The eight hours of sleep she needed wasn't possible, but she could get at least five hours and she wanted every minute.

CHAPTER 18

Expending his last ounce of energy, Blake shed his tux jacket, pants and shirt, dropping them on the chair beside the bed. He had maybe five hours to sleep and he desperately craved every minute of pillow time possible. A shower could wait. Even checking voice mail could wait.

The loud bang that crashed into his dreams caused him to roll to the floor, grab his jacket and reach inside for his gun before his eyes were clearly focused on the door. Listening intently, he realized that the noise was merely a bellman's cart that was overloaded or poorly controlled when it hit the wall outside his hotel room door. The crescendo of voices audible through his door from the hallway made him look at the clock to check the time. 8:15a.m.

Sitting on the floor, Blake seriously considered going back to sleep right there and then taking advantage of the hotel's Thursday brunch specials, but to arrive in time for the afternoon briefing at the agency he had to get moving.

Reaching for the hotel notepad and pen, he started a list:

- Shower.
- Call the airport to have the jet fueled and ready to go.
- Stop in town at Bahamas Financial Centre to engage a Bahamian attorney to handle the title transfer of the house. *Having a getaway house might be a good idea. It was worth keeping at least a year or so.*
- Arrange sale of that gaudy necklace. *Might get more money auctioning it in New York, but it's not worth the paperwork to bring it in legally.*

If all goes well, I might be back in time for a coffee break with

*Taylor at the waterfront bench before going to the briefing. Worst case
I have to wait to see her after work.*

Energized by the thought of seeing Taylor, Blake reached for
the phone to order breakfast then headed for the shower, singing
as he went. Blow drying his hair in the mirror, he noticed how
much he needed another dye job to turn his naturally blonde
wavy hair into Gabe's mousy brown, gelled look. No time now.
It may mean missing lunch. Interrupted by a knock on the door,
he exchanged a generous tip for his breakfast tray and sat at the
desk to eat. Reaching for his cell phone and the notepad, he
prepared to review messages left from last night.

6:55 p.m. "Yo, Prince, its Jack-o. Got your message, go get
'em! I'm at the Vinoy and Taylor is nearby. Don't worry. Get
back in time for the briefing. I don't want to have to explain
to the Director where you are."

7:30 p.m. "Are you on the man's trail or are you out partying?
These people haven't even ordered yet. I'm floating in prissy
nibble food. They're starving me. I'm more the stake out near
the taco stand kind of guy. This better be worth it."

7:44 p.m. "Gabe, it's Taylor. I'm stuck at the dinner party and
you must be busy so I'll say goodnight. You were right, the
Vinoy is lovely. I'd like to come here for a normal dinner.
I'm seeing another side of MACS and I don't know what to
think about it. I have lots to tell you. Look forward to seeing
you tomorrow."

8:32 p.m. "Do you realize that I have been looked over twice
by hotel security? They obviously wonder why I'm hanging
around. Anyway, the MACS crowd is getting boisterous so
I arranged to let Taylor bump into me. You know, I did the
accidental spill trick you taught me. I told her that I'm a friend

of Gabe's and she bought it. Thought it was a good move in case I need to intercept her. I'm not fond of swinging in on the chandelier to rescue the fair maiden. Try not to have too much fun, remember this is supposed to be work."

10:40 p.m. "Blake, it's Carla. Where are you? I'm sitting outside on the dock. Mother passed out after we got in from another business dinner. You remember the drill. The only change is that Father left town suddenly. Serena managed to sneak out of the dinner early. I wanted to stay, but our CFO Jordan said that we had to get Mother out fast to keep her from killing the deal. You know how she gets when she drinks during a mood swing. The worst part is that I left my friend, Taylor, with the late crowd. She's not the kind of person who will do anything to succeed. Won't that disappoint both of our mothers? I feel rotten that I didn't warn her. I walked away because that's what I've been trained to do. If people get used, oh well, that's the Girard method. Move on. Look the other way. You're right, I can't do this forever. Sorry for taking up so much space on your voice mail. Maybe we can meet for dinner again soon. Call me please Blake. Where ever you are, take care."

11:58 p.m. "Followed Taylor home to be sure that overbearing guy didn't defy my official police order to cease and desist his libido. Your family is a bunch of sharks, man, leaving that delectable flower of Southern womanhood to be ravaged by the Texan. You said they'd use anybody, anytime, anyway. Don't rush home for the grand finale. Taylor isn't as helpless as you thought. She nearly poked his lustful eyes out with her car keys. That's enough action for tonight. This is the Jackster, signing off for sleep. Don't call early."

Blake slammed his coffee cup down so hard the plate and

silverware rattled. He wanted to hit his head against the wall for being negligent, out having fun while Taylor was in jeopardy. He punched in the buttons for Jack's cell phone.

"Huh?"

"Wake up, Jack! It's Blake. Are you positive that Taylor is all right?"

"I followed her at a safe distance. Saw her go into the back of that big house in Allendale. Also saw some outside lights from the big house come on and go off a few minutes later like someone she knew was watching out for her."

"That was probably Sigrid and Lars, the caretakers. Thanks for taking care of her."

"I know you wouldn't want anything to happen to the source you have so carefully cultivated. That is the reason for your concern, Dr. Kendall's value to the investigation?"

"Sure. It's a professional interest, but you have to admit, she is a fine lady."

"Indeed, and your objectivity is so well preserved in this case that you probably aren't even bringing back a souvenir for her."

With his free hand, Blake reached inside his blazer pocket to touch the velvet jewel case containing the diamond and gold link bracelet. "No, Jack-o, I swear on J. Edgar Hoover's lace undies that I am not bringing back some tacky tourist memento. Besides that would cause her to ask too many questions that I can't answer."

"Are you back in Florida?"

"No, I have some personal business to attend before leaving Nassau, but I'll make it in time."

"Give me something to fantasize about; is the business a woman?"

"Regretfully I have to disappoint you and risk shattering my image. Actually I have to open a local bank account, dispose of some jewels and arrange the title transfer on a beach house."

"What are you doing over there? I thought you were tailing

Marco?"

"Right again. Since I couldn't sit in on his card game, I sat in on a different one. Sure would like to know which of us took home the bigger pot."

"Man, you're a freaking pirate."

Blake disconnected the call, knowing how that look of total amazement creeps over Jack's face. Satisfied that he had time to complete his errands, he made another call.

"Dr. Kendall."

"Good morning, doctor, I have this pain in my shoulder that needs a personal massage. Do you offer those services at MACS?"

"No sir, but the doctor does have limited hours at a waterfront location. Shall I book you for lunch?"

"Can't do, lovely lady. I'm working my way back home with a few more stops. Much as I hoped to be there for lunch, I don't see how it will work. Can I arrange an after-hours appointment?"

"Of course. I really need to talk to you. Did you get my message?"

"I sure did. Remember, no heroics. I sense that these folks are so busy chasing the almighty dollar that they would run over you without looking back."

"After watching Victoria and Serena's performances yesterday, I agree. But I think I'm on to something. I heard about another patient death. I'm going to use my research study as an excuse to try to get the records."

As with Carla, he wanted to warn Taylor, to tell her how dangerous it could be for her if they have any hint that she's onto something, but he had a job to do, a job that might require placing Taylor at risk, "Why don't you find out where the records are stored? Then let's talk about how to get a look at them. Okay? This isn't the day to push. Don't you think the entire office will be on alert to keep any skeletons from surfacing until after the visitors leave?"

"I think you're right. I can ask Ray, the program tech."

"We don't need much more than vital stats on the patient to find the death certificate. I told you that I would help you. Do you want to meet at the gallery after work?"

Taylor thought, deciding to make a bold overture, "Why don't you come to my place? I'll fix dinner, nothing fancy. Bring your swimsuit. I live in the guest house, with a luxurious pool practically in diving distance from my front door."

She proceeded to give him directions to her place. He listened, using his pen to doodle instead of write. He already knew where she lived and how to get there. He drove by enough times, late in the evening when the dim lighting suggested that she was asleep while he was doing his dreaming driving around.

* * * * *

"Hello."

"Sorry to interrupt your high rolling, but I've got news."

"Hold just a moment," Blake said, taking the Mont Blanc pen from his newly retained Bahamian attorney's desk to sign papers for the house transfer. Pushing the hold button on his cell phone, Blake made a bold signature on the four places marked, then pushed the papers across the desk. Walking outside on the office balcony for privacy, Blake put the cell phone to his ear and continued, "Okay, Jack, go ahead."

"Geek Boy found a return airline ticket for Dr. Marco."

"What time does he arrive at Tampa International?"

"That's the weird part. He's flying into Orlando this afternoon and he has a reservation at the airport hotel."

"It's only odd to the untrained eye. The shake-down is already underway. Victoria and Serena have to close the deal. Bringing Marco back in at this stage would be a mistake. He'll return after the contracts are signed. Believe me, the unholy trinity is rock solid when it comes to deal-making. It's the killer instinct, but it's also the closest thing to insight that any of them will ever have."

"So your mother and stepmother are going to make the score?"

"That's right. If the Magna team leaves before ten o'clock, you'll know they sensed the setup and got out with their corporate funds intact. If they are rushed to the airport barely in time for a late plane, they'll be lucky to escape with the elastic in their boxers."

"Man, that's calculated."

"Where do you think I learned to run a good sting? Think of it this way; all the Von Trapp children sang in the family act. Well, all the Girard children had roles in the family schemes. You know the family that steals together, stays together."

Taylor stepped off the fourth floor elevator, scanning the lobby. Seeing nothing unusual, she darted for her office. The patient files she was using for the research study were still on the lower bookcase shelf. Several memos littered her desktop; still more evidence that MACS decimated the rain forest merely to let people know about substantial matters such as how to use the new microwave in the break room, the latest change in the internal telephone extensions, and an envelope to add a contribution for an employee's baby shower. She opened her wallet, pulling out a ten dollar bill, then paused and put it back. *This is a big company with mostly pre-menopausal women. Five dollars is enough.*

At the bottom of the memo pile, she found a manila "Inter-Office Communication" envelope. Inside was a typed message on the back of a page from the MACS patient intake questionnaire. Using sixteen-point Matisse typeface, the words had the peculiar look of a crudely printed ransom note, "Want another view of MACS? Too bad you can't ask Martha Sanders, Greg Newman, or Peter Lane."

There was no signature. Taylor's eyes were drawn to the name Greg Newman. Jim King was probing for information on this patient's death and whether or not it was connected with MACS. Who were the others? Patients? Employees? Harriet's name wasn't there. The office door opened and Taylor shoved the page inside her top desk drawer trying not to look like a child caught with a hand in the cookie jar.

"Dr. K, no reason to panic," Brook said walking in and kicking the door shut with the base of her black platform shoe.

She placed a cup of steaming coffee on Taylor's desk, and then pulled up a guest chair. "Tell me all about the big evening."

"Not much to tell, lots of talk about business and the longest cocktail hour I've ever attended followed by dinner so late that I nearly slept through it."

"Did you end up with anybody?"

"End up? End up where?"

"You know, upstairs in the hot tub. Sally always books those kinds of guests into rooms with hot tubs."

"Obviously my concept of a business dinner is vastly different than the Girards."

"Good going! I thought you were too smart to climb the corporate ladder from a prone position."

"Tell me something: do the special guests know that employees are brought along for bonus entertainment?"

"Don't know. Of course the repeaters usually ask for Neva - at least that's the rumor. By the way, I checked downstairs. She's coming in late today," Brook reported with a shrug of the shoulders as if she were innocent to the implication.

Taylor decided to cast out a bit of line and see if Brook would bite. "Well, I did have to make an escape from Jim-Bob, I mean Jim King, Magna's CFO. He vacillated from pumping me for corporate information, which I don't have, to luring me upstairs to play rodeo."

"Ugh! He's a good looking guy, but drop the macho, please! Back home in the lone star state, I bet he drives a penis car."

"What?"

"You know what I mean. Guys get those tall SUVs with oversized tires and rumbling motors. From what I'm learning in Psyche 101, I consider it a new version of penis envy. They can't find transplant possibilities, so they impress with penis cars."

Taylor rocked back in her chair laughing. "Brook, I've got to tell Dr. Dale about your theory. That's definitely not the way I learned it in grad school."

The door opened again, Dr. Locke entered. "Too much levity going on here! Someone may think you actually enjoy your work," he said with mock severity.

"Pull up a chair, Sam," Brook offered, then turned to Taylor, "By the way, did you know that Dr. Locke has been looking at brochures for customized pickup trucks with wide traction tires?"

Taylor stuffed back another laugh.

"Okay, folks, I have a feeling that the joke is on me. Brook, you're going to hate this, but Victoria wants to give a copy of the PHP protocols to the Magna Group. Print it or make copies. Do whatever is easier."

"Neither is easier. And who reads those dumb protocols anyway except me when I had to translate your notes from PhD hieroglyphics into English?"

"See what happens when you send them to school? They get sharp tongues."

Brook picked up her mug, "Okay, Sam. I'll be at the copy machine for an hour or two. Answer your own phones."

Locke waited until Brook left, then spoke, "Taylor, did the evening go well?"

"I'm not sure what well means around here. Did I manage to stay out of Jim-Bob's clutches? Yes. That's my idea of well. Did I contribute anything to the evening? Considering the previous question, I guess not."

"I suppose you want to know why I didn't warn you."

"Yes, that would be interesting to hear unless nobody but me finds this whole thing odd."

"Quite honestly, Taylor, I expected to be at the dinner."

"Why weren't you?"

"I'm not sure. Serena pulled me out of the afternoon meeting to go to Plant City. She said there was a crisis situation and that the program nurse would explain when I got there. When I arrived, the patients were boarding vans per schedule. The program nurse had no idea what was happening. I called Serena's private line and got intercepted by Sally. In whispered tones, Sally insisted that they had a tip about a surprise Medicare inspection. She said Serena wanted me to stay there at least until five o'clock in case an auditor arrived."

"What happened?"

"Nothing. At five-thirty we locked up and I headed back. Traffic on the interstate going through Tampa's malfunction-junction was a nightmare. I phoned from the car to say I'd be late. Sally said that I wasn't needed for the evening as the table had already been filled. I took the hint and went home."

Taylor searched his face. Everything about his body language indicated he was telling the truth.

"As rotten as this sounds, it was hours later before I remembered that you were with the group, but I also knew that Carla was there and I thought she would watch out for you."

"That's okay. I know how to protect myself, but I wonder how Dr. Dale would feel knowing that MACS concept of a psychological residency included late dinner parties in the hope that the staff would put out for their benefit," Taylor said emphatically, "Tell me, do the male professionals have to sleep with female executives when a deal is at stake?"

Locke cracked the back of his neck as if to shake out the frustration, "There's plenty about the Girards that I don't understand. I can only guess that old habits die hard. Maybe that's the way they did business in Latin America."

"I don't think this is about culture or ethnicity. I think this is the universal concept of greed."

"On one level, you're right, but you've also worked with our clinical staff and you know we've got well-trained, dedicated people who care about their patients," Locke defended his turf.

"Okay, then how did you get Neva and Lorraine? Were they part of an HR campaign to hire the ethically handicapped?"

"Lorraine's been around the area several years working in psychiatric nursing and teaching at a local nursing school. She became Gina's very good friend, if you know what I mean. Gina arranged for her employment over my strongest objections. Later, when we needed more program nurses, Lorraine brought in Neva."

"I see your problem better now. I assumed you hired Lorraine and that didn't make sense. Surely you know that she constantly tries to undermine you."

"I know that, but as long as she and Gina are playing house there's not much I can do except contain the damage. I don't think she'll last long. Victoria and Marco may turn a blind eye, but Serena hates anyone who helps Gina gain status in the corporation."

"Does Serena dislike Lorraine?"

"Not exactly. Serena sees herself as the Queen Mother defending her son's right to the throne. I've actually heard Marco refer to Blake as 'The Prince,' so my guess is that he is as invested in the idea of his son's return as Serena is."

"What about Felipe? Isn't he their son too?"

"At the risk of being rude, have you spent any time around Felipe? The major part of his job description is trying to avoid his father's wrath and keep his dimwit wife in line. I'm surprised that Marco hasn't demanded a paternity test in the hope that he could deny responsibility for that loser."

Taylor thought about how out of place Felipe and Tiffany were at the dinner. Earlier in the evening, Felipe was rebuffed by the Magna delegation, Victoria and even by Serena - his own mother - when he tried to get into the business discussion. As the evening wore on, he and Tiffany moved away from the group turning their limited attention spans to giggling and groping. "Sam, why did the much-adored Prince leave and what does he do now?"

"All I heard was that Blake was in a doctoral psychology program but he left without graduating. That violated Marco's game plan, which he carefully crafted for all of his children."

"Did he flunk out because of too much playing around?"

"Doubtful. If you assume that even half of what Marco and Serena say about their son is true, the golden boy is also a genius. In her less moody moments, Victoria has even admitted to me that Blake is cunning like his father, yet brilliant on a level beyond the rest of the siblings. No, I think this was more of a clash of wills. As for what he does now, nobody knows. The family is forbidden to make contact since he was banished from the Girard kingdom."

Taylor almost said "except Carla", but she quickly covered her mouth as if to cough. Apparently Carla maintains contact with her half-brother in defiance of Marco's order. "Maybe he got into booze or drugs and the family would be embarrassed to bring him back."

"I don't think so. If his return were not a real threat, then why would Lorraine and Victoria be maneuvering in their own ways for Gina to get recognition from Marco?"

"This is all very sinister."

"The Girard concept of family is slightly off the curve. Perhaps Blake learned enough about family systems therapy in graduate school to get out while he could." Locke stood up to leave. "I have to hang around my office in case I'm needed during any remaining meetings. You can go back to your regular schedule in the clinic."

Taylor nodded, "I will be in for most of my schedule, but I'm also putting a full court press on the treatment effectiveness study that Victoria wants."

"If it will help, you can assign some of the individual sessions or intakes to the Social Workers?"

"Thanks but I'm up to date on the psychological testing. If we get new patients, I'll do my part of the workups and hand over the rest to other staff."

"Okay, sounds good."

"Sam," Taylor asked cautiously, "Who is Greg Newman?"

"Why do you ask?"

"Whatever happened to him, even Jim-Bob and the Magna crew got wind of it."

"It's a sad and complex case. I've got some newspaper clippings in my office that you can read about his suicide."

"Who is Peter Lane?"

"Where did you hear that name?"

"Just following up on possible cases that might skew the results on our treatment effectiveness study. You know, the statistical outliers."

Locke walked over to her desk, bent down beside her chair and in a whispered yet stern voice warned, "I'll tell you more about this later. We'll go for lunch away from the office. Meanwhile, I don't think it's safe for you to say those names aloud."

"Do you think it will cost me the residency?"

"No, I think it could cost your life."

* * * * *

Taylor arrived in the clinic as patients were moving into the second group period. A few stragglers lingered in the hall, some for food, some looking as lost as they probably felt. Her eyes scanned until locating her target.

"Ray, can I speak with you about a patient?"

He turned, handed off the wheelchair of an elderly woman to another tech and followed Taylor to the intake office.

"Close the door, please."

"Something wrong, Doc?"

"That's what I'm hoping you can help me find out, Ray. Is it safe to talk here?" she asked then immediately felt paranoid at the question.

Ray found nothing odd about it. He adjusted the mini-blinds on the window facing the hallway commenting that a slight upward tilt of the blinds makes the shadow of someone standing near the door easier to see from inside. Then he slumped down into the nearest arm chair, propping his feet on the adjacent waste basket.

Taylor began her carefully considered words, "I know that you think Harriet's death was peculiar and not given proper attention. Maybe that's due to carelessness. Maybe it's outright neglect. In either event, the police seem satisfied that there is nothing further that needs to be done. I'm wondering if maybe there is something more. As part of my treatment effectiveness study, I have to ask these questions."

Ray leaned over the desk, lowering his voice, "Dr. Kendall, you are the only one who doesn't look at me like a madman or a traitor when I mention her name. Yes, I'm certain something happened to Harriet here that pushed her over the edge."

As he continued to talk about Harriet's desire for recovery, Taylor remained focused on his casual, yet profound observation. *Can Ray be onto something without realizing it? Was Harriet's accident not an accident - or even a surprise - to the MACS hierarchy?*

"So, Doc…Did you hear me?"

"Yes, Ray. I was concentrating on your assessment of the situation," she said lamely trying to cover her distraction.

"Do you think we need to go to the police?"

"No! At least, not yet. We have nothing concrete."

"But what can we get that will make a difference now that didn't make show up in the original investigation?"

"I don't know yet, but here's an idea. Did you know a patient named Greg Newman?"

"No. That was before I transferred into this clinic, but I heard about it from my friend Harry, the social worker who got fired for no apparent reason."

Taylor looked up, her peripheral vision catching a change in light level outside the window. She wrote on her paper "Careful - outsiders" and pushed it toward Ray. Then in a slightly louder voice tone than necessary said, "So do you think I need to spend more time with Gary? Wait, is it Gary or Gerry?"

"It's Gerry, the new patient from the group home near 34th street. Don't worry about it, takes time to get to know all the names."

Lorraine pushed open the door. "Good morning, Dr. Kendall. Ray. I saw the closed door and assumed that there was a meeting. Did I miss anything?"

Taylor flashed her best plastic smile, "Nothing that concerns you, Nurse Lewis. Ray was asking my professional opinion about dealing with a few clients. Like our social work interns, he likes to learn and I like to teach."

"He isn't here to learn; he's a tech who has a hard time remembering his place."

Ray started to get up until Taylor motioned for him to sit. She rose and walked around the desk to stand squarely in front of Lorraine, "Speaking of knowing one's place, Nurse Lewis, have you ever considered either dressing like a nurse or like a business person? You're much too early for Halloween in your black with blood spatter jewelry. Or are you preparing a program for SRA survivors where your presence provides triggers for the patients' early life traumas?"

Lorraine's nostrils flared, her hands clasped in front of her as if she were trying to keep from clawing Taylor's eyes out with her long, pointed fingernails, "You are way out of line, doctor."

"And you need to spend more time working then meddling. As Dr. Locke told you recently, you aren't qualified to be my supervisor, so don't try."

An electronic squeal broke the tension. Looking at the message on the screen of her pager, Lorraine said, "This isn't over, Dr. Kendall. Don't mess with my clinic or my staff."

"For once we agree. This isn't over," Taylor replied standing firm. "Before you go, please remember that when it is over, you'll know it. I'll make sure of it. And don't come at me with your empty threats. I know who you are and what you are. In case you never read all the way through to Revelation, your team loses."

Lorraine grunted audibly, swiveled on her black boot heels and left, slamming the office door behind her so hard that the window rattled.

"Wow, Doc, you are either the bravest women I know or you have a death wish."

"Why do you say that? She's only a big mouth on a power trip."

"No, it's more than that. Last January we had a patient who was a former Catholic priest. He took one look at her and started babbling in Latin. When he got calm, he said he was performing an exorcism ritual to get rid of the demon. Now frankly, I've called her that and more, but this guy was stone serious. By the way, what is SRA?"

"Satanic Ritual Abuse."

"Is that what she's into?"

"I don't know, Ray, but look at the outfits. Black head to toe except for the blood red pendant she always wears. Sometimes she hides it behind a sweater like yesterday during meetings with the Magna Group. And that haircut, pointed toward her face with the burgandy streak. I've heard some older patients say that she dresses odd, but the schizophrenic patients, especially those who have had bad experiences with the occult must be terrified. Either she uses it as a power trip or she's the real thing."

"I have to admit that Lorraine scares me. The way she talks and gestures with those pointed nails like they were daggers. Then she shows up like she's clairvoyant."

"She has no power unless you give it to her. She's a cheap parlor trick, using her image and her bravado to keep the staff on edge. Stare her down and she'll leave you alone."

"Better watch out; she's taking aim at you, Doc. Come to think of it, she was being nasty to Harriet a few weeks before the accident. Does she think we are up to something?"

"A person with such an insecure grip on life as Lorraine

probably suspects that everyone is out to get her. We need to work quickly and carefully." Taylor took a notepad from her pocket and scribbled a phone number. "Here's my home number. It's written backward. Now you write down your home number for me." As he wrote, she continued, "I want you to ask Harry to speak with me, at lunch or in the evening, his choice. I need to talk with him soon about Greg Newman. I promise to keep you posted, okay?"

Ray rose from the chair, handing the note to Taylor. "Thanks, Doc. I hope that we find something soon so our names don't get added to the MACS disappearing act."

Taylor nodded. *If we don't succeed, how long will it be before someone else becomes curious enough to ask what happened to Martha Sanders, Greg Newman, Peter Lane and Harriet Logan?*

* * * * *

"You must be joking. This isn't the deal we came to discuss," Jim King responded indignantly after glancing at the summary page to the documents piled in front of him.

"Well, that's our deal. Take it or leave it," Victoria snapped back, folding her arms and glaring defiantly.

Now that the pleasantries were over and the numbers were out, even Douglas Parker, Magna's MBA became vocal, "The profit potential from the PHP programs will be eroded by the franchising for the Nutracuratives and that outrageous billing cost. We aren't stupid."

Serena gave her most alluring smile as she turned toward Jim King, "Of course not. MACS is too far advanced in mental health programs to deal with any company who is less than our equal in their own field, as Magna is in sports rehabilitation. Your company stands to gain substantially. Thus we need to insure that MACS is not giving away our most vital corporate edge, the Nutracuratives, without adequate compensation."

"Adequate? You're putting your hands into our pockets on

billing, training and whatever else this latest proposal dreams up until the PHPs generate enough to satisfy MACS. That's robbery, pure and simple," King replied, "No matter how sweetly you say it, Serena."

Jordan scanned the faces of the Magna representatives. "Gentlemen, I think we all need a break. Let's step away from the table, stretch our legs and take time to reconsider what we've heard."

Opening the conference room door, he shot a "help" look at Fiona. Not that she needed a hint. The jagged nerves coming out of the room were enough to send static electricity across the carpet. As was the custom, Fiona invited the visitors back into what was called the "private parlor", a small living room with phones and a fax, where they could retreat between sessions. Fiona's natural Irish charm was genuine enough to put strangers at ease. Checking to see that the water pitcher and coffee urns were filled, she pointed to the credenza; "If you need notepads or pens, please help yourself. This phone and fax are separate lines from our switchboard and are at your disposal to send or receive information." She took her business card from her pocket and wrote numbers on the back, "If you want to reach the MACS operator, dial 51. She can page Jordan or myself and notify our people when you are ready to resume your discussions."

Closing the door behind her as she left, Fiona walked up to Sally's desk, "Looks like they may be awhile. Where's Jordan?"

"He's in Serena's office," Sally replied without missing a keystroke in her typing.

"Maybe I need to be there, too."

"No!" Sally nearly shouted, then gained control over her voice tone, "Jordan wanted you to get back to the PR office. He'll call when he needs you again. You are right, this one may go slowly."

Fiona shrugged her shoulders, "Okay. You know where to find me. I'll keep my pager on."

The second day of negotiations was usually intense and

subject to private temper fits by Victoria, Dr. Marco or both. The first day of "show and tell" was much more fun. Bring out the pictures and the favorable news clippings. Order expensive catered food. Actually as Jordan suggested, order twice the food necessary so that the behind-the-scenes employees get the leftovers. Their little secret nearly backfired six months ago when Victoria actually went down to the third floor and saw filing clerks with plates of truffles and pâté. Jordan managed to convince Victoria that ordering excess food was a PR strategy. He told her that prospective investors or clients would see that from the first sip of imported Jamaican Blue Mountain coffee to the last bite of tiramisu flown in fresh from Italy, everything at MACS screamed *abundance*. Victoria complained about the excess costs, although Dr. Marco and Serena wholeheartedly supported the idea the way that Jordan sold it. Then again, excess was hardly a new concept to the Girards.

"Can you adjust the picture quality without affecting the recording?" Serena asked, settling back in her desk chair for a prime view.

Jordan tinkered with the video equipment inside the white Armoire on the far wall of Serena's office. What was sacrificed in resale value as an antique was more than offset by its function to hide the high tech electronic spying system. Setting the fine tuning button brought the whole scene into focus as if they were in the same room.

"Pour another coffee for me, Jordan," Victoria said stretching her legs across the sofa, "I think I'm going to like this show. What's it called, let's make a deal?"

As the ladies laughed, Jordan took his seat, preparing to take notes. The "private parlor" was anything but private. Unknown to the Magna Group, their every word was heard leaving plenty of time to plan a counter offer to their counter offer before it was officially presented.

"Don't you love to watch them sweat? We've got them on the

run. They want in with us."

"You may be right, Victoria. What is your opinion, Jordan?"

He turned to face Serena. *She doesn't want my opinion, not my honest opinion. Personally, I'd take the money and be glad for the extra Nutracurative sales plus the additional market penetration. But does she want to hear that? No way. She wants me to feed her ego. At double the pay of my last job, I'll tell her she's a Viking princess and float a frigging long ship in the lobby if it keeps her content.*

"Serena, you know that I'm only here to support your negotiations. You're the health care expert, not me. You say when to close the deal and I'll set it in motion."

Victoria rose up from the sofa, "This is no time to close. Look at them. They are disagreeing among themselves. This is the time to hit them hard while they're confused and tired. On the next round, let's throw in our training manuals free then stick them with two percent more on billing."

"That's a pretty expensive training manual, Victoria."

"Yeah, and while you were stroking Serena's ego you missed hearing Doug warn the owners not to let their real estate reserve fund get caught up in any deals. Jordan, get on the phone with our paid insider and tell him to find out how much money is in that fund."

"Victoria, I don't think this is a good time. I've never called the informer at their office, I always talk to him at his home number," Jordan protested.

"Have Sally make the call. Tell her to act like it's personal. Just get the information and get it now."

"But I still don't think that…"

"Jordan, we don't pay you to think. Make the call."

* * * * *

The knock at her door caused her to cringe until she heard Jordan's voice, "I need to speak with you, Carla, it's very important."

"All right. Come in," she said, without placing her phone call on hold so the person waiting could hear everything. "Hello, Jordan, what can I do for you? More contracts?"

"Not yet. I need to know if your mother has any extra medication around the office."

"I don't know."

"She's getting very manic, shaking and cussing. We have several hours left on the negotiations. I'm not sure I can keep her on track without the meds."

"What do you want me to do?"

"Will you please get her medication from the house or have it delivered. Make it fast, okay?"

"I'll do what I can, Jordan, but don't count on the meds working that quickly. You're probably on your own. Do I need to notify Father?"

"We could use him, but there's not enough time for him to get back."

"He could fly back to Tampa International and finish the meeting there."

"That won't work. We have to close here on our schedule. If they have the freedom to get away we might lose them. At least that's the way your Father designed the game."

His pager started to beep. Rolling his eyes toward the ceiling, "I have to get back upstairs. I feel like the announcer at a wrestling match."

As the door closed again, Carla put the telephone back to her ear, "I guess you heard."

His laughter was uncontainable, "That's the part of the family I miss most, those carefree days of conspiring together for the common greed."

"Blake, you can be so sarcastic."

"I'm realistic and you know it. It's past lunch hour. Sounds like it's taking longer than predicted to get into these guys' wallets."

"Sally and Fiona took them to the Don Cesar for lunch. If

Jordan and Serena can get things back on track, the deal will be done by the end of business day. I don't suppose you are close enough to meet for dinner?"

"No. Unfortunately, I'm heading into a meeting too."

"What kind of meeting? Are you working at a real job?"

"A job? You know I'm merely a miserable ingrate graduate school dropout with extraordinary fencing skills and expensive taste in clothes. Where's the market for that?"

"Are you running your own scheme?"

"Yes, my charming sister, you could say that."

"Will you tell me all about it?"

"Maybe. Maybe not. Why don't you pencil me in for dinner next week? How about Thursday? I have a gift for you."

"A gift? What kind of gift?"

"Expensive, extravagant and exquisite."

"You've got my attention."

"Works on all the Girard women."

"That was rude, but I'll live with it. Where do we meet?"

"I'll phone that morning with directions."

"You love being mysterious, don't you, Blake?"

"More than you know, Carla, more than you know."

CHAPTER 20

"All right, settle down people. The fishing forecast is too good for this evening to let this meeting run long," the Director tapped his pen on the pock marked conference table. Scanning the room, he took mental roll call.

"And in this corner, we have Blake Girard, who came in from the cold today for our benefit."

Jack Simms covered his mouth as if to cough and mumbled in Blake's direction, "If only he knew where you've really been."

Blake shot his friend a look that warned against further discussion then turned, smiling, "My pleasure to be here, sir. It's always uplifting for those of us who go undercover to see the fine talent that backs up our meager efforts."

"This isn't a game," Benny Murray, more accountant than agent, snarled from behind his nose high stack of files and reports.

"You are right, Benny boy. If it were a game, it would have tidy rules and three-part forms which means that even you could be a field operative. Now if you could add a few points to your firearms qual, we'd have to put Bambi in protective custody during hunting season."

The roar of laughter forced the Director to slam his notebook against the table to regain order. "Okay, guys, we've had our fun. Back to work. It's report time."

Blake took out the Mont Blanc pen his Bahamian attorney offered as a token of their new business relationship. As Marco said, "Mont Blanc is the only writing instrument suitable for a gentleman." He placed the pen horizontally, lying across his second finger. As his hand moved up and down, the pen remained in perfect balance. At least until Jack's elbow hit his. Looking upward, he noticed that all eyes were on him. Show time.

"Yes, sir."

"If it's not too much trouble, Blake, can you be here when you're here?"

"Yes sir. What do you need?"

"An estimate of when we can close off this operation would be nice?"

"At this point I can only tell you what Michelangelo told the Pope from his vantage point over the Sistine Chapel: it will be done when it's done."

"What kind of cocky attitude is that?" Benny rejoined the conversation, pulling out a bulging brown folder of accounting sheets. "We aren't making a movie. We are trying to prevent further waste of our government's money. If we can prove fraud, we need to stop it before it gets worse."

"If Medicare were a little more discerning in giving out our government's money, then the FBI and Justice wouldn't be spending more of our government's money to plug the leak," Blake fired back, sending daggered glares at both Benny and the latest lawyer from the Tampa Justice Department office.

"Enough!" the Director regained control over the undercurrent around the table.

Blake stood, walking deliberately to the marker board on the left wall. He drew a diagram with an outline of the eastern seaboard and the Bahamas to the east. Using a green marker, he made a prominent dollar sign then drew the money trail as he spoke,

"If you want to prove that MACS is ripping off Medicare, we can finish that with files we confiscate during the bust plus the information from leaks that we currently have. But if you want to find Medicare's money, start following the line in Jacksonville where the tap flows freely. MACS billing system is state-of-the-art to process claims quickly and gain a rapid turnaround. The money comes into MACS corporate accounts, and then the real shuffle begins. Using the eleven existing Partial Hospitalization Programs as conduits, creative accounting makes the money disappear from the books and reappear as cash. Large amounts of that cash is transported by courier to Nassau and scattered among three different banks. From there the money is sent out."

Using a blue marker, he drew three radiating lines, "My conjecture is that the money ultimately goes to Spain, Argentina and Venezuela or Chile. And that's why we need to get positioned immediately to intercept the funds in the Bahamas before we raid or Marco decides to close shop, whichever comes first."

"Wait a minute. How do you know this? Did your source find it out?"

"My source doesn't even know she's a source. She's not that highly placed in the organization. However Dr. Kendall did make a few comments that led me on this trail, and with the current deal-making that's happening this afternoon, MACS is drawing in another company."

"MACS has been steadily buying up small companies. What's unique about this deal?"

"Magna Limited is larger than prior acquisitions. In fact, it's larger than MACS. That's why I think that these new players are actually being drawn in to become fall guys. If MACS is already making large cash drains hidden by complex intra-corporate loans as well as positioning the pigeon, then they may be ready to move on."

Jack looked surprised, "Why would they leave such a sweet set up? They don't even know that the investigation is in progress. I don't get it."

"Of course you don't. We become too accustomed to the garden variety crooks that keep going back to the well until they get caught. Those people are dishonest and impatient. Truly evil people are capable of much more. That's why they are harder to catch. Look at the history of the California cellular clinics and the prior operations in South America. This Magna deal falls into their pattern," Blake tried to capsulate years of deal-making in a few sentences.

The olive-suited Justice Department attorney spoke up, "Sounds like hefty speculation."

"As I learned before dropping out of psychology training, past behavior is the best predictor of future behavior. Since I've been an agent, I've seen that proven over and over." Other agents nodded in agreement, obviously thinking about past cases.

"Okay, let's say you are right about skimming money and trying to leave," olive suit tried to set up his point, "They can't move that much money out of the country without a trace."

"As long as you underestimate the bad guys, they will beat you every time."

"So now you're telling us how to do the inside work," Benny spoke up.

"I'm simply asking Justice and the Bureau to get moving so that we can recover the money as well as close the operations," Blake said. "If the California investigation had done its job better, these principals would not have escaped prosecution."

"That case was different. It was all private money, no Medicare dollars," the olive-suited lawyer explained, "The billing from the PHPs and some tips from former employees gives us an edge in this situation."

Blake stared at the Justice lawyer, "The last thing you need is for Marco to beat you out of a prosecution by fighting you with millions of Medicare dollars he has stashed in other countries. You know, places where you can't touch it because you let it slip past while you score two minutes of fame on the six o'clock news. You'll be doing exactly what he expects. He's counting on Medicare or any investigative body to be so focused on the Florida PHPs that no one looks any further until he gets off scot-free."

"And what makes you think you have all the answers in this case?"

"He really doesn't know, does he?"

The Director shrugged his shoulders, "He's the third attorney that's been assigned to work on this case."

"I don't know what?" the young Justice Department attorney replied.

"You don't know that the reason I fought all the way to Washington to get this assignment. I understand MACS better than anyone."

"That's because you are such a hot shot. Typical agent..."

"No, you moron. It's because the Girards are my family. Marco and Serena are my parents. Victoria is my stepmother, in a manner of speaking. Running sophisticated cons is the family business and I was trained by Marco to be his heir."

The young attorney gulped audibly.

"That's why I know without a doubt that you'll never get him by following procedures. I can grasp his line of thinking, anticipate his actions. While you're worried about billing irregularities, I'm trying to hand you the case of your lifetime!" Blake turned to the Director, "Sir, I know I make your ulcer flare, but I only failed the Bureau once and it won't happen again."

Benny looked up, "You? Failed on a case? When?"

"San Diego, California. My second field assignment. I came in toward the end as backup. I was full of rules and regulations and I thought the good guys won by playing it straight. I watched from the sidelines as my family slid away on trivial legal motions, disappeared to South America, raised new capital and came back stronger than ever. The money from the California clinics funded MACS. The ante gets raised every time. Now they use a defenseless population of schizophrenics and endanger the careers of competent professionals while we scramble to take them down by the book."

The Justice lawyer was spellbound by the story, "What makes you so sure it's more than a case of hyped billing?"

"You are too dazzled by the corporate splendor and alleged

wonder cures from the self-acclaimed Medical Alliance for Community Services. You need a reality check," Blake took a blue marker and wrote MACS in large block letters on the board. Below it he wrote the letters in reverse, SCAM. A gasp rose from around the room.

"A worthy adversary telegraphs his move then dares you to follow. We failed to stop them in California. Left unchecked, they came back bolder and greedier. The result is MACS, an elaborate front for Medicare fraud, money laundering and… murder or murders."

"Murder? Are you sure?"

"All I'm asking, sir, is another week or two undercover, some extra support in the office and cut me some slack. I'll put ironclad proof on your desk or my letter of resignation."

"Is that enough time to make the bust?"

"I have reason to believe that it's all the time we'll have before Marco pulls the plug and gets away clean to a non-extraditable country."

"I hear they're foreigners. What makes you think that they even know which countries won't deal with us?"

"Mr. Junior Attorney General, while your mother was teaching you to recite Mary Had a Little Lamb, my mother taught me the names of safe haven nations."

* * * * *

Inside the Director's private office the three co-conspirators stood. He made them wait, not because the phone messages he was reading were important. No, they needed to cool their ardor.

"Well, well, Agent Girard that was quite a stirring performance. Now that you've rallied the troops, you might explain to me what other resources of my office have been under your command."

"This may take awhile, so you won't mind if we sit?" He motioned for the others to sit also.

"As if you give a rip what I think. Blake if you weren't such a good agent, I'd ship your insubordinate ego back to Quantico to work in the basement filing fingerprint cards."

"Sir, you know how you complain about my paperwork."

"Okay, make it fast, I only have two anti-acid tablets left so act accordingly."

"First of all, don't blame Jack. He made every effort to keep in contact with me as you ordered. I insisted that he help me by gathering some electronic information. That's how we enlisted Geek Boy…" Blake turned to his right and extended his hand, "By the way, I'm Blake Girard, what's your name?"

The young man shook hands vigorously, "I'm Derek Prentice. Honored to meet you, Agent Girard. You're a legend at the Academy."

"A legend? Don't buff that gigantic ego, he's already a renegade."

Jack interrupted, "No sir, he's a freaking pirate like his daddy."

"What! Have you all been watching Saturday morning cartoons?" the Director popped his last anti-acid, slurped down cold coffee and stared, "I don't want to know about this, do I?"

"Let's put it this way," Blake reasoned. "What you don't know, you don't have to report. And what I don't tell you, you don't have to tell Justice until we are sure that their latest wet-behind-the-ears lawyer won't screw it up."

"Gentlemen, we never had this conversation. As far as I know, you bumped into each other at the Y playing basketball. Keep it out of my office until you have something meaningful. And, Jack, don't let your pirate friend too far out of sight if you value your job."

"Yes sir!"

The three men stood up to leave.

The Director motioned for Blake to remain.

"Blake, I supported your request for this assignment even though I knew from working with you in Colorado that you were not a conventional agent. Frankly, I put my chestnuts in the fire for you on this one. You have to deliver."

"You know I will, sir."

"The chase is one thing, but there's a part of this investigation you underestimate."

"I don't think so. What do you mean?"

"You're an exceptionally talented undercover agent. You've faced down some tough characters, but that's not even close to what it's going to be like to put handcuffs on your mother and father."

Blake closed the door and froze in place. With so much effort going into the chase, he hadn't thought of the capture as graphically as the Director suggested. *Would Serena cower the way a fox does when surrounded by hounds and horsemen? Would Victoria sputter like a cobra, trying to attack regardless of the odds? Would Marco fight or capitulate or sense danger and slip out the side door? The idea of Gina and Lorraine in tasteful chains might actually be a turn-on for them. Maybe Tiffany will learn to bake refrigerator dough cookies to bring to Felipe on visiting day at the prison. And Carla…Oh my God, Carla. Somehow I've got to get her out of there before the ax falls. How? She knows things, probably too much about MACS. According to Taylor, Carla has total office access. That plus her role in Quality Management and her guilt by association means she knows way too much. And then there's Taylor. Shutting down MACS will crash her residency year. I've got to find a way to keep them out of this mess.*

"What mess, man? You're mumbling again."

"Sorry, Jack, I'm thinking."

"About Taylor?"

"Yes. And my sister, Carla. I've got to get her out."

Jack motioned for Blake to follow a few steps away to the supply room. "What do you mean you have to get your sister out? She's in it up to her patrician nose. She's an adult and according to you, she's a smart girl."

"She's capable, Jack, but she's never had a choice. The family runs her life."

"Get outta here, man, this is America. They can't hold her against her will."

"Yes, they can and they do."

"Do Mom and Pop Girard and Auntie Victoria start each day at the breakfast table by putting a gun to the head of your siblings to make them go to work? Or do they work for the cars and clothes and the expense accounts?"

"You can't possibly understand."

"Man, you left when you got their number. What holds sweet misunderstood Carla to this den of thieves?"

"Neither threats nor greed; they hold her with the tightest bond of all, their need."

"What you're talking about is more than a stunt. Freeing your sister could interfere with the investigation. Does the term 'obstruction of justice' have any meaning, Mr. Summa Cum Laude lawyer? That could cost you your FBI career, is it worth it?"

"If that's the price, then I'm prepared to pay it, but I promise we'll bring down MACS no matter what," Blake said calmly, "Now I've got to meet Taylor and find out what she has. She left a handwritten note for me at the gallery on her way into work this morning. She mentions that if anything odd happens to her, I need to find out about Greg Newman, Peter Lane and Martha Sanders."

"I'll put Geek Boy on it right away. Are they MACS patients?"

"Don't know. Get me anything and everything and make it fast. I have a sinking feeling that Taylor has stumbled onto some deadly secrets."

CHAPTER 21

I t's like the old saying, a watched pot never boils. The worse part of putting on hair color is sitting in the bathroom waiting for the timer to confirm that this boring task is done. He quickly blow dried his hair then put in the gray contact lens that camouflage turquoise blue eyes. Some slimy hair gel to tame his natural wave and worn Levi's with an old frayed Henley shirt transformed cosmopolitan Blake Girard into Gabe, unemployed actor and general nice guy.

When Taylor opened the French doors, all she could see was a giant bouquet of wildflowers and a pair of jean-clad legs.

"What is this? I've heard of special delivery services, but this is the first time flowers have walked to my house," she said reaching for his arm to guide him into the living room.

She took the flowers in her arms and laid them on the desk. Opening the attached card she read the words aloud:

"When I saw you coming,
I said to my heart;
What a pretty little stone
To stumble on!

Gabe I didn't know you are a poet too. That's so lovely, thank you," she said leaning over to kiss his cheek.

The touch of her lips sent quivers all the way to his toes. *Get a grip on yourself, man! You're no teenager. Remember why you're here; the official reason.* Then he looked into her hazel eyes and smiled broadly, "I have to be honest, I didn't write that. It's one of the Coplas, a classic form of Spanish literature."

"Who wrote it?"

"Don't know. There are many Coplas. They're four line songs

that have been passed down over generations. This one reminded me of you."

"My goodness, flowers and a cultural history lesson; you are an amazing man."

And you, darling Taylor, are a goddess with the compassion of Hippocrates, the analytical skills of Plato and the allure of Helen of Troy. Jack is right. I've crossed way over the line.

"Crossed what line? Were you talking to me?"

"No, I occasionally get wrapped up in my thoughts and a few words spill out. Makes no sense unless you hear the whole thing. Ignore me," he said trying to not look as gauche as he felt. *Blake would know how to act around her, but then vintage Blake would come on too strong. There were no women alive that he couldn't have on his terms in his time, until now. Approaching this woman confounds both of us.*

"Make yourself at home," she said handing him a tall iced tea with a sprig of mint floating on top, "I'll have dinner out in a few minutes."

"I hope you didn't go to a lot of trouble," he was mesmerized by her long legs in those short shorts walking gracefully back into the kitchen.

"Not at all. I'll have to impress you with my culinary skills on a weekend when I have more cooking time. Today it's simple fare."

He heard her singing along with the radio in the kitchen. Seemed like a good time to explore her house, so he said aloud, "I'll wash up, okay?"

"Sure, there's a bathroom in the hallway between the bedrooms."

He glanced in both directions. The small toilet and sink was what architects often call a powder room. There must be a full bathroom off the bedroom, her bedroom. He knew that the pool house was furnished by its owner, but it already had Taylor's distinctive imprint. The scent of Estee Lauder's Beautiful™

filled the tiny dressing area the same subtle way it clung to her clothes but not in the brash way that some women wore perfume intended to slap you into recognition. Taylor's perfume was an invisible frame for her impeccable style. He touched the satin covered pillow on her bed. *Lucky pillow. I would gladly offer my chest as a substitute.*

Back in the living room, he admired a collection of framed photos spread across the narrow table between the poolside French doors. In the center was an 8 x 10 family portrait that was quite different from his family. The Girard portraits were formal, stilted and preceded by fights over who sat where and who came out looking prominent. The smiles on the faces of Taylor's family were genuine almost serene; her father and mother sitting in front of the fire place, surrounded by Taylor and her lovely sisters.

"That was taken the Christmas before Daddy died," she said walking in with the salad bowl.

"Will you tell me about them?"

She walked over beside him, "I think I told you that my Daddy, Tom, was a family physician. He was the best at everything he did. My Mother, Julia, is a classic Southern lady; delicate as an orchid and dangerous as a thorn if you cross her. My middle sister, Savannah, graduated from Rhodes College in Memphis and teaches elementary school. She's taking a few classes toward her master's degree but mostly concentrating on her wedding next spring. My baby sister, Paige, graduates from high school this year. Hardly seems possible."

"Do you miss them?"

"Very much, but don't tell my Mama. She's looking for any excuse to send a plane ticket and fix me up with a job in Memphis. She thinks the time I spent in Florida for my doctorate was enough time away from home."

"Speaking of fixing you up," he said reaching for a small silver frame with a formally-dressed couple, "Is this Mama's idea of Mr. Right back home?"

"Actually it's Dr. Right. He's a surgical resident at Grady Memorial Hospital in Atlanta. Trey and I dated most of the time we were at Vanderbilt. That was the end of the story. This picture was taken years earlier at my Debutante Ball."

"Why?"

"Why what?"

"Why didn't two picture-perfect people end up together?"

"Because life isn't like the movies," Taylor replied recalling the emotional roller coaster of that failed relationship, "Trey's family is high in mid-south social circles. His father is senior partner in a top law firm. One grandfather is a professor emeritus at University of Tennessee Medical College and the other grandfather made his fortune on the Cotton Exchange."

"And exactly where is the downside for you?"

"His family wanted a daughter-in-law with a basic liberal arts BA who would be a gracious hostess, join Junior League, learn Ikebana flower arranging and gaze admiringly at her brilliant husband. Trey and I talked about setting up a joint practice in psychology and surgery where he would do orthopedics and I would specialize in pain management, but Trey's parents wanted only one doctor in the family and it wasn't intended to be me."

"Families can make impossible demands. By the time you get to graduate school, you ought to have enough self-awareness to choose between their plan for your life and your plan."

"Exactly. My family told me to do what I wanted. If it meant giving up grad school to get married, they were okay with it. All the pressure came from Trey's family. I needed time to think, so I took a year off after finishing my bachelor's degree to travel as a representative for my sorority. I was counting on the old 'absence makes the heart grow fonder,' but it didn't work out that way."

"Was the guy blind or stupid? You're perfect exactly as you are."

"Well, that wasn't the prevailing opinion. My absence gave his parents time to press their case for how hard it would be to make me into the 'right kind of wife.' Finally, I agreed with his Daddy

Warbucks; I wasn't going to be the right kind of wife. I left my snow boots and heavy coat at the Goodwill Store in Nashville and headed for Florida. Trey finished medical school and went to Atlanta for his internship."

"And you dropped off their radar screen that easily?"

"Yes. They dismissed me like last year's posh restaurant. I get cards at Christmas and my birthday from his maternal grandparents. They are precious people. If I missed anything about that family, it's being with them."

"Are you sorry it didn't work out with Trey?"

She looked into his eyes, so close that he thought she might see past the gray contacts, "Not anymore."

In a move that caught him as much by surprise as it did her, Gabe closed the narrow space between them and took her in his arms. *Her lips are sweet nectar. Hundreds of women on three continents say my kisses are masterful, but I have never received an ideal kiss until now. Kissing Taylor is magic. She is magic. I can't explain this, but I feel as if I have everything that matters in life right here in my arms.*

A kitchen timer rang in the distance. Taylor took a step back, with her hand still on his shoulders and his hands around her waist. "I think I better take the bread out of the oven before it burns."

Gabe lingered as if he were glued in that spot. He had a ridiculous impulse to take out his pocket knife and cut the carpet where they stood to kiss, in the way a victorious football team takes a section of goal post as a reminder of a great moment. *If I could turn back into Blake, I could make this work. Blake is the master of seduction, always suave and in charge. Sex is the game and he's the champion. This attraction to Taylor is more than sex or amusement. It's different. Could this be love? Do people really fall in love that fast? How would I know? I don't know anything about love. Worse yet, love in the middle of an investigation. Can love start with a lie and end who knows where?*

"Dinner is served," Taylor's sparkling voice cut through the fog in his mind as she set a steaming bowl of red beans and rice on the small glass top table.

He kept the dinner conversation light. She seemed to appreciate the time to regain her composure as much as he did.

"No more. Thank you. I'll curl up on the sofa like a lazy cat and fall asleep if I eat another bite. Dinner was delicious."

"I'm glad you don't mind quick cuisine."

"If I say I like it, do I still get the invitation for the four-course dinner?"

"Certainly and I'll throw in a second dessert."

Only if it's you, he thought.

His hand reached across the table to touch hers. For a moment, anything was possible.

RING! RING!

Taylor pulled her hand away from his and reached behind her for the wall phone.

"Dr. Kendall."

"Sorry to bother you at home, Doc, but I heard something you'll want to know."

"What's that Ray?" she repeated loud enough so Gabe could hear.

"Earl freaked out big time on the van and caused the driver to have a wreck, now Earl's locked up in a padded room at South Bay Hospital."

"Was anyone hurt in the accident?"

"The driver broke his nose and another patient sprained her ankle trying to climb out of the van before the paramedics arrived. Otherwise the telephone pole survived the hit."

"Ray, have you told anyone at MACS?"

"No. I left a telephone message for Dr. Locke and another for Neva. I was working late to finish charts at the nurses' station when the call came from the van company informing us that they were bringing in another car to transport the other two patients. I told them to fax an accident report to Neva tomorrow morning."

"According to protocol, do we need to inform anyone else?"

"Not that I know of. Oh, yeah. A doctor from the South Bay ER phoned asking about prescription drug information. Since I knew about the accident, I pulled Earl's file and gave him the history we had. Unless Earl is slipping something on the side, he's only on Nutracuratives and that's glorified vitamins. Was it okay to say that?"

"It might be crossing a line of patient confidentiality without written authorization, but it was an emergency. What's the MACS policy for emergency requests?"

"I'm not sure since I never have to handle these things. Was I wrong, Doc?"

"Maybe, Ray. You have to be careful to get a proper authorization before you say anything about patient information, even if it seems harmless on the surface. What if the caller wasn't an ER doctor?"

"Neva will write me up over this, won't she?"

"Not necessarily. Tell it to Dr. Locke first thing. Let him deal with it. Are you still at MACS?"

"No. I transferred calls to the answering service. I'm at home."

"Thanks for the information."

"Oh, yeah, Doc, one more thing I almost forgot."

"What's that?"

"Harry wants to meet you tomorrow after work."

"Harry will meet with me," she repeated, reflecting Gabe's thumbs up signal, "Where and what time?"

"Downtown Bar & Grill. Anytime after six."

"Downtown Bar & Grill. Where's that?"

"It's a St. Petersburg landmark. There's a whole subculture of Pinellas County that you are missing. This is practically a tourist attraction in drinking circles."

"Are you going to be there?"

"Sure, but I'll go on my own and meet you. It's not a good idea to leave work together. If there's any change in plans, I'll let you know."

"Thanks, Ray."

"One thing, Doc. Don't tell anyone, not even Locke that you are meeting Harry."

"Why the secrecy?"

Ray paused, cleared his throat, and then spoke almost in a whisper, "After he threatened to go to Medicare when he didn't get his final expense check, his apartment was trashed. Did five hundred dollars worth of damage that he had to pay, plus losing his security deposit."

"How terrible to be vandalized on top of losing his job."

"It wasn't vandalism; it was a message."

"Ray, it was probably kids looking for quick sale items to get cash for drugs."

"Druggies don't draw your face on a cloth doll, stick it with pins and hang it over your bed with a sign that reads 'Silence is golden. Talk is certain death.'"

"That sounds like a voodoo doll."

"That's what Harry's neighbor said. She's a Haitian refugee. Took one look at the weird symbols spray painted on his living room wall and ran out screaming. She said she could feel evil all over that place. He moved out and hangs with friends. He asked me to let it be known at MACS that he went to Citrus County. He doesn't want anyone to know he's in town."

"If he thinks his life is in danger, why doesn't he go to the police?"

"Harry says he doesn't want to end up like Peter."

"Peter? What happened to him?"

"You can ask Harry tomorrow. See you at work Doc."

Gabe wondered what was happening as Taylor dumped the contents of her briefcase on the floor and rummaged through the papers. She grabbed an odd looking printed sheet and shouted,

"It's him. It's Peter Lane; another missing link."

Gabe sat on the floor beside her. She handed him the paper. "This anonymous note was left on my desk in an inter-office communication envelope. It's starting to make sense. Jim King, Magna's CEO, asked if I knew about the circumstances of the death of a MACS patient named Greg Newman. I'm trying to find out about the other names."

"Bring me up to speed on what happened while I was out of town."

Taylor tried her best to condense the events of the last two days and yet explain the depth of her concern for the odd behaviors and general climate of distrust at MACS. What a relief to have a friend like Gabe, a nonjudgmental and extremely agreeable sounding board.

"I must sound as out of touch as my patients. Don't feel like you have to honor your offer to help me if you think it's all too outrageous."

"Why don't you make some coffee? Sounds like we'll need it to sort out this puzzle."

His expression showed no sign of being patronizing or shocked. Somehow he accepted it in stride without adding the "How did a nice girl like you end up in a place like this?" patronization or, worse yet, the explosive reaction that Dale would have if he thought that MACS was not a suitable residency site. "Good idea. It'll take a few minutes."

Gabe helped her up and then went over to the sofa to examine the paper. He realized that these were the names on the note she left for him at the gallery. The yellow sticky note on top of the copy instructed him to "Take this information and my briefcase, if you find it, to Dr. Sebastian Dale at Knight University if something happens to me." Taylor was a brave, assertive woman, not inclined to jump at her own shadow. Clearly, she was afraid and MACS was the source of her fears. That irked him. When he agreed with the Director to seek out and befriend a new female employee as an inside source, he didn't think she would be in danger.

The Girard pattern involves verbal and financial intimidation, nothing physical like assault or murder. What happened to change a successful pattern? How many times had Marco railed against the stupidity of drug dealers, bank robbers and kidnappers? As he often said, "Why would a gentleman soil his hands like a common criminal when money can be had so easily with charm, cleverness and, frankly, fine marketing?" Violence didn't fit the Girard equation. Who inside MACS is behind this change?

Scanning the built-in bookcase across from the sofa, Gabe spotted Taylor's DVM IV-TR. He walked to the bookcase, turning his head toward the efficiency kitchen where he could see Taylor's shadow. He called out, "Say, I think I would like a little dessert after all. Do you have anything?"

She appeared at the door. He dropped his hand away from the bookcase.

"All I have are some ready to bake cinnamon rolls that will take about ten minutes. How's that?"

"Great. I could use a sugar boost to charge my brain cells. Meanwhile, hope you don't mind if I get to know you better by looking at your books."

"I do that too. I learned it from Dr. Dale, my graduate advisor. He says that you can learn a lot about people from their book collection. While I bake, why don't you play psychologist and analyze my bookcase."

"Fair enough. I'll try," he said with relief at finding a viable excuse for snooping.

Once she was back in the kitchen, he reached for the large Diagnostic and Statistical Manual of Mental Disorders, Fourth Edition or as known in the profession, DSM-IV. When he started the doctoral psychology program, he used a prior edition. Deftly he flipped pages toward Personality Disorders.

Even as a grad student this section seemed more like my family tree than a diagnostic tree. There's plenty of Antisocial Personality Disorders at our family reunions. Most people would swear that the charming Marco could never be anti-social, since he is the life of the party. In diagnostic terms, antisocial isn't about being a recluse, quite the opposite. It's a rogue's gallery featuring deceit, manipulation, lies, con games, rationalizations, blaming victims, pleasure seeking, superficial charm and a total disregard for the rights of others. Some of the "associated features" are characteristics often seen in our frequently uprooted household, such as poor parenting skills, low empathy and the inability to sustain a monogamous relationship. In short, my father typifies the dangerous yet engaging white-collar psychopath.

As for those antisocial personality disorders who are aggressive, violent and comprise a large part of the incarcerated male population, they are the ones he and Victoria would hire as bodyguards, not as enforcers. Marco never wanted a trace of violence to be linked with him. Besides, as he often pointed out, "Psychopaths are a dime a dozen, my son, but true genius lies in using their craft well-hidden behind a choir boy image." As a psychiatrist, he knew exactly what he was, what they all were. I still recall how indignant he was when I confronted him with what I had learned about him. He laughed at me for suggesting that such an evil nature was problematic.

Turning a few pages forward, Gabe found Narcissistic Personality Disorder. Dr. Dale had been uncharacteristically complimentary of Blake's case study of this disorder. *Dale was actually speechless when I explained that my presentation of this disorder was merely a verbal portrait of my mother, Serena. She revels in being entitled, impatient, patronizing, demanding and exploitive. Even as a small child the rules were clear; her needs were imperative, everyone else's needs were foolishness or whining.*

Like a man falling through a time machine, he was again thrown back to that day as a child who fell from his pony into the rose garden. He was cut and bleeding, with thorns visible in his wind-reddened cheeks and tiny hands. Nanny went out to help him, but he pushed her away and ran up the winding staircase.

In spite of Nanny's insistence that his mother was unavailable, Blake knew she was home.

Earlier that morning, Nanny had dressed Blake in a velvet suit and told him that his mother asked for him to go into the music room and play the violin for her guests. Serena was there, sitting in her throne like chair wearing a silk dress with her trademark emeralds adorning her neck, ear lobes, and both wrists. He had run to hug her and this she time let him. Her dress was soft and her hair smelled like violets. He played his best so she would be proud. When her lady friends applauded, she smiled approvingly at him and called him "Our Little Prince." Then she summoned Nanny to take him back to the children's wing.

Hours later he was still elated by his mother's attention. That likely fueled his overconfidence in pressing the pony to jump the garden bench near the roses. The overconfidence extended to believing that Mother would tend his hurts instead of Nanny. Entering the partially open master bedroom door without knocking, he saw her sitting at the dressing table arranging her hair. She looked like an angel in a long white beaded evening dress. He ran up beside her and tried to climb onto her lap. She looked startled, and then saw a drop of blood fall from a thorn in his cheek to her dress.

She pushed him to the floor, rose up and went to the three-way mirror to examine the barely visible blood stain, "Oh, you horrid child, look what you did! I can't wear this tonight. All my friends are waiting to see my new Halston gown. Now I'll have to wear something less spectacular. How could you cause me such embarrassment?" Serena's ravings continued but little Blake heard nothing more. He cowered beneath the dressing table until Nanny came, picked him up and took care of him. Nanny pulled the thorns out of his skin, but she couldn't heal the ones that pricked the little boy's heart and lingered in the man's memory.

"I see you've chosen one of my favorites," Taylor pointed

to the book he held as she walked toward the sofa with a tray bearing two coffee mugs and a plate of hot cinnamon rolls.

He closed the book and sat it on the coffee table, "I was curious."

"Yes, it's fascinating reading. My sister Savannah calls it the All Purpose Catalog of Weirdness. Actually, it's a diagnostic manual used by mental health professionals," she reached for the book to show him. "I remember my first course in Abnormal Psychology. Dr. Dale warned us about a syndrome he calls OCDD."

"Isn't that where people wash their hands too much?" he asked, knowing the answer but allowing her the punch line.

"No. That's obsessive-compulsive disorder. Dale's version of OCDD is the Obsessive Compulsion to Diagnose any Disorder. He says it's common for graduate students to run around finding psychological symptoms in themselves and everyone else. As he predicted, it usually wears off by second year."

"Great coffee. Now show me how you might diagnose some of your strange colleagues."

She placed her coffee mug back on the tray and started to flip through the DSM.

"Okay, I'll take an easy one like Victoria." She slowed down page turning in the section on Mood Disorders.

Good choice, Victoria is definitely not subtle.

"Of course, you understand that I don't know much more than a few rumors about her social history and nothing about her medical or mental health history, but I have been in the room with her when she spoke rapidly about a flurry of grandiose ideas that had no connection. After nearly an hour of that, she suddenly became very withdrawn and sullen. Recently, in the Executive Staff meeting, she had a manic episode that seemed to surprise no one. Clearly they've seen it before and I've also seen her shift from low energy to explosive anger."

"Okay, Doctor, what's your best guess?"

"Well, I would certainly take a serious look at Bipolar Disorder. I would need to know more to be accurate. However, I also overheard Jordan practically beg Carla to get Victoria's medication before the big meeting finished. That tells me Victoria's disorder is known at least to some people outside the family."

"So Bipolar people would be hard to live with?"

"Depending on the stage of their mood cycle, yes. She's hard enough to work around in her better moods. If Sally weren't such a brown-noser, she'd never be able to survive Victoria's verbal abuse."

"Sounds complex," he replied. As she showed him how to follow the decision tree he thought, *Her first guess was right. Bipolar Disorder is the current equivalent to Victoria's original diagnosis of manic depression. As for medication, sometimes Victoria substituted her idea of a generic equivalent; a gin and tonic.*

"So Dr. Kendall, what about Serena and Marco?"

"Well, I don't see either of them that much, but watching Serena, I'd say she is very self-absorbed."

"Maybe she's confident."

"No Gabe, it's more than that. Just try to make a suggestion or offer another opinion and her eyes fire a look that would cut granite while she trashes your idea. She certainly behaves in narcissistic ways, but I'd be reluctant to label anyone a Narcissistic Personality Disorder without good reasons."

He struggled to maintain a poker face while thinking how her gut reactions were accurate.

"And what about the debonair Dr. Marco?"

She paused for another sip of coffee. "He has me puzzled. Granted he's a flirt and a manipulator among the staff, but I don't know if it's real or an act to support a business image he likes. And that's part of my confusion about what I see happening at MACS."

"In what way?"

"Dr. Marco seems sincere about the PHP programs and about professional training. So he made a pass at me. When I ignored it, he let it go. And while I think he went overboard in trying to explain away Harriet's death to the staff, I suppose he was protecting the programs. After all he is a psychiatrist with superb credentials. Did you know he was the founding President of the Inter-American Society for Psychological Research? He even told me how he pioneered treatments for schizophrenia in areas where these poor patients were still locked in prisons. He has a long professional history working with this disorder."

It took all of Gabe's determination to stifle a reaction. *With all she knows about deviant behavior, she's been taken in by a psychopath. Sure I know about the Society credentials. After all, we created that ruse together and then folded the organization after the first annual convention, but not before taking thousands of dollars in dues and contributions. The ornate, calligraphy certificate of appreciation from the Society's phantom board to the esteemed Dr. Marco was one of my best gift-giving ideas for his birthday. It's probably hanging on the wall at MACS, another of Marco's many awards that are easy to claim and impossible to check.*

"Taylor, be careful who you trust at MACS. From what you told me, there are a lot of inconsistencies. Nothing happens that isn't at least tacitly approved from the top. That means either Marco or Sam Locke know what's happening and approve or ignore."

"Not Locke. I don't believe he knows everything."

"Then the Girards, all of them, must be in on it."

"Wait a minute. The strangest reactions I've seen come from Gina Girard and Lorraine Lewis; and of course, Neva, Lorraine's clinic watchdog." Taylor shuffled through a notebook, opening it to an organizational chart of MACS clinics that was in her introduction packet. "Look at this. Locke is Clinical Director over the PHPs and Lorraine is the Director of Nursing. Both of them go out to visit other clinics, but Locke seems to be gone more often than Lorraine."

"What do you make of that?"

"I've also heard Locke complain about being given extra administrative duties that take him away from operational oversight of the clinics. Brook says that Lorraine constantly undermines Locke's orders but it takes weeks for him to find out. Plus Lorraine has a direct line to the royal family as Gina's live-in friend."

"What about the other Girards who work there?"

"Forget Carla. She's hard working and honest. To me, her best reference is that Lorraine obviously hates her and Gina resents her. Isn't that sad considering Gina and Carla are sisters? As for Gina, she's diagnosable on several counts. She and her mother, Victoria, are a few peas short of a pod."

Gabe laughed aloud at her remarkably accurate descriptions. "What about their brother?"

"Felipe, the gnome, or Blake the wonder boy?"

"Both."

"The way I see it, Felipe must be the postman's son. He is nothing like Marco or Serena. Maybe that's why they treat him with such obvious disdain. I get the feeling that he only works at MACS because he can't hold a job anywhere else."

"And their other son?"

"Blake? I've never seen him in person, only his stately portrait in the Executive Suite lobby. You ought to see it: tousle-haired, sun-blonde rich boy coming in from riding his polo pony. He looks bored with the planet. My first reaction was that he has a love affair with his mirror, like his mother does, but the rumor is that he's brilliant and charming. At the mention of his name, Serena sits up even straighter and gets that Queen Mother smile."

"Where is he now?"

"That's a big mystery. Only Carla speaks to her brother or half-brother or whatever he is. She told me that the family is officially forbidden to contact Blake until he returns and apologizes for whatever he did to offend them. Meanwhile, the rumor mill says that he runs around Europe and South America gambling, making fast bucks trading on the currency exchanges and having affairs with models and actresses. Frankly he sounds like an immature snob. Someday he'll meet his match."

He already has, Taylor.

"Be fair, maybe he's no longer the same guy you see in that old portrait. Since he left the Girards' cocoon, don't you think he's had time to come to terms with different attitudes, different values? You might even find that you like him."

"I doubt that. I saw my share of prep school boys at Vanderbilt. Now that I think of it, Trey was one of them. And besides, I sense that MACS isn't big enough for Marco and Blake to share control."

"Why is that?"

"If he's as much like Marco as Carla says, then they will end up in a struggle for domination that could split the family into two camps. Who knows what that would do to MACS?"

"Is there a picture of him in these promotional brochures?"

"No, there is just the portrait on the fifth floor. Carla says it was painted ages ago when he was home from college. It's the only picture of Blake that Marco allows in the office."

"Do you see it often?"

"No. I'm not among the simpering secretaries who look for excuses to deliver papers as a pilgrimage to gaze into his luscious blue eyes."

"I guess you think he's handsome."

Taylor reached over and placed her hand on his, "In a brash sort of way, yes. And his eyes are truly beautiful, even though they are probably painted as the artist's interpretation instead of the real color."

She ran her free hand into his brown, slightly gel moist hair thinking momentarily how much better he would look by letting his hair flow softly around his forehead the way Blake's does. "Actually, your face is a similar shape. You may be about the same height, difficult to tell. But I think you are attractive in a more genteel way. Besides he's probably gained a lot of weight and gotten leathery skin from too many nude beach parties on the Riviera."

He drew her into an embrace, initially to discourage further comparisons with his alter-ego. Jagged thoughts interrupted his enjoyment of her nearness. *So she likes plain, gray-eyed, slick-haired Gabe as the average yet sincere kind of guy. Blake gets typecast as, well frankly, as what he used to be. My God, she's good at reading people. Too good. Can she see beyond this disguise? Is she baiting me? No, that's not her style. She's direct. And if she thought I was Blake, she'd say so. Good going, man. She's falling for the phony and developing contempt for the real man. The Director warned me that this assignment was going to hit too close to home. I was prepared to deal with my feelings about the family. I wasn't prepared to be ambushed with feelings for Taylor Kendall. I'd given up believing that a woman like her existed.*

"Existed?"

"Sorry. My daydreams again."

"You daydream while you hold me?" she said with raised eyebrows and he could not tell whether they were indicative of real irritation or feigned amusement.

"Of course. I was thinking of you in a silver evening gown with me in a tux dancing on clouds across a star-filled surface where mundane things like MACS don't exist," he made a fast recovery.

"I think you've been auditioning for too many fantasy plays lately, but I do like the imagery. However, we better get back to mundane MACS and its latest bizarre episode."

CHAPTER 22

He picked up the anonymous letter and propped it up against a silk plant on the coffee table. He took her wire bound notebook and copied each name on a separate page. Next he drew a line down the center of each page. He labeled one side as "what we know" and the other side as "what it means". Using the pen as a pointer, he reviewed the facts, "Here are the names you were given plus Harriet's name. All we know is that something unusual has happened to each of them. We have to find the details to see if there is a connection and if MACS is that connection."

She turned the page back, "Greg Newman died from jumping off the Sunshine Skyway Bridge after he had been a patient at MACS. Here's some information I pulled off the computer from old newspaper articles."

She displayed three pages of news clips with nothing remarkable. It sounded like a garden-variety suicide by a depressed man. He left no note. Relatives weren't surprised considering his erratic behavior over the years. Those relatives did look twice at the MACS building and local agencies hoping to profit from the troubled man's swan dive off the 190-foot center span into the deep waters of a major shipping lane.

Gabe wrote down an abbreviated version of her comments.

"Peter Lane worked at MACS and now he's gone. Hank, Ray's friend, knows something but he's hampered by some bizarre, occult style threats. He either heard something or saw something that is dangerous to them as well."

"Dangerous to whom?"

"Certainly dangerous to Lorraine and probably to Gina too,

but I don't know how far up the corporate line it extends."

"What do you know about Martha Sanders?"

"Nothing and I don't even know where to start," Taylor admitted tapping her pen, a habit he noticed that she seemed to do while thinking deeply.

"I have an idea. I have some time off tomorrow; I'll take these names to the courthouse and check some records."

"What records?"

"I can start at the Vital Statistics office; look for birth and death certificates. Then I'll check on property ownership and professional licenses. Some of it I can even find using my computer," he offered, knowing that Geek Boy would have the full dossier on these people before the foam fell on his triple shot latte.

"That would be wonderful, Gabe. Are you sure you don't mind spending your day off doing research?"

"Not if I'm repaid with lunch at the bench?"

"That's a deal."

"And, Taylor, I'm going to tag along at the bar meeting." He saw her mouth open to protest and he touched her soft lips with his fingers, "I won't take no for an answer, but I do promise to say out of sight and not interfere unless you need me."

"Don't tell me that you've played a detective before? Or have you played the part of a secret agent like in the CIA or Interpol?"

"Nothing quite like that, however I'm willing to play Watson to your Sherlock Holmes."

She jumped off the sofa and dashed to the kitchen. Startled, he remained in his seat. She walked back in with something hidden in a hand behind her back.

"Okay, what's the game?"

"Your mention of Sherlock Holmes reminded me of the piece de resistance that I have in my hand."

"What is it?"

"Not so fast, Mr. Pretend Detective. This was tough to get. I want to enjoy the suspense a little longer."

He kicked off his loafers and propped his feet up on the adjacent ottoman, lounging back on the plush sofa. "Okay, Dr. Kendall alias Sherlock, tell me the gory details of your discovery complete with the show and tell item."

"Actually, the idea hit me when I was telling a social work intern how to better communicate with some of our older patients by using all powers of observation and never missing the obvious clues. Dale said that was like being a Sherlock Holmes. You remember: Sherlock got the call after Scotland Yard was totally baffled. Without DNA, modern forensics or even yellow crime scene tape, Holmes looked beyond the obvious to see the clues everyone else missed and that's how he solved the crime."

Another familiar Dale story. "Sounds promising, so how does that adapt to MACS?"

"Watch closely!" she exclaimed, bringing her right hand from behind her back to reveal a slim glass container about the size of a small jar filled with an orange liquid. She sat it gently on the end table between the sofa and matching overstuffed arm chair. Turning on the lamp, she held the container up to the light.

"Notice we have what appears to be orange juice or at least a harmless orange liquid, " Taylor paused, placing the container back on the table, "I was thinking about something Brook said about the Nutracuratives, 'Whatever it is, it's not what we think it is.' That made me wonder, what if the Nutracuratives aren't safe? As a nutritional supplement, they aren't FDA approved. What if there's a problem in the lab? Could too much of a good thing kill as well as cure? What if something or someone makes the formula toxic?"

Gabe sat up straight. Getting a vial of Nutracuratives was a stroke of genius. How he wanted to grab that container and fly it to the FBI lab tonight for analysis. He had to tame his enthusiasm and see what she had planned.

"You aren't doing any Jekyll - Hyde experiments with this,

are you?"

"Of course not! Remember, I told you about the time when Gina slapped the cup out of my hand so I wouldn't drink it? The next day, Neva made a point of standing outside my testing room while she told a new tech how the Nutracuratives have an unexplained positive effect on schizophrenia symptoms that might actually be unsafe for non-impaired people. She compared it to the way stimulants diminish hyperactivity in ADD children when the same stimulant could have an adverse impact on a non-ADD person. I asked Locke about it, but he doesn't know what's in the Nutracuratives. Apparently only Dr. Marco and Gina know. It's based on some secret herb from the Amazon jungles. I guess Neva's explanation is plausible if it's true."

Gabe's mind was racing at how to best handle this without appearing pushy. "I'm sure you want to have this analyzed for chemical content."

"Yes, I plan to do that. Since it's really important I only feel comfortable trusting that Federal Express will get it safely to the hospital in Memphis where my Daddy's friends are on staff. Someone there could get it analyzed."

He wanted to discourage any delays. "Listen, I have a friend at University of South Florida medical school; the 'chemistry is my life' kind of person who loves a challenge, plus the availability of the university's equipment. I'll take it tomorrow, and then go to the courthouse."

Sensing her internal struggle, he said, "I would never interfere in your work. You are taking the risk and you know what's at stake. I'm offering to help so that your absence won't appear suspicious. You decide. How did you get this?"

Taylor smiled, eager to tell about what she thought was a slick move, "Well, I heard the techs talking about how Mrs. Jerkin often gets indigestion after lunch and refuses her afternoon Nutracurative. So I stayed near her and offered to push her wheelchair into group. When she complained that she didn't want the drink, I took it and hid it in the planter on the high room divider. Another advantage of being tall; the other female staff can't reach that high, much less look up there for anything. After group was underway, I slipped out and reclaimed the drink. Unless there are hidden cameras in the philodendron, no one saw me."

Not bad for an amateur. "Very Sherlock. Are you a fan of crime movies and books?"

"Sometimes, but not as a steady diet. I like the more cerebral crime solving that Sherlock did rather than the car chasing, gun blasting, perfect-haired detectives on television."

He held the container with the orange liquid up to the light. It looked like ordinary juice, no trace of unusual sort of sediment. "Is this the same formula that you almost drank?"

Taylor winced at the question.

"What's wrong?"

"I don't think this is an 'R' code formula."

"Does that make any difference?"

"It must. The formula that Gina didn't want me to drink was an 'R' code," her eyes suddenly lit up like spotlights and her mouth slid into a big grin. "Ray also told me that Harriet's label was changed to an 'R' code the week she died, but most of the patients are coded with other letters. From scanning the drink trays, there are few 'R' codes."

"Could it have to do with patients who are allergic to something?" he questioned trying to search his memory of psychopharmacology. "Is it a different formula for patients who are either beginning or ending treatment? Or is it for patients who are taking some other kind of drugs?"

"I didn't know you were so familiar with medical procedures."

"I suppose saying that I watch 'ER' and 'Grey's Anatomy' isn't enough?"

She shook her head, folding her arms in a wait and see attitude.

"Okay, you caught me. I did some part time work with a medical clinic when I was in high school and college."

"What kind of work?"

"Strictly grunt work. File charts. Run errands for the doctors. It was only a summer job, but I did listen a lot. At one time, I even thought I might go into health care."

"Why did you choose acting instead?"

"I needed more variety, more challenges. My current work gives me that and still lets me explore the nuances of human behavior."

She gave a slight "oh well" shrug of her shoulders, typical of a driven career person who can't really understand anything that appears to be less than full throttle.

"Taylor, do you think you can get a sample of an R-code Nutracurative?"

She paused, mentally reviewing the schedule in which Neva or one of her nurses brings the cart out from the nursing station during the break after the community group session and again before the last afternoon group. "I have an idea where the Nutracuratives are kept," she revealed watching his obvious interest. "That's the good news. The bad news is that the formulas must be stored in Gina's lab."

"Didn't you tell me that getting into that place was like breaking into Ft. Knox?"

She smiled and walked over to the desk to get her purse. With a Cheshire cat grin, she pulled out what appeared to be a green credit card, "And here is the key to the kingdom."

He looked intently at the card with a good guess as to its significance but waiting for her to reveal it.

"This is the new, improved access card. With this I can get into any floor at MACS, even the second floor."

"Are you certain?"

"Yes. When Carla recoded it for me, she warned about full access and said not to tell Gina that the card also worked on the second floor. To be honest, I felt a little guilty about it all."

"Why?"

"Well because the approval came when Victoria was in a major manic mood and trying to show off for the visitors. Even Carla said that Victoria probably didn't mean full access but that it didn't matter since Carla knew that I could be trusted. Now I'm planning to use the card to spy on MACS."

How can she think she is being dishonest to the family who lived by what Victoria long ago termed a "toilet paper" code of employee relations; use for the dirty work, then toss. If the unholy trinity did catch Taylor in her spy game, they would be thrilled to have an instant scapegoat. Then he said, "Taylor, you told me that under law and ethics you have to protect your patients from harm. It looks like the potential for harm comes from the Nutracuratives. Let's say you check it out and find nothing, no big deal. But if you find something…"

"Then I head immediately for the police before someone else gets hurt!"

"No, if you find something, you take it to Dr. Dale. Let him make the proper contacts and you stay out of sight. I don't want to see any voodoo dolls hanging around here. Someone in MACS plays rough."

She failed to stifle a yawn. He looked at his watch. *All this intrigue was tiring her out and energizing me. Time to make a gracious exit, preferably with the sample.*

"I don't want to wear out my welcome," he said smiling and reaching out to touch her silky soft cheek. "You need to get some sleep. Let's meet for lunch at the bench tomorrow."

When he removed his hand to help stack the papers, she paused then asked, "What about the formula?"

"What about it? Do you want me to take it for analysis?"

"I have an idea. Why don't you take half of it and I'll send the other half to Memphis?"

He made a supreme effort not to let his face show how much

he hated that idea. *Chemical analysis with a small sample is tricky at best, inconclusive at worst. How many times has that concept been drilled into all the field agents by endless memos from the lab? Still, half is better than none. Besides, I'll have results long before she does.* "Okay, seems like a good idea for comparison." Not to mention the advantage he held in knowing the truth about Marco's Amazon jungle discovery.

"Tomorrow I'm going to look for an R-code and try to get a sample."

"Don't act suspicious or in your case, guilty. People with something to hide are always on the alert. I don't want to see your name on that mystery list of disappearing people."

They went into the kitchen. She took a clean container and poured out half. A few precious drops ran down the side and she wiped them with a paper towel. He took the sample and put it in his shirt pocket. They walked hand in hand to her front door.

"We never got to swim," she said pointing to the pool that appeared quite ethereal with overhead moonlight shining down to dance across the water surface amid a bevy of beams from the underwater lights.

"You're right. And I didn't get to see you in a swimsuit either," he answered using his eyes to survey her from head to toe, lingering at important spots.

She gave him a slight slap on the arm, "Is that why you invited me sailing?"

"Actually it wasn't, not consciously. Now that you mention it, what a fine idea."

He scooped her in his arms, kissing her ear, her cheeks and then moving to her velvet lips. *Her kisses make me wonder why we wasted so much of the evening talking about MACS. I have never wanted any woman as much as I want Taylor right now. An easygoing guy like Gabe might be used to waiting for what he wanted. Blake isn't. So why am I leaving? Walking away from her is physically and mentally painful.*

Taylor stood at the edge of the pool waving as he walked to his old sedan and backed out of the driveway. She closed the door, double-checking the deadbolt lock. Almost instantly, the underwater lights went dim leaving the faint amber glow from perimeter lights around the pool and patio. Either Lars and Sigrid were watching out for her or the lights were controlled by a pretty coincidental timer. With all of the disappearances at MACS, having a couple of live-in guardian angels around wasn't such a bad idea.

* * * * *

It was past midnight when Gabe climbed the stairs to his apartment. He flopped on the sofa, kicking off his shoes and reached for the phone.

"This is the Sims residence. At the sound of the tone, please leave a message…"

"Jack, wake up. It's Blake. I have to talk to you," he shouted into the phone as if his voice might jog his friend from sleep.

The line beeped then clicked off. He groaned aloud at the thought of getting up from the crater his body had molded into the sofa to find the note with the phone number he needed. He was drifting off to sleep when the phone on his chest rang like a fire siren. "Hello," he answered in a mellow tone.

"Obviously you weren't expecting me."

"Jack! I'm glad you returned my call."

"This better be worth it. I'm exhausted."

"Me too, but it is. I spent the evening at Taylor's."

"Wonderful. I'll hear your conquest story over coffee tomorrow. Now take a cold shower and go to sleep, man."

"It's not that kind of story."

"What! Blake the babe magnet didn't score? Stay where you are. I'll call the paramedics. You must be deathly ill."

"Give it a rest. You're ragging on me because I woke you up."

"Seriously, man, I'm worried about you. No action in Nassau.

No action tonight. What if the babes in D.C. hear about this? You'd be dropped from the list of Ten Most Wanted Men inside the FBI."

"I'll ignore that. Not that I owe you an explanation, but I'm keeping my contact with Taylor strictly business and it pays off like I said it would."

"Uh huh," a sleepy mumble went down the phone.

"Jack! Listen up! Taylor got a sample of the Nutracurative. I just got back from Tampa Airport where I had it packed in dry ice and sent for a rush analysis."

"Yo, man, good move!"

"Yes. I need Geek Boy first thing in the morning to get something solid on the mystery names. Every person named must to be located, dead or alive. We've got to find these people fast and interview the ones who can still talk. If necessary, get the paperwork started for protective custody until this thing is over. Taylor thinks I'm going to the courthouse to check on those names. Then we meet for lunch after she tries to get another sample."

"If somebody inside is as dangerous as you say, aren't we letting her get too exposed?"

"Don't worry. I'm watching her and she has a full access entry card. I'm going to finally accept her previous idea that we go snooping around over the weekend."

"Does the old man know about this? There's the danger of tainting evidence."

"Much as it pains me to admit, Jack-o, you're right. I'll tell him tomorrow morning," he yawned. "I'm out of gas. Got to get some sleep. We are closing in, I can feel it."

Jack echoed the yawn as he put down the phone. *Blake is finished with his story, so he's going to sleep. Now I'm wide awake at two freaking o'clock in the morning. Taylor Kendall must really be special for Blake to be patient with her when he is so persistently impatient with the remainder of earth and its lesser inhabitants.*

CHAPTER 23

When the alarm rang at six a.m. on Friday, Taylor was already up and curling her hair. After hours of tossing and turning, her mind refusing to quiet down, she gave up the idea of sleep and made coffee. Her efforts to reorganize the known information like a case history proved helpful.

Dale says that journalists have a simple formula for analyzing human behavior by asking the questions who, what, when, where and why. Determine those elements and the behavior, or response, begins to make sense. Even the irrational is rational for people who reorder their universe to support irrational thinking. Well draw a comic strip light bulb flashing over my head! That's what I've been trying to do. I've assumed that everything at MACS is rational and the patients are irrational. What if that's not true? I don't think it was true with Harriet or for the other names on that list.

At 6:40, she decided to call the hospital again. Daddy always said that an hour before the change from overnight to day shift was the worst period of pandemonium. Hoping to seize the advantage, she called South Bay, "This is Dr. Kendall. I need a condition report on Earl Hill."

"Sorry doctor, we can't give out any information."

"Excuse me! This happens to be my patient and I need to know!"

"According to my computer screen, there is no Dr. Kendall listed as the admitting or the consult. You'll have to call one of them."

"Fine, then I need the name and number of the admitting physician."

"If you're close to this case, then you already know that, don't you?"

The sound of the phone hanging up rattled Taylor. She picked up the phone again, dialed, and heard a familiar grumpy voice.

"Yes, I'll be at the cursed faculty meeting."

"Wait, Dale. It's me, Taylor."

"Ah, how's work going?"

"That's kind of what I called about."

"Taylor, I know it's not your dream job, but the written reports you've sent suggest that you are getting some good experience."

"I'm not calling to complain, Dale. I need your help."

"Case problem?"

"Yes, only I'm not sure who is more diagnosable, the patients or the staff."

"Welcome to the wide world of corporate-run professional psychology. It's different, but thanks to managed care, it's a world you have to learn," he replied pausing to pour another cup of coffee.

"I'm not calling to whine and this isn't what you warned as an 'adjustment disorder of the new job type.' At least one patient died mysteriously, a staff member was threatened and vandalized, and the wonder treatment may be not what it's supposed to be. In fact, it may be toxic."

"Those are pretty tough accusations. You'd better not say that to Dr. Girard unless you can back it up with facts."

"I'm saying nothing to him. His daughter and her playmate, the director of nursing, may be in it with him. Now we have a patient locked up in the South Bay psychiatric ward and I can't even get a condition report. I need to see you, Dale, today."

"Okay, come on in this afternoon."

"I can't leave, but if you can come over and make a surprise site inspection then I'll be in the clinic until three o'clock and then afterwards in my fourth floor office. Please, Dale, I wouldn't ask if it wasn't vital," her tone was uncharacteristically pleading.

"I'll see what I can do; if not today, maybe Monday." As he hung up, he heard her sigh and wondered, after all of the classes, tests, dissertations and clinic work what had happened to spook her like this.

* * * * *

The lukewarm pulsating shower sent water over his head and down his shoulders like the waterfall at the rear of Tio Pietro's cabin in the Andes Mountains.

BUZZ! BUZZ!

So much for enjoying the mood. He turned off the shower, buffed his lean body lightly with a towel and wrapped the towel around his waist. Pager or coffee? Coffee won. With the mug in his hand, he sat on a kitchen stool to look at the pager. He dialed that familiar phone number.

"I said I'd do my best to make the meeting; stop hounding me!"

"And a cheerful good morning to you, Dr. Dale."

"Blake!"

"I'm answering your summons."

"I got an odd phone call from Taylor Kendall at MACS. What's the international version of the Addams family up to now?"

There was always the chance that Dale would get drawn into this before it was over. Wait until he finds out that I've used him too.

"What's going on? It's more than what you've been telling me, isn't it?"

"Actually, Dale, it's a lot more. Now before you bellow, I can't talk on the phone, but I'll meet you for coffee later."

"Taylor wants to see me. She practically begged me to make a surprise inspection at MACS this afternoon. She sounds scared and that's not a common emotion for her. Do I need to go?"

"Yes, I think that's a good idea. Don't go witch-hunting.

Scratch that, bad example for MACS. What I mean is, keep it low key."

"Look, this whole business is making my blood pressure rise. What if I come over and meet you for lunch? It's confession time, boy, and it better be good."

"Not possible, I'm having lunch with Taylor."

"You're what?"

"Actually, I'm observing someone close to me, have lunch with Taylor."

"Now I know I need to get over there and find out what you're doing with her. This was not part of the deal."

"I know," Blake paused, well aware that the Director's wrath was puny compared with Dale's so he might as well face it. "Can we meet at Brenda's Breakfast Bar? It's a converted clapboard house on Fourth near Fifteenth Street. About ten o'clock?"

"Okay. You realize that chasing after you and Taylor will cause me to miss a faculty meeting."

"I sense your distress and guilt. The only person who'll be as happy as you are that you miss the meeting is Dr. Maxwell. Who knows? Maybe he'll actually get a positive vote on something if you aren't there to challenge him."

* * * * *

Seven o'clock. Enough time to try the hospital again.

"South Bay Hospital."

"I need to speak with Dr. Evans in ER."

"South Bay ER, nurses' station."

"Good morning, I need to speak with a resident, Dr. Evans."

"Evans? We don't have an Evans on ER rotation. Try Human Resources."

"Wait! Don't hang up! I'm looking for Dr. Evans, a psychology resident."

"Oh, yeah, him. He's not one of the real doctors."

Taylor bristled at the insinuation. *Let one of those scalpel-*

scavengers try passing a dissertation committee and we'll see who the real doctors are. Wonder where they keep the unreal doctors? "I'm Dr. Kendall and I need to speak with Dr. Evans as soon as possible. It's urgent."

"Everything in ER is urgent. What's your number? We're short two clerks and business is booming. I'll try to get it to him." She read back the number then said, "Wait a minute, I think I see him down the hall, hold on."

With that, the familiar hold music filled Taylor's ears. Dean Martin, Wayne Newton and Frank Sinatra sang without interruption. *Are they trying to make me hang up or torture me with lounge lizard fever? "On hold" is a kind of electronic purgatory where the caller waits an indeterminate time with no certainty of getting to the desired place.* Nearly ready to concede defeat, the phone clicked and a live voice said, "This is Dr. Evans."

"Jamal. It's Taylor Kendall."

"Hey Taylor! What's happening?"

"I need your help."

"That's a tough one. I owe my soul to this hospital and they take every waking moment."

"No problem. I need your help with a patient at South Bay Psychiatric unit."

"Why don't you come on over and see the patient? They're fairly good about letting community practitioners make visits. Who is the admitting?"

"That's what I don't know."

"But I thought this was your patient? Why don't you know?"

"What I'm about to tell you is extremely confidential, Jamal. Earl Hill is a patient that I work with in the MACS clinic. An ER physician who treated Earl phoned one of our staff who was working late with a request for prescription information. I don't think Earl was physically injured. All I get from several departments is a no comment on his condition. That's really strange. I want to know if he's okay," she explained trying to sound more empathetic than intense.

"Who would be the admitting from MACS?"

"Possibly Dr. Marco Girard's name would be used, but he's actually out of town."

"Why don't you get someone at MACS to inquire?"

"Jamal, I can't explain it all right now. Let's just say that I'm concerned about my patient's welfare and I think that MACS will want to get Earl out of there too fast for all the wrong reasons," she knew she had to tell him something to spark his curiosity. "I saw a patient die under peculiar circumstances my first day at MACS and she wasn't the first. That's why I'm concerned about Earl."

"Whoa, girl! That's heavy stuff. Have you talked to Dale?"

"Yes and he's concerned," she decided to embellish a bit. "He hoped you could help me and keep it low key. He'd consider it a personal favor."

"Anything for the main man. I can get up to the unit in an hour or so. What's the number at your office?"

"Don't call me through the MACS switchboard. I'll give you my cell phone number. And thanks, Jamal."

By the time she wrapped up her call with Jamal it was seven-thirty, six-thirty in Memphis. *Well, he probably still gets up early for rounds like Daddy did.* She dialed the number.

"Dr. Clifton's answering service."

"Good morning, this is Dr. Taylor Kendall, calling from Florida. I need to speak with Dr. Clifton as soon as possible."

"Is this an emergency, doctor?"

"Yes, it is."

"If you don't mind holding a minute, I'll try him at the hospital. All right, sugar?"

How nice to hear a gracious Southern accent; not a stern warning to hold or else. Rather a kind sort of "I really care about helping you" attitude that shows gentility isn't dead. No hold music, thank God. Taylor rested the phone receiver on her shoulder while gathering her briefcase, purse and the well-wrapped box containing the Nutracurative sample.

"This is Dr. Clifton."

Taylor hadn't heard his voice for years. Not since that last barbeque she attended with Trey, a strained event to say the least. She felt more seared on hot coals around Trey's parents than the ribs that were being roasted.

"Hello Papa Clifton, this is Taylor Kendall."

"Taylor! Are you in town?"

"No sir, I'm in Florida, but I need your help."

"Anything, just ask. Is something wrong with your Mama or the girls?"

"No, nothing like that. It's a medical matter with one of my patients," she paused. "Papa Clifton do you trust my judgment?"

"You've always been an honest, trustworthy young woman. I'm certain that you have become a fine young psychologist," he replied, knowing he had her attention he chose to digress. "In fact, I wish you'd come back to Memphis and work in my office. Several family practice physicians around here are adding psychotherapy. I'd be proud to have Tom's daughter working with me."

"And your daughter would have a heart attack knowing I was nearby," Taylor replied, recalling how delighted Trey's mother was that she remained in Florida.

"I swear I don't know how Sissy got to be such a controlling little snob. I like to think that she's influenced by Trey's daddy and his folks, but I suppose we have some blame too. Worst part is that her attitude rubs off on our only grandson."

"Papa Clifton, this isn't about Trey. I need a professional favor done in strict confidence."

"Name it, Taylor, and it's yours."

"You'll receive a Federal Express package containing a vial of liquid. I need to get it analyzed by the UT Medical lab as fast as possible."

"Is it toxic or viral?"

"No, it's supposed to be an herbal-based supplement in orange juice that is used with the schizophrenia patients at MACS. It's proprietary and not a prescription drug, so there's no published literature."

"I'm sure there's a good reason why you don't ask these people."

"Yes, sir, there is, but I can't explain it all right now. I may be totally off base and it's nothing more than the supplement it claims to be, but I need to know before I talk with my bosses."

"Okay, this is outside protocol, but I'll do it for you. Where do I reach you?"

"My numbers are on a note inside the box. Please don't tell anyone, anyone at all, what I've asked you to do or where you got the sample. It's really important."

"You have my word, young lady. Keep in mind that everything has a price. If I do this favor for you, do you promise to come over for dinner with me and Mama Clifton when you come back to Memphis to visit?"

She sensed a set up. "Yes. And yes, I think I know what you have in mind. I have to tell you that it won't work. I heard that Trey was seeing that Jarrett girl. My sister Savannah saw her looking at gowns at the bridal fashion show. Good thing I didn't wait around."

"Did you get married and not send us an invitation?"

"No sir, but I have a special man in my life."

"Well, all right, Taylor. But, it's not over 'til it's over."

* * * * *

At seven-fifty Taylor grabbed her things and ran to the main house back door. Stepping on the door mat sent a peal of bells announcing her arrival. The door opened.

"Good morning, Sigrid."

"Good morning, Dr. Taylor. Is this the package?" she said

reaching out her hand.

"Yes. It's all wrapped and I've phoned for a pickup before ten o'clock. All you have to do is give them the information on this card for the label."

"I prepare labels for every type of shipping. Miss M'etta sends packages all the time. She even has a personal account number if you need it."

"No, thanks, it's been prepaid. I sure appreciate it, Sigrid."

"Don't leave yet," she said firmly, then turned back into the kitchen. A moment later, she reappeared with an insulated sack. "Here's some hot honey biscuits to take to your office."

"Thanks, Sigrid! By the way, how's M'etta?"

"She's having a grand trip. Oh how that woman loves to travel."

"Next time she calls, give my regards," Taylor smiled, noticing how her mouth was watering already from the scent of those biscuits.

* * * * *

It was eight-ten when, while cutting across 38th Avenue ready to turn right on Fourth Street North, Taylor's cell phone rang. She fished around her purse to find it without taking her eyes off of the morning traffic.

"Dr. Kendall."

"Hi, it's Gabe. I'm ready to ferret out information at the speed of light."

"Would it be more time efficient if I meet you somewhere near the courthouse for lunch?"

"No! I mean, not necessary. After a few hours poring over papers I'll need a break at the best lunch spot in town. I'll see you at the bench."

"Thanks for your help. I don't feel so far out on a limb knowing you are out there with me."

"I'm happy to contribute to a worthwhile cause. Keep this in mind Taylor: don't act suspicious. You don't want them to think you're up to something."

"Then I better act paranoid to fit into the corporate culture."

Gabe flipped the cell phone shut and jammed it into his shirt pocket. Amazing how his casual, bordering on frumpy jeans with a worn plaid shirt and baseball cap pulled low over his eyes allowed him to move around the Federal Building without attracting attention.

The elevator doors were about to close when a huge hairy-knuckled hand intervened. Gabe stepped in, turning to say thanks. He hadn't felt so puny since before his growth spurt in high school. Those hairy knuckles were attached to an arm that went on and on before connecting to the torso of a man who must be at least 6'7". The other crane-like arm was on the shoulder of a petite spike-haired blonde whose skirt barely existed. She was holding on tightly to a baby stroller. If she bent over to tend that baby she'd surely be violating some nudity ordinance. The young mother continued a rapid fire conversation with an African-American woman and a frail senior adult woman. Their conversation appeared to be about various bouts with civilized society. Gabe smiled and nodded at the group.

The elevator gathered speed, and then stopped abruptly at the second floor. The casual banter halted as quickly as punching the mute button on the remote when two dark-suited men with poorly knotted ties entered. Gabe pulled the cap lower. *Why do bureaucrats insist on looking stereotyped? It's like a suit of armor that says "untouchable." Come to think of it, they do have that Eliot Ness expression.*

The giant man recognized them too, "Yo, people, better not talk. Big Brother's riding with us lookin' for somebody to bust."

Gabe marveled at the possibility of literacy from a Neanderthal. These guys must be IRS or bailiff trainees. Before the men left at the third floor, they had visually frisked the common folk in the elevator. He held the door open for them to exit. The shorter man turned back, "You better not be here to make trouble, boy."

"I'll do my best, sir, but I'm rarely successful," Gabe responded choking back a grin that veered close to rebellious. When the elevator door shut, the occupants laughed and cursed the representatives of the same government they were here to fleece, each in their own personal way.

At the fourth floor, Gabe gave high five to the Neanderthal and left. He purposely turned left toward the sign marked "Records" and waited for the next elevator to his real destination, "FBI Tampa Field Office". Trivial as it was, he chose to avoid letting his fellow sojourners know that he was one of those government stooges.

He didn't need to show his identification to the receptionist. He was well known, at least among the single women. Winding his way through the cubicles, he crept up behind a woman whose eyes were locked onto a computer screen and attached by headset to an audio tape player. He grasped her in a bear lock from behind her chair, his mouth pressing kisses on her neck, "My Moneypenny, how I've longed for you."

First startled, then delighted, she whirled her chair to face the kissing bandit,

"You scoundrel! You haven't checked in regularly." Her manicured fingers went straight to the cracked button in the middle of his plaid shirt, "You aren't on suspension, are you?"

"No, Gloria. This is part of my alter ego's wardrobe."

"Are you are getting your paychecks regularly?"

"Of course! I didn't have time to change this morning before going out to do the job so I can get paid."

She stood up to hug him, "Thank goodness. I count on you to bring style in here; not to mention how much I like your cute little butt in those tailored suits."

He stepped back, bending in a courtly bow, "Gloria, if I

can't find a woman like you, I shall enlist in the French Foreign Legion and forever mourn my failure."

"Get in my office before I call the French embassy and arrange your transfer," the Director's agitated voice rang out.

Blake paused to kiss Gloria's hand. She pointed to the gold coin necklace she was wearing and whispered, "If you weren't old enough to be my son, I'd keep you as my love slave."

"Do you think Lenny would approve?"

"Certainly, my husband is very liberal minded, particularly if you clean the pool."

"I'm waiting!" the Director bellowed.

"Yes, sir, here I am," Blake said, entering the office and pulling up a chair.

The Director shuffled papers in the third level of his in-basket, then checked a file in the fourth level. He pulled out a memo.

"I hear that you have my computer expert working for you again? Did I approve it?"

"Indeed."

"Since when? I have a monthly report backed up behind your monumental project. How do you figure I gave my approval?" the Director replied, reaching into his desk drawer for the ever-present roll of antacids.

"You told me to bring the MACS investigation to a close ASAP. I'm merely using the expertise of our highly efficient staff to make it happen."

"Shall I assume that what passes for a small scale national security alert that you initiated at the main lab is also about MACS?"

"Indeed. And I followed procedure to the letter."

He could not resist the urge to hear the answer, "How so, Agent Girard?"

"I obtained the sample from my contact late last night. At the earliest opportunity I personally drove the sample to Tampa

Airport for rush delivery."

"And that makes you special for something so simple a trainee could handle it?"

"I had two initial choices. Wake you out of a sound sleep after midnight or handle it myself. Because I value your expertise as my boss I wanted you to get a good night's rest, so I handled it. Now my first inclination was to fuel my plane and fly the sample directly to the FBI Lab. Since my car is at the townhouse in Virginia, I would have had to rent a car or get an expensive taxi roundtrip from Reagan Airport. Imagine how that would skew the expense reports. Not to mention, I wouldn't be able to check in this morning like I promised. As you can see, I did all of this for you."

Today he felt like what they called him, 'The Old Man', as he chewed two antacids and washed them down with flat cola, "Someday I'm going to stop being your straight man."

The door swung open and Jack strode in, "Hey, Blake, Geek Boy's on a roll."

"Jack, tell Derek to bring the information here. I might as well have some idea which wild goose chase my craziest agents are headed on today."

Derek "Geek Boy" Prentice walked in with an armload of papers. The Director took a pile of mail and files and tossed them on the carpet near his briefcase to make room for the printouts.

"Good morning, Mr. Girard. I think you'll be pleased with what I found," Derek said looking at Blake with undisguised admiration.

Blake smiled in return. Except for Geek Boy's fuzzy pilled knit tie, they were practically dressed alike. *Undercover work was my choice. I regret that I have but one fashionable image to give for my country.*

Derek started his explanation back at step one. Jack intervened to speed up the process, "Great work, dude. How about cutting to the bottom line? Our secret agent man has a meet shortly and

I've got to follow up on your leads."

"Oh, okay, sorry," Derek replied, nearly stuttering, "Well I made this chart."

Blake took the first copy from Derek, eager to see the results.

The Director gazed at his copy. "Look at this small print. Why so stingy with printer ink?" He took off his glasses and rubbed his eyes, "Jack, read it aloud."

"Greg Newman's suicide checks out. Police reports and autopsy report are unremarkable. Nearest relatives are in St. Augustine. We can get an agent from the Jacksonville office to do an interview. Otherwise, nothing more from the newspaper accounts."

Derek passed over a folder with the next name as Jack read, "Peter Lane, Licensed Clinical Social Worker. Last known job MACS. Left five months ago. Last month a complaint of professional misconduct was filed against him by Lorraine Lewis, RN."

"What kind of complaint?"

"Can't tell from here. Department of Health hasn't investigated yet."

"I'll have Gloria commandeer the information," the Director interjected.

Jack continued, "Apparently Lane moved without a forwarding address. No phone. And the notification from the state on the misconduct charge wasn't delivered. Checking his social security number, he's hasn't worked anywhere as a Social Worker since leaving MACS. Title records show he sold his car to a small time dealer in Clearwater who gives cash and isn't picky about clean titles. No record of another vehicle purchase. He registered with the Unemployment Office after he got fired from MACS, but he hasn't reported in again. He's missing in action."

Blake doubted the truth of that assumption. *Peter Lane is out there somewhere, probably in hiding. Taylor's meeting tonight with*

Hank may shed some light. He decided to say nothing about the meeting in case it didn't happen. He wanted to keep a full court press on finding all these people.

Jack looked at Derek, "Didn't you finish this?"

"Yes, sir, but I hit a lot of dead ends on the Sanders woman."

Blake read the sheet, "All we know is that Martha Sanders is a thirty-eight-year-old Caucasian woman, licensed as an RN in Florida and Alabama. She worked at the MACS clinic in Tampa. Last known address is an apartment on Davis Island." Turning over the second, then third page, he commented, "She has got quite a list of creditors. What do these codes mean?"

Derek took out his neon green gel pen to circle two sets of letters, "Basically the printout shows that Ms. Sanders left town suddenly without paying Tampa Electric, Verizon Telephone, Sears, and three gas cards. She even stiffed the Tampa Tribune news carrier. Say I use to deliver newspapers. People like that really tick me off."

"Stick to the subject, young man."

"Sorry, sir. Maybe she's with Peter Lane, since both disappeared suddenly."

Jack squinted at the information sheets trying to find the missing link, "What do you mean, they disappeared? Peter Lane surfaces occasionally. What about Martha Sanders? Is she working anywhere else in the state? Were her household goods confiscated for sale against her debt? Where is her car?"

"Don't know. Her apartment has been rented again. There's no credit card activity. Looks like she disappeared without a trace," Derek replied confident about his research.

"Did she file bankruptcy? Is she being sued by anyone? Is there a death certificate in Florida or any other state in her name?" Jack probed.

"No lawsuits. No death certificate, unless she died under an assumed name. I'll check on the bankruptcy filings."

As if the same thought hit them simultaneously, Blake turned to Jack and said, "Are you thinking what I'm thinking?"

"You mean that Ms. Sanders' disappearance is too neat and tidy?"

"Exactly."

"Would someone like to let me in on this?"

"How do you spell relief?" Blake said rocking back in his chair as a smug grin spread across his face. "Try, D-E-A. They have several nurses working undercover."

"How can that happen without us knowing about it, sir?"

"Go ahead, Jack, explain inter-agency cooperation to Geek Boy. Tell him why it's so hard for the good guys to stay ahead of the bad guys when the good guys are jockeying for territorial rights."

"Back it down, fellows. I'll shake down DEA for the information. Meanwhile, Blake, try not to alienate any other arms of the task force."

"Oh, come on, boss, you never let us have any fun."

A knock on the door interrupted the levity. Gloria opened the door barely enough to stick her head in, "Sorry to interrupt but you turned off the intercom button again. The men from Customs are here to consult on this case."

"Offer them coffee, then bring them in. We're wrapping up."

Blake stood up, "I've got to get back across the bridge for a meeting. My written report has all the details they need. Bluebeard found gold with less of a map than I've given them to locate the MACS numbered accounts in Nassau. Do you need me to stay or can Jack handle it?"

"Go ahead, all of you. I'll talk to them," the Director instructed. "Derek, stay on the computer research. Jack, you go back to St. Petersburg too. I want you within intercept distance of Blake from here on. And Blake, you stick as close as possible to Dr. Kendall. I want a live informant not a dead civilian and a PR nightmare."

Blake stifled the urge to say how much he enjoyed remaining close to her, "Don't worry about Taylor. She's bold, she's gutsy and she's out to set the world right. She won't back down under their threats."

"That's exactly what I'm worried about Blake. She sounds too much like you."

Jack stood up, put on his suit jacket and reached for his briefcase.

Blake gathered his papers and handed them to Jack, "Here, you keep this for me, okay?"

They walked out single file, Derek first, Blake in the middle and Jack close behind. The Director stepped over to the door to greet the two grim-faced Customs agents who were waiting to enter his office. Blake looked away to avoid making eye contact with the visitors. He recognized the shorter man as one of the men who rode up in the elevator earlier with him and the rowdy crowd. The Customs agent pointed toward the main office door as Blake was leaving, "Sir, you need to have someone watch that guy. He might be dangerous."

"You have no idea how right you are."

CHAPTER 24

Taylor arrived at the MACS clinic as green-shirted techs and social work interns were busy escorting the first van load of patients in the side door. She paused to speak to each patient by name the way Dr. Locke instructed all the staff to do each morning. He said it made a big difference in the patients' receptivity toward staff, which meant a potentially better start for groups. Taylor hoped that Locke would be here later when Dale dropped by. She wanted Dale to know that she did have onsite supervision from a working practitioner while Dr. Girard was jetting off to who knows where.

"Good morning, Dr. Kendall," Ray said with enthusiasm ringing in his voice. "I think this will be a very interesting day."

"Yes, Ray, I hope you're right," she replied, noting his emphasis on the word "interesting." She assumed he meant the meeting tonight with Hank.

During the second morning group, Taylor's cell phone vibrated in her lab coat pocket. She glanced down to see the number. South Bay Hospital; it must be Jamal. Trying to disguise her purpose, she called on Rocky, a loud-mouthed rambler to expound on his favorite subject, living alone. Once he got the floor he could go on indefinitely.

She rose from her chair, slipped out the door, and spotted a social work intern walking down the hall. "Angie, can you take over for a few minutes?"

"Oh, sure, Dr. Kendall," she nodded, taking the clipboard with group session notes from Taylor's hand.

The phone in the lounge was too close to the nurses' station. Nurses and techs were buzzing in and out, busy with charting and ordering lunch. Not wanting to go into the testing room at the opposite end of the clinic, Taylor ducked into the single seat staff rest room. She turned on the water faucet for background noise and hit the redial button. Luckily the call bypassed the switchboard.

"Doctor's lounge, Dr. Evans speaking."

"Jamal, it's Taylor."

"Say, I tried to check on your patient, but he's gone."

"Gone? Where? Who checked him out?"

"I was afraid you'd ask for details, so I copied the discharge order. It says that Earl Hill was released early this morning to his wife, Thelma. The order says the wife will handle transport."

"I thought that Earl was brought in by the police in an agitated condition? What doctor in his right mind signed him out in less than twenty-four hours?"

"You can find that out easily enough. It was your boss, Dr. Girard."

"No way, Jamal. Dr. Girard is out of town. Look at those discharge orders again. Is there any other name?"

"Oh, yeah, here's something. A nurse brought over the order from Girard and got a copy of Earl's inpatient record."

"Who is the nurse?"

"Someone with handwriting bad enough to be a surgeon. All I can make out is a big sweeping L, like that broad wore on her sweater. You remember the reruns of 'Laverne and Shirley' that we used to watch at the graduate lounge."

"Could the name be Lewis?"

"Yeah, could be."

"Thanks, Jamal. I need for you to keep this confidential."

"No sweat, my friend. Messing around with medical records isn't something I want to advertise around here."

"By the way, Jamal, how do you like being in the pioneer group for psychology in emergency room medicine?"

"It's fine. Good enough training and plenty of patient contact, but it's definitely not what I want to do after I get licensed. Too much like Friday night in the old neighborhood. Think I'd rather be in some posh little building where the abreactions are limited to nine-to-five with weekends off," he responded with a tone of envy.

"Actually, we limit them to nine-to-three followed by a few quality hours of paperwork."

"Psychology with banker's hours - you scored mama," Jamal said, yawning from a long night of overtime with another eight hour shift ahead.

"Maybe, if I can stay out of harm's way."

* * * * *

Blake walked into the restaurant that reminded him of a small New England family dining room with collector plates on high shelves lining the walls, overstuffed chairs and the smell of freshly baked bread. He spotted Dale near the far window table. From the moment he made eye contact, Blake knew his former mentor was indignant and it didn't take much to figure who was the immediate target of that wrath. Still, it was like going home again to see the man who radically changed the direction of his life.

Dr. Sebastian Dale rose from his chair. He hugged Blake with a fatherly, back-slapping hug. They sat down, delaying the conversation until the waitress poured a round of coffee and left. Dale spoke first, "You look great, boy. Clean living becomes you."

"I work too hard to get into trouble these days."

Dale stirred his coffee over and over as he always did when gathering his thoughts, "Okay, cut to the chase, boy. When I called you to ask if the MACS residency offer was safe for Taylor Kendall, you said it was. You also said that the MACS programs were legitimate..." he waved his hand, motioning for Blake not to interrupt, "...and you said that as far as you knew your bizarre family was serious about running real Partial Hospitalization

Programs. Now I've got a fine young woman caught in the middle. From the tone of her voice, I think something is extremely wrong. Explain."

Dale sat back, glaring at Blake the way he did at a student who foolishly showed up for class without doing the reading. Blake reached into his wallet and pulled out a one dollar bill. He wedged the bill into pages of Dale's calendar. "I'm paying in advance for a counseling session. You are now my therapist and I am your client so everything I'm going to say is strictly confidential."

"You know full well you are more of a son to me than a client, so keep your dollar and I will still honor the confidentiality. Let's hear your story."

"First, I want you to know that I didn't lie about MACS. They are doing serious psychotherapy groups. Their residency offer was a legitimate, albeit cheap, way to get talent that they probably bill out at higher rates for - same as with the Social Work interns - but that's speculation. The PHPs are the real thing with legitimate Medicare numbers."

"Then what's the problem?"

"At the time you asked me, there was some official curiosity into billing irregularities. I wasn't directly involved. Then more information surfaced and the situation took on a new urgency," he carefully stepped around the situation. "Since PHPs are directly administered by Dr. Samuel Locke and he checked out okay, I assumed that Taylor would be fine working with him."

"How generous of you to care about my students. How do you and the FBI figure into this?"

"I made contact with Taylor. She thinks of me as a confidante and a friend."

"Then she didn't go into MACS unaware? She never said a word to me. I even thought she was disappointed about taking that residency. Did she agree from the beginning to provide insider information for the FBI?"

"Not exactly."

"What kind of answer is that, Blake?"

"She did go in totally unaware and she still is. All she knows now is what she's found out on her initiative. That's one curious woman. Fortunately she has a new friend named Gabe who looks remarkably like me. The only Blake Girard she's ever seen is a portrait on the wall and the subject of highly romanticized office rumors."

"That means you're working undercover and she doesn't know it?"

"You know I can't answer that."

Dale paused again, putting his coffee cup down firmly. He leaned toward Blake and whispered, "Have you placed this woman in danger?"

"I didn't, but someone inside MACS may have."

"What are you doing about it?"

"I'm sticking close to her. All I can tell you is that this won't go on much longer. Either we move or Marco cashes out and heads for a neutral country. At this point, I'm not taking bets on which will happen first."

"Okay, your family is lying and cheating in business again. What's different this time than that nonsense they pulled in California?"

"This time may involve innocent people getting hurt and millions of Medicare dollars."

"I had a bad feeling about letting Taylor get anywhere near MACS. I wish I had objected when the university made that deal with your father, the devil, for that residency."

"I don't and I don't think Taylor would agree. She wanted to do her residency in Florida. She told me how it all happened."

"I'll tell you how it happened. That woman is as stubborn as you are. She blew off her options by holding out for South Bay then losing it. No wonder you get along well. You are the two most obstinate people I know."

"She's also beautiful, intelligent, funny and brave. And there's one more complication that even my boss doesn't know."

"What else?"

"I'm in love with Taylor Kendall and all she sees is what a great guy my alter ego is."

"Didn't you learn anything about dual relationships in my ethics class? This isn't a trash novel where the hero gets to keep the girl as a souvenir."

"I know, Dale. You're the only person I trust enough to tell. My contact agent is an old friend. I think he suspects how I feel, but we don't talk about it."

"Why don't you be up front with the bureau about your conflict of interest and walk away? Let someone else finish the job?"

"And what about Taylor? Do I walk away from her too?"

"How can you walk away from her? Blake Girard never walked into her life in the first place. She doesn't know the real you. Don't assume that the feelings she has for your undercover persona, Gabe, transfer to you."

"That's occurred to me." It was the subject of his worst nightmare, replacing his former subliminal fear of being paralyzed by a sniper's shot. In some ways he wished the case could linger a year, so he could avoid losing contact with her.

"I see it in your face, boy. You aren't prepared for this. It's not a macho problem or an intellectual exercise. Those you can handle. This woman reaches the vulnerable part of you that has avoided loving for fear of losing."

"Let's skip the inner-child symposium. We both know that my family is a textbook example of approach-avoidant behavior. I don't want to be that way with Taylor."

"Blake, listen to me. You don't need advice reserved for the lovelorn; you need a reality check. You took an oath to do a job and you have to do it. That job is essential to protecting Taylor. I trust you to do the right thing on both fronts, though God knows I can't imagine being put in a worse position than where you are now," Dale reached over to pat Blake on the shoulder in a supportive gesture.

"I didn't mean for this to happen. I don't want her to get hurt. And, Dale, I never wanted to mislead you about anything."

"I know you didn't. I taught you the value of truth and justice. Now I expect you to act on it. Evil is nothing more than perverted good. If you cross back over that line to bring them to justice, then you are one of them again. Beat them at their game but do it from the moral high ground. You can win, Blake, but don't win at any cost."

* * * * *

"Gabe! Wait up!"

He turned to see Jack cross at Fifth Street and run toward him. "Where have you been, man? I thought you were going back to the gallery. What's with Dr. Dale?"

Halting his stride, he turned to face his friend, "You mean, did I compromise the investigation? The answer is no. Will he blow my cover if he sees me with Taylor? No. Does he have a clue that something's going on? Yes. Dale used to be in Naval Intelligence. He reads between the lines very effectively."

"Okay, then he's cool."

"Yes. He wants to be sure that we can protect Taylor. I gave my word."

"Hey, man, you have the old man's blessing to stick close to the lovely doctor. How good can it get?"

"I'm not worried about that, Jack, I'm worried about how bad it can get."

CHAPTER 25

I t was only ten-thirty, but Taylor was ready to get out. The morning therapy groups degenerated into whining sessions. She lacked the energy or initiative to do much redirection. No luck in getting another Nutracurative sample. Sure, Mrs. Jerkin was ready to give hers away, but she's not an "R" code.

As Taylor tried to look at the labels under the guise of helping a new nursing assistant, Lorraine appeared. A long maroon fingernail pointed toward Taylor, "I thought you were told to stay away from distributing medications, Dr. Kendall."

"I was, Nurse Lewis, but according to our promotional material, Nutracuratives aren't medications unless you plan to send some to the FDA for testing."

"I dislike your attitude, Doctor."

"Really? I dislike everything about you, nurse," Taylor replied sharply, not in the mood to take any irritation from that viper.

"So you admit it. You're homophobic," Lorraine challenged, noticing that a few staff members had turned to listen to the confrontation outside the lounge.

"You're dead wrong. I don't care who you sleep with. I have a problem with who you worship, but even if you come in here with a birth certificate proving that you are Rosemary's baby, you still won't intimidate me. And don't bother to make any cute little dolls for me either," Taylor snapped, her knees locked as if to resist taking a step back.

Unaccustomed to such a face down, Lorraine turned and stomped down the hall. As she rounded the corner toward the nurses' station, the staff in the hallway applauded. It was a short lived ovation, ending abruptly when Neva appeared.

"You're made a powerful enemy, Dr. Kendall."

"Perhaps, but at least I know what she is. I never counted on her as a friend the way you have," Taylor said looking intently at Neva, "Surely you know that she'd dump on you in a heartbeat if it suited her purpose."

"Lorraine is a little eccentric, but she knows her job. If anything she's protective of her staff," Neva replied defensively.

"You mean like Martha Sanders?" Taylor was fishing and Neva took the bait.

"Martha was a good nurse until she started dipping into the drug samples."

"Did you see that happen or was that the official story?"

Neva paused, remembering the petite dark-haired woman who had such an easy rapport with the patients. Martha had the ability to take a room full of screamers and within no time persuade them to sit on the floor and sing with her as she played the guitar. "You ask too many questions, Dr. Kendall. Martha had that same problem. That's why she was transferred to the Tampa program. After she got caught doing drugs over there, she got fired. She's probably hooking on Dale Mabry to stay high."

"What a waste. Was she a good nurse before the problems started?"

"Yes, she was very good. I trained with her. She sure could handle the groups. Once Dr. Marco heard her playing guitar for the patients and getting them to move with the music so he suggested that she might retrain as a music therapist and she seemed excited about that. I guess the drugs were more exciting."

"Thanks for telling me about her."

Neva's defensiveness rose, "What do you mean by that?"

Taylor returned an innocent smile, "I'm pleased to hear that music therapy works well in these groups. I've been thinking about bringing in some CDs or homemade instruments. It's nice to know that it's been used successfully before."

Neva geared down. Taylor knew that she managed to diminish the importance of the information about Martha Sanders. She could hardly wait to tell Gabe what she learned and see if he made any progress digging into courthouse records.

"Phone call for you, Dr. Kendall," Ray said as he entered the group room.

"Take a message, Ray. We just got started."

Ray walked over to her chair and whispered, "You really need to answer this call, Doc. I'll hang in here with the group."

Taylor's first thought was that Jamal found more information on Earl's quick release. She smiled and made her exit appear casual. After picking up the phone and hearing who was on the other end, she felt anything but casual.

"Dr. Kendall, thank you for taking my call. I'm Harriet Logan's sister, Hallie."

"Well, uh, I suggest that I call you back later in the day. It's, uh…"

"I know you can't talk now, Doctor. Ray explained that your kindness and concern isn't appreciated by everyone at MACS. He also told me that I can trust you. Do you know what really happened to my sister? The official explanation is too cut and dry for me to accept."

"Well, I don't know anything yet. Or even if there is anything more to know."

"I'm flying in Sunday. I'll be here a few days to settle up Harriet's finances and pack the personal things at her condo. Would you meet with me next week? Any time, any place. You name it and I'll be there," the soft voice moving from assertive to desperate.

"Certainly, I think another place is a good idea."

"I agree. I don't want to cause trouble for you at the clinic. Ray will give you my cell phone number and national pager number so that you can contact me. I'll stay in touch with him. And Dr. Kendall, I want you to understand something."

"What's that?"

"My parents went through years of torment trying everything possible to help Harriet. We all did. Now they are devastated with grief over her death. I'm not looking for someone to sue. I'm looking for answers."

"I understand completely. I'll help in any way that I can," Taylor responded, feeling the weight of Hallie's despair transcend the fiber optic telephone cable.

Hanging up the phone, Taylor went back to the group therapy room. Ray turned to her, smiled and said, "I told you this was going to be an interesting day, Doc."

"And full of surprises."

A small voice called out to Taylor, "Come here, dear. I've got something for you."

Taylor turned to find a wheelchair closing in on her ankles, moving as fast as Mrs. Jerkin's stubby legs could shuffle. She handed the paper cup filled with Nutracurative to Taylor.

"What is this for, Mrs. Jerkin?"

"It's a present for you, dear. I know how much you like champagne and this is the finest I've had since New Year's 1939," the older woman said with a faraway look in her tired eyes.

Taylor checked the label. Not an "R" code. At the edge of her peripheral vision, she saw Neva watching them and decided to use it to her advantage, turning around as if looking for someone.

"Oh, Neva, can you help me?"

Neva walked over, "Another medication problem, doctor?"

"Mrs. Jerkin needs to get back to her New Year's party. She's trying to give me some 'champagne', but I told her that I don't drink. Can you handle it?" Taylor asked, handing the cup of Nutracurative to Neva.

Mrs. Jerkin's short arms reached out for Taylor. "But, dear, don't you love this champagne? I bought it for you. It's your favorite; you know it is."

Neva's firm grasp turned the wheelchair in the opposite

direction toward the community room. Over her shoulder, she said, "Now you're getting the picture, Dr. Kendall. Leave the medication problems to the nursing staff."

"Yes, indeed," Taylor replied trying to appear as cooperative as Neva assumed she was. *Of course, if that had been an "R" code.... then what? Grab the cup and run for the parking lot? Maybe I needed some of Mrs. Jerkin's "champagne" after all.*

BUZZ! BUZZ!

Taylor glanced at her pager to see the numbers, 07734. Turn the pager upside down and the numbers spell "hello". *That's Gabe's way of saying he's at the bench. This man is so much fun; I don't think there's a serious bone in his body.*

Taylor clipped the pager on her skirt waistband and hung her lab coat on the rack near the staff entrance. No one noticed her leave as the staff scurried to gather patients for lunch.

* * * * *

Even the summer humidity failed to dampen Taylor's mood as she took oversized steps toward the Yacht Club basin. In the distance to the left, she could make out a shadow at the bench. Gabe. Knowing he was there waiting caused her to quicken her pace to as near a jog as possible wearing heels.

He sensed her arrival, stood up and waved his arms with as much excitement as might be seen celebrating your team's winning field goal. Unexpectedly, for him as well as for her, he ran toward her, rapidly closing the distance between them. His strong arms wrapped around her.

"Taylor, I missed you. I could hardly wait for lunch."

She moved slightly back to look in his sometimes mysterious gray eyes, "Is there something wrong, Gabe? Is something bothering you? Is it me?"

He knew he had to get control of the urge to smother her like a bodyguard.

"No. I simply missed you and I'm looking forward to spending time together this weekend."

"Well, there are some new developments that may interrupt our time."

He remained quiet while helping her spread out the box lunch he brought.

"You think I'm going to work all weekend and dump you, right?" Taylor said.

"Are you?"

"No, silly. Actually I have an adventure planned and I want you to come along."

"What kind of adventure?"

"I'm playing Sherlock Holmes again and I definitely need a Dr. Watson. Interested in the role?" she asked with a mischievous glint in her brown eyes.

"Can we still go sailing Saturday night?"

"Probably."

"Okay, then count me in."

"Don't you want to know what we're going to do?"

"Not really. I don't care what we do as long as we spend time together," he replied, handing her the spare napkin he kept in his pocket to catch the honey mustard sauce that she nearly always left on her long delicate fingers from dipping the chicken wings.

She glanced at her watch.

"Don't worry. You have plenty of time for dessert."

"When are you going to tell me what you found out at the courthouse?"

"Can I interest you in a little cheesecake brownie and information?"

"Sounds great to me."

He took out his pocket knife to cut the string on the bakery box. Opening the lid, he let her peek at the decadent combination of cheesecake icing swirled with chocolate sprinkles spread on top of a brownie the size of a large index card. She bit into it emitting squeals of delight.

She's so different from the women I know. Taylor doesn't demand grand gestures or sets of jewels to be happy. She finds contentment in small indulgences like chocolate and sharing a waterfront bench.

"Okay you tell me your news and I'll tell you mine, but I bet mine's better," she issued a laughing challenge.

"Don't be too sure about that. I found out that Peter Lane is a Licensed Clinical Social Worker who worked with MACS from the first program until last fall. He suddenly got fired. Yet it was months later before MACS filed a complaint against him with the state licensing board."

"A complaint? For what?"

"Don't know that yet, but he has disappeared. My guess is that his friend, Hank knows where he is. Be sure to ask about Peter Lane when you meet with Hank tonight."

"Good idea. But that doesn't sound too odd from hearing the staff talk, the struggles with managed care is making drifters out of health professionals at all levels these days," Taylor responded, "What else?"

"I now know that Martha Sanders wasn't a MACS patient as we assumed."

She smiled, "Right. She was a program nurse in Tampa."

"I thought you didn't know anything about this woman? Did you send me on a wild goose chase?"

"No, I didn't. Actually, I found this out this morning. Neva said that Martha was fired for doing drugs. She thinks that Martha is still in Tampa."

"Working in healthcare?"

"Not exactly; Neva thinks she's a hooker working a street corner for drug money."

Gabe shook his head. *Another dose of MACS propaganda at work - trying to make the staff think of the Sanders woman as incompetent.*

"Brace yourself, Sherlock. Martha Sanders isn't in Tampa. She's spending quality time in a padded room at G. Pierce Wood

Hospital in Arcadia," he answered with satisfaction from being at least a small step ahead of her.

"You mean the state mental hospital? Did she freak out on drugs?"

"Maybe, but I think there's more to the story. Isn't it all a bit coincidental?"

"Neva says Martha was a terrific nurse one day and a crack whore the next. That's a rapid behavioral shift."

"What you don't know is that Martha started her nursing career at a drug rehab program on North Greenwood in Clearwater. I found a newspaper article about that program. Martha tells the reporter how she hates drugs and what it felt like to watch her two brothers die: one from a heroin overdose and the other shot during a drug deal. Does that sound like a woman who would become a drug user?"

"No it doesn't," Taylor contemplated trying to fit the pieces she knew into an image of Martha Sanders. "Speaking of hospitals, our patient who was in the accident last night was suddenly discharged from South Bay Hospital this morning under Dr. Girard's orders."

"What reason did he give?"

"You mean Dr. Marco? I don't know. He's not due back in the office until Monday. He sent the discharge orders via a nurse, probably Lorraine Lewis."

"Who forged his name on the orders?"

Taylor looked questioning, "I don't think anyone forged his name. I've seen Lorraine and Neva sign for him on treatment summaries and charts. Isn't that like a chief psychiatrist to feel too important to deal with routine paperwork?"

He reflected on years past in the various Girard medical ventures. *Yes, the great Dr. Marco Girard did perceive himself as too important for paperwork. He never had a qualm about letting support staff sign for him. Then if something went wrong with the treatment, he could claim that it was done without his approval and let the nurse take the fall. It certainly worked before, why not again?* "If Dr. Marco let a nurse sign out a patient could that same nurse sign someone in under his name, someone like unsuspecting Martha?"

A beeping cell phone interrupted his comments. Both of them looked at theirs. Taylor smiled, "This one's yours. I'll clean up."

She gathered the wrappers from their lunch, walking over to the nearest trash container. He checked the incoming message; "Missing nurse was DEA working on case. Call for details. Jack."

Taylor sat down on the bench. "I have to leave soon. Are you still planning to shadow me at the meeting with Ray and Hank?"

"Yes, I am. I promise to stay out of sight, but I have another idea for our weekend's entertainment."

"Okay, but remember I have secret plans for us Saturday morning."

"That's fine. Let's take a nice drive in the country on Sunday. Maybe stop for a visit."

"Is this where you take me to meet your parents for Sunday dinner?"

How I wish that were true, unfortunately you've already met my parents, you simply don't know it. "I was thinking about how lonely Martha must be in Arcadia. Why don't we stop by?"

Taylor clapped her hands and shouted, "Yes! Now you're getting into the spirit of this. You're even starting to sound like a real investigator."

"Oh, I think I can work up to it in time," he responded, pulling her close to him to both enjoy her nearness and prevent her from seeing his telltale grin. He kissed her with the sun streaming down on their faces. He knew he was holding on too long, but kissing Taylor was like reading a great novel; there's no good place to stop. She drew back from him, "I don't want to leave either. It's only a few hours until I'll see you after work. Okay?"

"No, leaving you is never okay. I suppose I can busy myself

for a few hours."

"Where shall we meet after I talk with Hank?" she asked, standing up and taking a step away while still holding hands with him.

"Take your car. I'll walk over and wait for you in the parking lot to be sure you get inside safely."

"Isn't that a long walk?"

"A mile or so. No big deal. I'd run a marathon if you were waiting at the finish line to kiss the winner," he flashed that irresistible smile and reached his arm around her waist.

"Stop that or I'll never leave here." She gave him a quick kiss on the cheek, sprang off the bench and ran toward the traffic light to cross at Second Avenue. Glancing over her shoulder, she saw him waving, watching her until she disappeared inside MACS.

I hate to let her go back into that place alone. In reality there's no way I can fulfill the official mandate and stay near her every minute. From the beginning of this case, before Taylor arrived on the scene, the Director warned me against attempting to operate inside any of the MACS programs. Even with the best undercover disguise, I could be recognized or at least questioned and brought to Marco or Victoria for their ever-popular interrogation. Being at a distance is usually a relief in undercover work, but being this far from Taylor, unable to help her once she's inside that building, is torture.

The only redeeming part of this is that she's one of the corporate showpieces who receive favorable treatment in return for trading on their good names and reputations. Employees in any Girard enterprise are well-compensated as a means to an end. The end, of course, was to support the Girard family in a lavish lifestyle built on the backs of other people's labor using other people's money. 'Rampant narcissism fueled by gargantuan greed.' Those were my final words to my family the day I left. Not particularly eloquent, but it was my declaration of independence, my resignation as The Prince of the Girard dynasty, and the most vicious slur I could think of on short notice.

Whatever the scheme, and there were many more that followed, the Girard family's overall plan never wavered. Build a high-profile, rapidly expanding business, front load income and leverage debt while sucking out the profits and assets acquired in mergers with other professional practices. When several million was safely hidden away in off-shore accounts, the family disappears slicker than Houdini, leaving a trail of debt, faltering mortgages and dumped employees. The only thing that seems to be different this time with MACS is that they are getting too flagrant in the ways they tap into US government dollars through Medicare. This may at last be Marco's undoing.

Walking along the sidewalk on the opposite side of the street, he peered through dark sunglasses at the MACS building. More money than usual went into establishing the Girard "do-gooder" image in St. Petersburg. It was a nicely revitalized classic building.

Noticing the staff door open and two women walking out, he quickly put on the baseball cap, pulling the brim down to meet the top of his sunglasses and crossed the street. It was Gina, in a white lab coat talking with a taller woman who, even with her back turned, could only be Lorraine Lewis. She flicked away a cigarette and strode toward the parking lot. Gina stood beside the door aimlessly looking up and down the street. She looked right at him without staring or giving any indication that he was anything more than another downtown bum.

It doesn't take much subterfuge to fool Gina. Carla is the only one who could see through this well-crafted disguise. No matter. When I step through the doors at MACS, no one will wonder who I am or why I am here.

* * * * *

Taylor was squinting to adjust her eyes from the bright sunshine to the fluorescent lights when she noticed Gina and Lorraine step out of the elevator. She reached for her lab coat as if putting on armor for battle. What now? Amazingly the two were locked in conversation and headed out the staff door without a backward glance. Taylor smiled, and then turned toward the first group room. A room full of hyperactive schizophrenic patients was cordial company compared to another confrontation with the wicked witch, Lorraine and Gina, the mad scientist.

"Did I do good work in group today, Dr. Kendall? Did I?"

She turned to find Bobby tugging at her sleeve and looking intently at her. "Yes, Bobby. I like to hear you express yourself."

"Are you sure, Doctor? You aren't just saying that, are you? I mean, like, if I, like, don't make it here, where will I go? Will I go away like Earl did?" his eyes began to dart around as if watching a tennis tournament that only he could see.

Taylor put down her clipboard and looked at him with the brightest smile she could muster, "Bobby, take it one day at a time. That's enough for now. And, Bobby, I think you are making a good effort. I'm proud of you."

His face raised and he focused briefly on her, "Wow! I feel great now." Before she realized his movement, he leaned over and kissed her on the cheek. Then he shuffled out into the hall repeating his new mantra, "Wow, I feel great. Wow. I am great. Wow."

Angie looked over at Taylor, "Wow, indeed, Dr. Kendall. You said the right thing to snap him out of the lethargy he's been in. I could barely get him to respond in activity group this morning."

"Before you crown me with what Ellis called 'great feats of therapeutic heroism', consider Bobby's problem. I could have said the same thing and he might have burst into tears," Taylor cautioned, reaching for the clipboard with group charting data, "You try to tune into each patient and give honest encouragement. And if it doesn't work, don't let it get you down. People with schizophrenia are extremely complex."

Turning toward the door, Taylor was relieved to see Dr. Sebastian Dale, from whom she borrowed that sage advice. Little did he know that he was being guarded by the Office Nazi.

"Dr. Dale, what a wonderful surprise," Taylor said with tone and facial expression that appeared convincing except to her mentor.

Sally stepped forward with her ingratiating attempt to appear civil, "Yes, Dr. Kendall. You forgot to mention that you had a guest visiting today. Did you also forget that there are procedures for bringing outsiders into the clinic?"

"Sorry."

"I hardly think that the university liaison to a fledgling psychology residency site is an unwelcome guest," he emphasized the last word with his famous raised brow of discontent, "Run along to your secretarial duties and let me know when Dr. Girard or Dr. Locke is available."

Stunned by the affront, Sally turned on heel and stormed back toward the nurses' station, choosing the stairway rather than a wait for the elevator.

Taylor pressed her lips closed to hold back the laugh building in her throat. She mumbled, "This way," leading Dale toward the testing room.

He stopped short of entering the room, stopping so quickly that Neva, who was following him, ran into him. "Who are you?"

"I'm Neva, the nurse in charge here."

"If I need a nurse, I'll call you. Meanwhile, don't you have something to do?"

"Yes, I suppose I do."

"Then do it, nurse!" he ordered with the same barking quality known to dispatch recalcitrant lab assistants and send first year students running for cover. He closed the door and took a seat across from Taylor.

"Classic Dale. I love it."

"Of course you do. It's the hidden agenda that all residents hold; the potential to use your doctoral status in dictatorial ways. I think it has something to do with post-dissertation repressed feelings. Enough levity, let's get down to business."

"I'm so glad you're here."

"Then make me glad for interrupting my day by getting to the point. What's not being said in the reports I receive?"

"I'm getting good experience with the patients. At least, after the first skirmish with Victoria Girard ended and I got out from under a paperwork project. I try to avoid Dr. Marco's subtle advances and Serena's chilly presence and I have a research project that I am trying to focus on. I have also been investigating the strange disappearances here."

He leaned back in his chair, "If I didn't know you better, I'd think that you're spending so much time around psychosis that you're sounding like your patients."

He was right. She sounded completely off the wall.

"Just a minute…" Opening her briefcase, she reached into a file compartment and pulled out a sealed letter. He held out his hand to receive it.

"I'm not completely comfortable with the Nutracuratives used in our treatment. It's not a drug and not FDA approved. I've seen odd reactions from patients and heard stories about others. Knowing so little about this 'secret-herbal formula', I wonder how to respond. It's not covered in psychopharmacology."

Looking at the back of the envelope, he saw that she secured it with sealing wax, an old fashioned touch that he hadn't seen in years. Holding it up, he said, "And I take it that for proprietary reasons, there are things you can't say about MACS programs in your reports to the university?"

Taylor looked relieved. He did understand her hidden message, "Yes, I want to keep the university informed of my work, but I have to avoid revealing sensitive MACS data. You were right; working in corporate mental health is far more challenging than I expected."

He took out his pen and wrote on the back of the letter, "Are we free to talk?"

She shook her head.

He nodded, "Okay, Dr. Kendall. Why don't you show me around the clinic?"

"Good idea," she replied, rising from her chair.

As she walked past him, he whispered in her ear, "Do you need to leave today? I'll pull you out of here."

"No, but thanks."

The staff seemed to pick up the vibes that this was an important visitor and showed greater than usual respect for Taylor. Since Neva had already been put in her place by the inimitable Dr. Dale and Lorraine didn't return, the atmosphere in the MACS clinic was practically collegial.

Taylor invited Rowena, a new nurse, to explain the Nutracurative dispensation procedure to Dale. Taking a cup from Rowena's hand, Taylor showed the label which corresponded to each patient number. The one she picked up wasn't an "R" code, but she made enough of the process that Dale would make the connection when he read her letter.

"Taylor!"

She turned to see Brook clomping down the corridor on black platform shoes that sounded like the Clydesdale horses on parade. "Hello, Brook."

"Hi. I wanted to tell you that Dr. Locke is on his way in from the Tampa clinic. He hopes to get back in time to meet Dr. Dale," she sputtered out the message, panting slightly.

"Dr. Sebastian Dale, I'd like for you to meet Brook, administrative assistant to the Clinical Staff and a part time student at St. Petersburg College working on her bachelor's degree. She aspires to move on to a psychology graduate program."

They shook hands. Brook spoke first, "Way cool to meet you, Dr. Dale. You seem like an okay guy. You know, wise and sedate. Do you really get your kicks from scaring new students?"

Taylor rolled her eyes.

"Yes, young lady, I do. It's quite an art actually. However, I suspect that if you ever enroll in my program, I'll have to come up with new material," he turned to Taylor, "Speaking of that university, I need to get back there."

Brook took him by the arm, "Come on, now. Are you going to leave without seeing Taylor, I mean Dr. Kendall, in action? The next group is about to start."

Good going, Brook, Taylor thought. "Would you join us?"

"Of course. And where are you going, Ms. Brook?"

"I'm going back to my dull little desk. When Sam and Lorraine are both gone and Taylor's busy, there's nothing happening but paperwork. How will I ever become a sports psychologist this way?" she waved her hands, purple glitter nails gleaming in the light.

"Sports psychology? Are you into athletics?"

"No, I'm into athletes. Guys only, of course."

"Of course."

She leaned toward him, "These days a girl has to be specific, if you know what I mean." She winked, squeezed his arm, and then pranced off toward down the hall.

Dale looked at Taylor, "What a project that girl is!"

"That's what I thought at first. Beneath the odd exterior is a skilled observer. Not to mention that Brook is one of the few totally honest people in this place," Taylor replied motioning toward the group room, "I'm still mulling over what she said recently about our miracle herbal potion."

"What's that?"

"She said that whatever it is, it's not what we think it is. The more I think about it, I'd say that applies to the entire MACS PHP operation."

CHAPTER 26

"What is Sebastian Dale doing in my clinic?" Marco's shout reverberated down the phone line slamming into Sally's eardrum.

"I don't know. He said it was an unannounced visit that the university does with all their sites, especially new ones."

"I don't like it. Where is he now?"

"When I left, he was getting a tour around the clinic from Dr. Kendall. She seemed pleased to be showing him around."

"Did he ask to see me?"

"Yes, but I told him you were presenting MACS programs at a conference."

"All right. Don't offer any details. Is Sam there or Lorraine?"

"No. Sam was called to Tampa on some staff problem. Lorraine is in Winter Park. Said she wouldn't be back until Monday. Do you want me to call her?"

"No, Sally. Let Taylor deal with Dr. Dale. After all, he's her advisor. Let's treat this low key and maybe he will go away."

"I can go downstairs and watch him."

"That's a bad idea. He's more cunning than he appears. Besides, Dr. Kendall can't say anything incriminating since she doesn't know anything in-depth about our programs. Does Victoria or Serena know that Dr. Dale is here?"

Sally swiveled her chair right, then left, observing that both of the women's office doors remained closed. "No. I decided to call you first."

"Well done! Now listen closely, I'm counting on you, as I always do my little flower. Keep Victoria out of this. She'll overreact. If anything negative happens, get Victoria out of the office and let Serena handle it. Ring me through to Serena and I'll explain what I want her to do."

Sally wanted to be Marco's deputy, to show him how important she was. Oh well, another time. If the situation turns foul, let Serena take the rap. Restoring her subservient voice she replied, "Whatever you say, Marco. And about Saturday night…"

"It's not possible this weekend. I won't even return from Orlando until late Saturday night and I need to spend Sunday going over some formula adaptations with Gina. Perhaps one night next week," he answered, leaning back in the lounge chair on the veranda of his Snell Isle home. The mansion was a five-minute boat ride from his dock to the Yacht Club where he could practically walk to the MACS corporate office.

Sally cupped her hand over the phone receiver and whispered, "I could drive over to Orlando after work and spend the night with you."

"No. I have business to attend to and so have you."

"Certainly, I'll connect you to Mrs. Girard," she stated, giving clear emphasis to "Mrs."

* * * * *

"Why do you think he's really here?" Serena asked after hearing about the site visit in progress downstairs.

"How do I know? Probably to gloat," Marco replied taking a long sip of cognac, "I haven't forgotten how Sebastian Dale refused to tell us where Blake went. I'm certain that pious professor talks to my son regularly. No respect for family. No respect for tradition. No respect for…"

Serena interrupted the certain tirade, "Now, Marco darling, let's not obsess over old wounds."

"You mean the pain your son caused when he told me that I was more like a fraternity brother than a father to him and that Sebastian Dale was the only true father figure he ever knew. That arrogant academic filled Blake's head with weakling, do-gooder philosophies. He stole our Prince."

"Marco, listen to me. Much as his absence pains us, Blake was merely another student to Dr. Dale. Blake's accusations were the growing pains of a young man testing his independence."

"Then where is he?"

"Marco darling," how Serena hated to cajole, but it usually worked, "Blake is out conquering the world much as you did at his age. When he builds his own empire, he will return and present it to you. Blake is strong, like you. He needs time to carve his own path. Remember when he was eleven years old and you took him hunting in the Canadian wilderness? You thought he was lost, but Abuelo Andres told you that Blake would return after he shot the biggest buck in the camp. And he did!"

"Indeed, and it took him a full day and night in freezing cold without food to drag his prize into camp so that some other hunter wouldn't find it and claim it."

"Don't you see, Marco, he's working his way around the world preparing to impress you. And we both know that you're indignation will melt when our Blake, your Prince, comes back to show you what he has accomplished on his own. Meanwhile, back to our business, shall I go downstairs and greet Dr. Dale or invite him to my office?"

"Much as he does not deserve your time or attention, I would like for you to make a brief appearance downstairs, my dear. I hear that Victoria is having a difficult day."

"Yes, I see evidence that she is heading into a depressed cycle. She bristled at my suggestion to go home early and totally refused the Lithium that I asked Neva to bring to her. I suppose Victoria squandered her energies this morning berating Felipe and the accounting department."

"Very well, keep her out of this. You handle it, Serena. Then hurry home. I think that we need to dine together and discuss a lucrative new business I found that is ripe for a takeover. I'll have the cook prepare a table for us in my room. Don't bother to dress up. We won't stay dressed long."

"As you wish, Marco," Serena said softly, replacing the antique white phone on its cradle. She rolled her chair back from her desk, picked up the Waterford crystal vase with roses and threw it against the far wall. The shattering glass and splashing water obscured the gritty sound she made spitting out his name like a curse.

* * * * *

Dale sat as patiently as could be accomplished in a cheap waiting room chair while Taylor made necessary notes on the group modality chart. The silence was broken by the sound of running steps and a sudden, "Hello!"

"Dr. Locke," Taylor said looking up, "We have a guest."

Dropping his briefcase on the nearest chair, Sam Locke extended his hand, "Yes, so I heard. Dr. Dale, I'm glad I got back in time to meet you. Would you like coffee or soda?"

"No thank you, Dr. Locke. I've already stayed longer than I planned."

"I understand. Can you spare a few more minutes?" Locke asked. He appeared to be struggling to catch his breath and perspiring after running from the parking lot.

Taylor took pity on him and asked, "I'll get the sodas while you get acquainted." She pulled the door closed as she went out to give the two men a chance to talk privately.

"Dr. Dale, I apologize on behalf of myself and Dr. Girard that one of us was not here to greet you."

"Accepted. However, I'm more interested in knowing how often a psychology resident is left in charge of a clinic filled with schizophrenic patients?"

Locke leaned back in his chair. This wasn't going to be easy.

"Normally, Dr. Marco or I are in the office during program hours. He's out of town until Monday. I was in earlier this morning, but got called away to an emergency at our Tampa clinic. There wasn't time to bring in an on-call psychiatrist and I didn't expect to be gone as long as I was."

"Patient crisis or another missing doctor?"

"We had a patient show up intoxicated and causing quite an uproar when the head nurse tried to have him transported to a detox center."

"Why didn't the on-site psychologist at that program handle it?"

Locke breathed deeply, wishing that Dr. Girard were here managing his own mess. *Forget that the MACS PHPs in Tampa are in dangerous waters by having only one psychologist officially listed as the program director and one psychiatrist as medical director for all three programs. Talk about being in more than one place at one time, particularly since both doctors rarely set foot inside the programs. Amazing how money motivates some doctors to sign Medicare documents that insure maximum billings for MACS and a tidy bonus for doing nothing more strenuous than compromising one's professional license. Of course, that's Marco's choice, not mine. But then it's not what Dr. Dale and his university committee wants to hear.* "Naturally our medical director, a psychiatrist, was involved in the situation."

"Why didn't he simply deal with the problem?"

"Well, it was more complicated than it seems," Locke stalled searching for a way to gloss over the truth that this practitioner-professor might accept. "The incident also sparked a conflict within the professional staff over how to deal with things. We have several new people in that PHP location so I thought it was best to show them how we at corporate would deal with such a problem."

Dale's expression indicated that he wasn't buying what Locke was selling, "And who would be dealing with a crisis in this clinic? Dr. Kendall, an extremely capable, but not yet licensed psychologist? The nurses? The techs?"

As soon as Taylor opened the door, she sensed the tension

between the men and remained in that spot awaiting the right time to enter the room.

Locke felt like he was under a laser beam from Dale's stare while another feeble excuse formed in his brain. The sound of Taylor's surprised "Oh, excuse me" broke the silence. He turned to see Serena Girard push past Taylor and come to his rescue.

"Actually, Dr. Dale, I can answer your question. Perhaps you remember me. I'm Serena Girard, a principal in MACS and creator of the Live Anew transitional programs," Serena walked toward the men who stood up from their seats until she took a seat in the chair between them, "Dr. Locke is such a busy man that he either forgot or that adolescent secretary of his failed to tell him."

"Tell me what?" Locke asked, offering to play straight man to what was bound to be a more creative deception that he could muster.

"How could you possibly forget? Our consultant, Dr. Rolando Quintero, a fine psychiatrist and eminent researcher, was in my office today. Neva, our program nurse, called immediately after you left requesting Dr. Girard to fill in during your absence. She didn't know that he was away. Thus I asked Dr. Quintero to remain on premises until your return and advised Neva of the same. It's my error if I kept Dr. Quintero in the Executive Suite. He was explaining amazing new research that impacts our Nutracuratives," Serena explained looking around to be certain the men were still paying close attention to her performance, "You know that I'm not a scientist and dear Dr. Quintero had to spend quite a lot of time helping me understand his work. If anyone is at fault for failing to have a senior doctor on the clinic floor instead of upstairs in the building, then I must confess that it is I."

"Understood, Serena. Thanks for clarifying that," Locke replied reaching out to take the soda that Taylor handed to him. Sipping the chilled drink helped his composure and occupied his hands, thereby reducing the urge to applaud such an elaborate fairy tale.

"Regretfully, I have to leave now. I've overstayed my welcome as it is."

"Dr. Dale, before you leave I have a question?" Serena asked, turning slightly toward the group. He paused and nodded.

"Apart from that trivial misunderstanding about staffing, don't you find our clinic to be the definitive model for schizophrenia group treatments?"

"On the surface, the MACS clinic appears to provide a suitable experience for Dr. Kendall's residency," he replied refusing to bite on the hook with which she fished for compliments, "Anything else?"

She lowered her voice and turned to face him with her back toward the others, "Yes. What do you hear from my son, Blake?"

"Mrs. Girard, I retain a keen interest in the progress of all my former students. As far as I know, he is doing well. He has matured into a man who is, shall we say, 'merciful, faithful, humane, religious, upright and balanced.' After all isn't that Dr. Girard's chosen formula for creating a Prince?"

* * * * *

"Well, Taylor, you said MACS was quite an experience and I certainly agree," Dale said sarcastically as she pressed the key code buttons for him leave through the main clinic door into the hallway.

"My cell phone number is on the report I gave you."

He patted the left side of his jacket, where the envelope was tucked out of sight in the inside pocket to indicate that he got her message. "If you have any doubts about anything that's happening at MACS, I want you to get out immediately and phone me. I'll deal with the fallout both here and at the idiots on the university supervision committee who approved this pricey asylum."

"Thanks. I'll be okay. I've got a good friend for backup."

She closed the door and paused. Seeing Dale leave gave her that same sinking feeling she had the day her Daddy drove away after unloading her suitcases at the Vanderbilt freshman dorm leaving her completely on her own. Jolted back to the present by her pager, she looked down to see the familiar 07734 message from Gabe. *That's the right motivation to get moving and finish those patient charts.* The meeting she anticipated all day was happening in less than two hours. She darted toward the nurses' station, passing Locke and Serena.

* * * * *

Locke slowed his pace, as would be expected, to hold open the elevator door for her. Pressing the close button, he waited for the doors to shut and the elevator motor to start before turning to face her. "I can hardly wait to meet him."

"Who?"

"Dr. Quintero."

Serena crossed her arms defiantly and stared at him, "That's impossible. More to the point, you have been gone all day and you need to catch up. The day is practically over. Perhaps we can arrange something tomorrow."

"Serena, tomorrow is Saturday. Since when do you work weekends?"

"Don't be truculent. The matter is tended to. That is sufficient," she replied sharply expecting him to take the hint from her marble-cutting glare.

He was in a strange mood. *Too much work. No lunch. Low blood sugar is as good an excuse as any to be irritating. God knows she does it often enough.* "I'm not truculent, but I am curious. So curious that I'm offering to take the good Dr. Quintero to dinner on the way to the airport or his hotel or wherever he's going. I'm interested in hearing more about his research."

"There is no research."

"No research," he said with feigned amazement. "What did you talk about all day? Did that scoundrel try to compromise you while Dr. Marco was away?"

"I think that will be enough for today."

"Now, Serena, as Clinical Program Director for MACS I feel slighted that I didn't get to meet Dr. Quintero. I want to know more about him," Sam said as the elevator passed the fourth floor heading to the Executive floor.

Serena waited until the doors opened. She took two steps out into the foyer then glanced over her shoulder toward Sam as if he were an afterthought, "There is no Dr. Quintero. I merely diffused an explosive situation as Marco asked me to do." She pressed the elevator down button, briskly walking away as Sam's roaring laughter echoed through the elevator shaft.

CHAPTER 27

Taylor took the pens and notes from her lab coat pocket and dropped them in the side pocket of her brief case. Next she removed her name badge and stuffed it into her purse, expecting to wear it tomorrow on her scavenger hunt around the office. With purse strap on her shoulder, briefcase in one hand and lab coat in the other, Taylor was lost in her thoughts as she walked toward the laundry collection bag in the far corner of the staff lounge.

"Watch where you're going!" an unfamiliar man's voice rang out.

Taylor blinked as she brushed her shoulder against a tall, hotel style clothing rack.

"Gosh, lady, I'm sorry. But you weren't looking," the man in the Clean Team Laundry Services shirt persisted. "Are you okay?"

"I'm fine. I guess you caught me daydreaming."

"Say, I do that all the time," the man said reaching out to take Taylor's wrinkled lab coat and toss it into a large basket. "I better not say that too loud. Some doctor around here will say I'm nuts."

"I am one of those doctors," Taylor smiled at his chagrin. "If daydreaming at the end of a long work day means you're crazy, then we better rent Tropicana Field and lock up most of the downtown work force."

He gave her a thumbs up sign and pushed the cart toward the community room to pick up the dirty towels and table cloths. That's when she noticed the green shirts hanging beside the pressed lab coats on the rack. Her eyes darted around. Only a CNA remained at the desk, painstakingly adding progress forms into charts. Taylor placed her briefcase on the top of an empty medicine cart in the hallway. She fidgeted around inside it to appear as if she was looking for something. The laundry delivery man paid no attention to her. When he took a handful of towels into the supply room, Taylor went over to the rack and grabbed a green MACS shirt. She dropped the hanger behind the chart cart and stuffed the shirt inside her briefcase. To conceal the shirt, she pulled some loose papers over the top. As the delivery man emerged to continue his rounds, Taylor wished him a pleasant evening then walked confidently out the side door to her car.

* * * * *

As Taylor drove west on Central Avenue, the buildings became more run down. Finally she saw a neon sign at the corner, marking the bar where she was to meet Ray and Hank. She pulled into the parking lot beneath the expressway ramp, noticing several rough-looking men get out of an old van and go inside. Her senses were on alert. Suddenly there was a tap on the passenger side window. She gasped, and then realized who it was. Pressing the unlock button, she released the door and he got inside.

"Gabe, I'm glad it's you," she said, leaning over to receive his kiss.

"Are you okay?"

"Yes. I was wondering about the crowd."

"As I suspected, you're not a bar-fly."

"I think I'm about to understand why my Mama warned me not to go to places like this."

"Most of these folks are blue collar workers looking for a cold beer and a place to unwind. It's not often that anyone gets out of line. You know, I would bet that the people in this bar are a lot less dangerous than some of the people you work with at MACS."

Their eyes locked. They touched each other's faces reverently, pressing sacred paths across her smooth cheeks and his hint of evening beard. The hypnotic moment was brutally interrupted by a ringing phone. Taylor reached in her purse and answered. The voice on the other end brought her to attention.

"I thought the pre-addressed stamped envelope was enough of a hint, but apparently I was wrong."

"Hello, Mama. I know I owe you a letter…"

"Letter? That's only if your phone is broken. I know your long distance credit is good, I've sent five prepaid telephone cards."

"You're right, Mama," Taylor admitted, tilting the phone so that Gabe could listen, "I have been so busy at MACS that my good intentions haven't translated into something tangible."

"Honey, don't you remember Granddaddy Dodd's warning that the road to hell is paved with good intentions?" Julia Dodd Kendall chastised her oldest daughter. "Not to worry, Taylor, I'm on the way."

"On the way where?"

"Well, you know that Savannah and I still have a list of things to add to her hope chest and we were going to shop in Atlanta or Dallas. But, since I was concerned about you, we decided to shop in Tampa."

"Tampa? When?"

"We'll fly in next Thursday. Don't take off work, honey, we'll get a rental car."

Taylor looked at Gabe in wide-eyed horror, "Mother, you can't come down next week. It's impossible."

"Don't worry about cooking or cleaning. We'll do that. We'll be busy during the day and be able to spend the evening with you. Besides I have to be back in Memphis by the following Friday when Paige returns from a band trip," Julia explained sipping her mint ice tea.

Gabe shook his head "no." Taylor knew what he meant. This was the wrong time for a cozy family visit with so many strange things happening at MACS. Daddy would have understood, but not Mama. *If I tell her something isn't right, she'll be on the next plane, train or camel caravan to correct it.*

"Mama, this is not a good time. Trust me and don't ask."

"Taylor Kendall, do you have a man living with you?"

"No."

"Well then are you living with some man at his place?"

Gabe turned away from the phone, covering his mouth to stifle a laugh. Taylor scowled at him.

"Mama, I'm living by myself and loving it, but I'm busy at work. At night I have a lot of things to study to learn about the PHP programs. I'm even going into the clinic to work this weekend."

"I have one of my intuitive feelings that something is not right with you."

Mama did have an uncanny ability to know when something wasn't right in her daughters' world. *Denial never works. It only makes her more inquisitive and more likely to fly down here to see for herself. Perhaps a creative twist will do.*

"All right, Mama, you caught me. I'll tell you what's up." Gabe turned around, this time his mouth open wide in horror.

"I'm listening."

"If you come to my house you'll find that the plastic seal is still on my vitamins and my refrigerator is full of junk food. There, I've confessed." She could picture her mother's all-knowing expression. "Now, I've saved you a plane ticket. Why don't you and Savannah do your shopping in Atlanta and visit your cousin? Isn't her house close to Perimeter Mall?"

"Listen here, missy, I don't care if you are a doctor, you are acting foolishly. You can't neglect your health. And use that high priced psychological training to put up some boundaries with these people. You're an employee, not a serf. And what's more, you're a professional. Your Daddy would tell you that if you want respect, you have to command respect and this is a good time to start."

"Yes, Mama, I'll do better. And I'll write."

"Even an email for me sent to Paige's computer will do."

"But Mama, when I was traveling for AOPi you told me that email was a low class excuse for correspondence. I believe you said, 'Either take a monogrammed notepaper with a fine tip pen and a touch of scent or don't bother to call it correspondence.'"

"True, that's the way genteel ladies correspond, but I have progressed over the years. I'm now prepared to settle for an email rather than nothing. I need to know you're all right. You are still my precious little girl, Taylor, and I love you. I know you have your own life and I'm very proud of your accomplishments. But since your Daddy died, I feel an even greater responsibility to protect you and Savannah and Paige."

Taylor noticed that Gabe looked away, as if contemplating something she didn't understand. "I love you too, Mama. If I need help, I'll call. I know from experience that nothing can stand up to you when you raise those claws to protect your children. I'm glad you're on my side."

"Taylor, honey, I'm always on your side. You have been an absolute joy to me since the day you were born. I pray every night that the right young man will come along who has the good sense to appreciate what a fine person you are."

Saying goodbye, Taylor ended the call. Gabe continued to stare as if fixated on something that only he could see. She broke the silence, "That was a close one. I certainly don't want Mama to have a hint of our worst suspicions about MACS."

"Do you realize how lucky you are to have a mother like that?"

"Like what? Intense, interfering and ready to battle my enemies whether I need her help or not?"

"No. I hear a mother who is concerned, loving, willing to inconvenience herself for you, and proud of you for doing what you chose to do."

"Yes, she's that too. But aren't all mothers that way about their children?"

"No, Taylor, not all of them."

* * * * *

"I'll go in first and blend in with the crowd. Wait three minutes and walk in. If you don't come through the front door in exactly three minutes, I'll come out to get you." Gabe reached for the passenger door handle.

"How will I find you after the meeting?"

"You won't. I'll call your cell phone and tell you where to pick me up. Is that cloak and dagger enough for you, Sherlock?" he tried to interject some levity to distract her concern with unfamiliar surroundings.

"Okay, Watson, the clock is running. Three minutes and not a second more," she acknowledged, rummaging in her purse. As she watched Gabe disappear inside the bar, she crammed her purse under the driver's seat, transferring the wallet and mace to her skirt pocket. At two minutes, fifty-seven seconds, she saw a jovial group of mid-thirties men and women walk past her car and turn toward the bar. They seemed like the perfect group to merge with rather than entering the bar alone. Taylor got out of the car. A young man from the group held open the bar door and paused to let her enter. Just as she hoped, she easily blended in rather than arriving solo and practically announcing she was a, what was that Gabe said, "bar fly." Heaven knows Julia Dodd Kendall would be shocked enough to see her daughter alone in a low class bar.

Squinting repeatedly, Taylor's eyes needed a moment to adjust to the dim lighting and smoky air. When she could focus again, she glanced around to notice Ray at a corner table waving at her. She nodded, looking around the room for Gabe. He was on a bar stool at the far end. She stared at him, but he gave no sign of recognition even though she was certain he saw her. He was talking to a guy who looked like an actor or an artist. For all she knew, this could be the place where Gabe and his theatre friends hang out.

"Over here!" Ray shouted, his mellow voice ringing out between stanzas of a twangy country music song on the juke box. Taylor slid past several tables to face the two men.

"Dr. Taylor Kendall, meet my friend Harry Brand."

Hank extended his hand, "Pleasure to meet you, Dr. Kendall."

"Please call me Taylor."

"Fine and I'm Hank."

The waitress appeared in a peasant shirt so low-cut that the bow at the neckline kept catching the belt hanging slightly off of a handkerchief-sized imitation leather mini skirt. "Hi, ya'll. What's your woman drinking?" she sputtered out the question between pops of chewing gum.

Taylor's feminist side nearly took issue with that comment, but she had a more important mission than raising consciousness. "I'll have a diet soda in a glass with ice."

"Sister, in case you haven't noticed, this is a bar. We use soda as a mixer," the waitress tapped her order pad, "How about a rum and cola? Or go a little wild and get a draft beer?"

"How about taking my order instead of critiquing my preferences?"

The waitress tossed her platinum hair extensions to one side, licked the pencil and wrote on the pad, "One Shirley Temple for the lady."

"Come on, Lurleen, stop teasing. This is my boss. Do you want to get me in trouble?"

Looking incredulous, the waitress turned toward Ray, leaning so close that if he sneezed, her cleavage would be splattered. With a kiss to his forehead that left a bold red lip print, she shuffled backwards quickly, a neat trick on Lucite platform shoes.

"Anything for you big boy. I'll get the boss lady a soda."

Taylor rolled her eyes. Ray and Hank were tripping over their hormones with locker room laughter. *Gabe wouldn't fall for such a blatant maneuver. If that trailer park hussy tries to put the moves on Gabe, well I'll. . . I'll what? It must be the smoky air that's making me go off on these weird thoughts.*

"Taylor, what did you want to ask Hank?"

"I guess I'm trying to understand some history of the MACS PHP programs. Not the PR version, the therapist-eye version."

Hank nodded, "You mean the good ole days before Lorraine was abandoned on our unsuspecting planet by the mother ship."

Taylor looked startled.

"You aren't some kind of friend of Lorraine's or Gina's are you?" Hank asked placing a clear emphasis on the word friend.

"No!"

"Not a chance, Hank. I wish you had seen Dr. Kendall face down the Princess of Darkness. It was butt kicking."

"This nice lady went toe to toe with Lorraine? You're the woman, Doc! Ask me anything. I feel like I'm in the presence of greatness."

Well at least her confrontation was worth something besides the tension headache that followed it. "Was there much of a difference in the program before Lorraine took over as head nurse?"

"Night and day, no pun intended. Dr. Locke hired me to work in the second program. In the early days, he was running back and forth between the program downtown and the one where I worked in Kenneth City. Even Dr. Marco spent time in the PHP with us. It was a small group of therapists and techs with one nurse at each location. We called ourselves the KC team and we really did work well together," Hank paused gathering his thoughts, "Come to think of it, I'm as proud of the work I did at the KC PHP as anything I've done in my career."

"You mentioned Dr. Marco, did you ever work with Gina?" Taylor asked, jotting notes on the cocktail napkin.

"Yeah, she came in occasionally with him. I thought she was a real odd broad until I met her mother at the MACS picnic."

"Okay, but what did she do? Did she interface with the patients?"

"Not really. She walked around with a clipboard and took lots of notes. And when she followed her father. It was like he dictated stuff to her in a foreign language."

"Probably Spanish."

"No. I learned a little Spanish when I was working at a cancer clinic in Mexico. That wasn't it," Hank replied. "There was even a Cuban nurse who couldn't understand them. Said she thought it was Brazilian."

They must have spoken in Portuguese. How clever. Spanish speakers are common in Florida, but very few people understand Portuguese. Carla talked about living in Chile, Argentina and Venezuela, all Spanish speaking countries. Brazil isn't that far away. Maybe they spent time there too. If Dr. Marco and Gina were speaking in Portuguese then they must have been trying to hide something from the staff.

"Hank, how did the patients respond to treatment?"

"In the early days, we had mixed results with a lot of dropouts but that's not unusual in treating schizophrenic populations. Then Dr. Marco said he had perfected the Nutracuratives and he must have been right."

"Why do you say that?"

"Because our success rate for people in the program skyrocketed. Before we knew it, MACS programs were popping up in Tampa, Orlando, Ocala, Lakeland and all around. That's when the corporate office moved out of the old Arcade building and into the place where you are now."

"Where did the PHPs begin?"

"The first one was in downtown St. Pete in an old boarding house with large rooms and narrow halls. They got written up weekly from the health department over something not being up to code. When Dr. Marco bought the building you're in now, the PHP was moved into the ground floor. It got renovated first. You remember the moving party, Ray."

"I sure do," Ray reminisced about that weekend, "Victoria

Girard called for all employees to work over the weekend to help move. She drove up in a truck that was packed with dollies and boxes. Dr. Marco followed in a van filled with beer on ice and food. We literally marched back and forth down Central Avenue rolling furniture and files from the Arcade office to the new building. While the guys did the moving, the women were painting and cleaning."

"Yeah, we bought into the line about pitching in to help the company be more profitable so we could get a bonus that never happened," Hank added, "A few weeks after the move I took some reports up to the Executive Suite and looked around. It's pure decorator with nothing but the best stuff. Bet the Girards didn't spend their weekend fixing it up. That smooth talking stud and his broads were using us again to line their pockets."

Ray nodded in agreement. Taylor had no difficulty believing yet another story of the dichotomy between the luxuries expected by the Girards and the extra effort demanded of the worker bees. Suddenly she made the connection.

"Hank, I saw you at MACS on my first day. You were coming out of HR after trying to get a check. What happened?"

"Yeah, I remember that day, but I don't remember seeing you. I was boiling mad."

"I also heard you tell Joanie in HR that you might report MACS to the medical board. Would you be willing to tell me exactly what you meant by that?"

Hank glanced over to Ray who nodded affirmatively, "Come on, dude, I told you she can be trusted. Tell her what you told me."

Taylor glanced toward the bar. Gabe was watching her intently. She smiled as a message that it was going well. He raised his glass in acknowledgement.

"This may sound really crazy, Doc, but I swear it's the truth," Hank prefaced his remarks. "I think the Nutracuratives are a way to manipulate the patients. Like Greg Newman."

"You worked with Greg Newman. What do you know about his suicide?"

"Suicide, huh? I don't buy that for a minute. Greg was doing great. He was looking forward to discharge from the MACS program to start a part time job. He even registered for night classes at USF. The guy had plans. People with plans and something to look forward to don't take flying leaps off tall bridges, now do they?"

"I agree with you, Hank, that people contemplating suicide are more likely to be at the end of their rope than ready to start a new life, but you know how complex schizophrenia is."

"That sounds too much like a MACS disclaimer to me. Besides, I knew this guy for years. Worked with him when I was a social work intern at a psyche hospital in north county. This time Greg was really on the brink of getting his life together and dealing honestly with his schizophrenia."

"How do you fault MACS or the Girards for what happened? The police didn't."

Ray jumped in, "Yeah, just like they didn't hold MACS responsible for Harriet's death either!"

"Okay, Doc, I'll tell you how I know," Hank took a slow drink from the long neck beer bottle, "The first time Greg was getting better he had a sudden relapse. I remember that day well. The nurse was busy on the phone, so she asked me and the other therapist to hand out the Nutracuratives to our group. Part of the typed label on Greg's drink was scratched out with a felt tip pen and the letter 'R' written in."

"I've seen codes changed too," Ray chimed in.

"An hour or so later, Greg flipped out. I called 911 to pick him up and transport to the hospital. I was afraid that I had made a mistake with those drinks so I filled out an incident report and gave it to the nurse. Next thing I knew, I was called to Dr. Marco's office where he quizzed me about the report then tore it up. Said he checked with Gina and it was a typo on the label, nothing more. He insisted it wasn't anything that could have harmed Greg. Guess I was a little too grateful to be off the hook, so I settled for that story," Hank tapped his fingers on the table nervously.

"Was that when Greg took his life?"

"No," Hank replied gulping down more beer, "After a few days, he was discharged from the hospital and enrolled in a different MACS PHP to start all over again. I was shocked at how far he had regressed. When I was sent to work two days a week at that program, I talked with Greg and reminded him how well he did before and that he could do it again."

"Did he?"

"Yes. A few months later he was ready to go again. This time he saw it."

"Saw what?"

"The 'R' code on his Nutracurative. We joked about it. He said, 'Hey Hank, now I know I'm ready to be released because my joy juice has an R for release on it.' Two days later, he was dead. Too coincidental for my liking."

Taylor felt a little less paranoid to hear that another professional found the 'R' code changes hard to explain. "Was that the only problem?"

Hank shook his head, "After Greg died, I started watching the codes closely. It seemed as if each time an 'R' code appeared, it was only a matter of days before the patient was discharged into a Live Anew program. Later I heard that most of them relapsed after Live Anew."

"Is it possible that the pre-discharge Nutracurative is less potent than what is used during treatment?"

"That thought occurred to me too. Then I noticed some program census comparisons in the waste basket when I went upstairs to Quality Management. Probably didn't get shredded like everything short of nail clippings does in that place," Hank said, "The numbers told the story. I looked over several old charts and found that 'R' codes, discharges and later relapses went hand-in-hand. And here's the clincher: Relapses in one program almost exactly match census increases in another. It's a new take on recycling."

"Are you saying that patients were made to relapse to keep the census up? What's the point?"

"The point? The point, Doc, is a decimal and the reason is the numbers in front of it. Big bucks. I used to date a secretary in billing. She told me that each patient is worth over $400 a day. Doesn't matter what shape they are in. Drag them in off the van. Let them spend the day talking to the wastebasket. Just keep the census count up. Money is the name of the game and the Girards are making a fortune," Ray interjected.

"What you are both saying is very serious."

"I know. And after I started asking questions among the staff, the nurses were instructed not to log the codes in the patient files. Next the Nutracuratives were brought down daily from the lab in time for use. No more keeping it in the nurses' station refrigerator. That's also when I started getting written up."

"What do you mean by written up?"

Ray answered, "It means that a nurse or a supervisory professional makes a note that damages your record. They wrote up Hank for stupid stuff like 'treating a patient with disrespect' when he would put the brakes on this older woman's wheelchair so she wouldn't deliberately roll over the toes of the woman next to her during group."

"That can't be the whole story, can it?"

"I was there, Taylor. I worked with Hank. Some of the charges they made against him were total lies. I always thought that Dr. Marco was afraid that Hank knew too much and wanted to get him out."

"You got that right, Ray. Except Marco didn't have the balls to deal with me man-to-man. He let his daughter's gal-pal Lorraine do the dirty work. She's a better man than he is," Hank let out a belch in the middle of his boisterous laugh.

Taylor wondered if there was truth in his angry outburst. Maybe Lorraine was willing to be the enforcer, but not likely to act without orders. "Where was Dr. Locke during all of this? Did you try to talk to him or tell him what was happening?"

"Officially I never got to talk with Dr. Locke so I came downtown several mornings until I caught him in the parking lot. He was nice about it. We walked over to the bagel shop to talk. I tried to tell him that the complaints they had written up on me were a crock. He didn't seem to know what to believe, but he did say that he'd tell HR to give me a good recommendation. That didn't happen."

"Are you sure?"

"You bet I'm sure. I kept getting turned down for social work jobs so I went to Tampa. It was the same deal. Spooky stuff started happening. That's when I left town. I'm staying with a buddy who lives off a country road in Hernando County. It's so remote that I'd have time to reload my shotgun if I ever see Lorraine turn in the driveway. She's the one. I know it."

"The one who did what?"

"The one responsible for filing malpractice charges against me with the state license board. She's done that to other people."

"You mean like what happened to Peter Lane?"

Hank and Ray looked at each other, surprised that Taylor knew about Peter.

Then Hank continued, "I was ready to leave Florida, but with a smear on my license I won't be able to get reciprocity to work in another state. MACS left me as tied up in knots as they did Greg and probably Ray's friend, Harriet."

"Do you think the charges against Peter are false too?"

"Let's just say we both got the same raw deal," Hank replied tapping his fingers on the table, "And to think, Pete and I helped them get started. We did double duty trying to make the programs work while the Girards raked in more money."

"Where is Peter Lane now?" she tried to make her question seem casual.

"Why do you want to know?"

Taylor sensed this was a conversation ending answer so she toned down her response, "I'm trying to see how all the pieces fit, Hank. From what I've learned, Peter Lane was an important part of the program just as you were. I'm wondering why you were considered excellent social workers one day and renegades the next."

"Watch out, Taylor. If you keep asking questions like that you could end up like me and Pete."

Taylor realized that his words were no idle forewarning. Clashing with Lorraine was becoming a regular event. No doubt word of it reached the Executive Suite. At least Carla acted as friendly as ever. Or was that an act to get information, the good cop-bad cop routine? Serena and Victoria certainly used it to their advantage in dealing with the Magna executives.

"Hank, do you have any proof? Anything written? Any report copies?" Taylor felt like even asking the question would make him wonder if she believed his story, but she had to know.

"No, I don't. I know what I saw and I take the word of a friend about what he saw. I guess you think I'm a nut case too."

"Not at all, Hank. I think you are on to something. I've questioned the 'R' code and have been thoroughly rebuked."

"Rebuked? It was practically a cat fight. Gina threw a punch at you then Lorraine rode in on her broomstick. If I hadn't found Locke fast, who knows what might have happened?"

"I would have been out the door. Guess I've taken your place on Lorraine's hit list, Hank."

"That's nothing to brag about, Taylor. When you get in the way of what the Girards want, they call out the enforcers and people disappear, some permanently. And don't think for a minute they care which one happens to you. MACS employees are about as valuable as used urine cups."

"Hank, I want to thank you for talking with me. And tell Peter Lane that what he's going through won't be for nothing. I know someone who is influential with the state psychology board. When I can put this together, well, I'm taking it to him."

"Good luck, Doc. Watch your back."

"Don't worry, Hank. I'm going to watch it for her. Taylor is the only person who is trying to help me find out what really happened to Harriet," Ray said.

"Lorraine is what happened, and we all know it," Hank gulped his beer.

CHAPTER 28

Taylor sneezed several times as the clear night air hit her smoke-assaulted lungs. She walked quickly to her car, locking the doors and turning on the engine. Before she left the bar, she saw Gabe head in the opposite direction toward the rest rooms. Maybe he went there or maybe there is another exit. He promised to call so she took her cell phone out of her pocket and sat it on the passenger seat. She was repairing her lipstick when it rang.

"Is this the beautiful lady taxi service? I'm a lonely guy waiting to be picked up."

"What do you expect from a taxi service, sir?"

"I want to gaze adoringly into the dancing brown eyes of the most exquisite, brilliant and amazing woman in the world."

"She sounds interesting. Will you settle for me?"

"I've been settling all my life, Taylor. With you, I don't have to settle for anything less than perfection," Gabe caught his own breath to stifle the declaration of love that he so wanted to give her, "I'll wait for you to pick me up on the corner at the open air post office."

Blake would have taken her straight to the airport for a moonlight flight followed by iced champagne when they landed. And after drinking champagne, he couldn't responsibly fly so they would have to spend the night. It's unbelievable how many times that old trick worked. But this wasn't the time or place to be Blake. His coming out party had to wait until the case was closed. Not such a tough assignment really. Stick close to her, like Bruce Wayne clearing away the grunt work so that Batman can ride in to rescue the fair lady. At least I don't have to wear tights.

Flipping open the cell phone, he spoke in a smoldering voice, "You have my total and undivided attention."

"I certainly wish that were true."

"Morganna! Why are you calling me here?" he answered, keeping a watchful eye on Taylor's car heading toward him.

"Blake, you ungrateful bore! I've been working overtime analyzing your sample and now you sound like I'm intruding. Are you with another woman?"

"I'm working."

"I'm sorry. I'll call back."

"No, wait. It's okay, but my contact is approaching so make this fast."

"Business first. You'll owe me playtime later. The Nutracurative is a fruit basket of herbs and natural substances. A few are tropical but nothing rare. The formula is no more lethal than a quart of juice from the local grocery."

"Well, there goes the prevailing theory that Nutracuratives cure schizophrenia."

"You must be joking. If that were true the local cops would be all over us to make the stuff in vats and dump it in the public fountains where Washington's homeless drink and bathe."

Taylor's car rounded the corner and pulled into a loading zone about fifty feet from him. She waved. Gabe pointed toward the phone. Taylor nodded.

"Blake! Are you still there?"

"Yes, my contact arrived so I have to go."

"Are you in danger?"

Yes, my heart has been captured, but that's not nearly the danger I once thought that it might be. "No, this is an informational contact. No gun play."

"Blake, you owe me for this one. I went beyond the call of duty and bullied my lab staff. I expect you to come home after this case. I want you to see me wearing the tanzanite necklace you sent. It looks great against my naked skin and black satin sheets."

"Later. I've got to get back to work. For my safety, contact me through Jack."

"When will I see you again?"

"I'll see you when the work is over. You know what this life is like," he artfully dodged the commitment she wanted. "I'm going to make a run at getting another version of the Nutracurative tomorrow. If I'm successful, would you put a full press on analyzing it? Please? You're the best in the lab," then he added as a lure, "and the best other places as well."

"Hmm. Glad you remember. Okay, send it up here, but the results will be the same. What you have there is a harmless nutritional drink. Add some serious anti-psychotics if you want to see a difference. Drugs control schizophrenia, not vitamin cocktails."

Gabe closed the phone and walked slowly toward Taylor's car. *Drugs! That's it!* He held his facial muscle taunt to appear like nonchalant like good ole, low key Gabe. Inside Blake was shouting victory. Tomorrow at MACS, he would find proof, now that he knew what to look for.

"Sorry for the interruption. I had to tell a co-worker how to handle an order," Gabe explained as he clicked his seat belt in place. *Oh God, how I hate hiding things from her. Deception is the essential skill of undercover investigative work. I'm not a pathological liar, merely a well-practiced one. Will she ever understand?*

"No problem, Gabe. Do you need to go back to the gallery?"

"No, but thanks for understanding. Let's get something to eat. I can hardly wait to hear what you learned from Hank."

"Now why do you think I know something new?"

"Because, good doctor, I watched your facial expressions and body language. You have a lot to tell me."

She stopped at a red light and gazed at him, "You amaze me, Gabe. There's a side of you that I don't think I know."

He paused. She was so good at reading people. He wanted to

tell her the truth, but that was totally impossible and dangerous to her well-being, so he resorted to the bland answer of his alter ego, "Then you have to spend more time with me. I'm a simple guy who simply wants to be near you."

Blake screamed inside his head desperately wanting to be heard.

* * * * *

Following Blake's directions, Taylor drove toward the old Gulfport Coliseum. Parking on the water side, they paused to look at the moon light bouncing off the incoming tide. Seagulls circled overhead, waiting for a hand out. He slipped his arm around her waist, pulling her toward him. "Taylor, no matter what happens I want you to remember one thing about us."

"What's that?"

"Believe me when I say that I have never been happier in my life than I am with you. And that has nothing to do with the circumstances. That's coming from the core of my being," he said softly, pressing small kisses across her forehead.

"Gabe, I've never known anyone like you either."

"I wish that we had met under different circumstances. Then I could tell you things I dare not say now."

"It's okay, Gabe," she responded, unable to grasp the true meaning of his words. "Just because I'm a professional and you are still trying to make it in acting doesn't mean that we can't care deeply for each other. Let's see what happens. Besides I'm sure you'll soon find your way to success in the theatre or maybe you'll learn the art business."

"You're right, of course," he said hugging her tightly. *Sweet Taylor, trying not to be as uppity as Mama Julia raised you to be. I bet she told you to find a doctor or a lawyer or a banker. At the very least he must be a well-bred Ivy League graduate with a promising future and enough money to make life comfortable. Too bad you don't know, that's exactly who I am.*

Taylor was relieved when Gabe guided her past the open air biker bar. That was a bit earthier than she could handle. Her clothes still smelled of smoke from the meeting with Hank and Ray. No telling what kind of smoke emanated from the leather and chains crowd. A few feet past the easy riders, she heard a Jimmy Buffet-style singer crooning out a fair imitation of Key West sounds. The small restaurant was packed with senior adults and yuppies, mixing amicably at the all-you-can-eat shrimp bar. Gabe noticed a couple stand up to leave so he made a dash to grab the table, motioning for Taylor to join him. She scanned the room, early attic decor mostly illuminated by candles dripping rainbow wax down the sides of old wine bottles.

"Nothing fancy but the seafood is fabulous."

"I've driven the shortcut through Gulfport from Pasadena over to 34th Street, but this is the first time I've gotten off the main roads. What a place untouched by time."

"Good description. You see, I've always searched for the more intimate places where the locals hang out. That's how you get to know the people," he replied subtly revealing what Marco taught him. *Wouldn't Marco be amused to know that the technique of mingling with the locals to check out the territory before a high stakes card game was remarkably similar to what I learned from a senior agent at the FBI Academy? At times, good and evil employ the same modus operandi.*

The waitress, a fresh-faced cheerleader type, began to enthusiastically regale the evening specials, when Gabe interrupted, "We'll have two shrimp platters, extra sauce and lots of napkins. And bring a pitcher of island tea."

"Would you like an appetizer? We've got totally outrageous stuffed crab and…"

Gabe flashed his disarming smile, "No thanks. We plan to gorge ourselves on shrimp and talk. You know, personal things."

The young waitress tossed back her hair and smiled. "You got it. I'll bring your dinner and disappear until you call me, cool?"

"Cool," he replied, turning toward Taylor in an effort to stifle a laugh.

"I think she likes you. It must be the smile, or maybe your tight tush."

"No chance," he answered, "Wait a minute. You never told me you liked my 'tush.'"

Her superior grin slid into a stammer, "I…I mean…I sound like a teenager."

"Dr. Kendall, do you or don't you like me for more than my witty conversation and my willingness to be your co-conspirator?"

She paused, hesitant about how much truth to admit, "Gabe, I like everything about you. You're different from the guys I've dated. You're more of a free spirit."

He reached for her hand, holding it tightly, "As beautiful and desirable as you are physically, Taylor, I can honestly say I'm most intrigued by who you are inside, not only how great you look outside."

"I'm equally fascinated by who you are. Not Gabe the actor, Gabe the man."

"I wish I could tell you about him."

The arrival of their food created enough interruption for him to regain his composure and resume his necessary deception. If the shrimp had arrived five minutes later, he might not have been able to suppress Blake's confession.

* * * * *

"From what you're telling me, Taylor, Hank is running scared," Gabe observed, stirring his tea while he mulled over her review of the earlier conversation at the bar.

"No doubt about it. Hank is a target. I told him to go to the police, but he laughed, saying he wasn't the hero type."

"Does he know where to find Peter Lane, the other social worker?"

"Hank wouldn't say, but I think he does. When I mentioned

that name, he and Ray exchanged nervous looks and quickly changed the subject," Taylor recalled her impressions.

"As far as we know, Peter Lane is still alive."

"I hope so. Why wouldn't he be?"

"Because when people within the MACS programs know too much, they have unfortunate accidents."

"Oh, Gabe, do you think someone at MACS is responsible for Greg's death, even though it was ruled a suicide?"

"Yes, I do. He was a very unstable person who may have been pushed to the breaking point by this 'R code' formula or something else. After all, he was surrounded by experts in psychology."

"Do you really think the Girards would resort to murder to keep their programs going?"

"It's a multi-million dollar operation based on the figures you heard from Hank and Ray. People have committed murder for a lot less."

Taylor sat upright in her chair as if suddenly pushed back by a strong wind. "I've seen that Victoria is ruthless, Marco is arrogant and Serena is narcissistic. I also know that Carla would have nothing to do with harming another person and Felipe is too stupid to be dangerous. Now Gina, that's another story. With goading from Lorraine, I think she would do anything... particularly if it gained her father's attention. Yes, I can see Lorraine and Gina as hit-women. I suppose your theory is possible."

"Sounds like you have them sized up rather well."

"I've only known the Girards a short time. I wouldn't want to falsely accuse anyone of such awful behavior. Harming a patient and terrorizing employees is extreme even for money. Don't they think they will get caught?"

"No, getting caught never enters their minds. From what you tell me, MACS is a sophisticated operation. Is that the work of novices, beginner's luck?"

"Apparently not."

"Well, Sherlock, what's the key, the missing element?"

"Blake Girard."

Shrimp sauce dripped down Gabe's lips and onto his shirt. He used his napkin to cover his open-mouthed amazement that followed her declaration. "What do you mean by that?"

"Blake must be the wild card in all this. Maybe we need to look for him. I know that Carla is the only one who can reach him."

"Why do you think Blake Girard would help you point the finger at his family?"

"I don't know exactly, but I'm certain from things Carla says that he must be more like her than the rest of the family. Maybe he's honest."

"How did you come to that conclusion?"

"Well, he was angry when he left and he's not here getting his share of the profits. Wouldn't it be ironic if his means of thwarting them was to reject their sinister ways?"

"Okay, precisely where do you think Blake Girard is?"

"I don't know. The rumor is he's an international playboy jetting from one high stakes card game to another. That's a bit cliché. Too much like a soap opera. Personally I think I'm on to him."

"You are?"

"Yes," Taylor's eyes sparkled with confidence as she reached for Gabe's hand. "I think that he gave his life to the mission field as the ultimate atonement while praying daily for the souls of his wretched family."

Funny as it was, Gabe's all out belly laugh seemed more generous than Taylor thought her meager effort at humor deserved.

With Taylor, Gabe almost felt as carefree as his persona was expected to appear. *She could be sincere one minute then confound him with her humor the next. There is no one who so craftily blends brilliance and assertiveness, except of course Blake Girard. They really would be the perfect couple. Wait, is it possible to be jealous of yourself?*

* * * * *

RING! RING!

Taylor kept one hand on the wheel while fishing in her purse for the cell phone. The ring continued. "Must be yours."

Her voice broke through his daydream and he answered his phone.

"I just got an earful from Morganna. What's happening?"

"Hello," he answered, purposely not saying Jack's name. "Do you need for me to check that inventory tonight?"

"Sure, man. Although given the choice I'd check out the lovely Taylor or the hot-blooded Morganna rather than some dusty antiques. Whatever does it for you."

"Okay, but I'll have to finish it tonight," Gabe said, winking at Taylor. "I have special plans with a friend tomorrow. We're leaving early and returning late."

"Now there's the man I admire. Setting up another seduction?"

"No, actually. I'll call you when I get back to the gallery. About thirty minutes, okay?"

Gabe hung up the phone. Taylor pulled up to a red light and turned toward him.

"Do you have to go back to your place tonight? It's already late."

"Yes, I'd rather do the work now than interrupt our day tomorrow."

"Oh. I was going to invite you to stay at my place so we could get an early start."

"Wish I could. I'll take a rain check," Gabe forced himself to make his voice sound upbeat.

The rode in silence as Taylor pulled up in the alleyway by the side door to the gallery. Gabe leaned over to kiss her. That was a mistake. Rationalizing that a good night kiss will be enough does nothing but lead the way to a cold water shower interrupted by steamy visions of Taylor. He pulled away from her embrace.

"I better leave now so I can get my work done fast and dream about you."

"You're such a flirt. What's the plan for tomorrow?"

"I'll bring coffee to your place about eight a.m. Is that too early?"

"No. Make it seven a.m. if you want."

Actually, I want to make it with you all night long, but that's a little too far over the job description for this case. It's not that civic-minded Blake hasn't given his body for his country, sacrificially compromising several blondes, a few brunettes and a red head in the line of duty.

"Gabe, are you falling asleep?"

"Oh, uh…not really. I mean, no. Or maybe yes. I think I could use some sleep."

He gave her one final, chaste kiss on the cheek then reached for the car door.

"Wait, Gabe. I have something wonderful for tomorrow."

Before he could respond, she got out the driver's seat and opened the trunk. Reaching inside, she pulled out a green MACS logo shirt.

"Isn't this great?" Taylor beamed. "It's the shirt that MACS staffers wear in the clinics."

"What's that for?"

"It's for you to wear tomorrow. I'll wear my lab coat so we'll both appear official."

"But you said we wouldn't run into the staff," he questioned, as she held up the shirt on his chest.

"Perfect fit."

"Taylor, are you hearing me?"

"Gabe, think of this as another role in a play."

"Very funny."

"Just wear the shirt. I went to a lot of trouble to get it for you."

"Exactly how did you get the shirt?"

"I took it from the laundry rack."

"You did what? Mama Julia will have me boiled in oil as a bad influence."

"I've never done anything like that in my life. It was very scary, but exhilarating. Besides it's worthwhile if we are successful," Taylor defended her action.

"You don't stop the bad guys by acting like them," Gabe nearly choked as Dale's words coming out of his mouth.

"Okay, okay. Besides, we're not stealing it, only borrowing it for tomorrow. I'll even wash and press it before I return it. Now do you feel better?"

"That's better. And Taylor, this isn't a fraternity prank. Try not to enjoy yourself too much."

Gabe closed the car door and watched her drive away. He fumbled for his key to unlock the side door. Taking the stairs two steps at a time seemed an eternity until he could fling his body on the sofa, green shirt draped across his chest. His cell phone rang.

"Coast is clear, my man?"

"Yes, Jack. What's so important that it can't wait until tomorrow? I'm tired."

"The tail we put on Lorraine Lewis followed her to the University today. She was hanging around the faculty parking lot near Dale's car."

"What was she doing?"

"Our agent couldn't tell if she tinkered with his car or not."

"Is Dale all right?"

"Yeah, man, he's fine. I phoned him as a friend of Blake's. Told him that his car needed checking and sent a tow truck. He was cool about it. I think he understood something was up. Took it to the nearest Sheriff's station and had the bomb squad look it over."

"If she hurts a hair on his head, I'll cut her heart out, assuming I can find it."

"Back off, man. No bomb, just a little present."

"What?"

"A cheap tracking device."

"Do you have it?"

"Yes. What do you think we ought to do with it? Find a long haul trucker headed north?"

"No. Leave Dale's car in the impound yard a few more days. We'll let Geek Boy lead her on a chase. He keeps begging to be where the action is."

"You're a wild man. Derek will love it."

"I need to be sure Lorraine won't show up at MACS tomorrow when Taylor and Gabe go on their scavenger hunt."

"No problem. I'll keep a tail on her. If necessary, I'll get St. Pete PD to pull her over on a traffic citation."

"And, Jack, I want you to bring Hank in for safekeeping. My guess is that when you find him, you'll also find Peter Lane."

"I agree, Blake. Are we ready to offer them immunity and safe house?"

"Based on what I heard tonight, yes, but not the Tarpon Springs house. I prefer that you get them out of state immediately. I want them to disappear completely until this investigation wraps up."

"And that will be soon?"

"I think our field trip to MACS tomorrow for the Nutracurative ingredients and looking in on Martha at the state hospital on Sunday will make sense of the rest of it," Blake paused making a mental checklist, "Are you sure Martha is still there? If DEA gets wind of this, they could move her."

"The Director said the same thing after he had Gloria make discreet inquiries. So he sent in a PRN nurse to watch Martha."

"Are you sure she can handle it?"

"Blake, this nurse is a highly decorated agent. According to her folder, she can out ride, out shoot and out rope the best DEA or MACS has to offer. And she's a babe. She might be right for you."

"I don't need your Oakie dating service. Besides, I'll be with Taylor."

"Keep an open mind. The nurse's undercover name is Ginger Gregory."

Blake yawned, "Where will you be tomorrow?"

"Within shouting distance of you and Taylor all weekend. Consider me your friendly neighborhood chaperone."

"Won't Mama Julia be happy about that?" Blake mumbled, hanging up the phone, unable to force his eyes open any longer.

CHAPTER 29

The double doors flung open. "Good morning, lovely ladies," Marco crooned entering Victoria's bedroom, "I brought your coffee."

He carried the tray toward the bed and surveyed the scene. Victoria, in her usual Asian embroidered red silk pajamas, pulled the sheets away from her bloodshot eyes barely enough to stare at him. Startled by the sound of a masculine voice, Serena emerged from the adjoining bathroom in a flowing pink nightgown with marabou feathers trailing the hemline. Marco sat the tray on the nearby table and turned toward Serena. He placed a gentle kiss on her cheek, "Cara Mia, I thought you reserved the diva sleepwear for me? Why wasn't I invited? You know how I enjoy these group activities."

"What do you want, Marco?"

"A vision of you, my charming wife, is all a mortal man could ask."

"Cut the sarcasm, Marco. It's Saturday morning, why are you awake so early?" Victoria quizzed, while rummaging in her night table drawer.

In three quick strides Marco was at her side, reaching his long fingers into the drawer and pulling out the silver flask. Holding it up, he shook it. "Seeking more hair of the dog that bit you?"

She lunged for the flask in his hand. Nimble as a soccer goalie, he read her move and veered in the opposite direction. The louder she cursed the more he laughed.

Serena crept up beside Marco, taking the flask from his hand and giving it to Victoria, "Now, now, children, let's play fair."

"Indeed, you are right, my darling," Marco replied, walking

over to the mirror to smooth his dark hair. "The yacht is fueled and ready for your day trip. I'm driving to Ocala to pick up the shipment. Don't wait for me at dinner. I'll probably spend the evening at the club in Ybor City and stay overnight in Tampa."

"Why isn't the shipment coming to the house like always?" Victoria asked.

"Too many undercurrents. Who knows, the local police may not be as bumbling as they appear."

"But Marco, there's no further investigation on that patient's suicide. At least, that's the assurance you gave us," Serena challenged.

"That's what I'm told. However there's the nasty matter of those disgruntled social workers. Lorraine saw one of them around town."

"I thought she gave them a warning."

"So I hear. Was that your idea, Victoria?"

"Well, it certainly wasn't mine. I abhor violence," Serena preened her hair as she leaned across the antique chaise.

"There is to be no destruction of property. That's for amateurs. Remember, ladies, this isn't Argentina, this is America. The police here have vastly superior forensic techniques. I'll decide when and if extreme methods are required, are we clear about that?" Marco spoke in what Serena described behind his back as his "tin general voice."

He glared sternly, and then swiveled on his heel marching toward the doors. Pausing to restore his composure, he adjusted his scowl to a naughty boy smirk, "No reason to bungle the details and destroy our multi-million dollar pipeline from Medicare. God bless the USA!"

As the double doors closed behind him, Victoria shouted, "Tell Sally that she has to be at work on time Monday morning."

If he heard, he made no retort, at least none audible over the women's playful laughter.

* * * * *

Taylor tossed her head on the pillow mumbling, "Come on, Mama, five minutes more, please?"

The continued ringing jolted her into the present. It was the telephone.

"Does the most beautiful woman in the world need an extra half hour sleep?"

"Oh, Gabe. I'm glad you called. I overslept. Are we late?"

"Relax, Taylor, its 7:30 a.m. I'm ready but it sounds like you aren't."

"I'll come over to get you in a half hour."

"Take your time. Why don't you phone me from the car when you turn on Central and I'll be waiting downstairs?"

"Okay, I'll do that. Gabe, I'm sorry. I mean, I was the one who was pushing you."

"No big deal. I'll be the guy standing outside in the obvious green shirt."

"I think I'll be able to find you."

She hung up the phone and dashed into the kitchen to turn on the coffeemaker. With one leg in and one leg out of the shower, her reverie was interrupted by the telephone. Expecting it to be Gabe, she wrapped a towel around her body and rushed to intercept the ring.

"I'm getting ready right now. I won't be late again."

"Sounds like you have a busy day planned."

"Papa Clifton!" Taylor recognized the deep southern drawl.

"Good morning, Taylor. Do you have to work today?"

"Well….uh…actually, I'm uh…I'm putting in some overtime on a project."

"Lucky co-worker, is it a young man? The one you mentioned?"

Taylor didn't want to get into a long explanation, yet she couldn't lie, "Yes. I am working with a gentleman whom I both like and respect."

"Well, you warned me not to get my hopes up. Since I talked

to you, Trey called and told me about that girl you mentioned. I still hope it's not serious."

"If he is happy, then I'm happy for both of them."

"Please, don't wish that on me. I have an airhead for a daughter. One per family is enough. I intended for my grandson to marry you and improve our gene pool."

"Gosh Papa Clifton, and you wonder where Trey's mother learned to be controlling."

"You're a smart woman, Taylor Kendall, but enough of that. You have to get to work and I need to catch up on reading EKGs. The liquid you sent for analysis is merely a fruit juice blend. Nothing remarkable. Lab report also says nothing toxic. At worst it may be snake oil. At best, it's similar to the base for those rum drinks at the poolside bar, the ones with the silly little umbrellas."

As he spoke, Taylor balanced the phone on one shoulder while setting out her makeup. "Thanks for trying. I have another angle on it, so I may send a second sample."

"Taylor, don't go tilting at windmills. Finish your residency and then you'll be in a better position to be a crusader."

"I understand what you're saying, but it's gone a little too far to ignore. Don't worry about me. I have someone backing me up."

"Are you sure he can handle it?"

How odd, that same concern continues to plague her. What does an underemployed actor with minimal education know about the kind of sophisticated web MACS is weaving? She wasn't going to let her doubts show.

"Gabe and I make a great team."

"You take care of yourself and stay out of trouble."

"Papa Clifton, what makes you think I'll get into trouble?"

"Simple. You have Julia's sense of curiosity and Tom's determination to right the wrongs of the world. That's an explosive combination."

* * * * *

Carla swirled cheese sauce around the eggs with the tips of her fork. Somehow that was more interesting than trying to turn Tiffany's monologue into a conversation. She droned on about nail tips and the difficulty of finding the right glue. Felipe's arrival interrupted the noise.

"Going shopping, Tiff?"

"I wish," she said with a practiced pout. "I don't have enough money. I'll go with you or stay at home. Where are you going, Felipe?"

With a look of surprise, or perhaps guilt, he paused. "I'm going to do some errands for Father. And…I…well, I'm also looking over some software systems. You know, search around the computer stores, the kind of thing you hate."

"What am I suppose to do all day?"

He reached for his wallet, pulling out several bills. She grabbed them and flung herself at him. Poor fool. He probably thought her purr of contentment was from being in his arms. Fortunately with her head on his shoulder, he couldn't see her stare with delight at the quartet of fifty dollar bills she caressed with her eyes.

He broke away from her and turned around, "Maybe Carla will go with you."

"Not a chance. Besides I'm going into the office to get that stack of quality control reports filed."

"Why, is your mother on your case about something?" Felipe asked, stuffing half a muffin in his mouth.

"No, I don't think so."

"Did my mother say something significant?"

"Felipe, the last significant thing your mother said was 'Voulez vous couchez avec moi, ce soir?' to my father," Carla snapped back. "The result was Blake."

"What does that mean, Felipe? Is that Spanish?"

"No, Tiffany, it's French. Felipe's mother never bothered to learn our language, but we were forced to learn hers," Carla enjoyed watching him fume yet lack the ability to engage in verbal warfare.

He turned on his heel, the only mannerism of his father's that he successfully copied, and stormed out the front door.

"Did I say something to make him mad?" Tiffany asked.

"No more than usual," Carla stifled a grin at her complete obliviousness, "Why don't you get an early start? You know, be there when the stores open."

"You can come with me if you want."

"Tiffany, do a favor for both of us and go alone. You don't want to spend the day with me anymore than I want to be with you."

With the sound of a horseshoe that's partially off the hoof, Tiffany clicked across the marble hallway in her leopard sandals. In the distance, Carla heard Tiffany greet Victoria. She jumped up from the table and went into the hall.

"Mother, I need to talk to you."

"Not now, Carla. Not until I've had coffee."

Carla sat down. The maid cleared the breakfast dishes. Nothing to do but make new napkin folds until Victoria was ready to be approached. Ten, fifteen minutes elapsed before she stopped pacing and refilling her coffee cup.

"All right, Carla, what do you want?"

"I need to replace a tire on my car. Which credit card is active?"

"Our personal card is at the limit. Use the MACS card. Can't it wait until Monday?"

"No, Mother, my tire has a slow leak. I'll handle it myself. I'm going to the office for a while so don't count on me for dinner."

"It's going to be quiet around here. Gina is out for the weekend. Marco claims he's going to stay over in Tampa tonight. Where are Felipe and his bimbo?"

"She's gone shopping. He left earlier acting a bit unsettled."

"What's that loser up to?"

"Who knows? Maybe he's following Father's example and went to find a mistress."

"Better check and see if large sums are leaving the operating account. If Felipe wants a little on the side, he's going to have to pay for it from his salary."

Serena stood at the door of the dining room, trying to ascertain the reason for Carla and Victoria's hearty laughter, "And what's the joke?"

"Your son, Felipe."

Serena raised her chin enough to look down on them, "Perhaps, but I'm also Blake's mother. Let us not forget that I produced Marco's heir."

"And where is Blake the magnificent? At least both of my daughters are busy with the work that supports our family."

Carla slipped out quietly as her father's wife and ex-wife replayed the endless argument. In a few hours, they will either kiss and make up or spend the afternoon shouting contradictory directions to the yacht captain. Either way, Carla had enough of the whole family for a while. Where better to escape them than at the office? Gina was the only one who ever worked on weekends and she was away with Lorraine. MACS headquarters would be a quiet retreat.

CHAPTER 30

Taylor pulled into the MACS parking lot as Gabe's eyes scanned the area.

"Is this your usual parking place?"

"Yes. Why?"

"Because parking here might cause another MACS employee to recognize your car. Let's park over toward the alley, near the back entrance," he pointed toward the spot. "I'm sure people going to the shops and the ball game park in business lots during the weekend."

It seemed extreme, but Taylor put the car in reverse, leaving her usual parking place to pull in to the left of the building to gain a little shade from the fledging tree in the median next to the alley.

"How's that, Dr. Watson?"

"Excellent, Sherlock," he replied, purposely molding his voice to a casual tone that would not reflect his sober mood. Snooping around the premises without a search warrant was definitely serious business. He had to snap out of this overprotective mode. MACS was Taylor's work place. Her presence on the weekend may be unusual, but not implausible. His presence, on the other hand, was a hot potato if he were to be identified by the bad guys or the good guys.

"Come on, slow poke," she shouted, bounding up the short flight of stairs. Her key card easily unlocked the back door. The heavy door shut behind them. The hallway was partially lit. She leaned close to him whispering, "There may be a guard at the front desk. We can get into the clinic without being seen, but we have to walk past him to get to the main elevators later."

"Do it now."

"What do you mean?"

"You go around the corner and say hello. Be friendly and ask if he wants coffee."

"Why are we going to spike it with knock-out drops?" her brown eyes danced with anticipation.

"You watch too many old movies. This is a simple observation not breaking into Fort Knox. Sometimes I wonder which one of us is the biggest ham."

She lightly slapped his shoulder, "You are. And if we get into trouble, I expect you to come up with some great lines to get us out."

"Never fear, my lady. Talking my way out of tight spots is practically my life's work."

"Oh, sure," she replied turning away from him to slide her key card in the door.

Taylor was surprised at Gabe's interest in the clinic. *Rather than boredom, he was alert to every sound and curious about the work. Could be that he is genuinely intrigued? Then again, he is an accomplished actor. Hard to tell when he's merely playing a role.*

She turned her attention back to the charts. He pulled a chair beside her and grabbed a patient chart.

"What are you doing?"

"I'm helping you. That's why you brought me, remember?"

"But you don't know what you're looking for?"

"Dr. Kendall, I don't have to be a psychological guru to turn to the yellow tab clearly labeled 'medications' and look for an 'R code,'" he snapped back.

Taylor rolled her chair over beside his. "I'm sorry, Gabe. My Daddy warned me that my take-charge attitude was great for work, but not great for relationships. I didn't mean to sound like I was the only one who could do this."

Her honesty shattered his defenses. He was used to demanding, even obnoxious women. She gave him the one thing that he wasn't prepared to handle: strength with caring. It reached too close to his core being, the Blake that he had never revealed to any woman. In psychological terms, this was the part of his inner child that Serena irrevocably wounded by her indifference. He vowed never to open himself to be hurt again. Now here was Taylor showing him how to be transparent without fear. As he reached out to receive her hug, he knew he wanted to be transparent with Taylor more than he wanted anything else in the world. If only this were a different time, a different place. If only he wasn't trapped inside another man's identity playing a part that she may or may not understand. If only...

RING! RING! RING!

The blaring phone startled both of them enough to break the embrace.

"Who's calling us?" Taylor whispered.

"Wait a minute. Don't touch the phone. There's bound to be an answering service." The phone problem was a welcome relief. It gave his mind a chance to override his feelings so that cool logic flowed to temper the hot Latin blood he inherited from Marco.

He closed the chart notebook firmly, "I think we're looking for the answer in the wrong place."

"What do you mean?"

"Well, you told me that Hank said the "R" code notation in the chart was dropped after he started asking questions. We don't know what the new notation is, so we don't see it here."

"I think you are right. I bet that only a few people, like Gina and Lorraine and maybe Neva, know what the designation for the old 'R code' is. Now what do we do?"

"Let's go to the second floor and snoop around the lab. Maybe there's some information up there that tracks the patients getting 'R code' Nutracuratives."

Taylor rose from her seat, carefully replacing the two charts they were viewing back to the correct places in the chart rack.

"The second floor may have extra alarms. It's a big secret deal."

"Yes, but you told me that your new key card allows full access."

"I think it does, but I've only been inside the file room. The only time I entered the lab side was on tour with Dr. Locke."

"Onward and upward. We'll never know if we don't try."

"What if we set off some alarm and the police come?"

"I rather doubt that the internal alarms are connected to the police station," he said drawing from his memory of past Girard clinics, "If MACS is doing something questionable, do you think they want the police to answer an alarm and wander around the place."

"Makes sense. Maybe the alarm rings at the Girard mansion? Or on Lorraine's pager?"

"No. If Dr. Marco was that worried about break-ins then he would have tighter security at the entry points. And he'd never give any employee a full access key card like you have. What you were told about the second floor security is a smoke screen to deter amateurs. I think it's another elaborate MACS hoax."

* * * * *

"Good morning!"

The security guard slumped in his chair nodded his head without losing eye contact with the DVD screen. As the entrant moved toward the elevator, he caught a glimpse of her and nearly fell out of his chair standing to attention.

"Oh, Miss Carla, it's you. I mean, I'm happy to see you."

"It's okay, Gus. Dr. Marco isn't with me."

"I don't usually see anyone on the weekend, except for the cleaning crew. It gets really dull," he stammered.

"Dull sounds wonderful to me. I'm going to my office," Carla replied reaching for the elevator call button. She noticed that the elevator was coming down from the second floor. As she stepped in the elevator, she thought she heard him say someone was there already. *No, he must mean the cleaning crew has been there. Anyway it doesn't matter, as long as I don't have to see another Girard all day long.*

* * * * *

Taylor watched Gabe as his fingers deftly probed the lab door and scanner. *He looks as if he knows what he is doing. Hopefully he doesn't moonlight in second story work. If he does, he certainly doesn't spend the money on clothes or a new car.*

Gabe heard it first; the sound of an elevator motor. He grabbed the key card from Taylor's hand, swiped it and pulled her inside the door just as the elevator opened.

Carla looked around. There was nothing out of place. That's one of the things she hated about multi-level offices; elevators with a mind of their own. Hopefully this one isn't starting the kind of erratic movements that preceded the last stuck-between-floors crisis.

Taylor leaned against Gabe's chest. She could feel his heart beating faster, his muscles tense. Moments later, he relaxed and drew out a long breath.

"What's happening?" she whispered.

"Get over there behind the file cabinet. I have to check."

She stood behind the cabinet, peeking around the corner to watch him. He opened the lab door about two inches to peer out in the hallway. Quickly, he shut it again.

"All clear. I heard the elevator door, and then the motor started again. Who could be here besides the security guard?"

"I don't know. Maybe it's the cleaning crew. Or maybe an employee forgot something."

"Until we know who else is in this building, whisper and avoid making any extraneous noises. Sounds carry in a quiet office building. Even closing file drawers sounds loud without the usual daily office noises. Okay?"

"Let's get inside the inner lab room. I've heard it's sound

proof." Taylor motioned for him to follow her to the door to Gina's secret kingdom. She reached for the door handle. "It's locked."

"Why don't you look around the files in this carousel while I try it. It may only be stuck."

With Taylor's attention focused on the files, Gabe pulled out the small nail file part of his pocket knife. Not a true lock picking set. No, those are illegal. However, as Dr. Marco often told Blake, "Pay attention, my son. You can learn something from a peasant as quickly as from a professor." As usual, Marco was right. The first guy Blake collared for industrial espionage taught him to use a harmless tool like this one to open the average office door. Deftly he popped the lock. "I got it. I think it was stuck," he told Taylor, who appeared skeptical yet silent about the ease of entry.

They walked into the stark room; white countertops, white tile floor and white walls as pristine as a store display. Three tall stools sat in front of workstations with the usual collection of vials, pipettes and containers. A lone microscope with a tray a clean glass slides sat in the corner. Gabe examined it carefully. He ran his finger across the platform, clearing a trail through the dust. Granted, it wasn't a sterile lab, but dust on a key piece of equipment in an otherwise sparkling environment said more about lack of use than housekeeping. So much for the "highest level of research" promised in the glossy MACS brochure.

Taylor sat on a stool, surveying the workstation, "Looks like my chemistry classroom in high school, except there are no Bunsen burners."

"I doubt that your classroom was this orderly."

"Labs are supposed to be organized."

"This lab looks more like a display than a working lab," he said, picking up a paper towel to avoid leaving fingerprints as he opened the cabinet above the adjacent workstation. Inside were more clean containers and a few simple mixing tools. Then he turned toward the rear workstation facing the outer wall. Opening the cabinet doors at counter level, he found four commercial blenders and nearly laughed out loud.

Taylor walked over to see for herself, "Is Gina running a smoothie factory on the side?"

"That's more likely than running a research lab. My guess is that this is where the Nutracuratives are mixed," he answered, leaning his nose toward each blender to sniff for chemicals.

"It smells like strawberry or peach; what's your pleasure?"

"Neither, sorry."

He started to close the cabinet doors when he saw a small pile of powder that must have been spilled during the mixing process. "Taylor, did you hear that?"

"Hear what?"

"I want you to walk out in the outer office and put your ear to the main door. Let me know if you hear the elevator motor."

"My you have good hearing. I'll be right back."

As soon as she left, he reached into his pocket for a small plastic zip top bag. Using his pen knife, he scraped the powder into the bag. He bent down to look beneath the counter for any other missed yet revealing messes.

"Gabe? Where are you?"

He rose immediately, bumping his head on the counter rim. "Ouch! Here."

"Are you all right?"

"Sure. Just another bump among many on this hard head."

She ran her fingers through his gel slicked hair pulling his head downward, "I can kiss it and make it better."

He wrapped his strong hands around her, raising his head until their lips were practically touching, "Then kiss me now and I'll feel better all over."

His kisses were soothing firecrackers that made her melt and soar at the same time. For him, it was different. To kiss Taylor was to genuflect at the altar of female perfection. After a lifetime of lust indulged by women of every nationality, he felt tremors that darted past his loins and made his heart quiver.

The thump of a motor start again, breaking the spell of the kiss.

"What's that?"

He turned his ear to the wall against which he had been leaning with her cradled in his arms. "It's coming from behind this wall. There must be a door somewhere."

She moved away from him and walked around by the free standing room divider.

"Here it is!"

"Shhh," he reminded, pressing an all too brief kiss against her lips. "We have to be as quiet as possible." Another simple office lock. He reached for the tool to open the door.

"How did you do that?"

With his adrenaline pumping from the kiss and the discovery of the powder, he forgot to distract Taylor's attention while he opened the door.

"Oh, that. It's an old theatre trick."

"Oh really?"

"Indeed. We bit-part players don't get dressing rooms, only worn out lockers. Those locker doors are constantly getting stuck and there's not much time to change between scenes," he wove his tale, "A prop man showed me this trick."

Taylor nodded yes while her expression appeared doubtful. Once he opened the door, they both stepped into a space the size of a large walk-in closet. The humming motor was a refrigeration unit with wide glass doors much like what you find in a convenience store. Neatly arranged on wire shelves on the left side were gallons of concentrated orange juice, tangerine juice and papaya juice. On the right side were paper canisters, similar to ice cream containers with numerical markings.

"Look at that," Taylor said picking up an orange juice container, "The famous Nutracuratives are nothing but a fruit juice cocktail. They don't need a chemist; they need a bartender."

* * * * *

"The cellular phone customer you are trying to reach is currently unavailable. At the sound of the tone, leave a message."

"Blake! Where are you?" Carla sighed and slammed down the receiver. She poured a canned cola into her glass and sipped the cool liquid. Then she pressed the telephone redial on her cell phone and left a message, "Blake, it's Carla. Nothing important. Don't get worried. Things are fairly quiet at the house. I'm at my office, but you can call my cell number. I may get a motel room on the beach and let our mothers think I've been out all night."

She turned the large amethyst and diamond ring on her finger, admiring its splendor, "Since you sent me the beautiful ring with that cryptic note, your mother and my mother took the bait. They are dying to know how I got it and from whom. Thanks again, little brother. I'm enjoying their dismay. Call me soon, please. Maybe you're right. I do need to get away from MACS and the family for awhile."

She dropped the cell phone back into her purse and with her other hand flipped the switch to turn on the computer. Her eyes were drawn to the miniature globe perched on the glass shelf near her monitor. She reached for it, spinning the tiny earth, "I wonder where in the world Blake is right now."

* * * * *

Gabe closed the glass door, "Do you have paper and pen in your pocket?"

"Yes," she replied, pulling a small note pad and black marker from her lab coat pocket.

"Excellent!" He focused on the top shelf, "I'll read off the numbers and you write them down."

"Why don't we open the door so you can see better?"

"No. Keeping the door open too long will fog the glass. What if someone comes in here soon after we leave? That would be suspicious," he answered, proceeding to read numbers.

Taylor started to write faster to keep up.

Why is it that men think all women take shorthand? It's not part of our genetic code.

"Am I going too fast?"

"Yes. Why is it that men think all women take shorthand? It's not part of our genetic code," she teased.

After a few more minutes of rattling off what seemed like random digits Gabe was finished, "That's the last number set."

"What's next?"

"Isn't there a coffee cart near the entrance to this lab?"

"Yes, but I don't think we're ready for a coffee break."

"Very funny, Dr. Kendall, however, we need something to scoop the powders. Would you mind looking to see if there are some plastic spoons on that coffee cart?"

"Okay, I'll be right back," Taylor replied heading out the narrow entrance.

He opened the glass door, carefully removing two cartons and placing them on the nearby table. Using a paper towel, he pried open one of the lids. *No odor.* He pinched a small amount between thumb and forefinger, touching it to his tongue. *Thank God, Marco hasn't resorted to smuggling street drugs. It's not flour or sugar. The markings are too precise to be phony ingredients. This is one or possibly two different substances. The numbers on each carton are handwritten in either blue ink or black ink. Subtle differences.*

What wasn't subtle was opening those containers. He desperately needed to know the contents. Granted, what he found couldn't become evidence. He merely wanted to be able to know where to look later so he could lead the investigators to the evidence when the search warrant was issued.

Is it possible that the powders are as harmless as the fruit juice? He shook his head. *No. Morganna may be a manipulative nymphomaniac at heart but once she puts on that lab coat, she's all business. Her suggestion that some type of medication would have to be included in the Nutracuratives to get a treatment result for schizophrenia is bound to be on target. Somehow these containers hold the answer.*

Taylor returned with four plastic spoons and a paper cup. "Will this do?"

Gabe ran his hand through his hair. God knows how he hated that gel.

"I don't know about this, Taylor. I think we better not touch anything."

"You must be kidding," she replied rising to his challenge, "We're here now and we have to find some answers."

"No. It's not right. Reading charts is one thing, but dipping into stuff is another."

She stood straight with that determined look flashing on her face, "Ridiculous. Here, I'll do it." She reached into her pocket and produced disposable plastic gloves.

"Where did you get those?"

"In the bathroom. I noticed how careful you were to avoid leaving fingerprints, not that I think it will matter. However, I remembered that all the bathrooms in the clinic have plastic glove dispensers. I checked the bathroom down the hall and there they were," she held up her gloved hands, "Sherlock couldn't do it any better."

Gabe smiled, amused at her enthusiasm and his ability to use it to get her to volunteer to do what he couldn't legally do.

Taylor teased open the container top and dipped in the plastic spoon.

"Hold it. Don't get greedy."

She grinned, obviously enjoyed her clandestine activity, "We need enough to get it analyzed."

"My lab guy says it doesn't take much."

"Oh really? Well maybe my lab contact needs more." The remark reminded her of Papa Clifton and the possible risk of the situation. She turned to Gabe, "You know, I think your guy works faster than my contact. Why don't we have him do this analysis? Can he do it quickly?"

Gabe smiled thinking of how efficient Morganna was both in and out of her lab coat. "Sure, my guy works a late shift and has lots of spare time most days. I'll take the samples over this afternoon."

"Great, I'll go with you."

"No, I don't think so."

"Why not?"

"Well, my friend is doing me a favor. His boss is a real tyrant and probably wouldn't approve. He'll only help us if he stays totally anonymous."

Taylor rolled her eyes.

"Hey, I thought you liked this cloak and dagger business, Dr. Kendall."

"I'll like it better if we get away with it."

"You and me both." *The old man would have a seizure if he knew I was here watching you do this. Watching? Helping and coaching is more like it. He doesn't understand how clever the unholy trio can be. Take the money trail for instance: the FBI could spend months shuffling official inquiry paperwork between Washington and Nassau while those millions disappear faster than ice in the Sahara. It's the same problem with the Nutracuratives. Marco has it planned to appear innocent if the most routine toxicity test are done. Morganna must be right. There has to be something else to it.*

"What do you mean something else to it?

"Oh, nothing. I was thinking about this whole fruit juice cocktail that claims to cure. Sounds like snake oil to me."

"That's what I thought at first, yet I see patients in group therapy who seem to improve. Then there's the sinister side of it. Like with Harriet."

"You didn't work with Harriet and you only have Ray's word about how well she was doing."

"That's true, but Hallie Logan claims that Harriet made great improvements during treatment at MACS. You'd think a twin would be able to read her sister better than anyone else," Taylor explained while closing up the last plastic bag of powder, "We'll get to find out when Hallie is admitted to the PHP next week."

"What! Why would she do something so insane?"

"Because, she wants to find out whether MACS helped or harmed her sister. Besides, I work in the program so I can watch her. If we sense trouble, Ray or I will get her out safely."

"I can't believe you would encourage her to take such a risk. The Logan's don't need to have another daughter in jeopardy."

Taylor glanced at her watch, "We've been here over an hour. I think we ought to leave. I don't know if the guard makes any kind of regular rounds on the weekends."

"You're right. Let's go. I'm getting hungry; how about you?"

Taylor closed the door to the refrigerated cabinet, carefully wiping the handle with a paper towel. "Before we leave, let's go to the fourth floor. I want to show you my first official professional office. And I might find something in Brook's desk that will tell us about the archive files locations. For a space cadet, her filing system is remarkably well-organized."

Gabe followed her down the hallway and outside the lab entry. No alarms. They rode the elevator to the next floor. He preferred to leave now, but that would be out of character. Taylor is proud of having an office after all those years in grad school. Naturally, as her guy, he would want to see where she worked. He hoped that the stop would be brief and uneventful.

"I usually pass the marketing department and take this short cut through the mail room to my office," Taylor explained leading the way.

Gabe thought he heard another set of footsteps, "Are you sure no one else is here?"

"Yes. We may be drafted to entertain clients at dinner parties but so far no one has said anything about working on Saturdays."

They reached the door to Taylor's office. Gabe looked around.

He saw Dr. Locke's office and a center desk with an oversize mug proclaiming in bold letters, "Brook's Daily IV".

Taylor opened the door, "This is my office. Not as fancy as the Executive floor, but not bad for a start." She walked over and sat in her chair. He took a seat in the guest chair.

"Very nice, Dr. Kendall and well earned."

"Thanks. I wish my Daddy could see it."

"You miss him a great deal, don't you?"

"I sure do. Daddy was my hero, personally and professionally. But I suppose it's natural to want your parents to be proud of what you do."

"I wouldn't know about that."

She stopped herself from asking about Gabe's family. The look on his face said it all. Clearly family was a touchy subject for him.

"Well, let's go check out Brook's lair," Taylor said standing up and motioning for him to follow her. "I've heard the nurses say that old records are kept in two storage centers not far from here."

"Why not on the premises?"

"They say it's for security and also so that if one storage center was damaged or destroyed, that wouldn't wipe out all the old patient records."

"Do you think that's where the charts for Greg Newman and Harriet Logan were taken?"

"Ray is almost certain of it. He told me that Harriet's chart disappeared the day before another box of records was taken to storage."

He stood beside her as she rummaged through Brook's side desk files. *Not likely to be as simple as you think, Taylor. Chances are the Newman and Logan files are at the Girard house or in a bank safety deposit box. Marco and Victoria would never take chances with potentially damaging information. At least not the real files, those have either been hidden or shredded. Anything we find in storage will be a reconstructed, less damaging version.*

While Taylor was busy with her file search, Gabe roamed around the hallway, mentally tagging the area in his memory for future reference. At the far end of the hall, he saw the ample kitchen. He rummaged through his jean pockets to get enough change to buy sodas for them. Stepping into the hallway, he heard her call out his name.

"Come on back. I've got a surprise for you."

Juggling the chilled drink cans, he replied, "Me too."

He stopped short of rounded the corner when he heard an all too familiar voice.

". . . so that's Mr. Wonderful?"

Taylor swiveled in Brook's chair in time to see a green shirted man practically leap into the men's restroom. "Gabe, wait a minute. I want you to meet my friend, Carla."

"A bit shy, isn't he?"

"Not usually. Maybe we startled him."

"What did you say his name was?"

"Gabe. He's an actor working at an antique shop between shows. He is quiet, but I don't know why he's avoiding us," Taylor answered, stifling her irritation.

"He's tall; at least his shadow is."

"Yes, for a tall woman like me, that's refreshing. I can wear heels when we go out."

Carla laughed, "That's never been my problem."

"Are all of your family members short?"

"Not all of us. My brother Blake is tall. It comes through Serena's side of the family and also from my grandmother's people."

"Are you going to be working long, Carla?"

"I don't know. I wanted to get out of the house. My mother and Serena are slinging insults. Coming to work was better than going shopping with Tiffany."

Both women laughed. Carla continued to look down the hall

toward the restroom doors.

"Taylor, what color eyes does Gabe have?"

"Kind of gray, nothing special."

"Do you know how tall he is?"

"Not really," Taylor closed her eyes to get a mental picture of walking beside him, "Compared with my height, I think he might be about my Daddy's height. Say around 6'3 or 6'4."

"And he lives near here?"

"Yes. He's renting this efficiency that's decorated like an overdone Chinese museum. Not his style at all. He's a simple guy who likes simple things," Taylor paused trying to read Carla's pensive expression, "Why do you ask?"

"Oh nothing. For a minute I thought I recognized his voice."

Gabe's stomach growled so arrogantly that he was certain the women would hear it from through the crack in the men's room door where he wedged paper towel to listen to them. *Oh, my God. Did Carla recognize my voice? I've got to distract her.* He turned on the water at the sink, and then ducked into the farthest stall. Hunching his shoulders toward the wall, he pulled out his cell phone and dialed. It rang a few times. He held on. Please let her hear it.

Taylor reached into her lab coat pocket to check her phone, "Not mine. Must be yours."

Carla glanced around. "Where did I sit that thing down?" She walked back toward her office.

Taylor followed the sound to the copy room. Carla's phone was on the cutting table.

"Here it is, Carla," she shouted, picking it up and walking toward her.

Carla grabbed the phone and breathlessly answered.

"Did I get you out of the hot tub?"

"Blake! I'm not at home. I'm at the office. Where are you?"

"I'm trying to hold onto my first class seat. I don't have much time to talk."

"Where are you going?"

"I'm at Orly. The gate agent is smiling and cussing in French. Wait 'til he finds out I speak the language. I want you to do something for me."

"Anything."

"Head for the mall and buy a disguise. Blond wig. Trashy clothes. Keep it hidden in your car. I've got an adventure planned for us."

"When?"

"Do it now. I'll be there soon. Call you later."

"Blake!" The line went dead. "That was my brother trying to reach me between planes. If I hadn't misplaced the stupid cell phone I would have had time to talk to him."

"Is he coming to see you?"

"Not today. He's at the airport in Paris going...wait, he never told me where he was going."

"It sounds like he lives a wild life."

"Yes, he learned that from our father, and yet every time I see him, he's fit and healthy. Not what you usually see among the jet setters."

"I thought they all had beautiful bodies."

"The best bodies money can buy, but after awhile the plastic surgeon starts running into old scars. Not to mention dowager's hump from standing over the tables at Monte Carlo."

Taylor looked amazed.

"It's not all it appears in the magazines. I vividly recall how some of the people that my father gambled with began to change in only a few years. The women aged worse. I don't want that to happen to my brother. He's out there trying to compete with our father's playboy reputation. It's not worth it. I don't think that's really what Blake wants. Too much champagne, too many indiscriminate lovers and, poof, the party's over."

Taylor put her arm around Carla's shoulder. "Sounds like you are the one person in the world whose opinion he respects.

Maybe you can convince him to settle down."

Tears threatened to spill over the edge of Carla's endless dark eyes. "My brother is the only person in our family who genuinely cares about me for myself. I wish he would come back, even if he doesn't want anything to do with the family."

"I guess he has his reasons."

"I suppose," Carla rubbed her eyes dry, "Sorry to pour out my problems to you. Maybe Tiffany had the right idea. I think I'll go to the mall. The work can wait."

"Good idea. A little shopping and a latte will brighten your day."

"Yes, it will. I'd invite you and Gabe, but he seems to be in hiding."

"Aren't men odd?"

"That's not the half of it. Blake wants me to go out and buy the oddest things."

"Like what?"

Carla held back her answer since it wouldn't be much of a disguise if someone in the company knows about it, "Oh, some different styles that he thinks I need to try. I'm going to lock my office and leave now." She walked a few steps, and then paused, "By the way, Taylor, why are you here?"

Taylor drew in her breath, "Well, uh...I left some paperwork in my office. I plan to set up my laptop by the pool tomorrow and run more statistics for Victoria's research report."

Carla looked at her strangely.

"I brought Gabe over to show him my office. This probably sounds silly, but after all those years in graduate school, having an office is a big deal to me," she tried to read her friend's expression, "I hope I didn't do anything inappropriate."

"Forget it. But I wouldn't mention it to Brook or anyone else. The paranoia level filters down from the top. My mother is certain that someone is out to get us. Well, say hello to Gabe for me," Carla walked down the hall toward her office.

Taylor rose from Brook's desk. Glancing around to be certain no one else was in the hall, she went over and knocked on the men's room door, "All, all outs in free."

Gabe cracked the door, "Is that woman gone?"

"Yes. She's in her office getting ready to leave."

"I'll wait in here."

"Don't be ridiculous! She knows you're with me. It's my friend, Carla Girard. I wanted her to meet you."

"Can we reach the stairs without passing her office or the elevators?"

"Yes, but why?"

"When I count to three, make a run for the stairs."

"That's absurd! I told you she knows you are with me."

"Taylor, don't argue," he opened the door glancing both ways down the hall. Then he grabbed her hand and pulled her behind him, "Let's go."

He closed the heavy fire door and started down the stairs, taking two steps at a time. Taylor hustled to keep up. At the first floor landing, she whispered as loudly as possible, "Don't open that door. It has an alarm."

He stopped short of touching the metal handle, "Now how do we get out?"

"The same way we got in, the lobby," Taylor explained having reached the lower landing beside him, "What's the deal? Why are you so jumpy? I told you that Carla is my friend. She knows about you. She only wanted to meet you."

"Wouldn't she wonder why I'm wearing a green MACS employee shirt embroidered with someone else's name on it?"

Taylor gasped. "Oh, no, I completely forgot about that!"

"Don't you think this would look suspicious even to your friend? That's why I thought it was better to get out of sight."

"You are so right, Gabe. Good thinking."

He pulled her into his arms for a quick kiss, "Even Sherlock made mistakes. That's why he needed a trusty sidekick to bail him out. Let's get out of here and get lunch."

"I'll say goodbye to the guard. You can go out the back door to the parking lot and wait in my car," she handed him her keys.

"Good idea. Do you have the samples?"

"Right here in my kangaroo-sized lab coat pockets."

"See you in a few minutes."

* * * * *

Gabe ran out the back door and ducked quickly into the car. He knew that the window from Carla's third floor office faced onto the parking lot. Pressing a familiar speed dial code, he had only a few minutes to set the next step in motion.

"Jack here."

"Yo, dude. I need help with a connection."

"God, Blake, you sound like an Ybor City drug runner."

"So if the CIA satellite is hovering over downtown St. Petersburg, our careers in the bureau are finished, right?"

"That about covers it. Speaking of career-ending maneuvers, I recognize that scheming tone in your voice. What's your latest ploy for pushing me into early retirement?"

"Oh ye of little faith. I simply want you to help with a little delivery, Jack."

"Where? To whom?"

"Morganna, of course."

"You want me to go to Virginia? The Director told me to stay in shouting distance of you and Taylor all weekend. You really do want to get me fired."

"No way, Jack-o. What's Batman without Robin?"

"Or Dr. Jekyll without Mr. Hyde, but wait, you don't need me for that one."

"Very funny. Wait, I see Taylor leaving the building. Check on the usual agency courier services or Federal Express. I have to get some samples to Morganna for a quick analysis. Got to go."

Gabe hung up as Taylor opened the driver's side door.

"Do you have to go back to work?"

"No. I was calling another actor about the rumor of an audition," Gabe skillfully changed his tone, "He's going to check on it and let me know where to send my tape."

"Tape? What kind of tape?" she asked clicking her seatbelt in place and starting the engine.

"You know, a video tape. It shows something significant about my work so that the right people can look it over."

"Does that mean you're leaving town?" she tried to prevent her voice from reflecting the sinking lump in her stomach.

"Not now," he replied gazing out the passenger window to appear as if he didn't notice her concern, "Of course, in my business, I never know where the next job will be, but that's down the road. Let's get back to having a great weekend together."

God knows I hate having to mislead her. Mislead. Polite term for lying in the line of duty. Untruth to discover truth. Can Taylor ever understand it?

CHAPTER 31

Taylor opened the guest house door and headed for the efficiency kitchen, "I'll make a sandwich tray with some fruit. We can eat by the pool."

"Sounds great to me," he said, lounging across the plush tropical print cushioned rattan sofa.

Taylor brought two tall glasses of mint tea. As he rose slightly to take the glass, she sat on the sofa end, pressing his head onto a pillow that she placed in her lap. "You deserve a break for helping me. Especially for quick thinking when Carla arrived. I guess I'm not such a great sleuth after all."

He looked up at her dancing brown eyes, "You have a few things to learn about being sneaky."

They sat silently. She tried to run her hand through his hair, but the gel felt creepy. If only he would give up that slick hair look. With the right shampoo or maybe a few blonde highlights, he would look so much better. Deeply engrossed in her make-over daydream, Taylor massaged his temples with her fingers. He felt as if he was falling into a gentle sleep, not from tiredness but from the rare feeling of total security.

Taylor broke the silence, "Do you think I need to put the samples inside another airtight container in the refrigerator?"

Her question was like an alarm clock, jolting him back to consciousness. He sat upright.

"Yes, I think you're right."

"I don't have to do that this minute. We earned a break."

"I don't think Sherlock and Dr. Watson rested until the case was finished. Besides," he said in a suddenly business-like manner, "I have to contact my lab friend and arrange delivery of these samples. We won't find out anything until the analysis is done."

Taylor stood up and pulled his hand to join her, "Let's go bag the loot."

He could have his way and pull her back down with him or do his job and move on. Duty won. He stepped away from her reach, "You can do the honors. I need to call my friend." He reached in his pocket for the cell phone.

She picked up the cordless phone on the nearby desk and held it out, "Use my phone. It'll save some airtime costs."

"Thanks, but I'll step outside to talk."

"Why the secrecy? Aren't we in this together?"

"Yes, lovely lady, we are, but my friend works in a secure lab and absolutely won't do this for us if it means dealing with anyone but me."

"Fine. I'll be in the kitchen."

Taylor left a chill in the wake of her path as she walked briskly past Gabe to the kitchen. He opened the French doors and looked around the pool area. There was no one around. The caretaker couple wasn't in sight.

He walked to the street side of the pool house near the garage and hit the speed dial.

"Aren't you lucky? I'm at home."

"Hello Morganna."

"Blake! Are you at the townhouse? Is this a surprise for me?"

"No, I'm in Florida working on a case, remember?"

"Don't tell me this is a business call?"

"Actually, it is. I have some additional samples for you to analyze, but this time, it's strictly off the record."

"Wonderful. I'm sure the Field Office will arrange courier transport. I can start on it Monday or Tuesday and send a report to your field supervisor."

He bristled at the icy tone. Morganna was determined to make this difficult.

"You know perfectly well that won't work."

"Well, darling, if you want to operate outside of agency procedure then you have to pay to play."

"What's the price? Do you want some earrings to match the necklace? Or maybe it's time for you to scan the fashion magazines for the latest runway hit?"

"You're the price."

"What?"

"You heard me, Blake. I want you and I want you now."

"I can't leave the field when I'm on assignment. Do you want to get me fired?"

"As if your lifestyle depended on that piddly paycheck," Morganna snapped back, "Not to mention that I could get fired for running your purloined samples at the FBI lab without an official paperwork request."

"Since when did you become rule-oriented?"

"Since you became distant. Are you with some woman? Is she another agent?"

"I can assure you that I am not shacking up with another agent. Besides my field contact is Jack. You remember him. I'm not his type and he's not mine."

"When are you making the delivery?"

"I'm handing it off to Jack. He'll arrange shipment and let you know."

"You haven't heard me, Blake. If you want your samples analyzed on the sly, then you deliver them in person today. And be prepared to spend the night."

"I told you we would have time together when I finish this case."

"And I told you that it's a package deal; you and the samples. That means you, tonight, in my bed or no deal," Morganna insisted.

"Fine. I'll get the jet fueled as soon as possible. You'll have to pick me up at the airport."

"It's almost noon. When will you arrive?"

"I don't know precisely. It may take an hour to get my plane out of the hangar and fueled. The flight is an hour fifty minutes if I push it," Blake mentally calculated, "I'll be there for dinner."

"Don't bother to pack a bag. Your silk robe is in my closet. That's all you'll need. I'll have food ordered in from the bistro."

"Morganna, you might as well know that I can't stay long."

"We'll have a great weekend."

"No, not even that long. I have to be back in St. Petersburg by mid-day tomorrow."

"Change it."

"I can't. This is crucial to the investigation. Another agent's life may be on the line, so don't play around with me on this one, Morganna. It's dinner and a cozy evening or nothing."

"Then you wouldn't get your samples analyzed."

"And I won't have the blood of a colleague on my hands either; it will be on your hands."

"Oh, Blake, you don't have to be mean to me."

"Don't interfere with my work. You'll never win that one."

She purred, "What terrible stress you must be under, my darling. Don't worry. I'll do my patriotic duty and comfort you as the brave soldier that you are."

Patriotic duty? No matter who's on top, it's easy to see who is getting screwed here. "Yes, Morganna, you're a real flag-waver. I'll call you when I'm starting my descent into the airport."

He slammed the phone shut. Taylor called out from the French doors, "Would you like for me to bring you a cold drink?"

"No thanks. I'll just be a minute more."

He pressed the speed dial again.

"You're been at her house nearly an hour. Why aren't you busy inside with the lovely Taylor?"

"How close are you, Jack?"

"In my football days, I could have hit you on the numbers with the pigskin my man."

"I'm impressed."

"If you want you could walk down to the corner and I'll pick up the samples."

"Sorry, Jack, but you're getting the day off."

"What do you mean?"

"I have to fly the samples to Washington today."

"Why? Aren't you and Taylor going to the mental hospital to look for Martha?"

"Yes, that's tomorrow. We were going sailing but Morganna changed that."

"How? You didn't tell Taylor about Morganna, did you?"

"No way. Nor vice versa. Morganna is demanding a few pounds of flesh in exchange for running the analysis on the sly."

"Whose flesh?"

"Mine, Jack-o, mine."

"You mean, literally?" Jack's laughter reverberated in the phone. "It's like a fractured fairy tale. Blake, The Prince, must allow the wicked Morganna to ravage his body in order to save the fair Taylor and restore good in the land."

"I fail to see the humor here."

"Is there anything I can do? Like go with you and work the second shift?"

"I refuse to dignify your sophomoric humor with a response. You can pick me up at Taylor's driveway in fifteen minutes."

"Short goodbye, buddy, you're slipping."

"Don't push it."

He ended the call and dialed again. The answer was nearly obscured by loud noise.

"Travis, is that you?"

"Yes it is. Hold a minute 'til I wave this guy outta here."

Blake heard the sounds of a small plane propeller.

"Sorry for the wait."

"Hello, Travis, Andrews here. I know weekends are busy for you, but this is something of an emergency. I have to fly out as soon as possible. Can you get my plane fueled and ready?"

"I can have it ready to go in forty-five minutes. Okay?"

"I really appreciate the favor."

"No problem, Blair, you're one of my best customers. Do you need any charts?"

"No, I'm heading to DCA and back tomorrow."

"I may be up with a student when you get here so check in at the desk. Mike's on duty. I'll tell him to look for you."

He crammed the cell phone into his pocket. This is not turning out the way he planned. He wanted a nice afternoon by the pool, to pick up Taylor's favorite fried chicken and salad order from Publix Deli and then sail out into old Tampa Bay to watch the sunset. It was supposed to be a promising romantic interlude between a nearly critical encounter at MACS to a Sunday afternoon visit at the state mental hospital. Instead he was going to have to watch disappointment cloud Taylor's magnificent brown eyes.

"Aren't you hungry anymore?" she asked leaning close enough on his right side to intoxicate him with her nearness.

"Of course, I'm always hungry. A growing boy, you know."

"Great. I've made a tray to nibble on while we relax at the pool."

He gazed the length of her tall frame. No more lab coat and heels. Taylor was in a bronze swimsuit and gold mules that made her legs seem like flawless columns for a Greek temple. The sun sparkled around her as a spotlight and appropriately so. Taylor was light and Morganna was darkness. Funny how the dark ways that once intrigued and amused seemed a lifetime ago.

"Well...are you ready?"

"Taylor, I'm sorry. I can't stay."

"What? This is our weekend together. You said you didn't have to work."

"I don't have to work at the gallery," he tried to keep as much truth as possible in crafting his excuse, "But my lab rat friend insists that I deliver the samples and do some other things."

Taylor tapped her right toe, a gesture he learned she uses when impatient, "You're no chemist. Why do you have to be there?"

"It's a trade off. My friend does the analysis and I do something else as a kind of payment for the favor."

"If it's a favor for a friend, why does he need payment?"

"This is an extremely unusual person, brilliant but demanding. I'll probably end up filing or pressing creases out of the linens. It won't take long."

"Are we still going sailing?"

"Not today. I'll probably have to make a run for pizza or cheesecake or satisfy some other peculiar taste that keeps my friend working. I think it's better if we meet tomorrow around noon. I'll come back here."

Taylor looked over his shoulder at the car pulling into the drive, "Is that him?"

"No, that's Jack. You've met him. He's going to give me a ride."

"Jack can go but I can't?"

"No, Taylor, that's not the way it is."

"You could have fooled me. I thought you were above the boy's club mentality."

"I am. Look, I'm willing to sacrifice myself to get the information we need," he sucked in his own cheeks to avoid laughing at the joke she would not have understood or appreciated, "Would you get the samples for me?"

He reached to squeeze her waist, but she pulled away. Waiting for her to return, he wondered if she had flushed the powder samples down the toilet. A few minutes later she returned with two sacks.

"The samples are here, double-packaged in zipped plastic bags. And this bag has food. At least share a sandwich with Jack."

Rather than being petulant, like most of the women he knew,

Taylor was overcoming her disappointment with generosity. Such a noble gesture made him feel worse as he kissed her.

"See you tomorrow, lovely Taylor."

"I'll be here, but if you don't show by noon, I'm going on my own."

He got into in Jack's car, nearly pulling the seat belt from its hinge.

"Patience, my man, you're hitting home runs all day."

"How do you figure that, Jack?"

"I keep binoculars in the car for surveillance. And checking out Taylor was the highest and best use those specs have had in years. Man, did somebody pour her into that swim suit?"

"Stop drooling like a teenager."

"And now, you go from sweetness and light to hot and nasty."

"Don't remind me."

"Do you want to stop by the gallery and pick up anything?"

"No."

"Oh that's right, you won't need anything. Morganna will keep you au naturale."

"That's not what I meant. I'll stop by my townhouse in Reston and get fresh clothes before I fly back tomorrow."

"Do you need for me to pick you up at the airport?"

"No!"

"Okay, man, your call. I do need to know when you get back so I can shadow your drive to Arcadia. Business, remember?"

"Of course. I didn't mean to take it out on you, Jack. Yes, I could use a ride from the airport."

"What time?"

"I'll phone you before I take off with the approximate arrival time. You might as well expect me in around eleven. Taylor gave me an ultimatum."

Jack jerked his eyes from the road to stare at him, "You mean she's dumping you?"

"No. She says if I'm not there at noon, she'll drive to Arcadia without me."

"She'll wait."

"No she won't," Blake answered emphatically, "If I do get delayed, I need you to break off and follow her. I'm convinced that finding out what happened to Martha will uncover a big can of worms and expand this investigation."

"You mean the double-dipping into government dollars is getting bigger?"

"I mean that instead of handing a Medicare fraud case to those nitwits in Justice, we'll deliver a few murder and attempted murder indictments as well. I'm trying to keep Taylor off the victim list."

* * * * *

Taylor stood in the shadows of an ancient oak tree adjacent to the driveway watching Jack's car pull away. Her feet clung to that spot as if glued. *Well there he goes on another sudden, peculiar departure. Is this how Lois Lane felt when Clark Kent kept disappearing? Of course, he was off to change into Superman and save the world or at least some part of it. But Gabe, he's no Superman. What's his excuse? Mama always says that when a man continually breaks his promise to you it's because he's keeping a promise to someone else.*

CHAPTER 32

"Pull up on the far side of that hangar," Blake pointed the direction as Jack turned.

A stubby dark-haired man in greasy striped overalls came toward the car, "Yo Mr. Andrews. The Citation is ready to roll."

Blake jumped out of the car and extended his hand, "Thanks, Mike."

Jack walked up beside him.

"Mike, the best jet mechanic in Florida, meet my land-hugging friend, Jack."

The two men shook hands. A pager squealed. Both men looked down.

"That's for me," Mike said, "If you want to start the pre-flight, Mr. Andrews, I'll be back out shortly to see you off."

"That's great, Mike, thanks."

When Mike was out of sight in the next hangar, Jack grabbed Blake by the arm, "Mr. Andrews, I presume?"

"Oh, yes. To the folks here at the airport, I'm Blair Andrews, president of Andrews Corporation. Remember, I told you that I had a closely-held corporation that officially owns the jet. It's a tax write-off thing," Blake explained, opening his bag and removing the pre-flight checklist.

"Wait a minute. Wasn't Andrews one of your aliases on an investigation?"

"Right again, Jack-o. You'd make a fine private eye, did you know that."

"Yes. And if I keep riding shotgun for your sideline ventures, I may have to get a PI license to make a living. Do fired FBI agents qualify?"

Blake rose up from checking the tires, "Jack, you take things too seriously. We have enough tension in our work. Shrug it off when you don't need it. It's a much healthier response."

"That's easy for you to say, Mr. Rich Boy Agent. While I'm sleeping soundly in my own bed tonight, I'll feel safer knowing that you're giving your all for our country."

"Not funny."

After the pre-flight activities were completed Jack ran back to his car to get the binoculars. He positioned himself in the shade of the flight office's awning to watch the take-off. Before getting into the plane, Blake pointed out which way he would be lifting off on the main runway. Like a silver bullet, the Citation Jet shot down the runway chewing up most of the 5,000 feet in seconds. The aircraft's nose lifted in the aristocratic way that Blake's own nose did at times. The plane executed a sharp left turn and made a slight tip of the wing before heading for the clouds.

"Andrews tipped his wing to you, bud, did you see it?" Mike asked walking up beside Jack.

"Was that on purpose?"

"Sure. He never does anything without a reason."

Jack nodded agreement.

"Yep, I first thought he was some pretty boy showing off with a flying hot rod. Not so. Mr. Andrews is a first rate pilot. I can tell, you know?"

"Really, how?"

By the way he takes care of his plane," Mike continued, "Yep, I always do extra for the Citation 'cause I know Mr. Andrews treats it right. Now I have to tell you something you may not know about your friend. He's no choir boy, but still, he's a top notch pilot. You know, the kind of guy who can take a chance sometime 'cause he relies on skill and not luck."

"I know exactly what you mean, Mike."

* * * * *

The persistent ringing intruded on Taylor's daydream. Realizing what it was, she threw the sunhat off her face and nearly fell off the lounge chair reaching for the cell phone. Maybe it was Gabe.

"Hello, Gabe?"

"No. I must have the wrong number. I was calling Dr. Kendall."

"I'm Dr. Kendall. How can I help you?"

"This is Hallie Logan, Harriet's sister," the soft voice replied, "I wanted to tell you that I have made all the arrangements to check into the MACS program next week."

Taylor pulled up a chair to sit under the umbrella table.

"What arrangements?"

"Ray helped me put it together so everything appears authentic. I even have an altered medical file and an admissions request from my old physician. He's retired now, but he wants to help me find out the truth about Harriet's death..."

"Wait a minute, Hallie. Do your parents know what you're about to do?"

"No. Not all of it. Not the part about checking into MACS as a patient."

"Who else does know?"

"Besides old Dr. Pratt and my secretary, just you and Ray know. Why, have you changed your mind about helping me Dr. Kendall?"

"I'm having second thoughts about your safety."

"Why worry now? No one at MACS was concerned about Harriet's safety. They made money as long as they kept her wallowing in her illness."

"This can be dangerous. You need to know that."

"Let me reassure you, Dr. Kendall, I look like Harriet but that's where the similarity ends. First of all, I'm not schizophrenic so I'll be totally aware of what's happening. And second, I'm a third-degree black belt and have run six marathons. I ought to be able to get out of trouble on my own," Hallie elaborated in crisp detail, "Ray and I are meeting for dinner to talk over strategy. Do you want to help us or not?"

"My plans have changed a bit. I can make it. You are going to meet somewhere out of sight I hope?"

"That's a good point," Hallie pondered, "I wanted to take in a seafood place on St. Petersburg Beach, but that might be too public. What do you suggest?"

"Where are you staying now?"

"I'm at Innisbrook in a condo that's rented under my secretary's name."

"Excellent. That's far enough in north Pinellas to be out of the Girards' way. Why don't I meet you there?" Taylor pushed aside the thought of how much she'd rather be sailing with Gabe. That was no longer an option. "We ordered a fried chicken dinner for pickup before my date had to leave. There's plenty for all of us"

"You don't have to do that."

"It's no problem. This will keep the food from going to waste."

"That's great. I'll arrange drinks and dessert."

"How will I find you?"

"Get a pencil and I'll give you the directions," Hallie answered, "Or you can ask at the gate for Cindy McConnell. That's the name I'm registered under."

CHAPTER 33

Getting close to the destination meant time to disengage autopilot and reengage his wandering thoughts. *Brooding over leaving Taylor alone by the pool won't make it any easier to pay attention to the control tower's instructions, or to deal with Morganna.*

Preparing for his turn to land, Blake watched another business jet ahead of him on final approach. The pilot was cocky and talking too much. A bit less talk and more action would have resulted in a professional landing. Blake pressed his microphone, "Citation to Tower. When the Lear stops bouncing, is it my turn?"

"Affirmative, Citation. Show us what you got."

And that's exactly what Blake did, guiding his jet onto the runway with the ease of a feather touching a pillow. Taxiing toward the private hangars, he recognized the red Corvette.

He spent more than the usual amount of time shutting down the engines and making notes for the ground crew. *Procrastination. Might as well get on with it.* He pulled the brown paper sack containing the samples from his flight case, snapped the case shut and rose from his seat. As he climbed down from the plane, Morganna rushed toward him, throwing herself into his less than waiting arms.

"Darling, how I've missed you."

"Hello, Morganna," he replied holding her away from him.

"But darling..."

"I need for you to get in the car and wait. I have to give instructions to the ground crew."

"Toss them the key and we'll call later from my place."

"This is a business jet; it isn't handled like valet parking. Wait over there."

Morganna stomped the heel of her Manolo Blahniks so hard that a thumbnail-sized topaz dropped off the side. She bent over to pick it up. Obviously $2,400 spike heels weren't the thing to wear when throwing a tantrum on a hard surface. Her anguish turned to amusement upon noticing that three suited men boarding a nearby twin engine plane ran into each other when they stopped to watch her. She knew they were wondering if her black leather pants would stand the strain. With topaz in hand, she rose up and blew them a kiss as she walked to her car. Flopping into the driver's seat, she took off the right shoe to survey the damage.

The car door opened and Blake crammed his long frame into the passenger seat. Peering over her sunglasses, she scanned him with x-ray precision.

"What an awful outfit. Did you dress from a dumpster?"

"I'm wearing what I had on when you summoned me. These are work clothes."

"Not exactly your usual Armani."

"No, my undercover identity isn't draped in designer labels," he replied, popping the gray contacts out of his eyes.

"Does the hair snap out too?"

"Not as easily. It's a color rinse."

"Thank heaven. I was afraid you had ruined your thick blond curls, you naughty boy," she said, slipping her right hand from the gear shift to his thigh.

He picked up her hand and placed it back on the wheel.

"Both hands on the wheel, please. I'm used to the safety of air travel. You beltway-babes scare me on these expressways."

"My driving is tame compared with what I have planned for this evening," She gunned the motor and passed other speeding cars as if they were standing still.

* * * * *

Blake picked up the glass and stepped onto the terrace. The sun setting in Virginia is ordinary compared to watching that same sun slide gracefully into the waters of the Gulf of Mexico. *Living again in Florida for this assignment reminds me how much I miss the water. Chances are the Bahamian house will be used more than I thought. Not that Morganna will ever hear of it. Or ever go there. Taylor's the only woman who will go to the beach house. It's open, inviting, gracious and serene. A house for Taylor to define in her image.*

"Blake! Where are you? The temperature in the hot tub is perfect."

Morganna's sharp voice cut through his reverie. He stared at the scotch in his hand. Maybe getting a little drunk was a good idea. This is one night not to remember. Then again, there wasn't enough time to get an overload of alcohol out of the system in order to fly back to Florida in the morning. He poured the liquid into the topiary. The sound of her gold mules clicked closer and closer until he felt her hands pull on the tie of his silk robe.

"You can run, but you can't hide."

Returning her embrace, he nodded, less from agreement than resignation.

* * * * *

"Jack, here."

"Hello, Agent Sims. Hope I didn't interrupt your dinner, but you said to report anything unusual."

"Sure. What's up?"

"Dr. Kendall left her home about a half hour ago."

Jack bolted up from his hammock, "What! Are you tailing her? Has she crossed the Skyway Bridge?"

"No sir. She's headed north on US 19. I assume you want us to pursue."

"I certainly do! Where are you now?"

"We turned her over to another pursuit car going north. I broke off and went to Belcher Road. If she continues north, I'll cross at Tampa Road and intercept."

"Who's on her now?"

"We have a male and female team, posing as an elderly couple. She acted as if she was checking us out."

"I'm on my way. Keep her in sight and get me a destination."

"Yes sir."

"Whatever you do, don't lose her."

"Understood."

Jack jammed one foot into his sandal and dragged the other sandal with his toe. *So much for a quiet evening at home while Blake's in Washington and Taylor's behind the security gates of an upper crust mansion. Blake will have a fit if she's gone off on some amateur sleuthing. Actually, he'll have a fit with me first. I have to handle this without alerting the office or the old man will want to know where Blake is. Where is that woman going?*

* * * * *

"Hi Taylor, come on in," Ray's mellow voice welcomed her. He reached out to take the grocery bag from Taylor's arms. "This chicken smells great. Drop your things on the sofa."

Taylor removed the shoulder strap briefcase and laid it on the ottoman, then followed Ray to the dining alcove.

"Hallie, Taylor's here." He pulled out a chair for Taylor, "You're going to like Hallie. She reminds me a lot of you, smart and outspoken."

"Thank you for coming, Dr. Kendall."

Taylor turned around to face Hallie Logan and nearly choked on her own saliva. Hallie Logan was a carbon copy of the woman she saw lying in the street; same hair color, same features. She was a living replica of the broken body sprawled across the intersection at Second Street.

Hallie came over and put her hand on Taylor's shoulder, "I

think I startled you. Perhaps I forgot to tell you that Harriet and I are mirror-image twins."

Taylor nodded mechanically, her mind swirling from what she just heard. *Mirror-image twins. They are the most identical of all identical twins and the most rare. They are literally a reflection of each other. If the sight of Hallie Logan unnerved her, imagine what it will do to Lorraine and Neva, not to mention Dr. Marco.*

Hallie reached over the table for a pitcher. She poured lemonade in a tall glass and handed it to Taylor.

"You're left-handed."

"That's correct."

"Was Harriet right-handed?"

"Yes, she was. Obviously you know something about mirror-image twins. For example, both of us wear prescription sunglasses to drive. Harriet's glasses are adjusted for defects in distance vision of her left eye and mine for my right eye. Even with those opposite characteristics, we are alike in so many ways."

"You were alike," Ray corrected.

"Oh, yes," Hallie sighed, "I can't bring myself to talk about Harriet in the past tense. I know she's dead, I'm not delusional. Being separated from your twin is like being handed a saw and told to amputate your own leg. I guess that sounds crazy."

Taylor extended her hand and Hallie grabbed it tightly, "Not at all. I've been told that the loss of an identical twin is one of the most devastating losses a person can experience. Were you and Harriet close?"

"Yes and no. When we were children, we were inseparable. Our parents didn't understand the modern thinking about twins needing their own identities. We were a matched set: dressed alike, hair ribbons alike, the whole deal."

Hallie opened a small photo book and showed a picture of them as children. Taylor had to admit that every detail, even their smile, was identical.

"When Harriet died, my mother started again with her old

fears that maybe she mixed us up as infants. She was so frantic about it that she wouldn't let my father order the headstone engraved." Hallie stood up and paced around the table, "Last week, I ordered the stone and had it delivered. They don't even know. It may be months, maybe years, before they can handle a visit to the cemetery anyway. I couldn't let Harriet lay there nameless. I know who I am and I know who she is. If the baby bracelets were switched, so what? It doesn't change anything."

Taylor wasn't sure where to take the conversation, but it was useful to get to know more about the sisters' relationship. "Were you always the dominant twin?"

"How did you know?"

"The fact that you are here willing to take this risk and what you described. If you were the take-charge twin for as long as you can remember, then you are the dominant twin. So you are who you think you are."

"You're beginning to understand us, but don't be mistaken in thinking that as the dominant twin I ran the show. More often than not we all reacted to what Harriet did. Not always bad things. Harriet was sensitive and attuned to every nuance of life around her. At times, she could create beautiful watercolor prints."

"When was the schizophrenia diagnosed?"

"When we were in middle school. At first, the school guidance counselor told our parents that her unusual behavior was probably hormonal and not to worry. Then it was blamed on her rather public and nasty breakup with a boy in our club. When she trashed the art room and cut her arms with the sculpting tools, it wasn't a puberty issue anymore."

"How did your parents take it?"

"They were devastated. That began years of psychiatrist visits on two continents. Come to think of it, most of our summer vacations were spent taking Harriet to another clinic. Chicago. Los Angeles. Atlanta. Boston. Then finally we went to Vienna, 'the birthplace of psychotherapy' as my father said," Hallie sat down again, tapping her long coral nails on the table, "I didn't even have to study for Intro to Psychology. I already knew the major counseling theories. Lord knows, we tried all of them."

Ray put his large, gentle hand on Hallie's shoulder. "Sometimes when Harriet was having lucid days, she would tell me stories about Hallie, how Hallie protected her when other kids teased her and defended her to the teachers. Not to mention those times during exams when the pressure was too much and Hallie went in to take Harriet's exams."

"It was easy. In fact, that's how I learned to be ambidextrous," Hallie explained, "By writing with my right hand. The few teachers who bothered to be observant thought I was Harriet. Meanwhile, Harriet went to my class and asked to go home sick."

"How long did that work?"

"It only lasted through high school," Hallie turned to a photo of their graduation, "We were both admitted to a prestigious women's college. I remember that day we were upstairs packing our bags when my father got a call from the dean. In some routine medical records that were transferred to the school's infirmary, she found out about Harriet's problems. She politely suggested that they had no way to deal with such difficulties. Two weeks later, I left for college and Harriet stayed home."

"The separation must have been hard on you."

"That's the pathetic part. Once I arrived on campus, I felt like an enormous weight had been lifted from my shoulders. I loved being at college," Hallie admitted, "And as selfish as this sounds, I was thankful that I didn't have to rescue Harriet anymore."

"There's nothing wrong with that. You had to go separate ways eventually."

"True, but I kept going. I ran from my responsibilities at home like Jonah ran from Ninevah. I heard my parents' pleas to spend more time at home over the summer, but I found ways to justify my absence; an archeological dig in Israel, teaching at a missionary school in Ecuador, interning on Wall Street."

"What were you running from, Hallie?"

"Myself. No matter how often the experts assured me that I wasn't destined to be schizophrenic, every time I looked at Harriet, I saw myself. I loved her and yet I resented what her disease did to her, to me and to our parents."

Ray knelt down next to Hallie looking up into her tear-stained face, "At least you didn't abandon her. A lot of families walk away. You continued to help. Harriet told me how much she appreciated your help. She said that you even paid for some of her treatments so your parents wouldn't drain all their retirement account."

Hallie wiped her eyes with a paper deli napkin, "I helped all right. I found the MACS program and showed it to her psychiatrist. I even paid the entry fees and her transportation to St. Petersburg." She rose and walked to the console, opened her purse, and pulled out a blue paper. She returned, laying the paper on the table in front of Ray and Taylor.

"Here's the proof. I killed my sister and now I have to bring my accomplices to justice. I'll do anything it takes, anything."

Taylor picked up the paper. It was a check for $5,000 written to MACS.

CHAPTER 34

He squirmed away from her embrace, reaching for his shirt and pulling it over his head as she tried to slither back into his arms. "Morganna, I have to leave. I told you that I have to be back in St. Petersburg before noon."

"Oh, Blake, darling, can't it wait? It's six o'clock in the morning and you only have to fly a few hours to get there."

"Yes, but I want to stop by my place. I haven't been home for months."

"Great. I'll slip on something decent, but not too decent, and drive you to the townhouse."

"No!"

"What do you mean, no?"

"I mean no in the conventional sense, unaccustomed as you are to that word."

He slipped his feet into loafers and walked out of her bedroom. She could hear his voice on the telephone. Realizing that he wasn't coming back into her room, she followed him into the living room a few minutes later.

"Okay, I'll be a good girl and accept your schedule. At least let me drive you to your place."

"No, Morganna," he curbed his impulse to tell her how much he wanted to leave. After all, he needed for her to handle the analysis of the Nutracurative. He put down his flight bag and pulled her into his arms, "Stop being such a temptress. You know I have to finish this case."

She snuggled under his chin so that all he could see was a profusion of long black hair. "That's the problem with loving a hero; he constantly has to go off doing heroic things."

"I'm not a hero, Morganna. I'm another agent doing his job," Blake replied, reaching his hand to turn her chin up toward his face, "And I desperately need your help."

"How desperate are you?"

More desperate than I ever thought I could be. Of course, as Marco always said, tell a woman what she wants to hear if you want to get your way with her. "Morganna, I'm depending on you. If you can make a fast analysis of the Nutracuratives without letting anyone at the lab know about it, then I can break this case ahead of schedule. Afterwards, I might be able to get a week off. I'm sure you could find something for us to do. That's enough time to go back to the resort on Bali that you liked so much."

"Oh, darling, I can hardly wait. When do you think you'll be free?"

"That depends on you. When do you think you can finish the analysis?"

"I'm up at this insane hour anyway and the lab is probably empty, so I'll go in after you leave. Can I phone you tonight?"

He drew her close to him, smiling at how easy it was to get his way. "That could be dangerous. Jack and I are going into a situation where we may have to get another undercover agent out. A ringing cell phone at the wrong moment could get me a well-placed bullet. I know you're mad that I can't stay, but..."

"Of course I don't want you in danger," she stared wide-eyed at him, then rained kisses across his chest, "I want all those luscious body parts in prime working order for Bali. I consider last night a mere deposit on what you owe me."

"That's my girl," he shuddered, "Wait until Monday evening to call or send a text message."

"You know I'll do anything for you."

A honking horn broke up the conversation. Blake gave her a quick kiss and darted out the door. She stood in the doorway unashamed in a flimsy red teddy that made the cab driver's day. She waved as the cab pulled away.

"Wow, mister, must be something important to take you away from that babe."

Something important - only one thing filled that bill. Not the FBI. Not bringing down the unholy trinity's empire. Not saving innocent people. Taylor. Just Taylor.

"Yes, someone very important."

* * * * *

The water poured over his head as he scrubbed. He scrubbed so hard that the loufah turned furry with arm and chest hair. Then he scrubbed again. He had to get Morganna's scent off his body. He couldn't go back to Taylor unclean.

When he stepped out of the shower, he absent-mindedly wrapped himself in his old faithful terry cloth bathrobe. Looking in the mirror he realized that the robe had been placed there, waiting silently for his return. *Bless you, Sedonia. No matter how long I'm away, you keep my home in constant readiness.*

Glancing at the clock, he had almost an hour before he needed to call another cab to take him from the townhouse in Reston, Virginia to nearby Ronald Reagan International Airport. He paused before entering his customized, walk-in closet. Opening the mirrored door, he laughed out loud. His master bathroom and closet together were larger than the apartment Gabe called home.

He turned toward the double hanging rods. Pants on the bottom, jackets on top, arranged by color. The adjacent rod was filled with his favorite Savile Row tailored suits and a rack of Armani for work days. He opened another mirrored door, inhaling the aroma of the cedar lined shelves that held his cashmere sweaters. His eyes fell on an aqua cashmere pullover before he slammed the door shut.

Taylor would like to see me in that sweater. She constantly hints that she wants to remake Gabe in a wardrobe exactly like mine, but I can't wear my Blake clothes for now. Even Gabe's underwear is strictly seconds, in keeping with his low rent image.

He stepped back into the bedroom, leaving behind his wardrobe to reach for the clothes he wore yesterday: Gabe's worn slick pants and olive drab shirt. If he hurried, he might at least get to change into clean, yet dull clothes before going to get Taylor.

Dressed in Gabe's clothes, he couldn't resist splashing on some of Blake's favorite after shave. The lecture on basics of undercover work played in his head, "As agents, you must never, I mean never, add even the slightest trace of your real identity when working undercover." *Yeah, so what? A few hours in the plane and a shower at Gabe's will remove the scent. Why not enjoy something from my own life?*

He walked downstairs into the kitchen where he could see his reflection in the gleaming brass knobs on mellow cherry wood cabinets. *Sedonia says it's too well-equipped to be a man's kitchen, but it's a great kitchen for whipping up serious paella and flan or rolling crust for quiche.* Growing up with the best food on two continents stunted his ability to adjust to burgers and fries at the student center. Learning to cook was the only way to get the food he really liked.

He reached into the oversized, practically empty refrigerator. As he liked it, there was a selection of boxed juices, about all that lasts when you only drop into your home a few times a year. He scanned the pantry for some snacks and chose a package of cheese crackers to eat with his boxed juice.

Sitting at the desk in the kitchen, he noticed a note pinned to the bulletin board with his name scrawled in bold print. He smiled as he read:

Welcome home Blake,

You didn't tell me you were coming, so you'll have to settle for box juices. If you plan to stay awhile, call me. If you know when you're coming back, leave me a message and I'll buy groceries.

If you're going back to work, be careful and come home in one piece. If you don't, I'll have to find the guy who hurt you and beat him to death with my mop. (Not a pretty sight.)

Raleigh sends his best and says that if you can't shoot straight, then duck fast.

Sedonia

Sedonia and Raleigh were a quirky old couple. Raleigh worked maintenance at the FBI academy. His favorite line to trainees preparing for their first simulated "street duty" on Hogan's Alley was, "I can paint 'em up as fast as you can shoot 'em up."

Raleigh proved to be an endless source of homespun one-liners. His wife, Sedonia, was a gentle yet blunt woman who was more like what Blake thought a good mother was. She was only seventeen when the first of eight children arrived. After raising that brood by taking in ironing and clipping coupons to supplement Raleigh's income after he retired, she decided that she wanted a "real job." A high school drop-out from the West Virginia hills, she stated that all she knew how to do was clean house and have babies. Since she was too old and too smart to have more babies, cleaning houses would have to do.

In two years, she had a crew of twenty-two working for her cleaning business, but Sedonia insisted on cleaning for Blake herself. She said that she appreciated how he helped her apply for the grant that got her cleaning business started. Fortunately, she didn't know that the $30,000 grant was really his money. She would have been too proud to take it directly from him.

Smiling, he tore a page from the memo pad and wrote:

My dearest Sedonia,

I'm only home for an hour and that wasn't planned. When I reached out of the shower and found my favorite robe waiting, I thought of how many things you do to give me a feeling of home for the little time I spend here.

You're the best,

Blake

P.S. I have a new house in the Bahamas as a personal getaway, but it's a secret. I'm going to send you and Raleigh over there soon to see it and give me advice on what needs to be done to make it special. You are the only people who know about it until I bring the future Mrs. Girard there.

Blake folded the paper, wrote Sedonia's name on the back panel and fixed it to the refrigerator between those awful cow magnets that she bought for him. He turned toward the door leading to the ground floor garage. Then he stepped away. *No point in checking on the Lexus. Raleigh takes it out once a week for a drive. Tinkering with the car would be as dangerous as slipping down into my favorite leather chair in the study. It's too easy to get comfortable in my real life.*

Pausing at the doorway to the kitchen, Blake picked up the local phone and called for a taxi. He surveyed the room as if he had never seen it. In his mind's eye he could see Taylor in a crisp gabardine skirt, silky blouse and ruffled apron standing at the cooking island. Two bright eyed children wiggled on the stools, sloshing milk from cereal bowls and laughing the same way she does; probably a little boy and a little girl. Taylor was singing a silly song with them as she reached into the pantry to get cheese crackers for their lunch boxes. A messy kitchen with the perfect family.

The alarm on his watch beeped. He pressed the clear button and rubbed his eyes. What he saw was depressing by contrast; a perfect kitchen, empty.

Walking toward the living room, his eyes drank in the ambience, the tranquility of his surroundings. He could imagine Taylor in every room. *If she hates the furniture, it's only wood and fabric - elegant, expensive, but unimportant. She could put up lace curtains and set a silk flower centerpiece on the mahogany dining table if it make her happy. And if she doesn't like living in Reston, we could sell the townhouse and build a home in Virginia or Tennessee or Florida. She can pick the city, state or continent.*

Like the diamond bracelet he bought for her in the Bahamas, a residence was merely something else that money and good taste could buy. He had both. All he lacked, all he ever wanted, was a woman like Taylor Kendall. The problem was, would she stick around when she found out the truth about him?

"Dr. Kendall speaking."

"Good morning Taylor. This is Gabe's friend, Jack."

She pushed the off button on the dishwasher to reduce the noise, "Hello, Jack. How are you?"

"I'm interfering and I have to fall on your mercy to protect me."

"How's that?"

"Well, I got a call from...uh...from Gabe. He's finishing up with the lab thing and heading back. I know he wants to surprise you, so don't tell him I called, okay?"

"I guess. Why didn't Gabe call? Did he ask you to call?"

Jack paused. He only called to try and prevent Taylor from becoming impatient and leaving for Arcadia alone. Protecting her alone down there would be too difficult, hence, a bit of well-placed interference was enough, he hoped, to persuade her to wait for Gabe. "I told you, Gabe wants to surprise you. Could you please act surprised?"

"I'll try. What's in this for you, Jack?"

Let's see. I'll avoid trying to tail you on a long stretch of lonely road, not to mention listening to the wrath of Blake in my cell phone mile after stinking mile.

"Oh, I'm a matchmaker at heart."

"How sweet, but I don't think we need you for that."

"Sure enough, doctor beautiful, I've never seen the man so smitten."

"That's an old fashioned word."

"I'm an old fashioned kind of guy."

"You know, Jack, I need to introduce you to my friend, Carla.

She's a gracious lady with old world manners and she can be funny too. You might like each other."

Carla. That must be Carla Girard, the man's sister. Yes, she's lovely but unattainable. If she's deep enough in that evil empire, the bureau might frown on corresponding with a woman I send to prison. Not to mention the possibility of Blake as a brother-in-law. I think I like him better as a friend than a relative.

"Are you interested, Jack?" Taylor persisted.

"Well, maybe another time. I've got my hands full right now with work."

"Let me know if you change your mind."

"When circumstances change, Doc, you'll be one of the first to know," Jack smirked at his tongue-in-cheek response. "Meanwhile, your man's on the way home."

"Thanks for telling me. I'll act like I didn't get this call."

Jack hung up his phone. *All right, Blake, catch a tail wind and get back here in time or we're both in deep trouble with Dr. Kendall.*

* * * * *

The silhouette of two figures, arms intertwined, made him shudder. As they approached, he shot them a look of unmistakable disdain. The shorter figure broke away and ran toward him with her arms outstretched. He grasped her hands and held them, but not as tight as his gaze held her quivering eyes.

"I don't care what you do behind closed doors. Don't flaunt it in front of me. Do you hear me?"

"Yes, Father. I'm sorry."

"You certainly are."

"Please don't hate me because I love Lorraine."

"I only hate weakness, Gina, you know that. If you want to work along side me, to be in command someday, you must push away from any encumbrances. Sex is fine. Take it wherever you want with anyone or more than one. I don't care. But don't let Lorraine lead you around. That's weakness. You know how I hate weakness."

"I know, Father," Gina answered, her eyes downcast.

"Did you get it?"

"Yes, sir, we did. It's in the car."

"Excellent. I'm going inside to finish my coffee. You and Lorraine can transfer the boxes to my car," he said handing her the keys to his Ferrari as he walked away.

Gina entered the restaurant after a few moments, looking around. There he was, sitting alone at a table.

"Father, we can only get three boxes in your car. What do we do with the other boxes?"

"Take them to Lorraine's house."

"Don't we usually keep the extras at home?"

"Not this time."

"Are we preparing to run again?"

Marco glared at her, tapping his hand on the table in a way that made his heavy gold signet ring sound like cymbals, "I will let you know when our time here has ended. For now, we simply need to make other arrangements with the extra ingredients."

"Lorraine is going to wonder why it's being stored at her place. That could implicate her in this whole thing."

"After all she has done, all you've done, you don't think you are both implicated?"

"Why would she put herself at further risk for us, Father?"

A waiter approached with his pad, assuming that the young woman would be joining the older man, yet he was waved off.

"Gina, if Lorraine loves you, then you have to persuade her to keep the boxes until I direct that they be moved."

"You want me to use her?"

"Why not? Sex is a powerful form of persuasion, regardless of one's persuasion."

"Father, I don't think I can do this. I really care for her. I don't want her harmed."

"Blake would do it."

"Do what?"

"He would do whatever he had to do, including sex, to achieve the goal."

Gina felt sucker-punched by his taunt. She slipped away, noticing that her father easily turned his attention to the Spanish language newspaper in his hands. She took deep breaths to avoid hyperventilating. Then she forced a smile as she approached Lorraine.

"We are going to keep the other boxes at your house."

"Why? What's Marco up to now?"

"Lorraine, this is a great opportunity for you as a sign of acceptance."

"In what way?"

"You already know the true 'secret' of the Nutracuratives. As a sign of trust, Father is allowing you to keep some of it. For him, this is a family gesture."

"He didn't look too happy when he saw us. Are you sure?"

Gina pushed a smile past her gritted teeth, "Of course. We can't disappoint him."

"I'm waiting for the other shoe to drop."

"This is our big chance to move up in power in the company... together."

"Then let's take this stuff home and celebrate."

* * * * *

"Faster than a speeding bullet...up in the sky, it's a bird, it's a plane, it's the man," Jack mumbled as he watched the Citation Jet land. Somehow Blake managed to shave ten minutes off his ETA. Jack waited at the back entrance of the hangar.

"Yo, Jack-o, let's roll."

"You are either the luckiest man on earth or the coolest."

"How about both?"

Did Blake have any idea how much he was like his father? Jack had seen Marco walking around the MACS building and a few other times when he tailed him. Marco had that certain swagger, a confident strut that said, 'Men call me sir and women call me often.' Blake tossed his flight bag into the back seat and got into the car. Jack turned back onto Ulmerton Road and pointed at the nearby Starbucks.

"Want to get a coffee?"

"No thanks, Jack. I need to make a fast change of clothes and get to Taylor's. I don't want her to leave without me. How can such an intelligent person can be so stubborn? It is so frustrating to work with somebody like that."

"Why Blake, I can't imagine."

"Are you sure she is all right?"

"Yes, she's fine. She hasn't left the pool house and no one entered."

"Are you following us to Arcadia?"

"No, I'm leaving ahead of you. As soon as I drop you at Taylor's, I'm going down there. I have two agents meeting me outside the hospital gates. I brought along the equipment if you want to be wired."

"I can't risk it, Jack. Taylor knows I don't wear a hearing aid, so how would I explain the ear piece? Besides, talking into those stupid lapel buttons works better on suits than on knit shirts."

"Then you'll be totally cut off from us and without a weapon. What if you need help? How will we know?"

"Welcome to modern crime fighting, Jack-o. I'll call you on my cell phone."

"How very Dick Tracy of you. Seriously, if you and Taylor aren't out of there by ten o'clock when they secure the outside gates, I'm sending in the cavalry."

"Okay, Jack, I promise to meet curfew. Will you be in this car?"

"No, I'm changing to a neon green Mustang. Strictly for undercover purposes since Taylor knows my car."

"Sounds like the drug squad is busting dealers with nice

wheels again. Have fun Jack, but don't get a speeding ticket."

"That's funny coming from you."

"Like Marco taught me - it's not what you do, it's what you get caught doing."

* * * * *

Taylor wrapped the last sandwich and packed it in the bulging tote bag. *Gabe suggested bringing snacks. This is too much food for one person, he better get here.* She was so absorbed that she didn't hear the door open until he spoke.

"Here I am, as promised lovely lady."

"Gabe!"

She ran toward him. He wrapped his arms around her and kissed her hungrily. Holding her to him, he was intoxicated by the pure, clean scent of her hair. She always smelled like rainwater and fresh flowers.

"Come on, let's get going."

"I suppose we'll have time to plan our strategy on the drive. Did you get the maps from AAA?"

"Yes. We can go I-75 south, then cut over at 70."

"Let's take the back road."

"What back road?"

"We'll go across the Sunshine Skyway and cut over to 70 from Bradenton."

"Why? Isn't the interstate faster?"

Why? Because it's a two lane, flat country road. Easy to see anyone following us. Easy for the backup car Jack has arranged to locate us if needed. Accurate, but too honest.

"Actually, it's more interesting, a glimpse of old Florida. Orange groves and farms. Nice break from the road ragers on the interstate," he explained, leaving out his initial thoughts.

* * * * *

"Car 10 to Control. Come in."

Jack fumbled with his right hand to find the microphone under a pile of fast food wrappers covering the passenger seat.

"Yeah, this is Control."

"We have a solid signal. The car is heading east on 70."

"Are you out of visual range?"

"Affirmative."

"See that the car makes it into the hospital, and then meet me at the diner in Arcadia."

"Is that when you'll present the plan?"

"If everything goes well, all we have to do is sit around."

"That's it?"

"Afraid so. I'm not expecting to lead the charge of the light brigade. Did you get a tracking device on the other car?"

"Affirmative."

"Did you hide it well?"

"Certainly."

"I hope so. See you at beautiful downtown Arcadia."

Jack tossed the microphone back on the seat. *Blake would be furious if he knew there was a tracking device on Taylor's car, but in reality there's too much space on the back road and too few places to hide in a small town. Of course, that's nothing compared with how mad Blake will be if he finds the tracker on his brown sedan. The old man said to stick with him until this case wraps up. Since Taylor's not the kind of girl to go for a three-some, electronic babysitting is the only viable option.*

* * * * *

"There it is," she pointed left to a long fence lead with a huge gate and a security guard station. "Almost a gothic kind of place, isn't it?"

"Taylor, it's a state mental hospital, not a health spa."

She pulled up behind a pickup truck, rolled down her window and heard the guard asking the men in the truck ahead for their names. Oops. She moved up to the guard.

"Hello, folks. Are you here as visitors?" the guard asked.

"Yes, we are."

"Fine. I need your names."

"Our names?"

"Yes, full names, please."

"Betsy and Bobby Browning."

"And where are you from Mrs. Browning?"

Mustering her best southern drawl, Taylor explained: "We're from Arkadelphia, Mississippi. Came to visit poor ole senile Grandpa. I feel so darned bad about it all. But Big Mamma, she says we have to go. So we borrowed her car and here we are."

The guard handed Taylor a visitor's card.

"You hang that tag on the mirror. There's a map on the back showing where you can park. Don't park in the staff spaces or your car will be towed."

"Thank you, sir, we sure enough won't cause any problems today."

Gabe practically swallowed his tongue to hold back his laughter, "We sure enough won't cause any problems today? Why? Will Big Mamma smack us down with her cast iron cornbread skillet?"

"So you think that's funny?"

"Yes, but extremely literate. I've never masqueraded as dead poets before?"

"Give me a break, Gabe. I didn't know we had to sign in at the gate. I was trying to think of a name for a husband and wife without using our names."

"And you went right to Robert and Elizabeth Barrett Browning?"

"That was less obvious than my first thought."

"Which was?"

"Lucy and Ricky Ricardo."

"You've got to stop watching nostalgia TV."

None of my undercover assignments have ever been like this.

With Taylor's creativity and serenity under pressure, she would make an exceptional FBI agent. Then again, as Jack says, she's stubborn and daring. That kind of behavior puts me in the line of fire too many times. Not a place for Taylor.

"Come on, get your gear," she said opening the trunk and reaching in. He jumped out of the car to see what she was up to now. Taylor pulled out two lab coats and handed one to him.

"What's this for?"

"We are going to see Martha by taking the path of least resistance."

He pulled on his starched white coat as she reached over to straighten the collar.

"Didn't you tell me that we needed to blend in and not be obvious?"

"Yes, ma'am, I did."

"Well, what blends in better in a hospital setting than two serious looking people in lab coats?"

"You think so. Who are we this time, Dr. Louis Pasteur and Dr. Marie Curie?"

"No, silly. Look at your name tag."

He looked down at the tag on his left top pocket. Turning it around, it read "Dr. Gabriel". He glanced over at her tag which read "Dr. Dodd".

"Interesting. Is there a history here?"

"Mine is my mother's maiden name. I didn't know your mother's name, so I did a play on your first name. I had these made at an office supply store in Clearwater."

"Clever. Now don't trap yourself."

"What do you mean?"

"You have to be careful when using a fake name...at least from what I've been told. Be particularly careful about signing your name when you're using an alias."

"I chose these names, why would I forget?"

"When you pick up a pen, you go on auto-pilot, writing

your real name before you realize it. If we have to sign anything, pause, better yet, pick up the pen with the opposite hand. That will make you think about what you're doing."

"What a marvelous idea. Did somebody tell you that?"

His mind flashed past a view of the FBI's top handwriting expert lecturing his rookie class, "You might say I heard it from a fairly knowledgeable guy."

CHAPTER 36

From behind the gates, G. Pierce Wood Hospital is arranged like a small college campus with several buildings, group home cabins and other no-frills staff housing surrounding the main hospital. Walking into the building, a newcomer is assailed with the scent of pine cleaner and futility. It's the place of last resort for adults with severe mental illness. Unlike a prison, most of these residents will never leave. There's no parole from schizophrenia, psychosis, dementia and other diagnostic labels that mark these people as rejects from a so-called normal society.

With complete confidence, Taylor walked past the visitor's registration desk, motioning for Gabe to follow. Getting past the metal detector was another story.

"Hold it, ma'am. You have to go this way," the security guard motioned.

"We're doctors. Do we look like we're here to hijack a gurney?"

"I don't know, ma'am, but you have to be checked like everyone else."

Taylor handed her clipboard to the guard and walked through. Gabe followed.

"That's good, now you doctors have to sign in. You aren't regular staff, are you?"

"No. We are here for consults ordered by Dr. Granger."

"On a weekend? That's unusual. Maybe I need to call administration."

"Listen, we are three hundred dollar an hour forensic psychologists from Palm Beach. Do you think we would leave our practice during the week and give up that much income? The only time we can afford to come here is on the weekend. Dr.

Granger was grateful that we would come at all."

The guard startled at Taylor's verbal assault. He glanced at the sign in sheet and then at her name tag.

"Well, Dr. Dodd, I suppose it's all right."

"If you aren't sure, we'll go hang out in the cafeteria until you roust poor Dr. Granger from his weekend break. At three hundred dollars an hour plus travel expenses, we can wait, can't we Dr. Gabriel?"

"Absolutely, Dr. Dodd, I could use a paid nap."

"Okay, go on. I'll list the chief's name as your authorization."

"Thank you. I'll mention in my report what a nice welcome you gave us."

Taylor and Gabe took the visitor tags from the guard and walked quickly down the hallway, turning at the first bend.

"I thought we were going to be low key, not annihilate the rent-a-cop."

"I tried, but he started it."

"And who is Dr. Granger?"

"He's the chief of psychiatric services."

"Do you know him?"

"No. I brought up the hospital's web site and wrote down a few key facts. I've been around hospitals all my life with my Daddy. Name dropping always works."

"Taylor, you scare me."

"Why?"

"This charade may be overkill. We could have walked in as regular people coming to visit a patient."

"True, but where's the fun in that?"

*****

"This is the third nurses' station we've tried. Maybe she's not here anymore."

"I see a staff lounge. Let's take a break. Might find a coffee pot," Gabe suggested, heading for the door and holding it open for Taylor, "You pour the coffee. I need to go to the restroom; be right back."

He closed the door, paused, then stepped across to the visitor's lounge and picked up the in-house phone.

"This is Dr. Gabe. I need for you to page Nurse Ginger Gregory and ask her to meet me at the nurses' station 3-A. Stat."

He hung up the phone to wait for his contact. Jack had told him how Ginger's first career as a Registered Nurse made her a popular undercover agent with the Medicare Fraud Squad. The Director arranged to pull her out of a Naples nursing home investigation to work weekend relief at G. Pierce Wood. Having her on the inside improved the odds. If anything went wrong, they ought to be able to get Taylor and Martha out or hold their own until he could summon Jack.

"Dr. Gabe?"

He turned from the phone toward a 5'7" stunning redhead with ample cleavage poured into a tight-fitting white uniform. If she managed to sneak in a weapon, he was hard pressed to imagine where she kept it.

"Nurse Gregory?"

"Yes. How can I help you?"

"I'm here to see a patient. The Director of my particular branch of service suggested that you could help."

"Nice to meet you, Gabe, is it?"

"That's right. Just Gabe."

"I wasn't expecting to see you as a doctor. Is there a change of plans?"

"Actually, I'm here with a friend. She's going by the name of Dr. Dodd."

"Is she fully briefed?"

"No. She's my inside contact on this investigation. She knows nothing about my employer. This costume party is her idea."

"Okay, if you're all right with it, I am too."

"I realize it's not procedure, but I had to bring her along."

"Where is she?"

"She's in the staff lounge getting coffee."

"Fine. Let's go in there and act like we just met in the hallway. I'll take you to Martha."

Gabe and Ginger entered the lounge.

"Dr. Dodd. This is Nurse Gregory. She knows the patient we're looking for."

Taylor looked up at Gabe. In a back country mental hospital where you expect to see Nurse Racket look-alikes, he found a nurse who looks like the star of a medical porn flick.

"What about your coffee?" she asked moving possessively closer to Gabe.

"I'll pass. Let's do what we came to do. Nurse Gregory, you lead and we'll follow."

They walked past the nurses' station to the elevator.

"The patient you came to see is usually in the game room at this time."

The elevator stopped on the second floor, entering a hall that looked like the starting line for wheelchair roller derby. A dozen patients were lined up headed toward double doors to the right.

"What's going on?" Taylor asked.

"Activities start soon in the game room. Patients from all the floors meet here. It's the hospital version of cruising the mall," Ginger replied.

"Can we talk with her in a more private place?" Gabe asked.

"Probably. I'll go in and get her. You two stay here. She may balk if she sees strangers."

Ginger leaned down to talk with a young man in a wheel chair. He nodded and she pushed him inside, disappearing through the double doors.

"Gabe, do you think we can trust her?"

"Taylor, we've asked several staff people how to find Martha Sanders and no one's offered to help. I asked her and she knew who I meant. Let's go with it."

"All right."

They stood aside as three more elevator loads of patients arrived. Taylor stared at her watch. Then the doors opened and Ginger came out pushing a chair with a dark-haired woman clutching a pillow. She motioned for them to follow, down the hallway and into a small room with a slit for a window.

"Martha, I want you to meet my friends. This is Gabe and, uh..."

"I'm Taylor, how are you, Martha?" She bent down until her tall frame was compressed enough to make eye contact with the timid patient. Gabe pulled up a worn metal chair.

As Ginger moved from behind the wheelchair, Martha reached out to grab her hand. "It's fine, Martha. I'm here. These people won't hurt you."

Martha's petite body seemed overwhelmed by the ill- fitting flannel robe. Strands of black hair fell loosely around her face, the rest tightly constrained in a pony tail. Graceful slim fingers ended abruptly with chewed nails. Her eyes darted side to side as if watching something they did not see.

"We know some of the same people you know, Martha," Taylor continued, "Ray Dwyer is a good friend of mine. He works as a mental health tech. He told me good things about you."

Martha's body resumed slight rocking movement, eyes darting side to side.

"And I met a friend of Ray's who knew you too. Peter Lane, a social worker."

No reaction.

"I also know a nurse who worked with you. She said you did wonderful work with music therapy. Her name is Neva."

Martha stopped rocking. A glimmer of recognition or total coincidence?

"You remember Neva? She works at MACS with Lorraine Lewis."

"Witch! Burn the witch!" Martha screamed, arms flailing.

Ginger moved toward the wheelchair, as Taylor held out an arm to block her path.

"Martha, why is Lorraine a witch? I need to know. Help me save the patients."

"Stop her. She makes the witch's brew. She makes them sick. I saw her. Stop her. Stop her!"

Martha jerked forward. Ginger's quick reaction caught Martha before she pulled away from the chair. She clung to Ginger like a frightened child. Taylor and Gabe stepped away as Ginger sang and patted the terrified woman's shoulders until she quieted down.

"I've got to calm her before we go back to the game room or she'll end up spending the night in restraints. There's a staff lounge on this floor, to the right of the elevators. I'll meet you there after I get Martha settled," Ginger directed.

Neither spoke as they walked to the staff lounge. Thankfully, they were alone.

"I knew Lorraine was behind it, I knew it," Taylor said, slapping the back for the door. "It's time to call the police on her."

"For what? Being the subject of an insane woman's nightmares?"

"Gabe, we found some substances that are being added to the Nutracuratives. Now we know, Lorraine's behind it."

"Hold on, Sherlock. We don't know that. We know that she terrorizes her nursing staff, but that's not a crime. And besides, how could Lorraine get away with this on her own without help?"

"She has Gina to help her."

"Do you really think Gina has the nerve to do anything at MACS without her father's approval? Would she tamper with his Nutracurative formula?"

Taylor paused; her forehead crinkled the way he knew it did when she was thinking intently. He waited for the conclusion to hit her.

"You're right. Gina may be Lorraine's bed warmer, but she would never cross Dr. Marco. If that's the case, then Marco knows what's going on."

"Knows, endorses or looks the other way?"

"Which is it?"

"That's a question without an answer. I believe, Sherlock, it goes directly to criminal intent."

"Martha said that Lorraine makes the witch's brew and she saw it. What if she means that she saw Lorraine altering the Nutracurative? And what if the substance she put into it was strong enough to push someone like Harriet Logan or Greg Newman into a psychotic state?"

As he feared, give Taylor a hint and she leaps to a huge, yet accurate conclusion. A conclusion that, if spoken in the wrong ears, could be life threatening. He had to back her down.

"That's a big leap. Let's stick with what we know."

"And what's that, my trusty Dr. Watson?"

"Well, Sherlock, at the risk of mixing literary themes, we know that something is rotten in Denmark. And we know that Lorraine is involved, which means Gina knows and Marco either approves or ignores it. I want you to be very careful about repeating this, even to Ray. There isn't enough to go on. It could mean trouble for you at MACS."

"How can I go back into that clinic knowing that someone may be trying to harm patients. Why are they doing this?"

"Money, Taylor, big money."

"MACS doesn't bill for the Nutracurative. They can't because it's not an FDA-approved prescription drug. Where's the profit in that?"

"The profit is in the virtually unquestioned daily rate paid for PHP treatment. At least the numbers you told me sound impressive."

"Okay, they make money providing treatment. So does every

other PHP in the country."

"Right, and didn't you show me your research on the success rate in treating persons with schizophrenia?"

"Yes. No matter what the program, it's a high risk population."

"And is the clinic full now?"

"Yes. I've peeked over Brook's shoulder when she types the weekly census reports. All the MACS programs together are running at about 97% capacity."

"Rather predictable for a non-predictable population. Do the same patients bounce back or do you see a lot of new patients?" he probed, wondering if she saw the same pattern he did, "Think about any patient who's dropped out recently."

"Well, one fellow, Earl, was involved in a serious incident and taken out for a few days for hospitalization," she recalled her conversations with Jamal trying to find out what really sent Earl into a tail spin, "Once again, the lowest common denominator is none other than Lorraine Lewis, who signed his discharge order at South Bay."

"Since when do nurses authorize discharge?"

"Lorraine was there. I know the psychology resident who worked on the case. And she signed Dr. Marco Girard's name on the release order."

"Then MACS lost a paying patient."

"No. He's been reassigned to the Clearwater program but it's really sad. Ray was up there last week and saw him. Ray's says the man is as bad off as he was when he first came to MACS."

"Didn't he make any progress at MACS?" Gabe probed in that clever and sometimes irritating way that Dale had of leading graduate students to the answer that they had been dancing aimlessly around.

"Yes, he did. Aside from a personality clash with another patient, he was doing well. In fact, I recommended him as a candidate for the after-care program, Live Anew."

"None of you saw the relapse coming?"

"I certainly didn't, but a lot of this is new to me."

"What did Ray say about it?"

"He was surprised too. Wait a minute. Ray and Hallie Logan told me that Harriet was ready for discharge. Then suddenly, without warning, she panics and runs into the street. That's not too different than Greg Newman. Ray said he was ready for discharge twice. Once, Greg had a sudden psychotic episode and came back to treatment. The second time, he left MACS and jumped off the Skyway Bridge. I see an ugly pattern."

"What's that?"

"Patients get better with therapy and the Nutracuratives. That makes the program's statistics look good. But some of them take a dramatic downturn and end up back in a program at another location."

"And how does that benefit MACS?"

"Like you said, it's about money. If they regress enough, they could come back enrolled in a different clinic. New clinic, new patient number, and more treatment until the full amount of annual reimbursement is exhausted, then the patient goes back to living under a bridge." Taylor's eyes glittered with excitement. She was onto something and she knew it, "It's the ultimate in recycling."

"Recycling only works to a point."

"Yes, and then somebody decides it's time to dispose of the problem. Only the problem is a person. That's not recycling. That's malpractice."

"You're too kind, Taylor; sounds like a motive to me."

"Oh my God, Gabe, we could be talking about murder here."

"That's why your life may depend on your silence."

CHAPTER 37

"Taylor, this is Mama. Are you working on the weekend again? Frankly, honey I think that clinic is taking advantage of you. You need a break. Why don't you get in your car and take a nice drive? Someplace relaxing, out of the city and out of pager range? And Taylor, when you get home, call me. I don't care if you are a grown woman; I need to know you're all right. You are all right, aren't you? Call me, honey. I love you."

Taylor's answering machine faithfully recorded Mama Julia's voice.

* * * * *

Taylor's head leaned against Gabe's shoulder. She had been quiet for awhile. Her turbulent thoughts must have exhausted her. He realized that she was asleep and he had zoned out too. Glancing at his watch, he saw they'd been waiting over an hour for Ginger to take Martha to the game room down the hall. Had she been called back to her floor? No. Honed instincts don't fail, something's up.

He gently shook Taylor. "Wake up, Sherlock, the game isn't over yet," he said, kissing her forehead.

"Oh, Gabe...I wasn't sleeping, was I?"

"Yes, you were."

"Did Martha get settled down?"

"I don't know. Ginger didn't come back."

"Well, guess we better go."

"I agree."

They started out the door, when Ginger ran around the

corner, crashing into them.

"Sorry," she panted. "No time. Follow me."

"Trouble?"

"Yes."

He grabbed Taylor's arms, pulling her along beside him. Ginger pressed the numbers on the key pad to open the "staff only" stairway door.

"Next floor. Hurry."

"If we're trying to get out of here, why are we going up?"

"Quiet, Taylor, keep moving," Gabe ordered.

They ran up the stairs behind Ginger. At the landing, she gave a hush signal, cracked open the door and looked around. Then she turned to them.

"Walk calmly beside me. We're going to the nurses' locker room."

They passed a male nurse, two patients and a ward clerk, none of whom showed the slightest interest in the fleeing trio. Ginger's eyes darted back and forth the way Martha's did. She pointed to a door, "Get in there."

They entered a room with all the appeal of the visiting team's locker room at a ghetto high school stadium. Two rows of green, dented lockers with a bench in between divided the room. In the back were curtained shower stalls and toilets and nearest the door, a thrift store reject sofa and chair.

"It's clear up here so far," Ginger said.

"What's the situation?" Gabe asked.

"I was stopped in the game room by a supervisor. She wanted to know where I took Martha. She said something about unauthorized personnel in the hospital. She was vague. Fortunately, Martha's still obsessing about the witch. I said she had another delusional outburst and I took her into a quiet room to calm down."

"That wasn't enough?"

"I thought it was, but then I saw the security alert flash on the computer screen at the nurses' station."

"Are they looking for us?"

"Probably. We don't need to be seen together," Ginger winked at Gabe, "If you get my drift."

She opened a locker and took out a Tommy Hilfiger duffle bag. Rummaging inside, she produced a navy jumper and blonde wig.

"Here, Taylor, put these on."

"You just happen to have a blonde wig?"

"I like to change my look from time to time. It's kind of fun."

Gabe rolled his eyes wondering if Taylor would buy that story.

"Why?"

"It's cheaper and less trouble than dying my hair when I want a new look. Enough questions. You can change clothes back in the shower stall," Ginger directed taking Taylor's lab coat, "Keep your white shirt on underneath and give me your skirt."

To Gabe's surprise, Taylor did as she was told.

Ginger opened a closet and took out a set of green scrubs, "Put these on over your clothes, Gabe." Moving closer to whisper she explained, "I need to get you out of here fast. I know I'm going to be questioned again about Martha."

"Who's asking?"

"I expect it's the DEA watchdog; she's their agent."

"That's what I suspected when we got stonewalled on the name inquiry. I didn't want to call attention to this visit."

"Do you have backup?"

"On the outside, I think he's drinking coffee at the Arcadia Diner."

"No other backup?"

"Yes, you."

"Oh, we are in deep."

"Can you get us out a back way?"

"I've only worked here once before this week, so I don't

know the layout that well. But I've got an idea." Ginger looked back, noticing that Taylor was still in the dressing area. Then she jiggled a lock on a locker across from her own. It popped open easily. "Bingo!", she smiled, picking up a key card on the lower shelf, "We aren't supposed to leave our key cards in the locker, but I hear it said that Cary does it all the time. They joke about how she's always losing her card, so no one will be surprised." She slammed the locker shut, handing the key card to Gabe. He tucked it into the pocket of the scrubs.

"Thanks. Is this a universal card?"

"It works on all exits, wards and main doors, but not administrative offices or medication rooms," Ginger replied, taking a pen from her uniform pocket she looked around for paper. Tearing a memo off the bulletin board, she drew a simple map. "Do you have a car?"

"Yes. Taylor's car is in a staff space near the main visitor's lot."

"That's good," Ginger nodded, "Follow the route I outlined. It will take you out of this building and around the group home cottages. Act casual. If there's any problem, duck into a cottage. At every entry door, you'll see three buttons behind a clear plastic cover."

"Okay. What do they do?"

"Red is the fire alarm, green is for escape and gold is for medical emergency. Push any button and you'll distract security until they can isolate the cause."

"Sounds like you've done this before, Nurse Gregory."

"Chaos is a good cover, at least that's what my field partner says."

"Thanks for the map," he shook hands with her.

As Taylor came out of the dressing area, she saw what looked like Gabe holding hands with Ginger and her jealously meter went off the scale, "What do you think?" Taylor spun around to show off her disguise.

"Interesting, and are you having more fun as a blonde?"

"I don't know," she turned to Ginger, "Do you find that you often run for your life as a blonde?"

Ginger's glossed lips turned into a smile, "More often than you'd believe."

As they left the nurses locker room, Gabe darted across the hall to get a wheelchair and motioned for Taylor to sit in it. He took the lap robe and arranged it on her legs to hide shoes that were too stylish for a patient.

"Let's go. Taylor, all you have to do is put your head down and look pitiful."

"Thanks," she mumbled.

"There's the elevator. Wheel her inside and I'll walk up after you get in," Ginger suggested.

Blessedly, no one pushed the second floor button and the elevator went directly to the first floor. Gabe started to move. Ginger reached over and pinched his arm. He turned to see her shaking her head "no." The elevator continued downward to a basement level. Two aides got off, holding the door for Gabe to steer the wheelchair. Ginger walked ahead and Gabe followed.

They ended up in the employee cafeteria - a large open room with one wall of high outside windows that was noisy and busy. Ginger went to get drinks. Gabe found a table to the outside corner between two large groups of coworkers enjoying boisterous conversations.

"Where are we?" Taylor asked.

"Looks like the cafeteria," Gabe answered, "Ginger drew a map for us. We'll stay here awhile, and then slip out a side door and onto the grounds."

"Do I have to play patient?"

"Yes, for now. It's a good disguise. By the way, I never thought of you as a blonde."

"Very funny, Gabe. I never pictured you as a blonde either."

"Life's full of surprises, Taylor."

Ginger returned bearing a tray with soft drinks and chips.

"The alert doesn't seem to bother these folks."

"Usually doesn't unless it's a major deal. Staff on break would rather not know about a crisis until they have to," Ginger replied, opening a bag of corn chips.

Taylor looked around. These people reminded her of MACS staff on break. They were happy to discuss anything but work. Then she noticed a security guard enter the room with two dark suited men.

"Gabe, look over there."

"Don't stare, Taylor. I'll look in a minute. Do you recognize anyone, Ginger?"

"I think the taller man next to the guard is from Human Resources. I don't know the short guy."

Gabe glanced, and then turned his head. He took a napkin, wrote, "He's Tampa DEA," and passed it to Ginger.

"Can he make you?"

"Probably not, but I don't want to chance it. How about you?"

"No. I'm clear."

"Am I missing something?" Taylor whispered, head down in her patient mode.

"Quiet, Taylor, I'll explain later."

"The men are walking through the cafeteria line. They must be doing a sweep of this room. You better leave."

"Right," he answered, moving Taylor's wheel chair a few feet in the opposite direction from the table. He stopped, locked the chair brake then walked back to Ginger, hugging her as if he were saying goodbye to a girlfriend. In her ear he whispered, "Do you need me to send in my backup to get you out?"

"No, I can handle it. The Human Resources guy is pointing this way. I'll stall them."

"Okay. Ginger. Thanks for everything. Call your contact in two hours or I'll have someone storm the gates."

"You better hope you're out of here before that time."

Keeping his head down, he walked slowly back to Taylor. He

bent down beside the chair as if having difficultly with the brake. Thankfully, Taylor remained quiet. The best way to leave the scene was slow and methodical, not running frantically like the characters in poorly-written detective shows. He heard the man speak to Ginger. He couldn't stall any longer without appearing suspicious, so he arranged Taylor's lap robe and began to slowly push the chair toward the exit door. A lull in the conversation of a nearby table made it possible for him to hear Ginger's diversion.

"Yes, sir, the woman got Martha's attention by saying 'You remember Lorraine Lewis, don't you?' There's no question that Martha knew who Lorraine was."

The short man wrote rapidly in a flip top notebook, "Do you know Lorraine Lewis?"

"No, sir, I don't."

"Who was the man?"

"I'm not sure it was a man...it might have been a woman dressed like a man."

Gabe picked up the pace. *Great fake, Ginger. That will keep them busy for a while.* He wheeled Taylor out the cafeteria doors and toward a maintenance entrance. It was like the engine room in the belly of a ship; grunting pipes, hissing steam and cramped corridors.

"The ride's over."

Taylor stood up and stretched. "Good. I feel too constrained in that chair. Are we going to make a run for it?"

"No. We're not trying to create a chase scene. What we are going to do is follow Ginger's map and take the long way to your car."

"Won't the guard stop us at the gate, Mr. Browning?"

"No, Mrs. Browning."

"Why not?"

"Because I'm relying on you to come up with another clever story."

"What if I can't?"

"It will work out somehow." *As soon as I can dial Jack's number on my phone and alert him to our problem.*

"Let's go. Bend down a little. These pipes are low," he cautioned, holding tightly to her hand as they weaved their way between the machinery to the red exit sign indicating an outside door. He pulled the key card from his pocket to swipe it, noticing the three buttons beside the door. *Don't need those now.* The door opened easily. They stepped out into the daylight. She started to follow the ramp.

"Not that way, Taylor, over here behind the dumpsters."

"It's smelly over there."

"Hold your nose; this is the shortest way to the cottages."

They walked past the trash area. He took her hand and pulled her with him, running toward a group of patients sitting at a picnic table under an oak tree.

"Can we join you?"

"Yeah, sure," replied an older woman, who was playing checkers alone. The others at the table made no comment.

Gabe turned to Taylor, "Lower your head and rock back and forth. I'm going to play checkers with this lady. Don't look up until I tell you."

To the security guards approaching, it looked like a mental health aide sitting with his patients. They walked by the table, then turned toward the far side of the hospital building.

Gabe squeezed Taylor's arm, "We can go now."

They walked between cottages, mingling when possible among the patients. Each time they stopped, she noticed that Gabe was scanning the area. He seemed to be alert and not frightened by their situation. Probably because of his theatre experience where he had to be aware of cues from other actors and improvise if someone muffed his lines. She could almost see the highway beyond the hedge. They must be near the parking lot.

Suddenly, he pushed her inside a cottage. It was a plain living room with vinyl covered furniture and a blaring television. The woman sitting in front of it was oblivious to anything beyond the screen.

"Stay in here while I check something."

"No, I want to go with you."

"Taylor. Stay here," he ordered, closing the door behind him.

Outside he walked over to the large hedge, looked around, then dropped to his knees between the shrubs. He flipped open his cell phone.

"Jack Sims."

"Jack-o. Trouble inside. Ginger's being questioned by a DEA guy."

"What do you need?"

"If she doesn't call her contact in an hour and a half, go get her."

"Done. We'll come in and get you out."

"Not yet. If you do, it'll blow my cover with Taylor. We're almost at the gate. You know her car. I'm going to create a diversion to get out."

"I've got back-up across the street right now. I'll be there myself in ten minutes."

"I'm in green scrubs and Taylor's wearing a blonde wig."

"Sounds interesting. Bring it on home, man."

He clipped the phone back on his belt and rose up slowly. A patient passed by who found absolutely nothing odd about a man sitting in a shrub talking. Then again, that same patient was having an intense conversation with two squirrels.

The door opened and Taylor startled. He hugged her, whispering, "It's clear. I heard something but it was another patient."

Taylor reached into her shirt to pull the spare car key from her bra.

"I could have gotten that for you. Did you put it there, to taunt me?"

"No. I always keep my keys in my skirt or jacket pocket. Ginger's jumper has no pockets, so I used what Mama calls 'nature's pocket'. Can we go now?"

"Good idea," he replied, opening the door for her. This was no time to sidetrack his senses thinking about Taylor's cleavage. As she stepped outside, he reached back to the inside door frame, popped open the plastic cover and pressed the gold button. Then he closed the door, took Taylor's arm and strolled casually toward the parking lot.

"Gabe, here comes a guard in a golf cart," Taylor said starting to pull away.

He held her tightly to his side, "Ignore him. Act like we only have eyes for each other." He leaned his face toward hers, depending on his peripheral vision to track the guard. The guard's radio crackled, "Medical emergency – cottage eight. Stand by to direct incoming ambulance."

"10-4," the guard replied, wheeling around toward the cottage service road.

"It worked!" Gabe cheered aloud, taking Taylor's hand, "Let's run to the car."

Two more guard carts drove past them as Taylor backed the car out.

"Drive slowly. Don't pull into the gate approach until you hear sirens."

"What sirens?"

"The sirens in the distance are headed this way. That's our escort out of here."

"That's an ambulance and a fire rescue truck. How did you know that?"

"Later. Pull into the exit line. When I tell you, hit the gas and don't look back."

She cut in front of a van and slammed on her brakes to avoid hitting the rickety pickup ahead of her car. The security gate was stuck as the ambulance turned off the highway and stopped.

Suddenly two plain clothes men flashing badges ran up to the guard and started shouting. The exit gate went up. One of the men motioned for the truck and Taylor's car to move forward so the ambulance could enter. She screeched out, making a hard right turn onto the highway.

"Keep going until you see the sign for the interstate," he said, looking back over his shoulder. That 'traffic cop' looked remarkably familiar. His cell phone rang. He opened it.

"The tail on you is our car. They'll get you to the interstate."

"You telephone solicitors never quit do you. I don't want to change my bank account."

"You've rattled enough people today, go home. I'm checking on Ginger."

"Thanks, but I really don't want to change."

"Don't I know it," Jack exclaimed, closing his cell phone and reaching for his fake U.S. Customs ID to show the flailing security guard. With all the illegal aliens in lower Florida, Customs credentials gain easy entry. He watched Taylor's car disappear out of the corner of his eye.

Taylor drove in white-knuckled silence along the highway. Gabe wasn't sure if she was trying to decompress after all of the excitement or still terrified.

"Let's pull off at the Fruitville Road exit."

"Why? Don't we need to go home?"

"Not as much as I need food. Head that way, Taylor; there's several fast food places off this exit."

"I know the area. I use to live a little north of here."

"Look in our mirror. No state troopers. No helicopter. We can stop if we want to."

"What if someone is looking for us, Gabe?"

"We used fictitious names to visit a patient. We aren't Bonnie and Clyde."

"Then why was there so much concern about us visiting Martha?"

"I can't say exactly, but if you're right about Lorraine being responsible for tampering with the Nutracuratives, Martha may be a witness to that. What if Lorraine has a nurse friend who keeps an eye on anyone visiting?"

"Okay, but how would Lorraine's spy be able to raise such a stink with the guards about us?"

"You never know."

Taylor pulled off the exit ramp, stopped at the traffic light and glared at him, "Were you responsible for that ambulance coming in at just the right time?"

"I pushed the medical emergency button in the cottage. That summoned the guard desk and the ambulance was called. It was a diversion."

"You did that?"

"Yes and it worked."

"I don't see how a nurse inside could send security after us."

"What if she told them we were drug pushers? After all, Martha is suppose to be there because of the aftermath of a drug overdose. I'm guessing any drugs she took were forced on her to keep her quiet."

"Oh, Gabe, that's so awful. What kind of woman is Lorraine?"

"One that won't make the cut for Miss America."

* * * * *

Taylor picked at her fries. Gabe finished his double cheese burger and the rest of hers.

I remember how she feels. The first couple of close calls I had as a new agent kept my nerves on edge for hours after the danger passed. Before I knew it, changing gears from normal to high alert became barely noticeable. Lasting on stakeout or hot pursuit is nothing more than an adrenaline rush. Once the danger passes, it's my stomach that screams for attention. Nothing pumps up my appetite more than escaping yet again. If Taylor knew that she'd find it hilarious.

"Do you want me to drive home?"

She tossed him the keys and opened the passenger door. He was talking to her about stopping for a walk along the observation road as they approached the Sunshine Skyway Bridge when he realized that she was asleep.

"Sweet dreams, Sherlock. That's enough crime fighting for today."

* * * * *

Taylor was awakened as the car stopped in front of the gallery.

"Why are we stopping?"

"I need to shower the hospital scent off me and gather my sailing gear," he opened the door, "You can go home and I'll walk over later."

"No!" her frantic answer stunned him. "I mean, can't you get your clothes and shower at the pool house?"

"You stay here and I'll be right back."

"I'll go with you."

"My place is a mess. I'd be embarrassed for you to see it. I won't be long."

He watched as she got into the driver's side and locked her door. Taking the stairs two at a time, he flung open the apartment door, and then quickly locked it in case she followed. He flopped across the bed, making the first ripple in a surface that would pass military inspection, and dialed the cell phone.

"Jack Sims."

"We're back in St. Petersburg. Did you find Ginger?"

"Yes. I did my Customs Inspector imitation, looking for illegal aliens."

"Did you find any?"

"Slam dunk, man. Two guys from Mars introduced themselves to me and offered a ride in their space ship."

"And what about Ginger?"

"She was doing fine without me. In fact, she had the DEA guys chasing their tails looking for Lorraine Lewis. She must have paid attention to the background briefing on this case."

"Nice work."

"That Ginger is one fine woman."

"Jack, you're drooling again. Is she pulling out?"

"Don't know. I called the communications room. Ginger checked in with her contact. I suppose she'll wait for an official decision. Do you think she needs to go back to watch Martha?"

"No, I don't, unless it's the best way to reduce suspicion. Obviously DEA has Martha on a short leash, which is enough protection. Whatever Martha knew, she can't retrieve it now. Other than allowing Taylor to see a little action as an amateur detective, it was probably a useless trip," Gabe spoke while pulling clothes from the closet and tossing them into a bag.

"Ginger told me that the medications ordered for Martha are given special clearance."

"What's that mean?"

"It means that DEA is protecting her mind as well as her body."

"How so?"

"The medications are prolonging Martha's incoherence."

Gabe tossed an extra pair of socks into the bag and walked over to the living room window to check on Taylor, "They don't know if she knows anything or not."

"Maybe. But Ginger was insistent on one thing."

"What?"

"She thinks that as long as Martha remains drugged, she's no threat to anyone. If Lorraine or Dr. Marco found her, they'd get what you got - nothing. No threat, no reason to kill her. Ginger thinks it's a good way to save Martha's life."

"I hope she's right, Jack. At this point, it's not much of a life. I'm going to stay with Taylor. She's shaken by our afternoon in the country."

"As the old man ordered, stay close, but then you're the master of undercover work, man."

"Get a box of donuts and use your imagination."

He zipped the bag, smoothed out the top sheet and headed out the door. The oriental carpet needed to be aired out and he hadn't had time to dust in a week. Stopping in at his Virginia townhouse reminded him of the style in which he liked to live. He couldn't demand ambiance in the places he stayed during assignments, but neatness, well that was uncompromising.

CHAPTER 38

"All right. Keep your pants on, I'm coming," a shrill voice shouted from behind the door.

"Are you Lorraine Lewis?"

"Yes, who's asking?"

"I'm Tom Lodge, DEA, and this is my partner. We need to come inside and speak with you," he said, holding up a badge.

"You can't push your way into my home like this. I refuse to let you in," Lorraine screamed. Gina listened from the staircase.

"Ms. Lewis, we have a few simple questions. If you have nothing to hide, you'll let us in. Or we can call reinforcements and take you to our office for questioning. It's you're call."

Gina ran to her side, "Lorraine, let them in. You're acting crazy."

Lorraine turned toward Gina, pointing a blood red nail tip toward the closet under the stairs; the closet where they dropped Marco's boxes.

Gina shook her head, "Don't assume anything. Let's talk." Cutting in front of Lorraine, Gina reached over to open the security door lock. "Come in, gentlemen. We weren't expecting guests. Are you sure this is the right address?"

Lodge and his partner walked in and looked around. The short, chubby agent noticed Lorraine's bare legs through the slit in her silk caftan and Gina's lace nightgown with sheer robe. Lodge rolled his eyes.

"Ms. Lewis, I need to know where you were from around noon until four today."

"I was here."

"And I assume this lady...uh...was with you?"

"Yes."

"What's your name ma'am?"

"Gina Girard."

"Do you live here?"

"No. I'm visiting my friend. We work together."

"I bet you do," the short agent mumbled.

* * * * *

Some things do work out almost as well as planned. The sun was sliding into the water, sending flashes of orange and gold over the water. He carefully trimmed the sails so that he could control the boat with one hand, leaving the other free to circle her trim waist.

"This is wonderful, Gabe."

"I knew you'd like sailing in the sunset. It's very..."

"Romantic?"

"Yes, but I wasn't going for cheap thrill. What I really like about sailing this time of day is that it's so peaceful," Gabe explained, leaning toward her to overdose on the rainwater fresh scent of her hair.

"I see what you mean. It is peaceful. After a day like today, I need that."

"Here, Taylor, you try controlling the sails."

"I've never sailed on my own."

"You can do it. I have a feeling that you can do anything you put your mind to. And you enjoy being in control."

She took a loose end of the sail rope and smacked him on the hip. He laughed.

"When did you learn to sail, Gabe?"

"I learned in college. A lot of my friends sailed."

"So you got this boat when you came to Florida?"

"Actually, this boat belongs to a friend who doesn't have much time to use it. He works too hard."

"This is a nice toy."

"He has lots of toys."

"So he's a real player, huh?"

"He has been in the past. I think he's finally growing up; been everywhere, done everything. It's time to find out what he cares about."

"He sounds conflicted."

"What do you recommend, Dr. Kendall?"

"I suppose he has to decide who he really is and what he really wants. If he wants to change his life, what is he willing to sacrifice?"

Gabe looked at her, wishing he could blurt out his thoughts. *Everything, Taylor. He'd sacrifice everything for you.*

* * * * *

"We have to call Father."

"And tell him that DEA storm troopers came over here fishing for information?"

"They didn't bring a search warrant, so they don't have anything on us."

"Not this time, but they'll be back. They may be at MACS right now."

"I didn't think about that. We have to call Father and warn him."

"For all we know, he tipped them."

"Lorraine, that's ridiculous. Father would never put me in jeopardy like that."

"Oh, so he'd hang me out to dry without a second thought? Maybe that's why he demanded that we bring the rest of the boxes to my house," Lorraine puffed frantically on a slim black cigarette.

"I think it's time for me to go home."

"Run back to the family. From what you've told me, they protect each other."

"Lorraine, you sound ridiculous. Why would Father lead

DEA to you when you can link him to the boxes and the Nutracuratives? Not to mention the things we've done that Father doesn't even know about."

"Are you serious? Marco didn't know we went after that mouthy therapist anymore than Don Corleone didn't know that, when he said someone needed to leave, the person turned up dead. Marco, Serena and Victoria know a lot more than they let on."

"Just remember that the voodoo dolls and trashing those apartments was your idea, Lorraine, not Father's."

Lorraine jumped up, grabbed Gina by the shoulders and leaned into her face, "And it was for us, not only for me. I'm the one who pushes your wimpy butt up the corporate ladder. No wonder Marco considers you a poor substitute for his precious Blake."

Gina pulled away and ran up the stairs sobbing.

Ten minutes later, Gina walked down the stairs carrying an overnight bag and purposely did not turn her head toward the living room as she reached for the door.

"Does this mean that we're finished?"

Gina turned, nose in the air in true Girard manner, "No, I never said that. I need space right now and you do too."

"What happens tomorrow?"

"I'll see you at work. Maybe can have lunch."

The door bell rang. Lorraine startled, sloshing her beer on the chair. Gina opened the door calmly, telling the cab driver that she would be right out.

"I can drive you home."

"That's okay. I don't want to get in another argument, Lorraine. I can't stand being pulled between you and my family. Let's not say anything we'll regret," Gina replied, opening the door and slamming it behind her.

* * * * *

Gina could have walked to MACS from Lorraine's condo. But she didn't want her destination known. She directed the cab driver to wait for her in the loading zone. Key card in hand, Gina waved as she ran past the lobby guard, took the elevator to the second floor and entered the lab. As she expected, no one was there on a Sunday afternoon. Entering her office, she closed and locked the door in case Lorraine followed her. She walked to the plant stand and felt around the base for the plastic bag. It was still there. Brushing off some dirt, she saw that the needle Lorraine used to inject Harriet Logan was safely tucked inside the zip top bag.

Father was right. Love is great but insurance is better. Gina smiled as she stuffed the bag back into the planter. *If Father did tip the DEA, then he has his reasons. If not, well, I have to protect the family. That's what Blake would do.*

* * * * *

As Gina entered the front door, she heard raised voices coming from the library. She removed her heels to slip quietly up the stairs. On the landing, she ran into Carla.

"What's going on down there?"

"Father came back early," Carla explained. "There was some trouble in the Orlando program this week. He and Mother got into a shouting match then Serena joined in. So much for a quiet evening at home."

"What kind of trouble? Is it about the Nutracuratives?"

"Not that I heard. One of the schizophrenic patients called in an abuse claim against a therapist. Now the place will be crawling with health inspectors tomorrow."

"What about DEA?"

"What do you mean?"

"You know, drugs."

"Gina, we don't use drugs. If patients bring in something, then we confiscate and destroy it. You know that."

"You don't know, do you Carla?"

"Don't know what?"

"The Nutracuratives. You don't know what makes it work."

"It's Father's secret Amazon jungle ingredients...or some such thing," Carla answered laughing, "My guess is it's like the cellular reconstruction clinic - plain old cold cream and the power of suggestion."

"That's all you know," Gina drilled, "Are you sure?"

"I'm sure that's what I think it is, but do I know? No. I thought only you and Father, and maybe Blake, knew the secret ingredient."

"Blake! He doesn't know anything, unless you've told him when you talk to him."

"Obviously I don't have anything to tell, Gina."

"Then why do you think Blake would know?"

"Because he was with Father when they flew into that Amazon village where the secret ingredient was supposed to have been found. You can't stand the idea that Blake knows more than you do about anything."

"This time he doesn't; I guarantee it," Gina replied.

"Don't bet on it. Blake has an uncanny ability to show up in the right place at the right time. When he does come back, he'll have Father's total attention."

* * * * *

Gabe tied the final line to secure the sailboat as Taylor gathered the trash from their deli snack bags. Things were happening so fast, he wondered if he would ever have the chance to take her sailing again. Her face framed in moon light, he knew that he had never seen a more perfect woman. She reached for his hand.

"I had a wonderful time sailing. Let's go again soon."

"You're quite a woman, Taylor Kendall."

"What do you mean?"

"You stand here with the wind blowing your hair like a delicate flower of the south, but I know you're the same woman who manipulated her way into a state mental hospital and played chase with the guards. You are fire and ice."

"My mama says that southern women are unique that way."

"If that's true, then you are the most unique of all, you temptress."

"Does that mean you're staying over tonight?"

His cell phone beeped and he allowed voice mail to intercept the call, but glanced at the number. The screen showed three other calls that must have come in while they were sailing. Morganna. Jack. Morganna.

"I have to go back to the gallery."

"Somebody wants you to work on Sunday night?"

"No. I can take care of those calls tomorrow, but, fair lady, it means an early day and I know I won't get enough rest if I stay with you."

"Okay. You're probably right. I have to steel myself to go back into MACS tomorrow and pretend to be clueless. Hallie Logan checks in tomorrow."

"I'm not convinced that's a smart move."

"Ray and I have everything under control. Don't worry about me, Gabe. As you said, you've seen me operate under pressure."

Yes, Taylor, but you haven't seen the unholy trinity operate under pressure. They play rough and they don't care what happens if you get in the way.

"Be careful, Taylor. The Logans don't need to lose another daughter and I couldn't stand to lose you," he said, wrapping her in his arms for a long kiss. He walked beside her to the car, loading her things into the trunk.

"Aren't you going to get in?"

"No. I think I'll walk back to the gallery."

"I'm going by there."

"I know. I need to stretch my legs. This way you won't be able to kidnap me in your car, take me home and have your wicked way with me," he said winking as he opened her car door.

He stood at the curb watching her car pull away before he started walking up Central Avenue. Waiting for the traffic light, he dialed.

"Morganna, here."

"Did you find anything for me?"

"Blake, darling, I certainly did. But it doesn't make any sense."

"What did you find?"

"I double-checked this. That juice cocktail has notable traces of a generic brand psychotropic and a little serotonin booster."

"That doesn't make any sense."

"No but the fruit juice is acceptable quality, but not organic."

"Wait a minute, what you are saying is that the Nutracuratives are a fake - a disguise for old fashioned pharmacology."

"That's the part I can't piece together. These drugs don't typically work together," Morganna replied, "I pulled the PDR off the shelves and scanned everything in the lab. Then I searched online for clinical studies. The combination doesn't make sense, unless it's some experiment. But you can't do those kinds of drug experiments with human subjects outside of a highly controlled FDA study environment."

"You can if no one knows it."

"Listen, Blake, you need more medical input than I can give. It sounds like a devious formula for forcing an adverse reaction."

"Such as?"

"It's not predictable, but a certain combination could cause some patients to become confused and clumsy, show rapid rise in blood pressure and breathe irregularly. Hype that with some verbal harassment or threats plus their schizophrenic hallucinations and it's like gasoline on a fire. This is really beyond my expertise. Do you want me to call in one of our physician consults or the drug company reps?"

"No, Morganna, absolutely not!" he caught himself raising

his voice. He stopped and sat on a vacant bench, a bench across from the MACS building. "This never happened. You never saw it or tested anything. You've given me enough to head in the right direction. My guess is that this 'R code' version isn't kosher by any standards."

"That's all I can do with it."

"Where is the sample?"

"I flushed it down the toilet like you asked me to."

"Did you leave any records in the lab?"

"No."

"Thanks, Morganna. You may have helped me break this case, even though I can't officially give you credit."

"The only thanks I want is a week with you, naked on the beach. Bali, wasn't it?"

"I can't think about that now. I have to stay focused on the job."

"Darling, I want you desperately."

"Take care, Morganna."

He started walking again, mulling over the information she provided. He had to know more. Flipping open the phone, he dialed Jack.

"Jack Sims."

"I talked to Morganna. What she found is really strange."

"Are you with Taylor?"

"No, I'm alone, crossing Central at the gallery. Come on over. We've got to figure this out and fast. I don't think we have much time."

"I agree and DEA didn't help any."

"What did they do now?"

"I'll explain when I get there."

"Say, Jack. Bring a large pizza. This may take awhile."

CHAPTER 39

Blake left the outside door unlocked for Jack. He ran upstairs, grabbed a legal pad and started making notes. *What Morganna found in the "R code" Nutracurative is unusual, but is it deadly? Or is Marco using accepted prescription medications to manage schizophrenic symptoms and pretend it's a miraculous cure from his proprietary formula, then using other drug mixtures to manage the relapse on schedule? Were Lorraine and Gina acting under orders or on their own? No, Gina would never double-cross Father, but Lorraine would.*

He was so focused on his notes that he didn't hear footsteps coming up the stairs. Without warning the door was kicked open and he dove for the sofa, reaching under the pillow for his gun.

"Hold it, I'm one of the good guys," Jack shouted, balancing pizza and drinks.

He raised up from crouching behind the sofa while putting the safety back on his gun, "Sorry, Jack. My fault."

"I know you, man. You're wrestling with this thing. What have you got?" Jack asked as he opened the pizza box, kicked off his shoes and pulled up a chair at the table where Gabe was working.

"Here, you take a look," Gabe passed the diagrams and notes to Jack.

Jack scanned the notes and the note maker. One of the most interesting aspects of working with Blake was his ability to accumulate details and synthesize them into an organized process, a flow chart for crime that was useful when it was time to go to court. Few defense attorneys ever put a wrinkle in his reports. As an agent, he could nail down the most obscure details and make the pieces fit. Working with him was poetry in motion, law enforcement style.

"What do you think, Jack? Is it as crazy as it seems?"

"I don't know, man. I don't see how it adds up."

"Me either. It's not the way the unholy trinity usually operates. They are devious and greedy, but not inclined to murder. Marco always said, 'If you have to do time, make it white collar crime.' Murder takes it out of that realm."

"Okay, what if they changed their ways since you left the family?"

"It's possible, but not probable. As Dale drummed into his students, 'Past behavior is the best predictor of future behavior.'"

"What about a wild card?"

"Such as?"

"Random mistake. Angry employee looking for revenge. One patient out to get another patient."

"That might work once, but there are two dead patients - Harriet Logan and Greg Newman. Since Taylor's been there a patient named Earl flipped out right before discharge and went to the hospital. And how does chance or revenge account for drugging Martha Sanders to near death and terrorizing Peter Lane? Too many coincidences."

"You're right. What's the common denominator among all of them?"

"The Girard family, MACS programs and fat Medicare reimbursements."

"Wait, you told me that Taylor's innocent research found an unusual pattern of patients bouncing back into the programs."

"Not the same programs. Taylor says the returning patients are transferred into a different MACS PHP where they get a new patient number."

"Why a new number?"

"New number disguises that it's the same person. Medicare has limits on various types of treatment for the same person in a given program."

"How do you explain that?"

Blake leaned back his head and laughed, "Taylor called it the ultimate in recycling."

"Okay, it's sneaky but is it illegal?"

"I think even the Justice Department lawyers can show fraud here. Not to mention the Nutracuratives are being used inappropriately with a failure to disclose that patients are receiving prescription medications."

"But they don't charge for Nutracuratives. How can that rip off Medicare?"

Blake stood up to pace. With the threads of the scheme dangling in his face, he had to tie them together. His brain scanned stored information. Jack poured another drink and waited. When that Cheshire cat expression crept over Blake's face, Jack knew the answer was forthcoming.

"I have an idea, Jack."

Blake reached for the laptop computer and entered the code for his personal mail box. From there he passed a series of firewalls to get to his contacts list. He scribbled down a number, exited the screen and dialed the cell phone.

"St. Raphael's Abbey, how may I help you?"

"This is Blake Girard, I need to speak to Father Francis."

"Please hold. I'll see if he can leave vespers."

"Give him a note with my name and mark it urgent."

Jack glanced at him, whispering, "Are things so bad that we need a priest?"

"Yes, but not the way you think."

"This is Father Francis."

"Franco, you dog. Are you keeping your vows?"

"The ones I like."

"Making any illegal substances?"

"No. I have an arrangement with an old farmer up the road. He sends me the occasional jar of moonshine and I give him absolution for it."

"Always the deal maker, Franco. Say, I need information."

"Don't run with that crowd anymore."

"It's not about people, it's about chemicals."

"Okay, I may be retired, but I'm still the best."

Blake explained Morganna's findings and the use of the Nutracuratives with MACS PHP for treating schizophrenia.

"Simple. It's an old street trick."

"Enlighten me."

"One of the reasons that schizophrenics stop taking the meds that keep them connected to the planet is that they hate the side effects," Franco explained, "Tossing in a little something extra_gives a kick - you know, an easy high."

"If the drugs are legal, patients can easily get them from doctors."

"Not in that combination, and street people are more generous in their own way. They trade drugs, sell drugs, screw for drugs. Take me to any city in America and I'll show you a veritable underground pharmacy. The best part about messing with prescription drugs is that you don't get busted for possessing it in small quantities. And if you're off on dosages, you get a free stomach pump at the county hospital."

"Or perhaps a slab in the morgue with a custom toe tag?"

"That's another possibility."

"Is it possible to purposely mix drugs to push a patient into reckless behavior?"

"How reckless?"

"Freaking out and running into traffic or taking a short step off a tall bridge."

"Certainly. Schizophrenics, particularly paranoid schizophrenics, already believe the world is out to get them. You don't need a lot of chemicals to kick their paranoia into overdrive."

"So by using legal drugs it wouldn't cause much attention at an autopsy, particularly if the drugs were reasonable for a person with known psychiatric problems."

"Exactly. There's no need to get caught buying arsenic or stealing biological warfare germs. You can kill with insulin if you administer it incorrectly."

"Could the drugs be mixed moderately, enough to cause a reaction that makes a patient appear to be regressing?"

"Yes, but it's a tough balance. It's like an arsonist who is foolish enough to climb a tree to get a closer view of the burning house, only to have the tree catch fire right under him. I wouldn't want to bet my professional reputation on accuracy. There's too many variables."

"Thanks, Franco. You've helped me make sense of all this."

"Glad to help. But, watch your back. People who would play those games with head cases are seriously evil. If they offer you a cup of coffee, don't take it. They could mess with your head too and you'd never know what hit you."

Blake shivered as he pictured Taylor's innocent face.

"I hear you."

"Go in peace, my brother."

"You forgot the absolution, Father Francis."

"Not until I hear the details. Call me back when you have time to describe the babes and what sinful things you did together."

"Go play with your rosary beads," Blake laughed, ending the conversation.

Jack slapped his hand on the bar, "How is it that we do the same job but you meet all the interesting characters? Where did this one come from?"

"Father Francis is a piece of work. Before taking his new identity under witness protection, the good father was the master chemist for a drug cartel. His idol was Carlos the Jackal so he learned how to be almost as good at disguises as he was at processing cocaine. He was a tough guy to bring down."

"Did you nail him?"

"Yes, shortly before I transferred out of Colorado. Stashing him in a monastery was my idea."

"Maybe he was ready for the contemplative life."

"Not really, but anyone who knew him in his former life would never think to look for that egocentric, atheist, sex fiend in sack cloth and ashes."

"Blake, you're the only agent I know who makes law enforcement look as good as the recruiting posters."

"I simply work with what they give me."

"No way I'm touching that line," Jack rolled his eyes, shuffling papers into a single stack. "The bigger question is, do we have enough to bust MACS?"

"Yes and I think we have to do it soon, before Marco gets edgy and pulls out. Didn't you have something else to tell me?"

"Oh, yeah, your visit to Martha Sanders got DEA all stirred up."

"They didn't follow Taylor's car. I don't think they can identify her."

"Thanks to Ginger. Unlike us, she pays attention to the information at the briefings. That's what made her think to drop Lorraine's name to cover Taylor. DEA picked up on it and paid a social call to Lorraine's house this afternoon."

"Even if it had been Lorraine, they can't arrest her for visiting a patient and they know from the joint task force memos that she's critical to the MACS investigation. Why would those morons tip her like that?" Blake stood up to pace again. "We've got to find out what they're after."

"The old man put a loose tail on all the Girards this week. Seems that shortly after the DEA guys left, Gina left in a huff, slammed the door and hopped in a taxi."

"There's a real committed relationship; a little shake down and she's out."

"On the way back to the family, she made a quick stop at MACS."

"Did she carry out anything?"

"No, but the agent tailing her reports that she went in sour and angry looking then came out, about fifteen minutes later all smiles. What's up with that?"

Blake turned around, shaking his head, "Chances are she went in to check her insurance policy."

"Why would she think of insurance policies? Does she think Lorraine's going to kill her?"

"Not traditional insurance. Her behavior tells me that she has a smoking gun hidden somewhere, probably in her lab on the second floor."

"What gun? I thought you said the Girards weren't violent?"

"I mean that metaphorically. Father trained us to find the weak spot in everyone - friends or enemies. He said that love and trust are fine, but insurance is better."

"I think I've got it; the family that blackmails together, stays together."

"That's one version of the Girard modus operandi. It's never failed and it's been tested on three continents."

"We need to know what she has and where to find it. Will Gina roll over when we make the arrests?"

"Hard to say. She'll never betray Father or Victoria, but she'd hang my mother by the short hairs if she could get away with it."

"What about Lorraine? Will Gina implicate her?"

"There's one thing Lorraine isn't counting on. Gina will never love her the way she loves the idea of gaining Father's anointing and my place in the family. She won't sell out the family. Neither will Carla or Felipe."

"Could Felipe's wife be a weak link?"

"Tiffany is a french fry short of a kid's meal. I doubt that she knows anything."

"What about Carla; how deep is she in this?"

Blake paused. *As important as it is to bring down MACS, Carla must somehow not be harmed by it.*

"Blake, are you ignoring me?"

"No."

"Well?"

"Let's talk off the record for a minute, Jack. I don't want Carla to be caught in the middle; she doesn't deserve it."

"Time out here: Carla Girard handles Quality Management. She has to know something about the PHP contracts and MACS operations. You can't shield her. This isn't a multiple-choice arrest. As far as I know, you're the only Girard who isn't up to the eyeballs in Medicare fraud and possibly murder."

"I hear what you're saying, but I don't agree. I think that Carla may be as innocent as Tiffany."

"But you admit that Carla is highly intelligent and trusted within the family. How can she not know what's happening?"

"Father, Victoria and Serena are extremely careful to dole out disconnected bits of information to their children and their managers," Blake explained, "They constantly mix up the puzzle pieces, so that people within the organization, even those who seem to know a lot, don't know enough to be dangerous. I guarantee you that if Carla knew about drug manipulation or murder; she would call me to get her out."

"I don't want to know what you're planning, Blake. I only hope you cover yourself on this one. Ex-FBI agents don't fare too well in federal prison."

"You're starting to sound like Dale. I told him and I'm telling you, I will not cross the line. I'll be under enough scrutiny when they go to trial."

"Can you do this, Blake?"

"I gave you my solemn word that I will not stand in the way of the guilty being arrested. Nor will I see anyone who is legally innocent prosecuted. Does that make you feel better?"

"Yes. Besides, you know that Taylor isn't going to be caught in this net. What little she knows, she's covered as our informant."

Blake nodded, turning to look out the window. *I'm not worried about Taylor, my friend. But I am getting Carla out, no matter what I have to do.* "Why don't you put on a pot of coffee? I'll be right back." He went into the bathroom and turned on the water before opening his cell phone. He dialed a series of numbers, call forwarding through three states to end up at a twenty-four hour exotic gifts line.

"I want eight dozen orchids delivered tomorrow morning to Miss Carla Girard's office in St. Petersburg, Florida...I'm not interested in how you get them there. If the local florists can't handle it, fly them in. Have them on her desk by no later than ten o'clock in the morning...I don't care what it costs, bill my account. And sign the card this way: 'All my love, I can't stand to be apart any longer.' Did you get that?...Substitute? No, I don't want substitute flowers. I want flashy and expensive. Thank you." He disconnected the call, leaned over the sink and tossed water on his face, enough cold water to wipe away a worried look.

* * * * *

"Talking to yourself, man?"

"I'm trying to figure things out."

"I couldn't find the coffee and it's probably just as well. My brain is fried. I'm going home to get some sleep and see if it all falls into place tomorrow," Jack said, gathering up his notes and jacket, "Are you coming into the office?"

"No. I'm staying close. Taylor is springing a surprise tomorrow and I don't expect it to be well-received."

"What surprise?"

"Hallie Logan, Harriet's mirror-image twin is checking into MACS pretending to be schizophrenic."

"That's crazy! What do they hope to accomplish?"

"Hallie's out for revenge and Taylor thinks that seeing Hallie will push the person or persons guilty of Harriet's death out in the open."

"This isn't an episode of 'Murder, She Wrote' where a stern

glance prompts the murderer to confess in glossy detail. We will be in a deeper crack for allowing another civilian to be put at risk."

"I know, but there's little that we can do. I've tried everything but the complete truth to get Taylor to change her mind about this."

"We could bust them tomorrow and pick up some of the missing pieces later?"

"No, Jack, that's a mistake."

"What if Lorraine or whoever tries to kill Hallie?"

"I don't think anyone will go that far in one day. If Hallie steps on too many nerves, we'll take her into protective custody."

"What about Taylor?"

"She's made too many waves already. If she suddenly disappears, Marco will know something's up. That will start the paper shredders working overtime."

"Maybe I'd better stay on this side of the bay," Jack thought aloud, "I'll have someone from the Tampa office meet me for a briefing."

"It's okay, Jack. I can manage on my own for a few hours."

"You can, but what about Taylor? There's no way you can go in to pull her out. At least she knows me and trusts me. If necessary, I'll go in for her."

Blake walked over and gave Jack a friendly slap on the shoulder.

"I can't ask you to do that, Jack."

"You didn't. I like Taylor Kendall and I realize that you're in love with her. If I'm ever going to be your best man, I better help keep the bride alive."

"I never said anything about..."

"Right and I never heard it."

* * * * *

Blake tossed around the bed, dodging nightmares. Not the

familiar one, where he gets shot at close range and paralyzed. This was infinitely worse. Taylor was branded as the mole inside MACS and tortured with hallucinogenic drugs by Lorraine and Gina. When he and the team came in for the arrest, Taylor was nearly comatose, unable to recognize him or respond to him.

He jolted awake from sleep's hold and stood up. The usual cold water to the face didn't break the tension. That dream was a message. He tugged an old Gabe tee shirt over his head, pacing around the small apartment.

If he couldn't take Taylor out of MACS, then he had to engage a misdirection play. He reached for his laptop computer.

I could pull more money out of Marco's Nassau bank accounts. No, that might push Marco to move all the money.

I could call in a false report to the fire marshal or local HRS. No, they might run if the heat got that close to the corporate office.

There's no choice left but to proceed with the plan to get Carla out, but step up the timetable as a diversion. The stage is set with the flowers and all the other mysterious gifts I've sent since the Bahamas trip. It seemed so much fun to make Marco and Victoria fear that Carla was getting attention from someone outside the family. Well, now it's time to make a decisive move in this game, not for fun, for survival.

He paced around the room again until the idea gelled.

Taylor can't disappear suddenly, but Carla can. That will throw the unholy trinity into such a panic they won't have time to be concerned about Taylor or Hallie Logan's arrival.

Satisfied with his plan, Blake turned off the computer, going back to bed for a few hours before daybreak.

CHAPTER

No need for the alarm today. Taylor beat the alarm clock on Monday morning by a full hour.

Reaching for her briefcase and cell phone, she started to dial Gabe's number then stopped. *He seemed tired and distracted yesterday, maybe he needs the extra sleep. Besides, getting the morning paperwork settled and the group schedules reviewed means more time to gain a front row seat for the fireworks.*

Taylor pulled into the parking lot behind Carla. As Taylor gathered her things, Carla rushed over to open the car door.

"Okay, let's hear everything about your weekend."

Taylor paused assessing the tone. Was it curious or critical? "I was really busy, how about you?"

"I was really bored. I tried to call you a few times but no answer. I even drove by your place Sunday afternoon to see if you wanted to go to a movie," Carla fell into step with Taylor as they walked toward the MACS building. "Let me guess, you were with Mr. Wonderful, weren't you?"

"Actually I was."

"That's why I couldn't find you. Where did you go?"

"We uh...we went for a drive...near the beaches I like in Sarasota. And then we went for a moonlight sail."

"I am envious. Sounds great," Carla reached over to use her key card in the entry door. "Are you getting serious about this guy?"

"I suppose I'm somewhat serious."

"Please, Taylor. You're hiding something from me."

"Why do you think I'm hiding something about this weekend?"

"It's the way you're answering me," Carla turned toward her, large brown eyes turned like a piercing x-ray. "This isn't a Likert scale: serious, somewhat serious, uncertain, not too serious, not serious at all. Come on, Taylor, if you like this man, for goodness sakes say so."

Taylor's near panic turned to amusement, "I hadn't thought of it quite that way. All right, yes, I really like this man."

"I knew it!" Carla exclaimed, opening the door and walking toward the elevator, "When Mother said she heard that you were acting strange, I knew it was personal."

Taylor was about to turn toward the clinic entrance, when she paused to pursue that comment, "What did Victoria mean?"

"Who knows? As you have seen my mother is prone to manic behaviors which result in bizarre assumptions. Come upstairs with me and get your coffee. You're early."

Much as Taylor wanted to get set up in the clinic, Carla's comments unnerved her. Riding up in the elevator, she turned to Carla, whispering, "Does your mother think that I'm not doing my job?"

"Relax, Taylor. You're this week's target of Lorraine's complaints. She gripes about everybody, even my father, behind his back. Look at it this way; you're giving Locke a break. He's been at the top of Lorraine's hit list for so long."

The last thing Taylor wanted to do was draw negative attention. She hoped that the new patient arrivals today would create such a stir as to reduce the heat she's been drawing from Lorraine, Gina and Neva. It wasn't going to be easy. Not after this weekend and the realization that something very wrong was going on at MACS.

"This is our stop," Carla said, holding open the elevator door for Taylor to leave.

Brook was standing in the hall, checking office supply boxes against the order form. "Oh, Carla? You've been keeping secrets again."

"Good morning, Brook. What do you mean?"

"I bet Taylor knows the big secret, don't you?"

Taylor drew in her breath feeling exposed. If the office queen of gossip knows about her weekend visit, then everyone else would know before the coffee got cold.

Carla turned toward Taylor, "Do you have any idea what she means?"

Taylor shrugged her shoulders.

Dr. Sam Locke came out of his office, "Oh come on Taylor, you must know more than you're letting on."

Taylor steeled herself, wishing she could disappear into the carpet.

"Stop picking on Taylor and tell me what's going on," Carla insisted.

Brook pointed down the hall, "Go to your office and see."

Carla pushed forward, opening her office door with a gasp. The small office was covered, floor to ceiling, with tropical flowers. An aquamarine ribbon hung from the largest spray, imprinted with the words "Te Amor" and a card that read, "I can't stand to be apart any longer, fly away with me." Taylor read the card as Carla walked around from vase to vase.

"Speaking of interesting men, sounds like you're story is better than mine."

Carla appeared pleased, yet not overwhelmed the way Taylor knew she would feel to receive such a floral tribute.

"Let's just say this gentleman is a dear friend."

Brook leaned into the office door, "Is this the guy who gave you that awesome amethyst jewelry? See you're wearing the ring now."

"Why do you think that?"

"Because you won't tell us anything and it completely ticks off your mother and Gina, so I think he must be one super hot guy."

"You could say that."

Taylor glanced at the clock on Carla's desk, "I need to get to the clinic."

"You're early," Brook commented, pulling a white orchid from a smaller arrangement and placing it in her hair. "I'll call you when Carla's new man shows up."

"Thanks, Brook."

"What about Taylor's new man?" Carla interjected, to deflect the attention.

Brook swung around so quickly that she nearly slipped off her platform heels, "What new man? I need details, lots of details. Do you have a picture of him?"

Locke leaned in the doorway, "I can see an abundance of corporate business is being transacted today, ladies."

"Dr. Locke, I need to speak with you later. Will you be in the office?" Taylor asked.

"As far as I know I will. Is there a problem?"

"It's some things I need your opinion on...therapy issues."

"Okay. Check your group schedule and come up to my office when you have a break. I'll do my best to make time for you."

"Thank you," Taylor said, trying to convey with her expression that the matter was more intense than the words she carefully chose.

As Taylor walked out, Locke fell into step behind her.

The elevator door opened and he held it apart speaking softly, "Is Lorraine bothering you again?"

"Not exactly, but my problem does have something to do with Lorraine and Gina and I suppose the Girards in general."

"Personal or professional?"

"Professional and extremely serious."

"Have you talked with Dr. Marco about your concerns?"

"No. I need to talk to you first. I'll be back in a few hours." Taylor noticed a shadow in the doorway behind Locke's left shoulder. The lines of the hair suggested that it was Tiffany, so the less said the better.

* * * * *

Taylor took a few deep, calming breaths before entering the clinic. Patient vans were arriving, staff were dashing around, and the phone was ringing. Business as usual. She spotted Ray wheeling in a patient and went over to appear to help. Taylor bent down until she was eye level with the elderly man and greeted him. Then she rose up and said to Ray, "No other new patients today?"

"Yes, Dr. Kendall, we are expecting two new patients. I believe they are coming in the van from Community Psychiatric Hospital." His wink assured her that Hallie was on the way.

* * * * *

"Carla Girard, Quality Assurance."

"What's going on down there?"

Carla gave the hush signal to Brook, pointing to the phone.

"Good morning, Mother. Is there something you need?"

"Yes, I need to know why your office looks like a Hawaiian luau."

"Can't be a luau, there's no pig on a barbeque."

"I'm not amused and neither will Marco be when he finds out. Who sent those?"

"Mother, you haven't even been to my office today, how do you know what I have in here?"

Brook reached for a memo pad and wrote, "Tiffany was here."

Carla nodded, still listening to Victoria's ravings.

"Mother, I'm over twenty-one. I don't need your approval to receive gifts."

Victoria's voice was so loud, that Brook decided to leave gracefully. Carla put the phone down on the desk, turned on her computer and started checking email until those familiar words rang out, "Did you hear me, girl?"

Carla put the phone back to her ear, "Yes, Mother. Can I get back to work? I have a lot of new OSHA reports to file."

"You haven't heard the last of this, Carla."

"I'm sure you're right."

"We don't approve of secret liaisons. I'll discuss this with your father and Serena when they come in and decide what we are going to do about it."

"You mean like what you did to Jay?"

Victoria uttered a Spanish curse and slammed down the phone.

Shaking from even a distant encounter with her mother, Carla reached across her desk to touch the cascade of miniature purple orchids placed on top of her inbox. *Jay. After all these years, that's the first time I've said his name to Mother since Father sent him back to India in disgrace. Clearly that's what she's thinking; this must be another Jay.*

How amused they would be to know the truth. No, they might be even angrier to know that the jewels, the flashy gifts sent to the office and now the flowers were a diversion from the man with whom I shared a playpen, a pony and a sense of humor. Thinking of him and how much he'd enjoy Victoria's distress made her smile again. She reached for her cell phone and dialed. A sleepy voice muttered hello.

"Is this what my secret admirer sounds like in the morning?"

"Carla", he raised up from the bed, shaking himself awake, "You deserve a more enthusiastic greeting. Sorry, I drifted back to sleep."

"Heaven knows what time zone you're in. Did I call too early?"

"No problem. Actually, I need to get going. Much to do today. I was planning to phone you."

"In case you are wondering, your credit card is maxed out."

"What makes you think that?"

"The evidence is all around me. Orchids of every size, shape and color. Mother is in a huff demanding to know why my office looks like a Hawaiian luau."

Blake let out his unique rolling laugh, "What kept her from tossing them out the window?"

"She hasn't actually seen the flowers. Brook told me that Tiffany arrived at the same time as the florist vans and let them into my office."

"It's nice to know that the Girard internal spy network operates as well as ever."

"Too well. I've had enough of them all," Carla sputtered, choking back a tear.

"I'm genuinely sorry if my gift put you in the way of Victoria's venom. Don't you see? This isn't the life for you. It's time for you to get out."

"Maybe I'll take a long weekend and make them wonder where I am. Do you still want to meet somewhere?"

"Yes. Today."

"Blake, where are you?"

"Closer than you think."

"Are you in St. Petersburg?"

"I can fly into Albert Whitted Airport downtown and pick you up."

"That would be great. We could have a long lunch."

"Carla, when I say it's time for you to go, I mean leave. Leave MACS. Leave the family. It has to be today, Carla, today."

"I don't know if I can do that so fast."

"Do you trust me?"

"Blake, I trust you completely."

"Then you have to listen to me because there won't be another chance to leave."

"Is something going on? Father has been really edgy. So are other people around here. Do you know what's up?"

He just asked for his sister's absolute trust and now he had to find a way to hedge.

"Blake, tell me if you know something."

"Will you run to Father? Will you sacrifice yourself to protect him and Serena and Victoria?"

"Not if I can help it. It's about MACS, isn't it?"

"You must see the signs. Marco is getting ready to run, isn't he?"

"Now that you mention it, there has been an unusual amount of wire transfers. So many that we had a few payroll checks bounce last week. Felipe covered them from a family account, but I don't think he knows what's happening."

"You know, Carla. Think about it. Past behavior is the best predictor of future behavior. "

"But we're making money. Why would Father want to leave now? We usually wait until some angry general or health inspector is marching in the front door."

Blake paused, allowing her to think about what she said.

"Oh, my God. Father senses trouble, doesn't he?"

"Why wouldn't he, since he's likely at the heart of it? How exposed are you with the clinic and the treatments?"

"I'm not directly involved in the clinics."

"Did you sign any major contracts for anything at MACS?"

"No, not contracts. I'm busy with quality assurance and government paperwork."

"What kind of government paperwork?"

"Medicare and Medicaid. It's fairly routine. In fact, I signed some things when we got started, but not any recently."

"Where are those papers?"

"In my file cabinet. It's very routine stuff."

"Let's say that Marco is, for example, overstepping his bounds and could be in trouble with the medical board. He's been there before. If that's what he's worried about, then you need to get away for awhile. And bring those papers with you. It's your insurance until things blow over," Blake prided himself on the clever way he guided her actions.

"I can't do that."

"You can and you will," he paused, making the effort to sound less desperate. "Right this minute, set the phone down and get those papers out of your files. Put them in your briefcase. Do it, Carla, now!"

She startled at his tone. Blake never spoke to her that way. He was either terribly angry with Marco or upset about something else. She unlocked the file, removed the papers and placed them in her brief case. Before she could pick up the cell phone, her office door burst open.

"You little fool. How can you speak to our mother that way?"

"Gina, this doesn't concern you. Go back to your lab."

Gina picked up the vase of cascading orchids and threw them across the room. Blake was furious listening to the sounds of breaking glass. He vowed silently to find the largest piece and slit Gina's throat if she harmed Carla. He was helpless to wait and listen, hoping that Gina would not notice the phone.

"Oh that's mature, Gina. What's the matter? Doesn't Lorraine send you flowers?"

"Shut up, Carla. There's a lot going on that you don't know. Things could get rough around here soon."

"I've long suspected that you and Lorraine like to play rough; not only with each other, but with a few former employees as well."

"You are so naïve. Lorraine and I do what we have to do to protect MACS and the family. We've done a lot more than we get credit for. You wouldn't believe what we're done to keep you and Father's French whore of a wife and even stupid Tiffany living in luxury."

"I resent being placed in a category with Serena and Tiffany. At least you didn't lump me with pseudo-Florence Nightmare, your bedside companion."

"You don't appreciate what Lorraine has done for us. Anyone less dedicated would have spilled everything when questioned by the DEA..."

"DEA? Isn't that a drug squad? What are you and Lorraine cooking in the lab?"

"Never mind. Forget I said that," Sweat began dripping down Gina's face so she turned from Carla to wipe it away, "Obviously you don't know everything and now you know too much. If you say a word of this to Father, I'll..."

"You'll what...send Lorraine to cast a spell on me? Oh, yeah, I'm scared."

Gina spun on her heels and slapped Carla's face. Even through the phone, the sound of Gina's hand striking Carla made Blake instinctively reach for his gun. How he wished he were there to protect her.

"You better be scared, and you better be quiet for your own good."

Gina left, slamming the door behind her. Blake saw the second hand on his watch move with excruciating slowness. Cell phone in one hand, he reached with the other for the apartment phone to call Jack, when Carla returned. Her voice betrayed her sobs.

"Are you still there?"

"Carla, I heard everything. Did Gina hurt you?"

"No. I'm fine...really...I'm fine."

"And you're going to stay that way until we figure out what's happening. Obviously there are things going on that even Marco doesn't know," Blake seized the opportunity Gina created, "You know that he can manage problems, but he can't manage what he doesn't know. Gina and Lorraine are loose cannons. Their recklessness threatens all of you. I want you out of their reach."

"How can I leave now if the family is in danger?"

"Carla, at least give Father time to get things back under his control. Then you can decide what you want to do. This is the perfect time. You had a fight with Victoria and Gina. They will think that you called your secret admirer and he rode in on his white horse to rescue you."

"Is that what you're going to do?"

"Exactly, only it will be with wings. Bring the briefcase and meet me at Albert Whitted Airport near USF Bayboro in an hour and half. Be there, Carla. I mean it."

"How will I find you?"

"Stand outside the flight office and watch for an incoming plane. Usual signal."

Carla knew that was his trademark wing tip. "Okay, but I have to pack."

"No deal. This is a come-as-you-are party. Stay away from the house and I'll buy you a complete new wardrobe. Please, Carla, be there."

* * * * *

"Jack Sims"

"Hey, Jack-o. I need some inside help."

"I'm on my way to Tampa. The old man was screaming your name in my ear at seven o'clock this morning."

"Why? I've been home in my bed, alone even."

"And yesterday? Did you forget that little skirmish in Arcadia? The DEA contact on our joint task force is freaking furious. They've put a tail on Lorraine and Gina. In fact, their tail car nearly ran into ours, literally."

"It's getting knee deep in federal agents around MACS. Don't you think that Marco will notice?"

"I don't know, Blake, what do we do?"

"We start the countdown for the bust."

"Do you think the DEA will screw it up and tip Marco?"

"There's a problem. I found out that he's moving large amounts of money. So much that they couldn't cover payroll last week. I need Geek Boy pulling bank records and cross-referencing with Medicare."

"Are you guessing or do you know something?"

"I know."

"Do you know in a way that we could get warrants or is this Girard intuition?"

"I'm getting more. That's why I can't meet you after lunch."

"Where are you going or do I want to know?"

"I'm trying to get to another source. I'll let you know. Can you get back in town soon? I'm concerned about Taylor."

"Aren't you having lunch with her?"

"I won't be finished in time. I'll meet you back at the gallery by three."

"Don't get too far out on that limb."

"Never do, Jack, not really."

"Looks like it to me."

"One man's limb is another man's high wire act."

CHAPTER 41

The woman who checked in at MACS was a shadow of the powerful executive that Taylor met a few days ago. Hallie Logan skillfully prepared herself for this charade. Her hair was tangled and pulled off her face with childish clips. What little makeup she wore was poorly applied. Her perfectly manicured nails were clipped below the finger line, not unusual with patients who are inclined to scratch themselves. And the mannerisms, she certainly knew how to play the part. After years of living with Harriet, Hallie insisted that she could imitate the symptoms of paranoid schizophrenia well enough to even fool anyone and she did. Ray and Taylor knew it was an act, but the other therapists were completely taken in.

Taylor was talking with the clerk about adding Hallie's name to her group list when she heard a scream and a clipboard drop. She turned to see Neva, shaking and pointing.

"What's this about, Ray?"

"Please lower your voice. This is a new patient from Community Psychiatric..."

"Sure. And I'm Madonna and we're going to film a new MTV video."

Taylor walked over to Neva, extending her hand to Neva's shoulder.

"Neva, I need to speak with you."

"In a minute."

"No, right now," Taylor pointed to a nearby testing office and gently tugged on Neva's arm. Surprisingly, Neva followed, closing the door behind her.

"Something weird is going on here. Ray's doing it. Are you

in on it?"

"Neva, it's not like you to overreact. You're upsetting the new patients."

"New patient? This is Ray's way of making a bad joke."

"No, it's not."

Neva started to pace around the small room, "You didn't know Harriet Logan. She was discharged before you started working here."

Discharged? More like drugged and frightened enough to run into the street and get run over like a stray dog. "Okay, so what's your problem, nurse?"

"This is creepy. I'm going to find out who that woman really is."

"I know who she is, Neva. She's Hallie Logan, a patient referral from Community Psychiatric Hospital. All of her medical information is on this intake sheet. Hallie is Harriet's sister," Taylor explained enjoying Neva's distress.

"Sister? She looks like Harriet's ghost."

"Of course she does. Hallie and Harriet are identical twins."

"What difference does that make?"

Taylor realized Neva was so unnerved that she wasn't thinking straight. "Neva, I'm sure you know that schizophrenia occurs in first-degree biological relatives ten times more often than the general population. With monozygotic, or identical, twins the risk that both are affected is astronomical."

Neva paused, scanning her memory. It sounded right.

"Here, look at the information for yourself," Taylor handed her the sheet, "And by the way, I'll be doing the intake testing for Hallie."

"Why you? I'll get one of the social workers who worked with Harriet to do it."

"But, Neva, Dr. Locke said I could do it."

"For what reason?"

Taylor had to think quickly, "Because it's a unique opportunity for me to work up a twin case. Remember, this is my residency. Locke did approve it."

"Yes, well...I guess...okay, fine. I'm going back to work."

If not for what Mama would call "good breeding and practiced manners," Taylor would have laughed out loud at Neva's total panic.

* * * * *

"Hey, this is Travis."

"Blair Andrews here," Blake replied with his most popular alias, "I need a major league favor and I need it fast."

"Wow, I'll have to pull out another plane to get the jet ready."

"That's not it. I need wings, but something different."

"You want the Baron?"

"No, this is a critical medical situation. It involves someone very dear to me."

"What can I do, Blair?"

"Get a small aircraft that can seat three for a quick round trip. Meet me at Albert Whitted Airport in a half hour and don't file a flight plan."

"I don't think I can do that so fast."

"I'll pay you one thousand dollars an hour, cash, from the time you leave until you return. The clock starts now."

"Are you serious?"

"Yes. A life depends on it, Travis. And you can't reveal this to anyone. Will you be there?"

"You bet. I'm reaching for the Piper keys now. Where do I meet you?"

"Here's what I want you to do..."

* * * * *

Taylor entered the group room. Hallie and the other new patient were already seated with the others. After this session, she would have a chance to talk with Hallie during the assessment.

No doubt about it, Hallie deserved an Academy Award for her portrayal of paranoid schizophrenic symptoms.

Neva looked in the narrow window. Group was in session which meant that Dr. Kendall would be busy and Ray was on break. She went into the medicine room off the nurses' station and dialed her cell phone.

"Hello, I'm busy, call later."

"Wait, I've paged you three times. We have a *crisis*," Neva emphasized the last word as much as possible without raising her voice, "When are you coming in?"

Lorraine put down the box she was carrying to talk on the phone, "I have to finish something. I'll be there in a hour or so."

"Lorraine, I need you here now!"

"Why? Either call Dr. Marco or dispatch the patient to the hospital."

"Not that easy. We have a new patient and you'll definitely want to see her."

"I'll check the new arrivals when I get there. What's the big deal?"

"Nothing if you don't mind working with a dead patient's ghost?"

"Neva, you've got to stop closing the bars. Did you do any drugs last night?"

"No, but you might when you see her."

"See who?"

"Harriet Logan's identical twin sister, Hallie."

Lorraine slumped onto the porch steps, "Harriet has a twin? Are you sure?"

"Yes," Neva responded, enjoying the alarm in Lorraine's voice, "I took the intake sheet and cross-referenced it with her insurance company. Same birth date. Same family. She's the real thing."

"Okay, but why would the Logans send her to MACS after Harriet died here, that doesn't make sense."

"That's what I thought. I called the referring physician in her hometown. He said that he thought MACS had been good for Harriet in spite of what happened. He suggested that Hallie enter treatment. He didn't think that Hallie was as fragile as Harriet and he expects good results. What do we do?"

"Call Dr. Marco."

"Not me. You do it; you're the head nurse."

"Has Locke seen her?"

"No, but a few staff members who remember Harriet have. A social worker fainted on the spot. Shall I send her home?"

"No. Throw cold water on her and put her to work," Lorraine barked, "We have to act like it's nothing. Why don't you call Locke downstairs for some pretense and watch his reaction. If he isn't shocked, then we know he's in on it."

"Okay, but it seems like something isn't on the up and up around here."

"Duh, Neva, you already know that."

Lorraine stuffed the cell phone into her pocket and picked up the last box. No way she was getting caught with boxes of drugs in her home. Granted they were prescription drugs, but still suspicious. *Damn that Marco. He knew the heat was on. He must have felt the DEA breathing down his neck. Gina is naïve enough to think that this was Marco's noble act of trust. Trust? More like scapegoat. Sorry, dude, it won't work this time.*

The last box had a dent in one side. She noticed that a trickle of powder fell out when the box was tilted. She dropped it into the trunk and retraced her steps. With her boots, she ground the powder trail into the grass and used her hand to brush a trace off the condo steps. In a hurry, she didn't go back inside the foyer to check for powder residue. The small trail of powder blended nicely into the beige carpet, except for the tiny tell-tale mound left in the hall closet.

Slamming the trunk, Lorraine gunned the motor and roared out toward Snell Isle. At the curve of the street leading to the

Girard home she parked in front of a vacant house, conveniently marked by a real estate sign. She took the boxes to the back yard and tossed them into the water. If anyone was looking, it would appear that the Girards had tried to hide something. She smiled, thinking that she had outwitted Dr. Marco.

* * * * *

"Unit two to control."

"Go ahead."

"We followed Lorraine Lewis to an unoccupied residence on Brightwaters Boulevard near the Girard house. She took boxes out of her trunk and tossed them into the water. Do you want us to fish the boxes out?"

Jack Sims nearly rear-ended the van in front of him on the Howard Franklin Bridge, "As soon as she's out of sight, get those boxes! I don't care if you swim for it, get what you can and photograph the site."

"Where do you want the stuff taken?"

"Drive it to Tampa as fast as possible. Tag it for this case. I'll call ahead and arrange for analysis."

"Well, I want to ask..."

"Get your butts in the bay and get that evidence! We'll talk later," Jack instructed. This could be a major break in the case and it was his score, not Blake's, this time.

CHAPTER 42

Ray escorted Hallie Logan into the testing room. Taylor stood to greet her.

"Welcome, Hallie. We are going to talk for awhile, then you'll go back to the group for snacks," Taylor gave her usual intake speech, "That's all for now, Ray."

He nodded, holding Hallie's hand a bit longer than necessary as he helped her into the chair. Talk about transference. He knew she was Hallie yet he looked at her with the affection he professed for Harriet.

The door closed securely.

"Hallie, you can relax, this room is reasonably secure."

The distant expression on Hallie's face became a grin, "It's working perfectly. I'm fooling them, aren't I?"

"Thus far you have given a totally convincing performance. How are you feeling? Can you handle this?"

"I have no problem with the patients. After all, I grew up around schizophrenia. But it's hard to restrain myself from getting into the face of some of the names that I remember Harriet mentioning."

"Like who?"

"That nurse, Neva, upset Harriet, but not as much as Lorraine. Where is she?"

"Don't worry, she'll be here soon. Neva, her puppet, will call her."

"Is she as weird as Harriet said?"

"How did Harriet describe her?"

"She said Lorraine was the nurse from hell who looked like she was from a horror movie - dark hair and eyes with blood red fingernails. Harriet insisted that this woman would dig those nails into her arm while appearing to help her stand up."

Taylor had heard that complaint from other patients although Lorraine claimed that they were exaggerating. "That's her, all right."

Hallie held out her hand, "Ray checked my bracelet. No 'R code'. He says I'm to watch for that."

"Yes, it's on the Nutracuratives that you will be given to drink."

"What if I get one? Do I drink it?"

"No!" Taylor realized that she nearly shouted, "Start some kind of fuss that gets my attention or Ray's. We need to get a sample of the drink if at all possible."

Without warning the door opened and Taylor startled. Dr. Sam Locke entered. Hallie turned her head and he flinched.

"Hello, Miss Logan, I'm Dr. Sam Locke, program director for MACS."

"Hi," she replied, quickly restoring a blank, dissociative expression.

Locke turned to Taylor, "Neva told me that I needed to meet the new patient. Have you done the assessment?"

"I'm trying to do that now."

"Do you need help?"

"No, thank you, Dr. Locke," Taylor replied. "I may need a second session so Hallie can be more relaxed. She only arrived in town yesterday and travel seems to have upset her greatly."

"Fine, take all the time you need. When you're finished, come to my office."

"I have a charting break after I return Hallie to group."

Locke nodded. He left the room, closing the door and leaning against it. He was so preoccupied that he didn't notice Neva beside him.

"Better than caffeine to wake you up," Neva said, watching him closely.

"You never asked if I have tendencies toward cardiac arrest."

"Are you going to tell Dr. Marco?"

"Are you going to tell Lorraine?" Locke continued after the rhetorical question, "Was there any actual business that I needed to handle here?"

"No, Dr. Locke, that covers it."

"Good. Report to Lorraine that I was as shocked as she hoped I'd be."

Neva groaned. Much as she wanted to catch Locke in some conspiracy, it looked like he was as clueless about Hallie's appearance as Lorraine. She was going to want someone to blame or frame.

*****

Travis called into the tower for clearance to land at Albert Whitted Airport. He turned to Blair Andrews, "Why didn't you come up to Clearwater to get the plane. Why the delivery?"

"I'm picking up a passenger who doesn't know that I arrived early to scope out the business deal. I'll bring the plane back later. Here's a hundred bucks. Take a cab into downtown for breakfast and hang around. I'll call you when I'm ready for you to pick up the plane. I'm still paying portal-to-portal from the time you left until I return the plane."

Travis nodded and turned toward the waiting cab as Blair climbed into the plane and took off.

It was a flight around south St. Petersburg, killing time for Carla to arrive. When he saw her number on his cell phone, he turned the plane and prepared for landing. As he descended, he tipped the wing and taxied the small plane as close as possible to the fence where she waited. He got out to help her into the plane, then took off again heading for the long but less used airport at Sebring.

Carla immediately noticed something unusual about Blake, but when they took to the air, she felt like an eagle soaring over the MACS building. To her amazement, she was relieved. She leaned her head on Blake's shoulder and fell into the most restful sleep she'd known in months.

* * * * *

"Wake up! We're landing."

"Where are we?"

"I'll explain on the next plane."

"What plane?"

"Look over there. See that Beechcraft twin engine? That's your next ride."

He lifted Carla down from the plane and pointed her toward the larger aircraft, "Get on the plane, I'll be right there."

Blake entered the spacious aircraft where Carla was settled into a leather seat of a roomy cabin, infinitely more comfortable for long trips than the Piper. A tall, distinguished man emerged from the cockpit.

"Hey, you got my flight plan?"

Blake took some papers out of his suit pocket, "Yes, here. Look it over and tell me if you have any questions."

The pilot studied the charts while Blake walked back to the small galley and poured a cup of Cuban coffee. He brought the coffee and a wrapped sandwich to Carla.

"Are you being served?" he grinned, securing the tray to her seat.

"Thank you. I didn't know this flight had stewards. Any more surprises?"

"Actually, there is one more."

"Does it have anything to do with your bad hair day?"

Although he took out the gray contacts, there was no time to rinse the light brown color from his blond hair.

"I was trying something different. Women do it all the time."

"Well it's not your best look, unless you're hiding from an outraged husband."

"I assure you, sister dear, that I follow Father's advice about women, scrupulously avoiding those who are underage, married or with prior arrests for partner abuse."

"In your own way, you're as outrageous as Father. Now tell me where are we going?"

"That's the other thing I have to tell you. I'm not coming with you today, but I will join you shortly."

"Why not?"

He ignored her question and motioned toward the pilot, "Carla, this is Jerry Tobias. He's a retired Marine. He may actually be as good a pilot as I am."

"I can out fly you with one hand tied behind my back."

"Well, don't do that with this lady on board."

"Okay, just as long as you and I have another dog fight soon. I miss it."

"Dog fight? In the air? That's dangerous!" Carla instinctively interjected to protect her brother.

"Don't worry, Miss. We occasionally fool around with vintage aircraft at the air shows. It's all good fun. I'm going to get ready to take off."

"I can't begin to thank you, Jerry."

"No thanks needed. I owe you big time."

After Jerry disappeared back into the cockpit Carla asked, "What did he mean?"

"Remind me to tell you about it, sister dear. Now, do you have the papers?"

"Yes, here in my briefcase."

"Open it and let me see."

She took out the contracts and extended them toward him.

"No, you hold them; I only want to glance at them." Marco often said that "a peek was worth two finesses." That advice seemed to apply here. He couldn't hold evidence that was removed from MACS under less than optimal circumstances, but he could sneak a peak at the papers she held. As he suspected, her signature and Marco's were on documents that could be trouble. *If that's the only tie she has to Medicare fraud, this gets simple. There'll be plenty else around MACS to link Marco to the conspiracy.*

"Okay, that's fine," he said handing her a large manila envelope. "Put them in here." She thought it odd, but did as he said. He placed the envelope in the bin next to the cockpit door.

"What's that about?"

"Nothing, I'll deal with it later. Enjoy your lunch. You'll arrive at your destination shortly."

"You aren't telling me where I'm going, are you?"

"It's a pleasant surprise." He leaned over to kiss her cheek, "You're safe now. Remember that you must not call the family or anyone else. When I get there, I promise to explain everything. Trust me, Carla."

"I trust you. Finish your work and join me. Looks like you could use a vacation too."

Blake walked toward the cockpit and pushed open the curtain. He tapped Jerry on the shoulder and Jerry pushed his headset off one ear.

"The material in the bin needs to disappear."

"Whatever it is, consider it shark food over the Atlantic, my friend."

"A car will be waiting at the air strip for the lady. Be sure she's okay."

"Are you kidding, Blake? I'll protect her with my life," he ran his hand through salt and pepper hair, "I've never forgotten. If you didn't have the guts to charge that guard, I would have rotted in a Shining Path cell. No negotiations for prisoners of the undeclared war on drugs."

"It goes to prove, I'm as crazy as you are," Blake said, a picture of that night raid flashing across his mind. The Peruvian army commander refused to let the joint American military and FBI teams go back to the rebels' mountain hideout for Jerry. With the unofficial blessing of the Marine Captain, Blake and a young marine volunteer slipped out after dark while the two commanders argued about protocol. The makeshift plan made as much sense as charging hell with a water pistol, but it worked.

"Not really, you're crazier. And I still think you would make a fine Marine. You're more of a commando than a college boy fed."

"True, and it drives my field director over the edge. Keep it to yourself, the lady does not need have a 'need to know.'"

Jerry saluted and Blake returned the salute as he left the plane. He secured the door, rolled away the steps and gave Jerry the all clear signal. When the Beechcraft King Air was airborne heading south, Blake got into the small plane and returned to Albert Whitted Airport.

Unbuckling his seat belt, Blake opened his wallet, and counted out four crisp, non-sequential thousand dollar bills and handed them to Travis, who returned as the Piper was on final approach.

"Wait, Blair, that's too much for such a short trip."

"Travis, it's my way of saying thanks and insuring my privacy."

"Not a problem. As far as anybody knows, you've been out shooting take-offs and landings to check out this plane for possible purchase. Haven't seen anybody all morning," he winked, and then put on his aviator reflective glasses.

CHAPTER 43

Blake walked to the side of the building, his back to the wind that blew from the waterfront. He took off his dark sunglasses and reinserted his gray contacts. Looking at his watch, he missed lunch. He decided to walk from the airport back to the gallery. To be safe, he went up Second Avenue South, knowing that most of the MACS people traveled on Central or First Avenue.

Rounding the corner at the gallery entrance, he saw a car near the apartment door. He ducked behind three older men waiting at the bus stop. Then he heard a familiar, mocking voice:

"Freeze!" The man pulled a badge from his coat and quickly flashed it before grabbing Blake's left arm and twisting it behind his back, "I need to talk to you sir. Please come peaceably and there'll be no trouble."

Blake rolled his eyes. One older man standing on the street corner clasped his chest in terror, another shuffled aside while the third whistled, oblivious to the situation.

Around the corner out of the bystanders' sight, Blake jerked away from the grip, spun and had Jack in a strangle hold before he could speak. Laughing, Blake let him go, opened the door and ran up the apartment stairs. Jack ran after him.

"Assaulting an FBI agent is a federal offense, boy."

"Sure. And scaring the crap out of the locals isn't offensive? You need practice at the gym. A grandma from a self-defense class can take you, Jack."

"I was going easy on you compared to the arm twisting I got from the old man this morning."

"I took a few hours to put together some details of the case. I didn't even cross state lines, I swear," Blake defended his absence.

"The only way I can work with you is strictly on a 'don't ask, don't tell' basis. But you are going to be envious when I tell you what you missed."

"What? Is Taylor all right?"

"Yes, as far as I know. She hasn't left the building. Our tail on Lorraine paid off. They followed her to a house near the Girards' rent-a-mansion. She dumped boxes of drugs in the water and then went to work."

"Did we recover anything?"

"Sure did. Let me see...I wrote it down," Jack said, thumbing through his pocket notebook, "We salvaged two boxes of prescription drugs, labels intact. DEA guys showed up as our men were climbing back onto the sea wall. It's in our Tampa office getting bagged and tagged."

Blake's delight was greater than Jack knew. Those boxes are what he needed to secure specific search warrants without revealing the unauthorized Saturday search he made with Taylor or Morganna's unofficial analysis at the FBI lab. *Never ceases to amaze me how any investigation can turn on what Dale calls PDL, pure dumb luck.*

"Blake, you aren't listening to me."

"Oh, sorry, I was contemplating our good fortune. We have to consider this find in preparing the search warrant."

"The word is that it's time to wrap this one up."

"Agreed, I don't think there is much more to know about MACS' operations from the outside. I do think that there is more to know in general, particularly about the two dead patients and the attack on the DEA nurse."

"Blake, what are we going for?"

"It's a Medicare fraud case that grew into two counts of murder and assault, at the least "

"How do we tie it together?"

Blake kicked off his shoes, propped his feet on the ottoman

and reached for his laptop, "Those floating pill boxes are a huge break. Great work, Jack. Let me show you how I have this diagrammed," he explained as he brought up a chart on the screen.

* * * * *

Regardless of how many times Sam Locke stepped off the elevator onto the executive floor, he knew it involved him groveling, shuffling or evading. Dealing with the Girards required nothing less.

Sally glared at him, pointing toward Marco Girard's bronze door, "They're waiting for you."

The "they" meant Victoria and Serena were riding shotgun for Marco. What he didn't expect was to see Lorraine, pacing like a cougar ready to spring on an unsuspecting prey.

"Good morning. I'm glad you are all here. There's something we need to discuss," Locke said, trying to seize the initiative.

"Screw discussion, we need damage control," Victoria sputtered.

"Let's give Dr. Locke a fair opportunity to explain this unfortunate situation," Serena interjected, playing her good cop role.

"Obviously we are all talking about our new patient, Hallie Logan."

"How do you explain this, Locke? Why didn't you warn us?" Marco demanded, slamming his fist on the conference table.

"I first heard about it this morning from Neva. She called me to the clinic where I met Ms. Logan. She certainly is a dead ringer for her sister."

"'Dead' is the operative word," Lorraine interrupted, "Something is odd about her being here. What have you done?"

"What have I done? I've long wondered what you had to do with it, Lorraine. I do know that you were one of the last people with Harriet Logan before she ran out of the door and into traffic," Locke fired back, "Care to tell us the type of crisis intervention you were using? Seems you got the desired result."

Lorraine lunged toward him as he stepped back behind Serena's chair.

"Silence, both of you!" Marco shouted. "I don't have time for recriminations. I want her out of here today, and I don't care if she leaves in a van or a body bag the way her sister did."

Locke flinched, "Acting in haste is a mistake, Dr. Marco, after what happened to Harriet. If we treat Hallie differently than other new patients, we could be setting ourselves up and placing the MACS in jeopardy."

"What do you mean, Locke?"

"I mean that the Logan family could be watching us to see how we deal with Hallie. If we fail again, they come after us with a wrongful death suit for Harriet and some kind of malpractice action related to Hallie's treatment."

Serena nodded, "Dr. Locke is right, Marco. If anything, we must pamper Hallie. To do less would face a plethora of annoying legal actions."

"I get it, now," Victoria said, "This is the Logans' way of getting back at us. They send us their other schizo kid and dare us to make a mistake."

"I think you're right, Victoria," Locke responded. "So that means we have to be careful in the way we deal with Hallie."

"Fine, but I want her out of MACS."

"I understand Dr. Marco," Locke scrambled for a compromise, "We can work with her a few days and determine that she isn't suitable for our programs. That gives us a solid reason to send her back to Community Psychiatric and makes us appear to be acting in her best interest."

"What about our best interests? We pay you twice the going rate for program directors, Locke. For that price, we buy your unqualified loyalty, is that understood?"

"Yes, Dr. Marco. I know what you're asking."

Marco stared at Serena, then Victoria as if he could read their thoughts. Then he sat straight in his chair giving the majestic impression of the Pope making an "ex cathedra" pronouncement, "It will be done as Dr. Locke suggests. Lorraine, instruct your staff to note even the slightest indication of non-compliance by this patient. We have to build a case for discharging Hallie Logan from MACS. Can you agree to that, Locke?"

"Yes, Dr. Marco. I'll handle it personally."

"And, Locke, I give you three days to make this work. If you don't," Marco said as he pointed to Lorraine, "I'll find someone who can do what needs to be done."

Lorraine folded her arms and smiled. She knew he would fail.

Locke walked out of the office, closing the door behind him.

"Lorraine, keep an eye him. We only want results, not excuses."

Invigorated by the possibilities, she replied, "If I solve your problem, Dr. Marco, I expect something meaningful in return."

"Such as?"

"Full recognition of Gina as your heir and second in command of MACS."

"Never make demands before earning the reward."

"I'll earn it. I do much more for your family than you realize."

Lorraine turned to leave, confident that she had secured the future for herself and Gina. Drunk with the scent of power, she pushed aside earlier thoughts that Marco was setting her up with the DEA.

As soon as the bronze door closed, the three exchanged glances.

Victoria spoke first, "She's getting too familiar with us. She has to go."

"She's as dangerous to Gina and the family as Jay was to Carla," Serena added.

"Calm yourselves, mother hens. I see what's happening. Let

her serve our purpose. Once Lorraine eliminates Hallie Logan, we will turn her in to the police."

"But Marco, that could bring unwanted attention on our business dealings."

"Serena, Cara Mia, I fear that it's time to plan our departure."

"Why Marco? We are doing so well here."

"Yes, darling, but we are attracting attention. Even the Bible tells us that 'the thief comes in the night' to avoid excess attention."

"How long until we leave?"

"Good question, Victoria. I was estimating sixty days, enough time for two more large Medicare deposits. However, if the Hallie Logan matter becomes a problem, we have to be prepared sooner. Say, three weeks to a month."

"Will you leave first, then send for us?" Serena asked. "Perhaps we all need to leave together."

"No, we must not appear to panic. Why don't you and Victoria start talking about a shopping trip to Paris in a few weeks? You can also suggest that Carla will be attending a conference. That will circulate among the office gossips."

"What about Gina?" Victoria demanded.

"I'll speak with her tonight," Marco answered, "It depends on whether her loyalty is with the family or her lover."

"You mean you would cut my daughter out of our business that easily?"

"Why not? You agreed to the same treatment for my son."

* * * * *

Shoulders slumped, hands in his pockets, Locke walked back to his office.

"Looks like they worked you over pretty good," Brook's voice broke his stupor.

"It was the usual happy family gathering with their bulldog, Lorraine, straining at her leash."

"Well I hope you told them that this bouncing paycheck game has to stop."

Locke rubbed his eyes. He completely forgot to mention it.

"Sam, you didn't say anything about it, did you?"

"No, Brook, I'm sorry. I intended to but I got ambushed when I walked in."

"Listen, Sam, the natives are getting restless. There's talk that MACS is in financial trouble. Do you know anything?"

"I think it's Felipe screwing up on the deposits. When I look at the program census and the billings, there's plenty of money coming in even if Medicare is late on some payments." He paused to look at his phone messages, "Hold my calls. I need to think."

"Okay, but you have a visitor. Dr. Kendall is waiting for you."

"Thanks, Brook." *That's right; I told Taylor to come up and talk to me during her break.*

"Hello, Taylor, how is your day?" Dr. Locke attempted to sound casual as he sat in the guest chair opposite her.

"My day is fine, but the staff was extremely unnerved when Hallie Logan checked in."

"Yes, I can see why."

"I wonder what Lorraine will do when she sees Hallie."

Locke knew what she wanted to do and what she would do if he didn't get Hallie out soon.

"Do you think Hallie is in danger?"

"Quite honestly, I don't know."

"Can't you make Dr. Marco understand that Lorraine is out of control? There are staff who believe that she had been threatening Harriet before her death."

"Threatening? For what reason?"

Taylor decided to give him a little more information and see how he responded, "The way I heard it, Harriet was trying to get an outside psychiatric consult and Lorraine blocked it. Harriet felt that someone was trying to impede her recovery."

"I never heard anything about the consult request," Locke

answered, "Patients always have the right to get a second opinion outside of MACS."

"They do if they ask the right person. Obviously you didn't know."

"No, I didn't. In fact, I filled in for process group two days before Harriet's death. I knew that she was on the list for discharge to a step-down program so I paid particular attention to her responses. I distinctly remember thinking how much progress she had made."

"Less than forty-eight hours later, she's dead following a psychotic episode. How to you account for that, Dr. Locke?"

"I didn't see her after that, so I don't know. Some of our patients unconsciously fear discharge and begin to regress closer to that date."

"That's not the way staff members saw her. Of course, since her chart has disappeared we can't verify that."

"Disappeared? No, it's probably been sent to the archives. There's a secure storage center where inactive MACS files are kept for all programs."

"Wrong again. I tried to get it...I mean I asked to see it. Because of Hallie, I wanted to...to compare their assessments," Taylor stammered.

"I know that Marco took the file to dictate a response on the incident to our liability insurance carrier. If it's not in archives then it must still be in the building."

"Yes and no. There is a small file with summary data and a copy of the intake, but Ray says there are no group notes or original assessments in Harriet's file."

"So Ray is your source. I thought so. He was close to Harriet and he took her death very hard. Why didn't he come to me with this information?"

"He didn't know if he could trust you."

"But he trusts you?"

"Yes."

"That's good. You have managed to gain the trust and respect of most of the staff in the short time you've been here, Taylor. That's an important part of being the clinical professional leading a treatment team," Locke had been meaning to give her that compliment and this seemed the right time, not to mention the distraction value.

"Thank you. I also need to tell you that some staff in the clinic are upset for other reasons."

"Yes, I realize that the bounced checks last week caused a lot of distress. Felipe assured me that everyone would be paid before the end of business today. Do you need your check replaced Taylor?"

"No, my check cashed as usual. Isn't that odd?"

"I don't know what to think of it."

"Well I think the Girards don't care about the problems of the little people. I bet Felipe's check cashed."

Locke nodded. *Of course it did. And so did the checks for Serena's collagen injections, Victoria's bar tab at the country club and Marco's mistresses.*

"Sam, I've heard about another patient, Greg Newman, who jumped off the Skyway Bridge. Word is that Lorraine didn't like him either. Have you noticed that Lorraine's disapproval makes people leave, whether they plan to or not? Face it, the suicides are getting a bit too convenient around here."

Locke shook his head, "And you think MACS is responsible?"

"Not MACS, certain people at MACS."

"I assure you, I never even linked the two incidents. I don't even see how they can be compared."

"What if they are linked? What if there's an attempt to recycle patients back into the programs by forcing relapse?"

"Well, we do occasionally re-admit after a patient experiences a relapse. You know that's common with this type of diagnosis."

"Occasionally? Check it out, Dr. Locke. Patients are being recycled through MACS PHPs. Don't just look at the census numbers. Compare the names. It's the same people back with different patient numbers."

Locke paused. He knew that Victoria and Serena had under-the-table arrangements with several local psychiatrists for referrals. He also knew that Serena was insistent about the potential success of her Live Anew step-down care program even though he advised against it. *Several programs of that type have been tried in this market and all of them failed. The reality is that the billings on Live Anew were insignificant compared to the MACS PHP cash cow. I assumed that Marco let it continue to pacify his wife.*

"Taylor, have you discussed this with anyone else at MACS?"

"No."

"How did you discover this? Did Ray tell you?"

"No, Ray hasn't put it all together. Actually, I saw the pattern when I did that busy-work patient analysis for Victoria. At the time, I noticed that the success rates in treatement for MACS patients were much higher than the national averages. Considering how unpredictable this population is, it didn't make sense that MACS kept such an even census.

I've run the numbers again recently after Brook started sending me a copy of the weekly patient census. It's a statistical miracle. If the Orlando PHP is down 5% one week, then Brooksville is up 5% the next week. It's never more than a percent or two off. Sorry, Dr. Locke, but that kind of balance demands a second look."

Locke stood up and walked behind his desk. He picked up the census report for last week. *By God, she's right. There must be more manipulation than I knew. More than the payoffs to psychiatrists as medical directors in programs they rarely visited. Victoria defended the practice as no different than the pharmaceutical reps offering continuing education cruises to entice doctors.*

When they wanted him to order all discharges into the Live Anew program, he objected weakly. Serena suggested that, to ease his conscious, he offer three program choices: Live Anew, a county program with no real therapy and a community organization that was run by a support group. Once the patients saw the attractive group room and outdoor patio, they chose Serena's program. *There's nothing as lucrative as running your own patient recycling system.*

"Dr. Locke, what are you going to do?"

"Taylor, I appreciate that you brought this to my attention first. Can you to give me a week to get up to speed on these problems?"

"All right, but I have to remind you that the law requires reporting irregularities in patient treatment."

"I know that and I give you my word that I'm not going to turn my back on it. Not this time."

"I have to inform Dr. Dale."

"Wait, Taylor, give me time to get a handle on this before you call him. I have to neutralize Lorraine or she may try to implicate you. That wouldn't be good for your residency."

"I haven't been here that long. Any records I saw, Victoria gave to me."

"True, but Lorraine doesn't play fair. She'll want a sacrificial lamb and she's not too fond of you."

"I stand by my work. Let her challenge it."

"She won't go for that," Locke replied, "The last time she got mad at you she was complaining to me. I told her your work was exemplary and to back off. She said that you were seen in the crowd at Harriet's accident and she would get the social worker who was also out there to make a case that you contributed to Harriet's death."

Taylor jerked backward as if she had been punched. She hadn't told anyone at MACS about what she overheard about Harriet's ramblings. Lorraine must be bluffing.

"That's not true!"

"I know that, Taylor, but she can cause a lot of trouble for you. That's why I don't want you to discuss this with anyone, not even Ray. I know what I have to do and I'm ready to do it. If I think you're in jeopardy, I'll call Dr. Dale."

"Okay. I couldn't bring myself to believe that you were involved in anything illegal."

"Thanks for the vote of confidence. Now keep working and stay away from Lorraine," he said, extending his hand to shake hers.

Taylor smiled and stepped toward the door.

"And Taylor...thanks. You helped me more than you know."

After Taylor left Locke reached into his top desk drawer for a calculator. The more he worked the census numbers, the more he saw the pattern. He turned on his computer, entering patient names, then program names.

What a shell game. Maybe the rumor is true that early in their marriage, Marco and Victoria fled a bad business deal in Montevideo by posing as gypsies in a traveling carnival. That must have been a learning experience.

They certainly know how to spot a mark. After all, they found me. Given a fat salary, new lease car, important title and freedom to create a pilot group program the way I envisioned it in graduate school, they bought me. Then they set me up with a persistent adversary. As long as I was busy battling Lorraine for my job, I had no time for details. I gave them good programs and well-trained staff. Meanwhile, she was undermining my authority, sleeping with the boss' daughter and who knows what else to keep those almighty dollars flowing into MACS. Sorry Marco, you bought my title, but you didn't buy my soul.

He typed a short note and printed two copies, placing one in a sealed envelope and the other in his pocket. He picked up his briefcase and closed the office door behind him. "Brook, I want you to take this note directly to Serena. Don't let Sally stop you. Put it in Serena's hands."

"Sure, Sam. Do you have an appointment that I don't know about."

He paused to formulate a plausible explanation, "Yes, my

dentist called. He had a cancellation and can work me in this afternoon. I may not be back."

"Okay. See you tomorrow."

Locke nodded. *I doubt it.*

* * * * *

Taylor watched Hallie Logan get safely on board a transport van at the end of the day. She'd have to wait until later to find out more. Hallie promised to phone Ray each evening after she returned to the group home near Tyrone Square Mall.

"Looks like insanity runs in the family."

She turned to face Lorraine Lewis, "Insanity is a criminal court issue. We work with schizophrenia. Surely you know the difference, Nurse Lewis."

"What I want to know is what you heard about Harriet?"

"You mean Hallie."

"No, I mean Harriet. I think you heard something that day and I want to know what it was."

"I told Dr. Marco and the police exactly what happened. Read the report."

Taylor turned to walk away when Lorraine's arm thrust outward and a hand with sharp fingernails grabbed Taylor's arm.

"I want to hear it from you."

"All you're going to hear from me is an assault complaint if you don't let go of my arm this minute."

Ray looked up from his paperwork to see what was happening.

"Dr. Kendall, I need your signature before you leave," he shouted.

Dismayed to find a witness, Lorraine released her with a warning, "You're out of your league, sorority girl. Stay away from Hallie Logan."

Taylor stepped back, moving toward the nurses' station. Ray handed her a chart with a yellow sticky note asking if she was being harassed.

"Yes, Ray, we all know how that therapeutic approach works." She rolled her eyes in Lorraine's direction.

Ray nodded, "Can I walk you to your car, Dr. Kendall? One of the nurses told me that the pedaling purse snatcher was seen nearby. You know, he's the guy who rides up on his ten-speed and grabs purses."

Taylor wasn't sure if that was a ruse or reality, but she welcomed his company. She wasn't in the mood for another round with Lorraine.

* * * * *

"FBI Tampa Office."

"Hello...I need to speak to someone about Medicare fraud."

"Sure, I'll transfer your call to the Medicare fraud squad. What is your name and who are you with?"

"I'm Dr. Samuel Locke, former program director for MACS in St. Petersburg."

"Would you hold a minute, please?"

He had walked for an hour along Redington Beach preparing to make this call, only to be stuck on hold.

"Gloria, this is Didi on switchboard. I've got a Dr. Samuel Locke from MACS who wants to talk to somebody in Medicare fraud. Do you want to take this call?

"Thanks, Didi, put the call through to the Director. I'll slip him a note to explain. And if anyone calls from or about MACS, let me know right away."

* * * * *

Taylor pulled into the driveway, eager to get a hot bath and wash the sensation of Lorraine's clammy handprint off her arm. Her head was spinning with conflicting information. Brook's comment about the Nutracuratives seemed to describe the whole operation, "Whatever it is; it's not what we think it is."

"Hello, Dr. Kendall. I have a surprise for you," Sigrid's

cheerful voice was a contrast to Taylor's dark mood.

Taylor took the medium size box from Sigrid's hands, "What's this?"

"It's a gift from Miss M'Etta. She sent one to Lars and me too. It's a box of chocolates and treats from Switzerland."

"Thanks for telling me. I could use chocolate right now."

"You look tired. Come to the main house and I'll fix a hot dinner."

"That's nice of you, but I'm entertaining later."

"Tell that nice young man to take you out to dinner."

"We may order pizza."

"Pizza? That's no dinner. You need meat and potatoes, something to stick to your ribs. I can bring over enough food for both of you."

"Sigrid, you sound a lot like my mother. I promise that I'll get something good to eat, after I have a handful of chocolate for an appetizer."

Sigrid laughed and headed back into the main house as Taylor entered the guest house. Her phone was ringing.

"Taylor, how did it go at the clinic?"

"Gabe! It was okay. I'll tell you all about it later. Are you coming over?"

"Probably. I need to check on a few things first."

"Better hurry. I got a box of Swiss chocolates and I'm breaking the seal."

"Oh, do you have a secret admirer? Should I be jealous?"

"No, silly, it's from M'Etta, my mother's friend who owns the property where I'm living. Hurry over; I have so much to tell you."

"I'll be there as soon as I can. Bon Appétit."

He hung up the phone and finished printing the action sheet from the investigation chart that he and Jack worked on earlier. Satisfied that every detail was covered, he turned on the shower and stepped in. After all, he had orders to stay close to Taylor.

That's one order he was looking forward to fulfilling. The ringing phone caused him to miss a beat in his shower solo. He stepped out, wrapping a towel around his water glistened physique.

"Yes?"

"I've got your Christmas gift."

"Save it for December. I'm going back to my shower."

"Not 'til you hear this, my man. Samuel Locke called the Tampa office. He's ready to turn them in for immunity."

Blake dropped the towel and sat naked on the kitchen stool, "Are you serious? What happened today at MACS?"

"Don't know yet. I'm going to meet Locke at the Belleair Country Club for dinner. We aren't bringing him in until we know if his story is for real or if he's fishing on behalf of the Girards."

"Who else is coming?"

"The old man is driving over now. I'm turning at the golf course. Where will you be later?"

"I was going to Taylor's place."

"That's perfect. I'll call you when we know something."

"Okay. I'll stay at Taylor's until you call."

"Another thing: after Locke phoned, the Director started the paperwork for warrants. Your time with Taylor is almost over. Score a home run, man."

"I can't, Jack, much as I want to. I can't love her and leave her."

CHAPTER

"The buffet looks divine. You and Cook may leave now. We have family business to discuss," Serena waved her hand toward the server in a disinterested manner. The events of the day were nerve wracking. She wanted to create a calm atmosphere when Marco came home.

If he becomes too anxious, he either broods in his study or leaves to spend the night with one of his mistresses. With any luck, he won't know about Sam Locke or Carla. Victoria might not even know yet. How delicious it would be to ambush them both!

The front door creaked. Serena gathered the skirt of her brocade hostess gown and opened the double doors to the dining area to greet the arrivals.

"Felipe! Why are you and Tiffany here now?"

"We live here, Mother."

"Don't be impertinent!"

"Mother, I've had people in and out of my office all day - screaming, cussing, crying and begging. I need a drink."

"This is absurd! Paychecks are delayed a few days and these people make such a scene. Where's their gratitude for their jobs?"

"I know Mother. As you say, it's the revenge of the little people," Felipe replied rubbing his temples, "Are we having a dinner party?"

"No, my son, I thought we needed some family time, thus I arranged this buffet and dismissed the staff. Why don't you and Tiffany serve your plates and eat in your room?"

"I think she wants to get rid of us, Felipe."

"How uncharacteristically astute of you, Tiffany."

"Maybe we don't want to leave."

"Have it your way, Tiffany. I have to give Marco some unpleasant news. After the events of the day, he's going to look for someone to blame," Serena explained. "Do you want Felipe to face his father's wrath?"

Felipe grabbed his jacket from the chair where he tossed it and took the plate from Tiffany's hand pulling her with him. "Let's leave while we can. Tell Father that we have dinner plans out."

"But Felipe, I thought we wanted to..."

He shook his head.

As they walked away, Serena called out, "Get a thrifty motel room if you must and don't hurry home."

She paced across the entry hall, arranging and rearranging the flowers on the marble table. Finally she heard cars pull into the driveway. She opened the door to greet them. To her dismay, Gina didn't go home with Lorraine. She was riding with Victoria. Marco spun the Ferrari to the side parking area. Serena pressed her lips into a welcoming smile and breezed past Victoria to embrace Marco.

"My dear Marco, you've had such a trying day."

"Yes, I need a glass of brandy, a large brandy."

Gina scurried into the house to do his bidding.

Serena waited until they were seated and on the second glass of wine. Then she pulled two letters from underneath the silver coffee tray where she placed them earlier.

"I'm afraid that I have more distressing news. I carried the burden of this all afternoon to allow the rest of you to continue your work."

"Did you carry it to the spa for your massage?"

"Yes, I did go for a massage. I needed to regain my composure in order to help you through your difficulty, Victoria."

"What difficulty?"

"Did you see Carla this afternoon?"

"No, and I told the cleaning crew to trash all the flowers in her office. Marco, I warned you that this secret admirer business was getting out of hand."

"And for once, Victoria was right. A mother's instincts never fail."

"Make your point, Serena, and get it over with."

"Carla left the office before lunch. She's gone for a tryst," Serena passed Carla's handwritten note to Marco. He read it then threw it at Victoria.

"Why didn't you call me, Serena?"

"Marco, darling, I didn't find out until hours after she left. I quizzed that silly secretary, Brook, who seems to know nothing. Supposedly Carla said she was starting early on a long weekend and would be back next week. That's all I could find out."

"Did anyone see this man?"

"No, and her car is in the parking lot. I assume the man sent a taxi."

"If he can afford all those orchids, he can afford to send a limo," said Gina.

"Shut up, Gina, unless you know something useful," Victoria barked.

Marco reached for the decanter and poured another round.

Serena continued, "Carla is merely asserting herself with this casual romance."

"We don't have time to trail her. She'll be back and we'll deal with her then."

"How very wise of you, Marco. There's another, more serious, matter," Serena interjected. Unfolding the second page she held, she began to read:

Effective this date, I resign as Vice President and Program Director for MACS. It was clear to me today that my authority in the programs and with the staff is compromised by Lorraine Lewis. Since she has no intention of leaving, I will.

I understand that by leaving without the contractual sixty days notice, I forfeit the next performance bonus. I will contact Human Resources to process necessary papers.

Thank you for the opportunity.

Sincerely,

Samuel Locke, Ph.D.

"He can't do that to us," Victoria shouted.

Marco paused, holding his anger in check, "We have to focus on the big picture." He noticed the broad smile on Gina's usually dour face. "Gina, I need your help with this matter."

"Yes, Father, what can I do?"

"I'm not going to accept Locke's resignation immediately. I will insist he return for a transition period. Perhaps you could visit Lorraine tonight and suggest that she begin to formulate a transition plan for me."

"Do you want me to go now?"

"Yes, I do, but there's one thing you must communicate to her."

"What is that, Father?"

"Lorraine is not to tell anyone about Locke's resignation letter. Not even Neva. No one is to know until I'm ready to make the announcement," Marco instructed, "If a word of this leaks out, I'll fire Lorraine and make a complaint against her nursing license. You must assure me that you can keep her in line."

Gina thought of the syringe with Lorraine's fingerprints hidden in her office, "Father, I have some insurance. Forget the licensing board. What I have can get her arrested."

Marco raised his bushy eyebrows, stood up and went over to embrace his daughter, "Well done, Gina. And you've answered a question that plagued your mother and me for some time."

"What's that?"

"It's a simple question of where your loyalty lies - with the family or with Lorraine."

Gina winced at the thought of making such a choice, "As you taught us, Father, I will protect the family first because the family protects me."

He hugged his daughter then waited for her to leave.

"I thought you wanted to put distance between Gina and Lorraine?" Victoria asked, "Why did you send her back?"

"I need for Gina to keep Lorraine in the wings while we deal with Locke."

"Why not accept his resignation and give the job to Lorraine? She's bowed to us long enough to get it."

"Patience was never your virtue, Victoria. Are we alone in the house?"

"Yes, Marco. Felipe and Tiffany are out for the evening and I dismissed the servants early."

"Excellent. We need to plan our departure, ladies. I want Locke at the helm to take the fall from the Department of Professional Regulation when we go. They are more likely to assess fault for the programs to a psychologist than to a nurse. I need to offer them a substantial scapegoat in my place. Locke has no idea how we've groomed him for that role," Marco smiled, pouring himself yet another brandy.

"How long have you planned this, Marco?"

"Actually, I only began thinking about it last week. Something doesn't feel right."

"Is that why you moved the payroll out of the account?"

"Yes, it is. Did Felipe find it?"

"That imbecile can't find his zipper without Tiffany's help. I knew it was you."

"I will not have you malign my son. At least he's here working while your daughter takes off on a romantic holiday without warning," Serena sneered.

"Ladies, ladies! We have to talk business," he said, putting the stopper back in the decanter, "Let's have our meal and coffee then we'll set the table and start making lists."

"How much have you sent to the offshore accounts?"

"Enough."

"How much is enough?"

"For your tastes, Serena, there's never enough. However if we can secure one or two more major deposits from Medicare, then we will all be set for life. Not only us, but I have set aside generous accounts for all of my children."

"Does that include Blake?"

"Yes, Victoria, it does. I still expect him to return to the family," Marco retorted in a way that told both women the subject was not open for discussion.

* * * * *

"The Taj Mahal, the beach at Maui, the sun gleaming on a glacier in Antarctica - none are more spectacular than your smile."

"Gabe, that sounds like a line from a play."

"No, I'm being completely serious and totally original," he said as he stretched out beside her in the double lounge chair by the pool.

"Oh, yeah, and you've seen all these places to make a fair comparison?"

"In my own way, I have," he answered. *Well, Blake has, but I can't tell her that. I can't even tell her how I really feel or what's about to happen. Why can't the end of the world happen right now, before she finds out who I am and why I pushed my way into her life in the first place?*

She nestled closer to him. He had to taste her lips again. She was as eager as he. If he wasn't careful, this woman would destroy his control.

Then it happened; the phone rang. He sat upright and answered, "Hello."

"This is Jack, it's over."

"What happened?"

"He rolled like an SUV on recalled Firestones."

"What do you need me to do?"

"Meet us at the bar on Ninth Street. Make it fast. Sorry to ruin your big evening, man."

"It's the curse of the working class. See you later."

He closed the phone, observing Taylor's glistening lips and puzzled expression.

"Is something wrong?"

He sat down and wrapped her in his arms, "You are perfect, but life is not. I have to go."

"Why?"

"Jack's involved with some trouble. I need to help him."

"I'll go with you, Gabe."

"No, Taylor. Besides, after the kind of day you've had, you need to rest," he said, kissing her nose gently as he pulled away from her. "I have this feeling that if I stayed, neither one of us would get any sleep."

"I've heard that before. Is this a promise or a threat?"

"Let's say it's a promise. I want you, Taylor, make no mistake. But it has to be the right place and the right circumstances. I can wait."

"Will you be back tonight?"

"No. I'll try to join you for lunch at the bench. And Taylor, promise me that you won't annoy Lorraine and you'll keep away from Hallie Logan."

"I'm happy to stay away from Lorraine, but why Hallie?"

"From the way you described things today, Hallie is like ground zero for an explosion. Anybody near her could get hurt if things go badly."

"Gabe, you worry too much. I already decided not to spend

too much time around Hallie. It will make Neva suspicious. From what she said when I talked to her earlier, once the shock of Hallie's appearance wore off, groups went on as usual."

Taylor stood up to walk with him to his car. He gave her a quick kiss and got into the car, cranking the noisy engine. He assumed she was saying goodbye so he nodded and smiled. What he didn't hear was her question. She took his nod to mean, yes, go ahead and call Dale. She went into the pool house, locked the door and dialed Dr. Sebastian Dale's home number.

* * * * *

It was nearly eleven when he left the meeting. They were in agreement. The raid had to go down soon. The Director would brief the Joint Task Force in the morning. Jack would be there to get the details.

His phone rang, "What now?"

"That's what I want to know," a familiar voice barked at him, "What's going on at that nut shop your parents call a treatment program?"

"I can't explain it now, Dale."

"What is the FBI waiting for, an engraved invitation? From what Taylor told me about the games they play with the patient census, you ought to have enough to take them down."

"Let's just say that what you know is the tip of the iceberg. Trust me, I'm watching out for Taylor and I'm doing my job. Don't ask me anymore."

"All right, Blake. Do you want me to come in tomorrow and remove Taylor from the residency?"

"Absolutely not. Taylor is protected, that's all I can say."

"What about her residency?"

"I have a plan. Give me time to make arrangements. I won't let anything harm her."

"What about you? If you need to talk, come over to the house. The key is in the same place."

"Thanks, Dale. And thanks for trusting me."

"Just because I trust you doesn't mean I'm not going to rake you over the coals when this is finished."

"Understood. Listen I've got a call waiting and I need to check it."

Blake pulled over into an empty grocery store parking lot to answer his call waiting. *What else could happen tonight?*

"Hey, man. I got a call from the office. Locke spent three hours giving his statement and it's priceless. Not to mention all the copies of internal documents that he brought with him."

"Will Justice give him immunity?"

"They're jerking him around and sending him back into MACS, but in the end, you and I know he'll be covered."

"Is he going back tomorrow?"

"Like he has a choice? Said he would go back, apologize and kiss butt with the speed of light. He thinks they'll let him work out at least a few weeks until witchy woman takes over."

"That's perfect."

"Do you think Dr. Marco will let Locke keep the keys to the executive washroom after resigning in a huff?"

"You bet he will, Jack-o. And you can also bet that Marco has been setting Locke up for the fall since he arrived. It's the Girard tradition. We recruit top people and pay well. Our sacrificial lambs exceed the USDA prime standards."

"Ouch! Your family scares me."

"Me too."

"Will Taylor be all right in there?"

"Definitely. The unholy trinity has enough crises to occupy their attention. Pulling Taylor out suddenly would put her in greater danger than leaving her there, under their patrician noses."

"If you have anything else that I need to present at the Joint Task Force meeting tomorrow, email it to the office."

"So we're on for Friday?"

"Negative. I can't wait for the fat lady to sing. After the good doctor's performance, the timetable may get moved to Wednesday."

Blake paused, mentally calculating his hidden agenda, "Jack, I'm going to be out of touch tomorrow."

"Where are you going?"

"Don't ask, don't tell, my friend."

"What do I tell the old man?"

"Tell him that this case is going to take a lot out of me. I need a day alone to get mentally prepared for the bust."

"I forgot about that, the family thing and all. I'll cover for you. See you at your place about five tomorrow. I'll bring food."

"Thanks, Jack. You're a good friend," Blake ended the call. As Marco taught him, the ability to deceive enemies and bystanders is not nearly as valuable as the ability to deceive a friend.

CHAPTER 45

Rays of the rising sun bounced off the Citation Jet's wing Tuesday morning, causing Blake to rub his sleep-deprived eyes. Methodically, he walked around the plane with the preflight checklist. Satisfied that he and the mechanic had done everything possible to make his metal marvel fly, he boarded and secured the door.

Marco taught him to fly before he was old enough to drive a car, but little about the mechanics of flight. That was too technical to capture his father's mercurial interests. No, Marco taught him the spirit of flight. Many times he told Blake, "When you put on your headset to contact the tower, it's like a bride receiving her cherished wedding band. The headset is a connection to another world, allowing you to leave this gravity-bound planet and become one with your airplane, soaring together in the clouds. Flying, my son, is like an orgasm; you must be totally involved to savor every moment." Marco would be pleased to know that the thrill never diminished. Flying was the one of the few legal skills acquired from his father.

The usual advantage of leaving St. Petersburg/Clearwater Airport at dawn was the lack of traffic. Not so today. He pulled up third in line behind a UPS cargo plane and a smaller commuter jet. Probably a good thing. Gulping down another shot of black coffee, he secured the thermos and smoothed out his air charts before it was his turn to move onto the active runway. He relished takeoff the most, piercing the clouds like an arrow. Once airborne, he guided the plane into its approved cruising altitude, heading south.

Blake wasn't lying when he told Jack that he needed to get

mentally prepared for what would happen tomorrow. He had thought about it...dreamed about it. He knew it was right, but that didn't make it easy. Dale and the Director said almost the same thing, "Evil as they are, they're still your family."

His thoughts drifted to Marco and their adventures. The last time they flew together was that trip to the Amazon jungle. The local pilot they hired was afraid to attempt a landing in the narrow clearing Marco pointed out. When they returned to the outpost, Marco thrust a handful of money into the pilot's hands, shouting at him to refuel the plane and motioning for Blake to take the pilot's seat. That's where Marco found the substance he claims to be the secret ingredient in the Nutracuratives.

A voice from the Miami control tower interrupted Blake's reminiscences. He made the necessary adjustments to line up in one of those imaginary sky decks that air traffic controllers use to separate crowded air space. When his turn came, he landed and then turned toward a private hangar off the commercial jetway to park where directed by the ground crew within a marked circle. Walking down the portable stairway, he shouted instructions to the crew chief.

A young man in a bronze silk double-breasted suit swaggered toward him. "Mr. Girard? I'm Raul Hernandez, Miami office."

Blake met his handshake with a "Viva Cuba libre," which was heartily returned by Raul. As he thought, this young agent was Cuban.

"I can drive you anywhere you want to go or take you to pick up a loaner car from our office. Your choice."

Blake wanted to handle this solo, but he was tired and it was destined to be a long day. Besides, he didn't want much about his visit known at the Miami office. Using one of their cars would force him to document his destination in the city. That could cause questions. It was best to leave it the way he had Geek Boy explain it to his Miami buddy, a scouting trip to check some possible MACS properties.

"Raul, I'll leave the driving to you. Been a while since I drove around Miami. No telling where I'd end up."

"Where do you want to go, Mr. Girard?"

"Miami Institute of Psychological Research. I have the address if you need it. And, skip the formalities. Call me Blake."

"No problem, Blake. I know exactly how to get there. The Institute's a swanky private place across the street from the hospital where my Abuella - that's my grandmother - had surgery last year. Here's my car."

He pointed to a silver Porsche Carrera and opened the doors. Blake looked over the younger agent's fashionable clothes and fast car, "Salaries must be higher in your territory."

"Not really."

"Then your office's idea of a company car is different than ours."

"No sir, we drive standard issue vehicles."

"Is this what they call a standard issue sedan in Dade County?"

"Oh, you mean this car, no. It's my personal car. See, I got this girlfriend who works down at the Dade cop shop. She lets me know when the primo seized merchandise goes on the auction block. That's how I got this car. It belonged to a second rate drug dealer. He was ripped about losing it when he got busted. May have been a low life, but he sure kept a shine on this baby. No question, it was hand-waxed regularly."

Raul looked over to see Blake's head slump against the window. "Long assignment, huh? I know how that feels. Sleep on, man, Raul is at the controls." He roared down the interstate, probably coming closer to breaking the sound barrier than Blake did in the jet.

* * * * *

Taylor woke up feeling like her legs were crammed into a box. Then she remembered lying down on the sofa, hoping that

Gabe might come back. Standing up to stretch, she went to the kitchen to turn on the coffee pot then opened the door to get the newspaper. A note was taped to the door.

Good morning, beautiful lady,

Wish I was here, but I have to make an early round of deliveries.

Call you later,

Your Gabe

My Gabe? What does that mean? I wonder what I mean. Too much to think about before coffee.

* * * * *

Half an hour later, Raul announced an interim stop. Gaining no response, he shook his passenger's shoulder. Startled from a restless sleep, Blake twisted around, swinging his left arm up in a defensive posture.

"Chill, man, we're on the same team. Nothing going down here."

Blake got out slowly to stretch, feeling ridiculous for his overreaction, "Sorry Raul, I didn't mean…"

"No big deal. You look whipped. That's why I stopped at this McDonald's. Thought you might want to throw cold water on your face and the back of your neck. That always helps me clear my head. You do your thing and I'll get coffee and sandwiches, okay?"

"Great, make mine a tall soda and any kind of breakfast sandwich. I drank a week's worth of coffee on the flight down here," Blake mumbled walking toward the men's restroom.

Getting some food was a good idea. Wonder if Raul is the intuitive type or tying to make points with a superior? He's a friend of Geek Boy so he must have heard inflated stories about me. Either way, after this break, I'll be ready to do what I came for.

* * * * *

"Good morning, Dr. Locke. Come in and help yourself to coffee."

"Thank you, Dr. Marco. I didn't know if you would see me."

"We're both highly-skilled professionals and we both know how easy it is to become intensely protective at perceived invasions of our territory. Obviously the way we handled matters yesterday was offensive to you. I would have preferred that you came to me first and discussed it."

"I don't want to work with Lorraine breathing down my neck, but I feel I owe you the proper notice. If you want, I'll work out the sixty days."

Marco looked triumphant, "Excellent. I accept. Perhaps during that time we can consider a different division of power that will persuade you to remain with MACS."

"I'll listen to what you have to say."

"That's all I can ask. Serena and Victoria will be pleased to know that you are staying."

"Lorraine won't be pleased."

"What makes you think that Lorraine knows?"

"Doesn't she?"

"I'll see to it that Lorraine backs off while you either phase out of your position or transition into a new role that I'm contemplating for you. Is that acceptable?"

"Yes, Dr. Marco, and I'll try to avoid confrontations with her."

Marco took Locke's resignation letter from his pocket, tore it up and tossed it in the trash. "That's that. You handle the Logan girl. You can bring me up to date on it at next Tuesday's executive staff meeting." He pumped Locke's hand and escorted him to the elevator.

As the elevator doors closed, Sam Locke knew beyond a shadow of a doubt that he was again in the hands of the Philistines.

* * * * *

Raul drove to the north side of Miami Institute, stopping at the entrance marked "Doctors".

Good move! A Porsche wouldn't be remarkable amid the luxury cars in the physicians parking section.

"Stay close by. I don't expect to be more than an hour," Blake instructed, "And if you see anyone from your office, you don't know why I'm here."

"I don't need to know. Derek says you're the main man. If he says you're cool, you're all right by me. Here's a card with my cell phone number. Let's put it this way, I memorized every episode of 'Miami Vice'. Snappy getaways are my specialty."

Blake nodded, left the car and fell in step behind two doctors heading for the same entrance. He moved effortlessly past the security guard and the lobby receptionist by breathing the magic words, "Dr. Guitierrez needs to see me. Confidential research matter."

He did his homework well enough to know that at the Institute, "Dr. G" reigned supreme. Dr. G was the prize lured away from the National Institutes of Mental Health by the Miami Institute Board of Directors in a bidding war with Duke, Vanderbilt and UCLA.

The last roadblock between Blake and his quarry was a sixty-ish champagne blonde secretary whose desk plate identified her as Rhoda Carpenter. His line didn't work. Rhoda knew a bluff when she heard it. She also had the advantage of keeping Dr. G's appointment calendar.

"Okay, pretty boy. Tell Rhoda what you're selling."

"Nothing. Actually I have something to give."

"More drug samples? We have enough of those to turn South

Beach into mellow-yellow land. But, of course, we're too late."

"I hate to pull rank on you, but I have to see Dr. G."

"What rank? You're not a board member and you're not from NIMH. Tell Rhoda the truth and you might win one date, all expenses paid, with my daughter. Great girl. She likes tall men like you."

"Rhoda, much as I enjoy sparring with you, we're both busy. I'll make you a wager that you can't refuse."

"I'm listening, pretty boy."

"Tell Dr. G that Leander is here. If he calls me in, I'll never mention that you doubted me. If he doesn't know me, I'll throw myself out and take your daughter on my sailboat for the most romantic weekend of her life."

With a sly wink, Rhoda dialed the extension, "Dr. G, a guy calling himself Leander wants to see you. He doesn't have an appointment and frankly I think…"

The inner office door opened. Dr. Celio Guitierrez stared at Blake, smiled in recognition and directed Rhoda to hold all calls. She was speechless, a rare condition for her. He motioned for Blake to enter and then pushed in the door lock to secure their privacy.

"Sit down, Leander. Is there a problem?" Dr. G asked as he glanced at the 8 x 10 photo of his wife and son building a sandcastle on the beach outside their Biscayne Bay home.

"No. This is not about your family. I am here to collect on a debt," Blake replied, then reached over and picked up the picture. "They look well and happy. Enrique has grown so much. How old is he now, seven or eight?"

"Eight. He is not much of a scientist, but he can crack the bat at Little League."

"I'm glad that I helped make it possible, Celio. Do you remember the day I delivered your family back to you, safe and sound on your doorstep in Maryland?"

"Of course. My Enrique talked nonstop for months of his

hero, Leander, who made the bad men go away."

"He was a brave boy," Blake flashed back to the memory of a narrow escape from the men who held Enrique and his mother, Ella, captive in a cabin outside Medellin, Colombia. The delicate Hispanic woman and her wide-eyed son spent five terrifying weeks in that dirt floor shanty after being kidnapped during an Easter visit to her mother's home in San Salvador. The older woman died from a blow to the head with a rifle butt while fighting to shield her only grandson. Ella was even more shocked to discover that they were kidnapped as bait in a dispute between her brother-in-law and a rival drug lord. The family connection to the Medellin drug cartel was embarrassing to her husband and so well-hidden that she only learned of Celio's roots from her captors.

Dr. G reached into his center desk drawer and pulled out a checkbook, "I understand. It's time to pay up. I said then that what you did was more than your job required. You not only rescued my family, but you did not reveal my fraternal connection with the outlaw Benito. Clearly I would deny you nothing for your bravery and your discretion. How much do you want?"

"I don't want your money, Celio. I need something more valuable...your influence."

"How so? You are already a powerful man. What can Leander, the lion man, need from me?"

"I'm asking you to save my friend's career. As your wife once was, my friend is in the wrong place at the wrong time," Blake handed over a folder with Taylor's university transcript, resume' and letters of reference. As Celio looked over the material, Blake continued, "She won't be able to complete her residency that has barely started for reasons I can't disclose at this moment."

"What an unfortunate situation. Dr. Kendall has a strong academic record, but I don't know what I can do at this point."

"You can do what I did for you...move mountains."

Celio's eyes darted between Blake and the picture of his family.

He vividly recalled the frustration he felt when the American and Columbian governments offered nothing but excuses for their inaction; excuses why a raid in the heart of the drug cartel would fail, excuses about creating a diplomatic incident if not handled properly, excuses that kept his wife and son prisoner for day after agonizing day. Then he found one man among them, Leander, who was willing to think outside the box, the way he demanded of his research assistants. Celio was successful as a researcher because he never cared about what other people said can't be done. Try the unexpected and expect results. The diplomats made excuses. Leander took action. "All right. Exactly what do you want me to do for your lady friend?"

"Taylor needs to finish her residency at a credible place. Under your leadership, this Institute's reputation is impeccable. When her residency is complete, she's going to need someone like you with serious clout to convince the Board of Psychology of her worth in spite of the initial interrupted residency. I don't want her career affected because of a situation beyond her control."

Celio jotted notes in the margin of Taylor's resume' and circled an area of her transcript, "Here's what I can do. I'll develop a new post-doc position. Rhoda can crank out the paperwork fast. I'm constantly developing ideas while out fishing or playing bocce. In my mind they are half-underway before the rest of my staff hears. Rhoda says I need to order benzodiazapine-laced chocolates for the Human Resources Department to offset the panic I frequently create there."

"Will that be suitable for her residency?"

"Yes, indeed. I'll make it one of my pet projects under my personal supervision and appoint Dr. Kendall as a clinical assistant. She'll have to work hard, but if she can keep up with our pace, she will earn my full support."

"Thank you, Celio."

"Your Dr. Kendall must be a special woman."

"She is. One more thing," Blake said, reaching for an envelope from his inside coat pocket and pushing it across the desk, "I don't want her to be inconvenienced by the change. You'll find one hundred thousand dollars in new bills in that envelope. Consider it a donation toward your new project."

"That is generous."

"See that she has accommodations at a safe place near here as well as a modest salary appropriate to such a program."

"That can be arranged. I'll tell her it is part of a grant."

"Good. When she's finished, keep anything left over as an anonymous gift to your research."

"Thank you."

"There is one condition, Celio. We never had this meeting. Neither Taylor nor anyone else can know I was involved. Her university advisor, Dr. Sebastian Dale, will contact you in a few days."

"I'll be ready."

Blake rose from his chair, "When Taylor's residency is complete and you have made the appropriate recommendations to the licensing board, I will consider your debt of honor to be paid in full." With a slight bow of respect, he left the office.

Blake felt relieved as he left the building. Raul drove up immediately.

"Got some time to look around the city?"

"Not today, Raul. Head back to the airport, please."

"Say, I heard on the radio that there's a four car pile-up on the Causeway. Could take an extra forty, forty-five minutes to get back to the airport. Why don't you catch some more z's?"

Blake leaned his seat back to rest confidently now that the last loose end was tied up in preparation for his confrontation at MACS.

*****

Arriving at the airport, Raul asked to see the plane up close. He followed Blake around during the preflight check with unbridled enthusiasm.

"This baby isn't exactly standard government issue either, is it?"

"You're right. The airplane is my indulgence like the Porsche is yours. Would you like to go inside?" He opened the door and motioned for Raul to follow, "Watch your head."

Raul beamed, slithering into the copilot's seat. "What a rush. I wish I could fly in this baby."

"If my schedule wasn't so tight I'd take you up, but I have to get back to my post. Duty calls."

"Sure, man, I understand."

"Next time I'm in Miami, I'll take you for some serious flying time."

Raul saluted as he left the plane. He moved to an area where the mechanic said it was safe to watch the plane taxi to the runway. Mesmerized by the sight of Blake's jet surging northwest into the afternoon sun, Raul began to feel that his beloved Porsche was much too tame on the drive down A1A.

Taylor walked out the back door into the MACS parking lot. She needed a break in the warm afternoon sun. To her disappointment, Gabe didn't call for lunch.

"Want to go get an ice cream?" Brook asked walking up beside her.

"I'm not particularly hungry."

"Then come with me. It's on the next corner and I have hot news."

They crossed the street. Brook looked over her shoulder, than started to talk at warp speed, "Did you know that Carla left town?"

"No, I didn't. A business meeting?"

"All pleasure and no business. She took off with her secret admirer. You know, the guy who sent all those flowers?"

"Are you sure, Brook?"

"Yes. She kind of told me, but I didn't pay much attention to it. Later Victoria called me to her office and grilled me for an hour. It think little Carla pulled a fast one on the family. Serves them right."

"Why do you say that?"

"They use her. Carla cleans up all their messes. They work her so hard and you'd think she wasn't even family. Of course what have you got left? Wimpy Felipe, personality-challenged Gina or Tiffany who's more of an airhead then I am."

Taylor laughed at the characterizations. "When will she be back?"

"Never, if she's smart."

* * * * *

Blake touched down at about two o'clock. There was plenty of time to change back into his Gabe attire and see Taylor before meeting Jack. He called from the car, hoping it wasn't a bad time.

"Dr. Kendall."

"Hello, beautiful lady. I'm back."

"Gabe," she said, causing Brook to turn her head so fast that she got strawberry ice cream on her nose. Taylor laughed.

"Now I'm funny."

"No, not you. It's Brook wiping ice cream off her nose."

"Where are you?"

"We walked down the street to the ice cream shop. Are you coming over for dinner? I'll cook."

"No can do. I have to help with a building project." She was quiet with obvious disappointment. "Can I call you later?"

"Yes. I even saved the last brownie for you. Does that entice you to come over?"

"Not nearly as much as you entice me, beautiful lady. I'll call later."

Brook stared at her, "So, what are you doing this evening?"

"Nothing, he has to work."

"Bummer. Sounds like you both work too much."

"We probably do."

* * * * *

Blake opened the door in time to grab the sub sandwich sack from Jack's overstuffed arms as he dumped the files on the table.

"I'm the man with the plan."

"I can hardly wait to hear it. There's drinks in the fridge," Blake offered, spreading out the files and papers in an orderly manner.

"Are we still going tomorrow?"

"Yes. We got the warrants signed today and we're waiting for your recommendation on the time."

Blake sat back in his chair, mentally reviewing what Taylor had told him about a typical day at MACS.

"Does Locke understand what he's to do?"

"Yes, he asked Marco to move up the Executive Staff meeting from next week to tomorrow. I think he said they start around ten or ten-thirty," Jack said, checking his notes.

"Okay, let's go in about eleven-thirty. That ought to catch the unholy trinity and most of the key staff before they leave for lunch."

"I'll pass the word to the task force," Jack agreed, watching Blake stare at the blueprints of the MACS building.

"You don't think Locke will tip anyone?"

"No, man, he's scared...really scared. He said that Marco was way too nice about the whole thing."

"I told you Marco would welcome his scapegoat back to the herd."

"You were right, Blake. We told Locke that we were sending in an agent disguised as a tradesman measuring for wallpaper. While there, our agent could take a look at the executive staff during their meeting and get familiar with the inside of the building."

"And you think he bought that?"

"He did and there's the extra inducement."

"Such as?"

"The old man told Locke that if anything leaked out before we are ready, then the immunity deal is off. Plus he'll be slapped with obstruction of justice."

"He can still play hard ball."

"He's got a lot riding on this case. So do you, Blake. If we screw up anything that lets the Girards walk, we can kiss a promotion goodbye. That's a lot to lose."

"Not as much as I'm losing."

"True. You're losing your family."

"I let them go a long time ago, Jack. What I'm losing is my

future and the family I may never have with Taylor."

* * * * *

"Precisely why are we changing our Executive Staff meeting to suit Dr. Locke? One would think that he needs to accommodate us."

Marco refilled her coffee cup, then took his time pouring a brandy before he sat on the sofa beside her.

"Cara Mia, we need to keep Dr. Locke in his position until we are ready to leave MACS. He wants the meeting to affirm his status. With all the arrangements I have to make, it better suits my schedule to have next week's calendar clear."

Victoria poured her own brandy and pulled up the ottoman to sit near them. "This isn't sitting well with Lorraine. Gina says that she feels slighted."

"That's unfortunate. Or maybe it isn't. Keeping those two sparring with each other distracts them from what we are doing."

"Speaking of what you're doing, when were you going to mention liquidating the MACS pension fund?"

"My dear Victoria, one would think that you don't trust me - your partner, the father of your children."

"Spare me the phony indignation, Marco. I've never loved you, but I've always understood you. You are consistently greedy and manipulative."

"Thank you. Coming from one who personifies those characteristics, I appreciate the compliment," he said raising his brandy snifter in a mock salute.

"This isn't productive," Serena chided.

"You are right, Cara Mia. Let me explain. I split the pension portfolio placing half in a different account and the remainder in our payroll account to cover next week. On paper it appears as if we have made a new pension investment decision. By the time of the next reporting, we will be gone."

"And the account numbers? Does Felipe have them?"

"No. I'm handling it and he looks the other way."

"Then you need to give the routing numbers to me."

"Of course, Victoria, I'll get information for you before I leave."

"Or you could give it to me now."

"Alas, I don't have it with me," Marco answered, then turned to Serena, "I almost forgot the very important task I have for both of you. I need for you to make a list of the most sensitive, incriminating files that pertain to the areas under your control. Those will need to be shredded."

"You're right. We can have Sally begin tomorrow."

"Serena, why would we allow Sally to be in charge of something so vital and so private?"

"Why not? I allow her to use my husband's privates."

CHAPTER 47

"Come on out. You can't hide in there any longer," Brook chided knocking on Sam Locke's office door. "It's Executive Staff meeting time. Leave now and get a good seat."

"What constitutes a good seat?"

"One that's off angle from Serena's marble-cutting stare, too far away from Victoria to be kicked under the table and to Marco's right since his peripheral vision isn't as good on that side."

Taylor laughed, "And where do I sit?"

Brook turned to leave, "In your car, driving away from this loony bin."

"Come on, Taylor, we might as well get there before the blueberry muffins are gone," Locke suggested, allowing her to pass first.

When they entered the elevator and the doors closed, Taylor turned toward him, "I'm glad that they didn't accept your resignation."

"Don't mention that to anyone else. I only told you because I didn't want you to alarm Dr. Dale and the university. When I do leave, and I don't expect to stay much longer, I'll help you get settled with a new supervisor," *Although I don't really see any way to salvage your residency this late.*

The elevator doors opened. Several department heads were mingling beneath the chandelier in the foyer. Taylor looked over her shoulder at the life-sized portraits of the Girard family. Her gaze landed on Carla's delicate face. She hoped that Carla was having a fabulous time and in no rush to return.

The meeting followed its typical format. Marco opened with his corporate loyalty speech followed by Victoria's teamwork theme. When Marco was present, Victoria's ramblings were curtailed. Serena invited Sam Locke to stand by her side and show the various color-coded charts illustrating the progress of the Live Anew program. Taylor found herself straining to hear Serena's voice as a din arose from outside the conference room. Two secretaries scurried past the glass doors shrieking.

"Is this a fire drill?" she whispered to the accountant sitting to her left. He shook his head.

Two men opened the glass doors, displayed badges and ordered everyone to step outside.

As Taylor walked out and moved to the side, a crowd of unfamiliar faces - men in dark clothing wearing vests marked "DEA" - were lining up outside the conference room. The next wave in the sea of strangers wore FBI vests and flanked an inner core of men and women in banker's attire with badges.

Victoria pushed past the man at the door, "What do you fascist thugs think you're doing here? Our attorneys will arrive momentarily and have your jobs over this invasion of privacy."

Her empty threats fell on disinterested ears. The "vests" moved down the hall and toward the file room. The "suits" moved in closer.

Dr. Marco stepped forward with Serena on his arm, appearing unruffled, "Now gentlemen, please excuse our associate. I'm sure this is an honest mistake on your part. We can settle this misunderstanding without terrorizing my employees if you will return to the downstairs lobby. I'll speak with one of your representatives. This is a secure medical facility and I cannot allow strangers to rummage through confidential records."

"Dr. Marco Girard, stand aside or you will be moved," replied the "suit" nearest him.

"I will not be moved! I demand to see the person in charge. I never deal with the hired help."

Just as the Red Sea parted on Moses' signal, Marco's words caused a parting of the suited FBI agents. At the end of the line, near the elevator doors, one man stood. A tall, broad-shouldered man in a custom-tailored suit stood apart from the others. Something was very familiar about that purposeful stride. Recognition came with the force of a lightening strike.

"Blake!" Serena cried.

"Gabe?" Taylor gasped.

He walked directly to the Girards.

"Good morning, Mother, Father, Tia Victoria. Checkmate, the game is over."

"What is the meaning of this foolish charade, Blake? If you want to come back, you know the conditions," Marco countered.

"Let me make this clear," he said, stealing a glance at Taylor, "I am Special Agent Blake Girard of the FBI. We're here to close down this scam, or shall I say MACS. Yes, Tia, I continue to admire your penchant for twisted humor and word play."

Pushing her way past a shaking secretary, Gina spewed her anger, "Blake, you bastard, how can you do this to your own family?"

"Wrong as usual, Gina. You can't get over the fact that our father's passion to have a son drove him to make certain that the wedding took place in sufficient time to make me quite legitimate."

Marco stared at Blake with a peculiar mixture of fury and pride, "My son, my Prince, you could have had everything. What you are here to tear down, we might have made into an empire together. You waste your brilliance playing tin soldier."

"Have you become so deluded in building your empire that you forgot the philosophies you drummed into my head? Let me refresh your memory. Your hero himself wrote, 'For the difficulties that attend conspirators are infinite and we know from experience that while there have been many conspiracies, few of them have succeeded.' I have succeeded, Father, but not in the way you planned."

Blake locked eyes with Marco. The electricity that flowed between them mirrored many a timeless struggle - Michael the Archangel and Lucifer, Luke Skywalker and Darth Vader - a fierce clash in which only one could be left standing.

Using Tiffany as a human shield, Felipe leaned around her, "Well isn't this great? Blake comes back into our lives quoting J. Edgar Hoover."

"Shut up, Felipe," Marco demanded casting a disdainful scowl, "At least show respect for the words of Niccolo Machiavelli, even if you have no ability to comprehend them."

Shoulders slumped, Felipe moved back behind Tiffany. Marco never stopped comparing them. Even in this situation, Blake was favored.

"Get your kicks, super cop and read us our rights."

"No, thank you, Tia. One thing you and father taught me is to have someone else do your dirty work. Agent Sims, please take these three people aside and very carefully read them their rights. Then proceed with the others named in the warrants. Call the agents on the ground floor. The woman who just ran down the stairway exit is Lorraine Lewis."

Serena was probably the only person who recognized the expression on Marco's face as one of pride watching his Prince in command.

The employees' names were called and divided into two groups, those being held and those not. Taylor heard the murmur of those staring and pointing alternately between the portrait of a younger Blake and the live version. Blake glanced across the room, struck by how poorly art imitated life. It was all smoke and mirrors that never measured up.

The buzz of conversations increased as FBI agents mingled among the employees. Blake paused to watch the parental figures he long ago named the "unholy trinity" escorted by Jack and three other agents into the elevator. *Outraged as they are, they will never know that I gave the order allowing them some measure of dignity by asking Jack to delay placing them in handcuffs until they were outside the building and inside the van. You see, Mother, I do value family.*

Dozens of scenes flashed through Blake's mind. Memories of times he and his siblings were pushed aside to nannies and extended family while the status-seeking trio courted the socially and politically elite. Try as he might, he could not recall a single warm, maternal memory of Serena. Her tears today were as phony as those she shed the day he renounced their reprobate lifestyle and left the family. *Watching them leave under armed guard lacked the satisfaction I expected. Dale was right; revenge is its own kind of evil.*

* * * * *

Blake's concentration was again interrupted as he heard Taylor's name called. He pushed past the team who was sealing file cabinets and darted through the mail room, a shortcut she had shown him to her office. She wasn't there. Blake took deep breaths to quell his racing heartbeat the way he learned to do when the adrenaline rush of the moment threatened to overtake him. Closing his eyes to visual distractions, his nose honed in on the scent of her perfume. He followed the scent down the hall to a storage room.

"Taylor, we have to talk."

She looked up, than cut her eyes away from his, picking up two empty boxes and walking past him. He followed in silence. Hands full, she kicked open her office door. Dropping the boxes, she sat down on the floor beside the bookcase to begin packing her books. He sat down and started putting books in the second box.

"You can't imagine how many times I wanted to tell you, but I couldn't. It's been hard trying to balance protecting you with doing my job."

"Nice to hear that I was a convenient pipeline for your cops and robbers game."

"You know better than that, Taylor."

"It was really all business to you."

"Once you got a hint of the deception going on here, you hated it as much as I did. You became a one-woman vigilante committee when you realized that people were being harmed. At least that's what you told me."

"For the record, that's what I told my friend, Gabe. You remember, Gabe? The nice guy I thought I could trust?"

"Taylor, you can trust me. You know that."

"Know? I don't know you. I assume from comparing you to the portrait in the foyer that your real hair color is blonde, not brown. But how about the eyes? Gabe has gray eyes and Blake has aquamarine eyes as distinctive in real life as in the portrait," Taylor looked closely at him, "I've spent hours with you, or some semblance of you. I thought I knew you."

"The hair color rinse and tinted contacts were props for the job."

She rolled her eyes in disbelief. *How could I have been so easily fooled? I'm a trained observer of people who missed something so obvious. The truth is, Blake doesn't look that different from Gabe. It was the aura of his hypnotic presence that was his real disguise. He played the part so completely that I suspended disbelief. I fell for a trick used by stage magicians. The truth was out there for anyone to see who looked beyond his diversions. I'm an idiot. How did I miss it?*

"By the way, I suppose I ought to thank you for doling out to me those occasional nuggets of truth that you, Mr. Who-Died-To-Make-You-God, decided I could handle."

"Wait a minute, Taylor Kendall!" His indignation suddenly matched hers, "I have never directly lied to you. I evaded your questions and distracted you. Have you forgotten the day we met? You asked if I was hiding my identity and I told you that I only did so when I was working. That's the truth. Law enforcement is my work."

"I thought you were an aspiring actor, Gabe."

"Undercover work is nothing more than character acting. In that sense, I do aspire to become a better actor. My life often depends on it."

Struggling to restrain her emotions, Taylor thrust out both hands in front of her, "Okay, Danno, book me."

In a gesture that surprised them both, Blake sandwiched her outstretched hands between his, turned her palms over and kissed each one.

"Stop it! This isn't the time or the place. What happens next? Am I going to be arrested?"

"Of course not, Taylor. You and most of the MACS employees are mere pawns in their game. You will be asked to give a statement, but not today."

"What's going to happen to Sam Locke?"

"Nothing. He already made arrangements to testify for immunity."

Sam too? This morning he was assuring me that everything was fine at MACS. All the time he knew it wasn't true.

"You will be contacted by federal prosecutors from the Justice Department to assess what you know. I've already told them that you know very little about the MACS operations, but I hope you will tell them everything that you uncovered in your research."

"Of course I will. Are they using anything that Gabe and I found on our feeble attempts at investigation?"

"No, not unless you mention it."

"And what if I do?"

"You could give some sharp defense lawyers an out for Lorraine and Gina. And confidentially, Dr. Kendall, sufficient evidence against those two has been obtained in another way," he responded watching her react to the message between the lines.

"So our Sherlock and Dr. Watson game accomplished nothing but to distract me?"

"Not so. While it didn't yield anything that could be used in court as evidence, it filled in an enormous blank that led me to look in the right places."

"Well, Agent Girard, congratulations on your investigation. While you were busy working, I was hanging out with a friend. Now I'm going to have plenty of time on my hands. Maybe I can get Gabe's old job at the gallery. My career in psychology is trashed."

"No it's not."

"Yes it is. You're a cop, not a psychologist. You don't even understand."

"Fine. Then let Dale reassure you that there are options. Will you believe him?"

"How do you know Dale? Did you read about him in my dossier?"

"The venerable Dr. Dale was my graduate advisor too."

"Are we talking about the same Dr. Sebastian Dale?"

"Yes. Ask him about me. Without Dale's influence, I would have become the son that Marco and Serena wanted."

He stood up and helped Taylor to her feet. Picking up a box of books under each arm, he walked down the hallway with Taylor following. At the elevator, he handed the boxes to a uniformed officer with these instructions, "See Dr. Kendall to her car."

Almost imperceptivity, Blake squeezed Taylor's hand and whispered, "I have to finish here and tackle a mountain of paperwork tomorrow. Meet me Friday at the bench for lunch. I'll bring the fried chicken and explain everything." He leaned further to kiss her cheek, but she turned away.

CHAPTER 48

Friday morning Taylor went on the Internet to compare headlines in the Florida cities where MACS operated PHPs: "Wings Clipped for Jet Setting Trio", "Deceiving the Mentally Ill", "The Great Medicare Billing Robbery", "Medicare and Murder – the Ultimate Scam." She was torn between disgust at the mention of MACS and the kind of prurient curiosity that makes people crave another information fix from the media.

Local television news replayed scenes outside of the MACS corporate offices. Serena actually paused and smiled for the cameras as she, Marco and Victoria walked into the courthouse. Taylor could only imagine what was going through their minds. Wouldn't that make an amusing psychological study? She enjoyed the arrest scene so much that she taped it from the news channel to watch it again and again.

Taylor made a valiant attempt to dawdle, unpacking her books and rearranging the linen closet. Blessedly the phone rang.

"Are you ready to move back to Memphis?"

"No Mama. I have to stay here and work out my residency problem."

"Looking at my clock, I'd say you need to be leaving soon."

"I'm not going anywhere."

"Yes you are, honey. Go meet him."

"Why? There's nothing to say."

"Taylor Kendall, I didn't raise you to be small-minded. I know for a fact that you listened to a dozen ridiculous excuses from Trey and came back for more."

"I was young and stupid then. Maybe I still am since I didn't see what was right in front of me."

"That's pride talking, honey. Granddaddy Dodd warned that an unforgiving person would ride his pride straight to hell."

"I don't think that's theologically accurate."

"Don't get sassy with me, missy. Remember where you came from. You never used to be sanctimonious." That was strong language for Julia Dodd Kendall.

"All right, Mama, I'll hear his story."

"That's better. If you don't, you could spend a lot of years regretting it. Don't you care for him?"

"I was falling in love with Gabe, but he doesn't exist. The man who stole his identity is a different man, a man who could not trust me."

"No, honey, the man you love is Blake Girard; you merely called him by a different name."

"I don't know if I can love him or trust him."

"I understand. I was married to two men and both were your father."

"What do you mean?"

"When your Daddy came home from Vietnam, he was a different man. Oh, he had the same face as the man in our wedding pictures, but he was different and he never changed back."

"Didn't you resent that? You didn't get what you bargained for."

"No, in the long run I got more. Your Daddy lost his youthful innocence in Vietnam. Once he readjusted to his life and to me, his character was deepened by harsh experiences. Tom Kendall was two different men and I loved both of them."

"That's just...weird."

"I know, Taylor. Life is weird. The strong survive and those who love unconditionally will triumph. Call me after you talk to Blake."

Taylor reached into the closet for a better outfit than the jeans and cut-off tee shirt she was wearing. As she applied makeup she rehearsed aloud, "I'll listen to him like I promised Mama. Then I'll tell Gabe...I mean Blake, how I feel about being used and I'll leave."

Driving through downtown, past the gallery, Taylor turned toward the Pier. Every time she saw it she marveled at it's upside-down pyramid shape poised on the end of what was originally a historic fishing spot in St. Petersburg.

She parked and walked in the bright sunlight toward the green bench that she and Gabe had previously considered theirs. There he stood. He was unmistakably Blake Girard; a man of style, sophistication and confidence.

How many times did I want to change Gabe's appearance? I wanted Gabe to stop slicking down his hair with that gel, wear a button-down collar shirt, shave the hint of a beard and buy a tasteful navy blazer. With those things accomplished, Gabe the carefree, underemployed actor easily morphed into Blake Girard, champion of justice.

The wind carried her perfume toward him and he turned to greet her, "Taylor! I was afraid that you would stand me up."

She sat down beside him. He handed her a box of her favorite crispy chicken with curly fries and a large cola. They ate in silence until he wiped a spot of barbeque sauce from her lips.

"Gabe or Blake or whoever you are, I can't decide whether to hate you for spoiling my residency or applaud you for bringing down MACS before anyone else got hurt."

"Please, Taylor. I want you to get used to calling me Blake."

"So where did you get the name Gabe?"

With the naughty boy grin that she adored, he explained, "If you recall from the portrait, my real name is Blake Andres Girard. In crafting an undercover name for this operation, I reversed my initial to G – A –B and added the E to make Gabe."

"Creative."

"Playing with words and acronyms is an old trick I learned

from Tia Victoria. That's why she named the corporation Medical Alliance for Community Services. Reverse the letters in MACS and you have S-C-A-M, which was always their intent."

"You mean you knew that all along?"

"Of course I did. The bureau had some unsubstantiated tips from the medical community. Since it involved my family, the Director of the Tampa FBI office requested my help early on to analyze the situation."

"But MACS seemed genuine and the treatments appeared to work."

"That's the hallmark of a good scam, a legitimate appearance. When I heard about the Nutracuratives and the miraculous secret ingredient, I knew it was a scam. I needed time and information to prove it."

"Then you already knew about the Nutracuratives?"

"I didn't know what it was, but I had suspicions. In fact, I was there when the miracle cure was found."

"You were?"

"The summer before I started graduate school at your alma mater, I traveled with my father to South America to pursue his latest fascination with psycho-active plants as healing agents. He heard about a tribe that claimed to use such herbs. We flew into their village to see for ourselves."

"Of course," Taylor brightened making the connection. "The MACS program brochures claimed that the Nutracuratives contained some unknown herb that Dr. Marco discovered in South America. The idea of an all-natural substance to moderate symptoms of schizophrenia appealed to a lot of our patients' families."

"And he made it sound noble, didn't he?"

"Yes. The programs didn't even charge for the Nutracuratives since it wasn't FDA approved as a medication."

"But the real prescription drugs mixed into it were FDA approved."

"Is that what we found in those boxes in the lab?"

"Good work, Sherlock. You're right. Fortunately a cache of drug boxes were also found away from the office when someone tried to destroy them."

"Then there's no crime since they used legitimate prescription drugs?"

"No, the patients were not given complete disclosure about the drugs. The problem isn't the drugs per se, it's the way they were used and misused to manipulate patients into relapse. Your statistics gave me the first clue to what was happening. But it took awhile, and a little extra-curricular snooping to figure out how it was done. The rest was old fashioned analysis."

"And I was a means of obtaining inside information since you couldn't walk in there yourself."

"Initially that's why I made contact with you, but you know that's not the way it is now." He reached for her hand and she pulled away.

"I don't know what I know anymore. What I do know is that when you and the cavalry rode in to corral the bad guys, my residency was an early casualty."

"Don't give up, Taylor; it's not that bad."

"Not that bad? You were a psychology graduate student; you must know how prejudicial it is to fail to finish a residency."

"It's not your fault."

"Who cares? All the residencies are taken. I'd have to wait until next year and begin again. I have a better chance of winning the lottery than getting a decent residency after all this mess and you know it." Taylor punctuated her anger by crushing the chicken box and twisting it.

Blake took it out of her hands, brushed the crumbs from her lap and sat quietly until the storm in her eyes subsided. "Taylor, you may not trust me, but I know you trust Dale. He's in his office working on the situation."

"Now you're a psychic?"

"No, if I were, I would have found a way around this impasse between us. However, I do know that there is an answer in process for your residency problem. Dale is faxing out the university's approval today if you agree."

"How do you know that? Do you have his house bugged, Mr. FBI Agent?"

"No, I found out the easy way, I was there."

"You were at Dale's house? How do you have time to make social calls between raids on major corporations?"

Blake chose to ignore the sarcasm. "After securing the MACS offices and filing preliminary reports, I was worn out. Even my supervisor saw it and told me to take off. I drove around going nowhere for several hours. I didn't think I'd be welcome at your place. Then Dale phoned me after he heard about the situation on the evening news."

"What did he say?"

"He ordered me to get my butt to his house. Half an hour later I was sitting in his den pouring my heart out about my bizarre family and about you. When I exhausted myself, he lifted my feet up on the couch, put a pillow under my head and covered me with an old blanket."

"I never thought of Dale as a caregiver."

"The empathy didn't last. At seven o'clock this morning he slapped me on the shoulder and handed me a cup of oil slick coffee. Then he picked up his lecture notes for the eight o'clock class and told me the pity party was over."

"That sounds more like the Dale I know."

"When I didn't move fast enough, he shouted at me to get off his couch, go home, take a shower and face you. I've faced many dangerous situations in undercover work without shirking. Frankly, I needed Dale's swift kick to get here. I didn't know if I could do it."

Taylor began to wonder if Dale knew all along what was going on. "I still can't grasp your connection to Dale. He never spoke about you yet he often talks about his most successful students."

"He knows what I do. He helped get me into the FBI Academy."

"That doesn't make sense. Dale trains psychologists not police."

"When I started at the university, I intended to be a psychologist. Actually, that's what my family intended. My esteemed and controlling father made career choices for all his children. He decided that too much time would be wasted moving me through medical school to a psychiatric residency, so he selected a psychology doctoral program. He wanted his heir to be a doctor and this was the faster, cheaper way."

"Too bad you couldn't finish grad school."

"Dropping out of the psychology program was done with Dale's encouragement."

"He told you to drop out of school? To give up?"

"For your information, I finished first in my class at law school before joining the FBI."

"Dale turned you into a lawyer?"

"Indirectly. He showed me that ethics was a way of life, not merely a college course. That was a radical concept for me. My father raised me with conditional love and twisted logic, believing that any form of weakness was a tragic flaw."

"If you believed that, how did you get where you are?"

"Dale shattered that delusion. In him I found a genuinely moral man with strength and abilities equal to my father. They simply approach life from different perspectives. I am Marco's seed, but Dale is the only real father that I've ever known."

"It almost sounds like Dale is Marco with a conscience."

"You may be right. You've seen Dale rampage around campus when thwarted by lazy students and insipid administrators. He's no shrinking violet. Yet he relies on motivation instead of manipulation."

"That's true. At first, I thought he was Captain Bligh looking for some poor student to walk the plank, but after I came to know him, I realized that he knew how far to push each of us toward our personal best."

"With me it took a big push. We were walking down the beach one afternoon to go fishing and talking about my crazy family. He told me to get my head out of Machiavelli and contemplate Augustine's take on evil as the absence of good rather than make excuses. He said I either needed to be an honorable man or a competent sociopath, but stop trying to play it both ways. Then he stopped, took the pole and literally drew a line in the sand; him on one side and me on the other. He made me decide that day whether to live my life in the pursuit of good or evil."

"That's when Blake, The Prince, left the castle."

"Yes, I decided to quit the psychology program, leave my family and work my way toward law school. You know the rest."

"But there was a constant preoccupation at MACS about Blake's whereabouts. The rumors about you were quite outrageous."

"I made contact regularly with my sister, Carla, as you know, and I always sent a birthday card to my mother. But Marco and I had not spoken to each other for years aside from the words we exchanged at MACS this week."

"Blake," she said, pausing at the unfamiliar sound of his name, "Why didn't the family search for you if Marco wanted you back so badly?"

"Simple. Marco's pride, Serena's narcissism and Victoria's jealousy would never allow them to search for me. They preferred to wait for the prodigal son to crawl home from the pig pen."

Taylor's lips slid into a broad smile, "There's one problem with that notion; the pig pen was at home and so were the prodigals."

They laughed and walked together along the sidewalk, neither knowing what more to say.

He broke the silence, "Dear God, I feared I would never hear you laugh again, Taylor."

Blake took her hands in his and this time she didn't pull away. He looked intensely at her, "Revenge isn't as sweet as I thought it would be and that's not the worst of it. I nearly compromised my job. I am an effective agent because I never let my feelings interfere with my work, but this time I did. That could have cost the Joint Task Force months of work and millions of dollars if the family had completed their plans to flee before we took them down."

"Perhaps you had an unconscious desire to give your family another chance."

"No, it wasn't family loyalty. It was because of the feelings I have for you. I wanted to delay the investigation to spend more time with you and give you as much time as possible to finish your residency."

"Then why move now?"

"Marco started shuffling money, Lorraine was out of control and you were inside playing detective with extremely lethal people. Things started happening too fast. We had to move. As it is, millions of dollars from Medicare and Medicaid have been wired out of the country to secret accounts."

Taylor shook her head in disbelief. Brook joked about evil as a corporate value in MACS. She even drew a cartoon of Taylor as a tiny figure in a white lab coat against a huge granite column with eyes. In place of the bronze engraved sign at the entrance that read Medical Alliance for Community Services, the cartoon sign read "EVIL INC."

Blake gave her a few minutes to process all that he told her. She seemed overwhelmed. "Sorry, Taylor, but you wanted only truth between us and what I've told you is the truth. I made a rookie mistake by allowing myself to get personally involved during an investigation. I knew it was happening and I couldn't stop. I didn't want to stop."

She moved toward the railing overlooking the yacht basin.

Blake went to her side, slipping an arm around her waist. He cherished the feel of her hair against his cheek. There was so much he wanted to say, but now it was up to her.

"Let me see if I've got this right. You interfere with my career and I interfere with yours. This isn't going to work, is it?"

"I don't know; maybe not today or next week. I know you want to finish your residency and get your license, but I've become a patient man. I learned it from hours of bad sandwiches and stale coffee on stakeouts. I can wait for you, if that's what you want."

He reached for the velvet box from his inside coat pocket and handed it to her. "Call it a deposit on the future. Wear it and think of me."

At least it's the wrong size for a ring box. Opening it, she found the gold and diamond bracelet he bought for her in the Bahamas. She took it out and held it for him to clasp on her wrist. It was elegant, the kind of gift Blake, not Gabe, would know how to buy.

"If I wear this bracelet what does it mean to you?"

"What does it mean to you, Taylor?"

The tension was broken by the squeal of Taylor's cell phone. Blake moved quickly to the bench and grabbed the phone that was protruding from her purse. He spoke briefly then walked back and handed it to her.

"Hello, this is Dr. Kendall."

"I knew it wasn't freaking Anna Freud. Her number's unlisted."

"I was going to call you."

"I know but I'm a busy man so listen. If you want to salvage your residency, get down to my office this afternoon. There's a psychology associate position with the big shot director at Miami Institute of Psychological Research, but you have to move fast."

"Are you sure about this?"

"Since when am I not sure about something?"

"Yes! Yes, I want it. I'll leave today if I have to. I can't begin to thank you. This is fantastic! Blake, it's Dale with incredible news..." She turned in time to see him walking down the steps toward the yacht slips. She closed the cell phone and put it in her pocket, all the while watching him. He took off his navy blazer, tossing it onto the sailboat. Then he rolled up the sleeves of his pin stripe button down shirt before dealing with the lines that held the boat to the dock.

"Please understand, Blake, I have to finish my residency. I've worked years for this, surely you understand. You already have a career."

If she intended for him to hear, she grossly miscalculated. The wind carried her words away from him. He maneuvered the sailboat out into the water with ease. Each second was an emotional battle for her. *Follow him. Stay here. Go after him. Stay here. Shout for him to come back. Tell him that you love him, whoever he is.* The sailboat turned, ready to make a run.

Tears welled up in her eyes. She had no tender words of consolation for Blake when he confessed to delaying and nearly ruining the investigation for her sake. This time, she was the victim of her own delay. All that remained was to wave at him as he sailed away. Squinting in the midday sun, she tried to focus on his familiar broad smile until he was out of sight. The sun danced off the diamonds in her bracelet. She held it to her heart.

Tears formed in his eyes as he cursed the midday sun, knowing that his excuse was a lie. The blazing sun was puny compared with the light of his life, standing alone near the same waterfront where he met her.

EPILOGUE

<u>Agent Jack Sims</u> coordinated the evidence of the Joint Task Force for the FBI, IRS, DEA and interfaced with the Florida Medical Board in the cases against MACS. These diverse, and occasionally territorial, forces spent months preparing a stunning presentation that scored major political points for the Assistant Attorney General. Sims received a commendation and promotion. Frankly, he deserved an ambassadorship for extraordinary diplomatic talents and a purple heart for surviving the inter-agency skirmishes.

<u>Dr. Samuel Locke</u> received immunity for his testimony. He returned to private practice, developed a new and totally legitimate group therapy model, and became a best-selling self-help author.

<u>Peter Lane</u>, Licensed Clinical Social Worker, was brought out of federal witness protection to testify. He had plenty to say about Lorraine Lewis.

<u>Hallie Logan</u> returned home, satisfied that her twin sister's death would be avenged, even if she didn't get to do it herself.

<u>Martha Sanders</u>, RN and DEA agent was sent to an advanced neuropsychological rehabilitation program in Colorado. Gradually she recovered her long term memory enough to testify convincingly against Lorraine and Gina.

Considering them a flight risk, the Judge denied bail and sent

Marco, Serena, Victoria, Gina and Felipe to jail pending trial. The Girards were charged with various counts of fraud, conspiracy and cheating the IRS.

Gina Girard and Lorraine Lewis were charged with manslaughter in the deaths of Harriet Logan and Greg Newman and with assault with deadly intent against Martha Sanders. Faced with the prospect of hard time, Gina led FBI agents to the syringe hidden in her office. That "insurance" secured a plea bargain for Gina and left Lorraine Lewis accountable for the deaths.

There was never a question that **Tiffany Girard** knew anything.

MACS, Live Anew and the affiliate corporations went into bankruptcy, using the paperwork that was already typed and stashed in Marco's desk drawer. The final paychecks from the last week of operations bounced, leaving employees with nothing. Work friendships were maintained and others renewed as former employees socialized with each other at the Unemployment Office.

Using Victoria's word games, Blake located three numbered accounts in Nassau banks. The $29 million recovered in these accounts turned the Attorney General into a media celebrity. Over $10 million remains missing.

Agent Blake Girard took a leave of absence from the FBI. The Director called it "burnout". When Blake arrived at the house on Eleuthra Island, he recapped the events for Carla. They talked nonstop for almost twenty-four hours and then he became practically mute, hardly speaking. For weeks, every day was the same; sleep late, run on the beach to near exhaustion, then collapse in a lawn chair listening to a continuous loop of Jimmy

Buffet's Margaritaville.

No charges were filed against **Carla Girard**, for lack of evidence linking her to decision-making aspects of MACS. She flew into Tampa for depositions and returned to an undisclosed location. Carla understood the sacrifices Blake made for her freedom and to put an end to MACS reign. She stayed for a month at the island house with him until he shook the depression and declared that it was time that they both move on with their lives. She decided to go back to Chile and live with Tio Pietro's family. To make certain that she was financially secure, Blake used an elaborate series of transfers to move $1 million US dollars into an investment program that would pay a monthly life income into Carla's account at Banco Chile. Blake found that money the way he found the other four numbered accounts, which were coded with each Girard sibling's birth date. He turned over the accounts designated for him, Gina and Felipe to the Justice Department. At the very least, he would see that Marco and Victoria provided for their often neglected daughter's new life.

Dr. Marco Girard managed to weasel out of the worst of the fraud charges. He had been careful to have Victoria and Serena sign the most potentially incriminating business and financial documents for MACS. A name stamp was used to order the drugs, which could not be proven to have been done by his hand. The only original signatures related to shipments of the prescription drugs were Gina's and Lorraine's. Imagine his relief when the only other papers that could tie him to the conspiracy, the papers that he thought were stored in Carla's office, could not be found. That left him with lesser charges and a hearing on revocation of his medical license. The ink wasn't dry on his half-million dollar bail agreement when he dusted off a phony passport and fled the country to avoid prosecution. He has yet to surface in any nation with an extradition treaty.

<u>Dr. Taylor Kendall</u> found the residency under Dr. Celio Guitierrez of the Miami Institute of Psychological Research to be the most fascinating experience. She was the envy of her classmates, even the ones at South Bay, when her work earned a mention in another of Guitierrez' renowned studies. His name and the prestige of the Institute erased the stigma of MACS. She qualified for the October Exam in Practice of Professional Psychology and passed. The day she received the congratulations letter from the Florida Board of Psychology, the first number she dialed was no longer in service.

<u>Dr. Sebastian Dale</u> walked into the lecture hall with a new class of psychology graduate students who thought they had something to offer the profession. He gave his usual introductory speech designed to weed out the faint hearted. He surveyed their faces. Was there another idealist like Taylor? Another maverick like Blake? He clearly hoped so.

ACKNOWLEDGEMENTS

Thanks to my family for their encouragement; my husband, Bert, who is my proof-reader; my daughter and favorite Coffee Master, Kelly; my daughter Robin and her husband, Gunner, who made possible the most amazing grandchildren in the universe, Faith, Grace and Joseph.

My faith in God is my "firm foundation" for life, providing the strength and assurance to take the ethical stand regardless of what others choose.

Jane Till, Director of Applied Ethics Institute, St. Petersburg College. She instantly identified this book as an "Ethical Thriller."

Clinton Lee of Brentwood Photography, an artist with a camera who captured the mood of this story for the cover, and his lovely canine assistant Konica.

Stephen Durnin-Moore, my dear friend and consultant on fine art and antiques.

Dr. Crystal Waterford and her colleagues, you know who you are.

My loyal assistants Par (cockatiel) and Star (sun conure), who stayed up late while I wrote, preened my hair and snuggled my shoulders. Star, our rescue bird, died before this book was published or she would have saluted me with her ultimate compliment, "sweet bird."

ABOUT THE AUTHOR

Blending backgrounds in broadcasting, business, psychology and education, Dr. K.T. Erwin has a broad palate of experiences to bring to her writing. A true "GRITS" girl, she was raised among the horse riding, tea-giving ladies of Memphis, Tennessee. She attended Rhodes College and her writing voice and love of learning emerged at Eckerd College in St. Petersburg, Florida where she earned a BA in Political Science. Dr Erwin earned an MA in Counseling from Liberty University and Ed.D. in Counseling Psychology from University of Sarasota (now Argosy).

Heavily influenced by Mary Tyler Moore's "make it on your own" philosophy, she began her broadcasting career at WLCY Radio/TV and became the first woman to host an issues-oriented talk show (*Encounter*). Other broadcasting achievements include being the first Consumer Reporter with daily features (WRBQ's *Tell Kathie*) and first female news producer in the market (WTOG).

The author of five professional counseling books, Dr. K.T. Erwin is an accomplished speaker and is considered to be an expert in her field. She has taught in the Applied Ethics Institute of St. Petersburg College and for Troy University. She is a Licensed Mental Health Counselor, National Certified Counselor and Board Certified Clinical Psychotherapist.

Presently Dr. Erwin is an Assistant Professor of Counseling for Regent University and a Certified Health Coach for Take Shape for Life. Her most important role is as "Mimi" for four fabulous grandchildren.

DON'T MISS K.T. ERWIN'S

UPCOMING NOVEL

TAYLOR KENDALL:
BESIDE MYSELF

After a near career-ending residency, Dr. Taylor Kendall settles into a private practic group. No more research projects, following on the coattails of master practitioners or wrangling with other residents for the best cases. Finally, Taylor is a Licensed Psychologist able to work with clients in a calm, professional environment...or so she thought.

Taylor panics when a kindly senior adult client mentions being threatened and then suddenly disappears. Taylor takes drastic action to try and protect her client and learns that two other clients in the practice are also mysteriously missing.

As the search expands from a quest to an obsession, Taylor tries to lose a dangerous stalker while keeping tabs on her ethical boundaries.

www.ingramcontent.com/pod-product-compliance
Lightning Source LLC
Chambersburg PA
CBHW020455020726
47493CB00001B/37